# THE FATHER

## AMERICA LEAVES THE AMERICAN CENTURY

A NOVEL

Volume 1 in *The Father* Trilogy

# BRETT ALAN WILLIAMS

**COMBUSTIBLE**

Combustible Books™
"A fire of the mind."

COMBUSTIBLE BOOKS FIRST & ORIGINAL EDITION,
MARCH 2014
Revised September 2019
Originally as *The Father*, revised as, *The Father: America Leaves
the American Century*

ISBN-13: 978-0-578-59141-4

THEMES
1.  Multigenerational family epic—History—20th century—
    21st century—Literary fiction.
2.  Philosophy—Political philosophy—Religion—
    Science—Literary fiction.
3.  Societal evolution—Social movements—The human condition—
    Civilizations—Literary fiction.

Published in the United States of America

Combustible Books; the burning mind logo; "COMBUSTIBLE" when associated with said logo; and "A fire of the mind" are trademarks of Combustible Books Publishing.

Interior layout and format by Combustible Books – 12 pt. Times New Roman font. Cover design by Combustible Books. Further information about *The Father* trilogy or its author, and his blog concerning political philosophy, science, religion, and current events can be found at TheFatherTrilogy.com or Goodreads.com.

Dedicated to my parents and their generation.

# CONTENTS

**PART ONE:  YOUNG AGAIN**

# 1. First Light

Rainless thunderheads blazed with internal fire. Sky linked to ground with a flicker of current in the distance.

Joseph waited. Ground rumbled beneath his feet.

Vast flocks of geese honked overhead in a migration south with the onset of summer. Snow fell from clear space above. The moon took a bite from the sun. Joseph watched it all, spellbound. He shook his head at the improbable scene.

He kneeled, tilted his straw hat, and massaged withered leaves of a corn stalk. Tiny roots about its base peeked above ground. He crumbled a clod in his hand. How do I feed my family on this? he thought.

A hawk streaked groundward. It caught Joseph's eye as it disappeared behind a tree line with their many limbs broken in submission to windstorms past. He squinted at the sun nearly eaten by the moon. He studied the old farmhouse scarcely able to hold itself up, knowing what was about to happen there. It's a fistfight for all of us, he thought. After all the battles, dashed hopes and failed dreams, is there salvation? In this world, or in another?

Hoisting his spade, he struck Illinois soil. His shovel wrenched under crust. Wind moaned past a barbed-wire fence.

All these machines make it harder, not easier, he decided. More machines; fewer men; more product; lower price per bushel. And Europe don't need our grain no more. Maybe that old woman's Bible is right: the more we hurt, the greater our reward. Ample reward on the way then. But don't have time to wait for it. Man and his family could starve out here and nobody'd know it.

He smashed a blood-laden mosquito, its stinger lanced in his arm. He scratched white streaks across dry skin. He peered at the sun, threatened by thunderheads, swallowed in crescent mouthfuls by an eclipsing moon. Shadow soldiered over land and its irregular contours in a muscular march about to push over the house. The solar disk vanished behind lunar blackness. Birds returned to nests. Nocturnal animals awoke.

Again in the dark, Joseph battled the earth, attacking what he could not see or understand. Thrift and hard work will get you to The Promised Land, he thought. The real one, abundant with food. Food in your belly, that's salvation.

Drawn by the noise of a motor, Joseph saw an airborne craft glint the last light from a lost sun. "No mail needs gettin' from St. Louie to Chicago that fast," he muttered. "Gonna get yourself killed in that fool thing, Mister Lindbergh." It evaporated into umbra with a final flash from heaven that triggered sights and sounds in his mind—an old man coiled on the ground, cut to pieces; guards hammered his attacker with rifle butts; a wail from the library filled the world, horrified by the utmost of fears.

He turned away from the vision. They can't know this, he thought. They think I'm strong. A soldier.

Inside the farmhouse, a midwife spanked the newborn boy. "I swat 'em like they gonna be swatted in life, sister. Harsh world out yonder."

Bloody and soaked in sweat, Claire raised on elbows. Her wooden bed rocked and squeaked. "Enough!" she said.

Grandmama entered with a pail of water. She rinsed her hands and turned for the midwife to steal the infant. "This boy's got value only if he lives longer than the last one," she said. Be two years closer to help on the farm if she'd not had a girl the time before that." She lifted the crying child. She looked for imperfections in the boy. She laid him on a table and snatched strips of cloth from the midwife's arm.

The midwife's body jiggled, chin forward over large breasts and blood-spattered apron. "Grandmama, just *what* are you doing?"

Grandmama pecked at the child. "Got to make sure this one ain't weak or deformed somehows." She poked a bone-dry finger in the boy's mouth. Crying, he turned his head to expel it. "Folks are born into this world as animals, son. Firm lessons and fear of God will cleanse thy savage impulses. You be still now."

The boy lay silent. Without expression, he watched Grandmama's eyes. She leaned sideward. His eyes tracked hers. She straightened. "Got too much pride in him. Or not pride, but—"

"Old woman," the midwife said, "spear your grubby finger in that child one more time, and I'm gonna do the same to you." She stuck her index finger into Grandmama's buttocks. "And I won't be pokin' your mouth, that's certain."

Grandmama lifted the boy's hindquarter by his feet. "Gotta check my boy."

"Ain't your boy, sister. Claire's boy! You ain't doing the birthing around here, I am!"

Grandmama delivered the child to Claire. "Daughter, we might finally got a worker." Grandmama pulled the boy's ear and looked inside. "The Good Lord has called on Americans to restore the world. One worker at a time. One boy made into a man. Men to make sacred the profane. Sooner you get up and around, girl, sooner you can have another."

The midwife opened the bedroom door. "Sonny!" A four-foot-tall, brown-eyed boy appeared. "Momma and child are alive. Go tell the Mister he got his self a son. 'Bout ten pounds. Good field hand to come. Run along."

The boy jumped over rows of emergent corn. He shouted, "Mister Whitaker! Mrs. Whitaker's fine, and she gave you a son! Big one too! Ten pounder!" He panted, eyes wide. "Gonna hop or holler or something, Mister Whitaker?"

Joseph considered the words as though they were in a foreign tongue. He could see the sun fight free of the moon to chase shadow from landscape, to reclaim the fields, to save the house. He began to dig. "Be in when chores let me."

The boy turned to run back.

Joseph fixed tight his hat. "Ten pounds, you say?"

The boy stopped. "Ten whole pounds. A gift from God Almighty!"

"Another field hand's the only gift we need," Joseph said.

The boy ran and shouted back, "They all waitin' on me, I expect! Momma brought me to spread the news!"

Joseph counted rows to estimate potential harvest. He owed

money to the midwife. He owed the bank for seed grain. He had a son to pay for. He looked overhead, wondering if delivery of mail from the sky was easier than pushing dirt on the ground. But his father was a farmer. How could he be anything but a farmer?

***

Sounds of Joseph's feet mixed with crickets singing each other to sleep. The stars above were calm. On the horizon, they pulsed for reasons he did not comprehend. He grabbed a bucket to draw water from the pump. Crickets hushed in tall grass near the pipe. He paused. One began to speak to others, and they answered. Joseph drew the pump handle high with a screech. Crickets muted. He washed hands, cleaned boots, and headed for the farmhouse. A pillar of smoke slanted from the chimney.

His lantern cast rims of light across Joseph's face. His boot soles thumped on floor planks. Through the bedroom doorway, Joseph saw Claire asleep, as was their son in a basket next to the bed. Light from Venus leaked through a window on the boy, immobilized by cloth wrap so as not to touch himself in a sinful manner.

Joseph lifted him near the window. He whispered, "Twixt them slits for eyes you got, I see a likeness…sort of." He tilted and rotated the baby for a full three-dimensional view. "Look pretty near like a mirror to me, boy. A very big boy. What'd we decide to call you anyhows?"

"We'll call him Little John for now," Claire said, "but John D'Wayne Whitaker's the name."

"Don't I get no say in this? After all, he's—"

"My son," she said. "Name's John D'Wayne."

Joseph paused. He nodded. "John D'Wayne." He studied the boy, stared his future in the face, and thought about the past. He murmured, "Now that you're here, there are expectations. Roles you don't choose. Nothing's more important than family. Our name and way of life will live after us."

"Put him down, Joseph. Needs his sleep."

Joseph laid the newborn in his basket. He left the room.

Claire reached down to stroke the boy's face. "*My* boy. I'll never give you up for nothing, not to no one, never. Not like momma did

6

Little Orville. You're my boy, you hear?"

The boy coughed. Claire sat up. Joseph stopped in the hallway.

The boy coughed again and kept coughing, wheezing.

Joseph ran back. He unwound cloth that bound the boy's chest.

"Joseph, you shouldn't do that!"

"Says who, your mother? We don't need a second lesson in stupidity." He handed the naked child to Claire. "Hold him close, skin to skin." He covered them. He stoked the fireplace. He watched them, waiting for the boy to stop coughing.

In the kitchen, Joseph pulled a sweat-stained paper from his overalls pocket. He withdrew handfuls of newspaper clippings and groped for the stub of a pencil.

He sat. The chair creaked. He moved the lantern close and turned his ear toward the bedroom. Hesitant, he reached for the Bible. He checked darkness down the hallway. He opened the Bible to read. Shaking his head, he snapped it shut. On its smooth back cover, he placed paper, turned toward the light.

To My Son:                                        Tuesday, June 22, 1926

You were born today. You got a sister, Helen. Grandmama lives with us, for now. I'm a farmer. You will be too.

You come to quite a place. Always something new, including you. Radio down at the feed and seed. Hear people talk you don't know and can't see. Prohibition's on, but don't apply in this house. A Tennessee teacher went to jail for teaching people come from apes. Papers say a captain from Kansas got cross county roads started. Cement ones, mostly for something called a Model-T. People are back at stadiums to see Babe Ruth.

It's the fiftieth anniversary of Custer's last stand. Hundred years since the death of Jefferson and Adams. Hundred fifty years ago, America declared independence.

A son, he thought. Need you as a man. Can't afford you as a boy. He reread the letter. He folded it, lingered, slipped it in the Bible. He whispered toward the bedroom, "If you're gonna follow in my footsteps, I better be surefooted. But before all that, you gotta survive the night, the week. One step at a time."

7

# 2. Premonition

Grandmama approached Joseph from behind his back. She badgered, "I expect to be buried beside the only one I serve 'sides Jesus. James Waldo Pilcher would never give up an leave Illinois."

Joseph did not turn to face her. "I ain't JW. You want to stay? Stay."

"Then what are you waitin' for? From the looks of these scrawny little ones, shoulda left here long ago."

Joseph closed his eyes, mumbling to himself, "Don't pretend to take my mother's place."

He looked over fields bare of all but the hardiest of weeds. He wondered, What's to become of America? When the plain man works himself to the bone, still short of a meal; when bankers pilfer power behind a wall of words; when honor and virtue are too expensive to keep.

The sun was high and hot. Claire held hands with the twins, Rachel and Thomas, almost five years old. Two years more familiar with the world, Little John ran around the auto. He counted laps with each pass. "Helen taught me how to count to a hunnert! Numbers follow in order, way breaths do!"

Joseph faced Claire. "Uncle Wendel says fields are good in Iowa." He tapped the car. "This is how we get there—brother Harry's Plymouth. Been run hard. Hope we make it, and me back here in a week. Hitch rides back to Iowa."

Joseph leaned in. Claire drew back. He glared at her, paused and whispered, "Don't much care for living under another man's roof."

Claire watched the ground. "Until we get back on our feet."

Joseph caught Grandmama's eye. He stood straight and turned

for the car.

Little John ran by Claire and touched the car for another lap. "Does it see from them big eyes up front, Ma?"

Claire leaned down, whispering on John's next pass, "Don't you get excited. You know what happens."

Grandmama stiffened near the rear bumper. "Running without a purpose is like laughing because you feel like it. Remember what our Good Book says about discipline and the devil, daughter."

Joseph pushed on belts under the car's hood. "Boy's learning to count, Granny. One less thing he'll depend on from others." He knew she loathed the name Granny.

Little John passed Grandmama again. He snagged the toe of her boot. Claire hesitated, then lunged to catch him, short by the distance of her indecision. John's chin met gravel to roll a pattern up the side of his cheek.

Claire lifted the boy. "This ain't Orville Clem, momma!"

Grandmama's eyes flared, her mouth gathered air. With an about-face for the house, she said, "Better hurt him now 'fore he hurts you later."

John wheezed. Claire whispered, "Stop that or Daddy's gonna think you're weak." John nodded, eyes panicked, throat constricted. She dabbed blood from his face and shirt with a handkerchief.

Joseph watched Grandmama leave. He crouched to examine tires. "Son, have you read about the boy who discovered Planet X?"

"Wait, Joseph. Gotta clean him up," Claire said. She kept scrubbing the same spot. "Breathe even, John."

She brushed dust from his knickers. She licked her fingers and pressed down hair on his head. "That's it. Now Daddy asked if you read one of his stories."

John ran to his father, now under the car. "Don't know how to read, Pa. Too much to learn on the farm."

Claire followed the boy. She spit on the handkerchief to rub again the stain on his shirt.

From under the auto, Joseph's voice sounded as if from a cave. "Read me a snippet about a farmboy named Clyde from up north in Streator. Searched the sky for heavenly bodies. Folks laughed at him, but guess what?"

"What, Pa?"

"He moved to Arizona and discovered Planet X."

"He found a planet in Arizona, Pa?"

"Persistence, boy. Counts for more than all the smarts in the world."

"Persistence. I'll remember, Pa."

"So, what was it you were doing when Grandmama got in your way, son?"

"Counting to a hunnert, Pa."

Joseph shoved on a spring shock absorber. "Finish?"

"No, Pa."

"What'd that boy up in Streator learn about people laughing at him?"

John hopped over his father's outstretched feet. "Twenty-two! Twenty-three!"

Claire tapped his shoulder on the way by. "Slow down."

Joseph drug himself around the perimeter of the Plymouth. He pulled coils, pressed joints.

"A hunnert!" Breathing hard, John bent down at the car's rear bumper. He ran to its front, where his father hatched from beneath the vehicle. "I did it, Pa! I finished her off!"

Joseph stood and beat dirt from his pants. Through a cloud of dust, he checked windows in the house to see Grandmama's spying eyes slide behind a window frame. Joseph spit sand from the tip of his tongue. "Got yourself a start anyhows," he said.

Joseph pulled a letter from his pocket, held in John's face. "See this? Uncle Wendel wrote it a month ago. Words from the past here to change the present."

John snatched the paper and smudged it with blood. "All that in them marks? Don't see how!"

The man took his letter as John followed its path to his overalls pocket. "Gotta read to see, boy."

Joseph turned to the others. "This rig ain't a tractor. This trailer and the hitch we fashioned won't pull the house. Best of the best gets packed. Start to it."

Within hours their trailer was full. Joseph surveyed their hill on wheels as Grandmama surged out of the house, down steps, and over the dirt yard a step at a time. Like the advance of a glacier, till rolled either side of her possessions.

10

Joseph grimaced. "More Bibles."

"And Sunday programs!" Grandmama grunted.

"Think all them Bibles say something different, Grandma?"

Grandmama found a place for her property. She sat next to the children in the back seat. Claire reached in to seize John. "Sit up front with your momma."

Joseph took the driver's seat. "Everybody quiet, so I don't get nervous, needful of relaxation." Liquid swished in a flask pulled from his pocket. He watched Grandmama in the rearview mirror, her jaw muscles flexed.

The Plymouth groaned. Its transmission rattled. Possessions clanked and rang over gullies.

Joseph patted Claire's knee. "Apples in a basket," he said. "Shake 'em up to settle 'em down. Nothing but junk following us anyhows."

She twisted toward the door and tugged her dress at the ankle. "Yes, but it's our junk," she said.

The Plymouth shivered when a ridiculous squeal and snap emerged from the engine. Joseph braked.

Grandmama nodded. "Not even on the road yet and look what you did. Won't Harry be pleased when I tell him."

***

The Whitakers watched children drink from roadside puddles as Joseph drove by them. Skin-and-bone calves cried for dead mothers. Broken-down autos, overloaded like their own, served as mile markers under threatening skies.

In a village on a gravel road, the Whitakers saw the Oaky Doky restaurant beside a gas station. They passed beneath a sign reading *Standard Oil Ethyl*, in white letters on a blue background. Joseph nodded and said, "Rockefeller says it's seventeen cents a gallon."

Grandmama broke her long silence. "With the money you got, we'll run outta gas, middle of nowhere."

One of a half dozen used and worn out fan belts pulled from a rafter in the barn for one last life caused the car to shimmy as it slowed. Four gas pumps topped by glass cylinders were manned by attendants. A clean-cut man in a white jacket, black slacks, and black polished shoes tipped his hat to Joseph.

Whitakers left their car to stretch as attendants flitted about the auto and under the hood. Grandmama started for a bench shaded by an eastern wall. Joseph held her forearm. He placed one arm about her waist. Others stopped to stare.

He seated the woman, left, and returned with a tin cup of coffee.

Grandmama yanked it from his grasp. Water splashed on his boots.

He looked toward the car. Claire and the children turned away.

"Grandmama," he said. "I owe you plenty for matching your daughter and me. She's a fine cook and a good mother. JW must a been quite a man."

"And don't you forget it! I lost him when your good woman was thirteen."

"I know when—"

"Lost Alda Mae at ten months. Cora Bell, not quite a year, and my Little—" Grandmama stopped herself.

"I remember Orville Clem," Joseph said. "I know you're plenty angry. More sad, maybe. Or maybe you feel guilty. But past lives, sacred in memory, were not meant to taint the here and now. Now I got all the respect in the world for elder wisdom and right raising. When the kid deserves it, you crack 'im. Nothing wrong with it." He leaned down, one hand against the wall. He looked up into her face. "Better be the right reason. Otherwise, you touch my boy or the rest of 'em—who I feel for as you did for your own—I reckon I'll strike the first woman in my life if I have to.

"Follow?"

Welling, her eyes met his. She whispered, "But I miss them so."

Joseph stood straight. He sucked a snippet of air between tongue and teeth. Drops of rain began to mark his hat. He walked in the station to pay an old man for gasoline and return the cup.

Grandmama neared the Plymouth. Joseph crossed behind her. Tiny Rachel held her grandmother's hand and walked with her to the car.

Claire met Joseph. She brushed lint from his shirt, mouthing, "Will we get there?"

One attendant bowed. "Thank you, sir. Please stop by again, sir."

Seated in the car, Claire turned to check her children settled in the back. She straightened Helen's dress.

"Momma, I'm hungry," Helen said.

"Soon, child. Drink some water. Fill up your tummy."

John appeared in a trance. From the back seat, he studied a pump island lit by a shaft of sunlight.

Claire tapped his hand. "John, why, you little stinker. Come sit by your momma."

She checked the emptiness to see what he saw. "Little John, don't put your nose against the glass. You'll dirty Uncle Harry's window."

John's eyes looked down the road. He placed his palm and outstretched fingers against the window. Grandmama watched him.

Claire reached for her handkerchief. "John D'Wayne Whitaker, get your dirty fingers off that glass. And what are you looking at, boy?"

The shaft of light disappeared. John relaxed and folded hands in his lap. He looked once at the floor and back out his window. "Nothing, Ma."

# 3. Work Was Sacred In 1933

Joseph and John stood in the barn. Both stared above. Joseph saw multiple beams support the roof by a single apex nail. He looked down at his seven-year-old son.

"Today we'll cut the field and bail it," he said. "No dilly-dally. Wendel wants his work done quick." Through open barn doors, Joseph scanned the horizon. "Shoulda been done already. Hay's pulling nutrient back to root. Livestock won't survive a hard winter on it."

He handed John a sickle. "Your first job for Aunt Arlene and Uncle Wendel. It's pretty clear we want to keep Wendel happy if he's to see a fair trade for temporary quarters and food in the belly. No labor, no matter how humble, is ever demeaning, John."

Joseph leaned under the flatbed to tighten a bolt, rocking the vehicle. "Ain't just the rules of nature you gotta follow, John—rules of man too. As you have noticed, FDR is a touchy subject. Wendel don't like charity, and he don't like cripples. Don't expect you'll bring up neither. But the last thing we want is to anger the man that give us work and shelter."

Joseph harnessed Cleveland and Wilson, Wendel's Ayrshire ox team. A breed known for its stamina and temper. He yoked the flatbed to a labyrinth of leather straps and metal rings. "Beware of luxury and too much comfort, John. Avoid crowds and their approval. These things corrupt character. Doing makes a man, not display."

"I'll beware, Pa."

Joseph pulled hard on a strap. "All that pleasure-seeking had something to do with the Great War. People tried to make up for

14

whatever we lost over there, and it wasn't the battles. Look what it got us. Another nightmare. Full-fledged depression."

"Still having bad dreams about the war, Pa? Like Grandmama says?"

"Only weak men have nightmares about hard times, John."

"That's right, Pa, you're strong. Grandmama says the war was wrath of God come down on us for sins of the drink, gambles on the railroad, and bringing Catholics from across the sea to build 'em. Time to follow fundamentals like Mister Dixon says in his book."

Joseph shrugged. He cinched reins. "This land will strengthen you as a man, and in ways you interact with other men, John. No better way to independence than working the land and fair dealing with neighbors you know. Can't do neither in the city with strangers. Whole country seems to be packing up for them cities."

Joseph lifted his sickle to the flatbed. "One day soon we'll teach you on that twelve-gauge, John. Add hunting to your skills, help feed the family. Hear there's a place couple hours walk, called the Castle Patch, full of game." Joseph looked down at John. "Remember, son, out here we harvest nature, don't savage it. Something city folk don't understand—harvest, savage."

"I'll never live in the city, Pa."

"Do you remember what I said about problems, John?"

"Problems were made to fix, Pa. Farmers are problem fixers."

"Well, I found me a problem." Joseph disappeared behind bundles of hay and returned with a sleepy puppy by the scruff of its neck. "Here's the problem. Collie. Uncle Wendel says we oughta shoot him. Keep him from going hungry."

The dog yawned, its mouth open wide.

"Don't shoot him, Pa! I'll work twice as hard, feed us both!"

"Here you go then. Somebody to see the world with."

The dog wagged its tail and whimpered. Saliva formed froth in corners of its mouth.

John held the dog. He laughed. "Bubbles…"

"What's that?"

"He's making bubbles in his mouth, Pa." John giggled. He inspected his new friend and all his parts. "Do I get to name him?"

Joseph nodded.

John repositioned the dog's face. He intercepted its gaze as it looked about. He laughed. "See that? He keeps making bubbles...Bubbles! That's your name, boy. Little John and Little Bubbles. You and me, we're friends!"

He sat the animal down, grabbed his sickle, and ran for the fields. "Come on, Bubbles, let's get to work!" Bubbles chased him.

Joseph climbed the flatbed. He whipped the reins. "Heya! 'Mon now!"

With a bent axle, wheels wobbled out of balance. Absent wooden spokes made a round wheel elliptical. The flatbed pitched and yawed in a drunken sway.

In the field, John trailed the flatbed as he cut grass with a sickle. Bubbles attacked John's pant leg, shaking it. John set him back. "Don't let Pa see you shirk or he'll plug you one, feed you to the pigs. Gotta work, boy, twice as hard."

Bubbles barked.

"Don't worry, I'll protect you. You'll protect me too. Pa says there's nothing more important than family. You're family now."

Repeated commands seemed to have little effect on the dog until finally, Bubbles sat still. Bubbles watched the boy recede, then ran to catch up and sat again, focused on John.

Farmyards dotted the expanse as islands on a field ocean. John saw his own farmyard. Towels flapped on the clothesline.

"You know I've been able to count for a while, Bubs, but Pa just taught me how to average." His sickle slid through grass. "I know the average number of trees in the average farmyard, and number of kids in the average house. Average number of locusts is three per swing."

Locusts were everywhere to compound troubles and compete for food, even eating paint off buildings. Under John's nose was a fierce contest for scarce resources, where winners won the right to live another day.

Like the pendulum of a clock, John whipped the sickle back and forth. Joseph cut grass thirty yards ahead. Up and down the field they went. A fistful of long blades, taut and twisted, served as twine substitute to wrap and tie each parcel thrown on the flatbed. Sweat split dirt trails down the side of John's face. Hours passed as the sun met its horizon. Songs from animals and insects began to be sung.

"Wendel wants this field done today, John. We're three quarters there, but we'll break for the nightly show and water the team. I'll turn the boys for our next run. You scoop 'em some drink from the creek. We'll eat and rest a bit."

Next to their flatbed, father and son carved out niches in the field. They pulled cornbread and spicy dried meat from denim bags. Bags made from legs of worn-out overalls scissored off and stitched at the knee. Bubbles lay close to the boy. John shared his cornbread with Bubbles. They all watched light depart the earth with a pygmy portion of melancholy.

"Thomas and Rachel are out there playing while I'm here working, Pa. Guess that makes me a working man."

Joseph nodded.

"More work we gotta do in the barn, right, Pa?"

Joseph hummed a quick note of agreement.

Yellow cirrostratus wisps intercepted sunlight. Lower in altitude, as if strewn from coins in a jar, red-rimmed silver-dollar clouds deflected the sun into fans of sequin light. Lower still, cumulus clouds turned purple and Prussian blue.

Joseph stood. He dusted his seat.

John hopped to attention. "Let's get to it, Bubbles."

Joseph pointed. "Man in the moon is smiling big on us."

"Full moon, Pa. Think there's really a man in the moon?"

"Don't suppose."

"Think there'll ever be folks up there, Pa? Like you and me, looking back our way?"

"Don't reckon so."

"Me neither, Pa."

From the valley came Wendel's voice. "Work's to be done, Joseph! You doing it?"

Joseph stepped around the flatbed to see Wendel. He motioned to clean fields.

"And what about the rest ya ain't cut yet? Need it done now, not next week!"

Joseph nodded and mounted the flatbed. John lifted Bubbles to his side.

Wendel trotted up the rise, patrolled grass cargo, and counted bundles. He checked ox reins and tugged straps. "Joseph, there's a penny auction coming to Grozier's place. Owes them bankers eight hundred dollars, and they're gonna hock everything the man's got. Folks organizing to stop it. You in?"

Joseph considered the dusk. "Got no affection for them bankers, Wendel. But stringing a noose from the haymow ain't right either."

"Why not save a farmer from the likes a that bunch, Joseph?"

"Penny auctions are organized by the same fellas who started Milo's Farmer Union, Wendel. You know what they say—buy nothing, sell nothing. How right is that?"

"We're on strike to save our farms, Joseph. If them bankers say what we do is illegal, well I say there was a Tea Party that was illegal too."

"Wendel, I hear them unions are communist. The whole world is turning communist." Joseph shook his head. "Opposed to it."

"Don't forget, Whitaker, you got the work you got 'cause of my favor as in-law. Without me, what then?"

Joseph nodded once and whipped reins. He rolled past Wendel. John jumped aboard, Bubbles held close.

Wendel paced the flatbed. "No difference between Grozier, you, and me 'cept time. Them bankers got nothing but a piece a paper and a rag-tag military backing 'em. And we all know what their man Douglas MacArthur did to vets at Anacostia, don't we. Burned 'em down!" Wendel punched his own chest. "They're calling us fly-speckers and woe-be-tiders! And we work the land to feed them bastards so they can take it from us? No sir! They come for my property, I'll use the noose on 'em, and I'll have plenty of company. Won't turn my back on neighbors. They won't turn theirs on me!"

Wendel watched Joseph leave. John and Bubbles kept eyes on the man packed with rage. "Pa, what's a penny auction?"

"Bankers sell off everything to pay up on mortgage and loans farmers fall behind on."

"Neighbors stand with neighbors, Pa? Like Uncle Wendel says?"

"Give ya the shirt off their back if ya need it."

"So why don't you stand with 'em, Pa?"

With his thumb, Joseph polished a spot on leather reins. Robins picked the ground for grubs sacrificed to the avian exodus. Valleys took on autumn hues, warning of change.

"Did we make Uncle Wendel mad, Pa? Ain't that the last thing we wana do?"

# 4. Citizen Training

John sat in the back of the classroom. Pa says I gotta learn all I can to be an independent farmer, he thought. Feed the family. Free from them monopolies and wage slavery.

Miss Pancake clapped once. "Children, rise," she said. Classroom chairs clattered against floorboards. "Our national anthem is four years old. It took one hundred seventeen years to make it official. Respect it."

She pointed to the blackboard, chalk lyrics written over its surface. Hands over hearts, facing stripes with forty-eight stars, her class of five to eleven-year-olds sang in unison.

Miss Pancake stood erect in her white blouse and black ankle-length wool skirt. Her tight bun of sandy brown hair was tinged with gray. Wireframe spectacles perched on her nose.

Singing complete, students pledged allegiance.

"Do not slouch, children. Proper posture." Palms opened wide, Miss Pancake pressed down the air before her. All took their seats, shoulders back, hands folded on desktops.

A pine scent rose from timbers replaced in the floor. Warped windows distorted fallen prophecies from snowflakes outside. Wood beam roof supports met at the zenith where flags of tattered spider webs waved over forgotten landscape.

Helen leaned forward to whisper, "Have you seen him, Rachel? That man, Stevens, he waits for Miss Pancake every afternoon. Says the same thing every day, 'How can anyone ask for a prettier day?' Even when it rains. They got a thing going on, that's what I think."

"How do you know?" Rachel murmured.

"I do what I gotta to stay current. They'll talk for an hour or

19

more. At the end of which he waves goodbye and says, 'Wish upon a star tonight, Miss Pancake. Wish for another day just like this one.' I think he's a lonely man with nobody to visit."

"Or a happy man with no one he'd rather see, Helen."

Miss Pancake interrupted. "Ladies?"

The girls straightened, red-faced.

Hands folded, heels together, Miss Pancake spoke. "Today, children, history and government meet reading and writing. You will read about President Thomas Jefferson. You will write about similarities and differences between the president and yourself, his times, and yours." Miss Pancake walked down the aisle with two canvas-bound volumes. "As Abraham Lincoln said, we use books to converse with the dead, the absent, and the yet unborn. Books are a sacred thing, children. We're fortunate to have these precious vessels to share. Gather in two groups." She handed books to her class. "And remember, penmanship is an art. Graceful continuity, please."

Nine-year-old John opened the book for his group. He turned pages as though one of his grandmother's Bibles. From one hundred thirty years ago, John read aloud this message from a dead man: "I am not an advocate for frequent change in laws and constitutions. But laws and constitutions must go hand in hand with the process of the human mind. As that becomes more developed, more enlightened, as new discoveries are made, institutions must advance to keep pace with the times."

Two people away, around the human circle, Kevin Crownauer taunted John. "What'd ya find in there, Whitaker? Whitaker—"

Sitting between the two, Candace Jane Spaulding spun toward Kevin. "Silence, Crownauer."

Kevin coughed and leaned forward. "Hey Whitaker, gonna find smarts in there?"

As Candace spied authority, her hand seemed not so much to move but appear behind Kevin's head. She grabbed short red hair to pull back his skull. Her eyes met his. "I said, *silence*, Crownauer, or you'll wish you had not done injustice to man and God by your birth. So help me to kingdom come—"

At once, Candace released her grip, rested her hand on Kevin's shoulder, and glanced at the text for reference.

"Miss Spaulding?" Wooden footsteps were upon them. "I had no idea you and Mister Crownauer were so fond of one another."

Candace gasped. "We most certainly are not…so fond as it may appear, Miss Pancake."

"I see. Then what have you gained from our assignment thus far today? And so quickly." She bowed forward toward them, hands clasped behind her back.

"Most assuredly, Miss Pancake…I was demonstrating for Kevin the benefits of Jeffersonian succinctness and…clarity, ma'am."

Miss Pancake smiled. "Very well. Explain for me what led you to conclude President Jefferson would have such a grasp of another's attention, at recess. Both of you." She straightened and turned toward her desk.

Candace withdrew, flashed Kevin a foreboding look, and faced forward. Both responded, "Yes, ma'am."

John tried to ignore them but found himself reading the same line over and over. He raised his hand.

Miss Pancake nodded. "John?"

"If laws go hand in hand with the—" He paused to read from the text. "'Process of the human mind,' does that mean right and wrong change too? Aren't there truths that are true forever?"

"Good question, John. Who thinks right and wrong can change over time?" No one raised their hand. "Children, what if I should be the mayor? There is a law stating all witches are to be burned at the stake. Furthermore, I, as mayor, have the power to declare who is a witch, and I decide that you, Miss Spaulding, are a witch."

Candace Spaulding hailed Miss Pancake and was granted permission to speak. "I am not a witch, Miss Pancake. There are no such thing as witches."

"Indeed, but in my fictional scenario, I am the mayor. I decide who is a witch, and this is 1692, Salem, Massachusetts, where and when they did believe in witches. What then?"

Candace raised her hand and was acknowledged. "You can't be the mayor, Miss Pancake. You're a girl."

"Use your imagination," Miss Pancake said. She walked past Candace, patting her shoulder. "You are not a witch, dear girl. You are an angel." Speaking to the class, she said, "Now, in time, people of Salem found the idea of witches and witch-burning absurd. So

21

you see, children, laws had to change to keep pace with this process of the human mind."

"So laws are stupid," Kevin said.

Miss Pancake peeked over the top of her eyeglasses. "Kevin?"

"Sorry, ma'am."

"And?" she said.

Belatedly, he raised his hand, then put it down.

Miss Pancake approached the front. "I do not intend to create confusion on this matter of right and wrong. There are absolute truths. There are right and wrong ways to live one's life. We are a nation guided by moral virtues that temper our impulses and restrain our urge. This confers meaning to our natures. These virtues come from God and give birth to laws, which come from man. First-principles—the morals and their laws—are foundations of a true community. Society is held together by faith in God and enlightened agreement, children. Not chains, not the rule of a king.

"Yes, John?"

"But if men make laws, how do we know they're right?"

"Our Constitution has the final say, John, with a Bill of Rights protecting communities from federal intrusion. But on God's moral matters, powers above the law may intervene, as Mister Lincoln argued in his debates with Mister Douglas on the matter of slavery. Notice, moral laws can differ from local civic laws. It is illegal for one man to own another. It is also still illegal to carry firearms on your person in Marion, though no one today would do such a thing. This is not the wild west anymore. So, do not confuse objective moral laws with subjective local laws, or you risk presuming that law, and perhaps morality itself, are matters of mere preference.

"Yes, John?"

"If I always please other people, will I always be right?"

"You must find what is ethically right, John. Practice that. Popular opinion, though domineering in a democracy, is not necessarily right. This the Founders knew, and thus created for us a republic, not a democracy."

One question begot another. Ethics on the farm versus the city; personal rewards of moral practice; the fate of America if it should lose it.

Kevin Crownauer's reluctant hand was granted permission. "I

know a man that says, 'Do as I say, not as I do.' That means what he does ain't right, jus' right for him, sorta. And whatever it is ain't right for long. But when I get to be in his shoes, I can give orders that ain't right neither. And…well, I guess that jus' goes to show there ain't no right or wrong."

"Do you all understand what Kevin said?" Miss Pancake wrote on a slip of paper and verbally clarified Kevin's point simultaneously, a feat that left younger students awestruck. "Who made this remark, Kevin?"

He shrugged.

Miss Pancake placed a folded slip of paper in Kevin's shirt pocket. "Whatever guidance this statement might provide is negated by actions of the speaker," she said. "As a violation of ethics, we call this *hypocrisy*. Do as you *should*, children. Would you set a record long-distance run by taking a short cut? By riding a horse? Such actions would make great achievements a lie. Process is a moral matter, as our Founders enshrined in our Constitution.

"Remember, children, the world responds to truth and honest struggle. To see in another human being that commitment to climb the highest places moves something in us all. We celebrate the gallant soul that reveals our essence. Cheaters are quickly forgotten.

"Yes, John."

"Did you learn ethics in school, Miss Pancake?"

"Some. More by example, as we all do. Exemplified by those who lived by the highest standards of character and virtue. I practiced to be like them."

"Who, Miss Pancake?"

"Funny and compassionate, caring, and steady, my father and brother. Now time for recess, children. Off you go."

Higher matters than morals sent children for the doors. As they struggled to fit into coats and mittens, Miss Pancake tapped on her desk. "And, children, 'jus'' and 'sorta' are not proper pronunciations. You know that."

She moved to the window and sat on its sill to watch them play as was her habit. Seated, Miss Pancake's palm opened like catching rain. "Miss Spaulding," she said. "Mister Crownauer. Shall we?"

Both halted their escape.

\*\*\*

The school day ended. Miss Pancake walked to the exit. She pulled a rope hung from space above and rang the school bell. In the distance, parents were alerted their students would be home soon.

She opened the doors. Children walked down stairs in order. On solid ground, restraints released as each ran away.

There in his place beneath a pair of trees, Mister Stevens waited for his cue—the last of the children to fade into fields and forests for home.

John lingered at the stairway's base. He examined something not there. Miss Pancake watched him. "What's the matter, John?"

John twisted his mittened grip about the wood railing. He squinted in the afternoon sunlight. "My Pa says to be an independent man and a good citizen means you've gotta be a good farmer, and to be a good farmer you've gotta know just about everything. How long does it take to learn all there is to know, Miss Pancake?"

"John, you won't have time to learn everything."

Terror leached over his face. "But if I don't know everything, how can I know I'm right? And how can I know what's true?"

"John, there is more I do not know than I ever will." Miss Pancake smiled and glanced at Mister Stevens. He stepped back with a tip of his hat. She descended stairs. "In every earnest life, John, these questions are of enduring interest. Let us tackle being right first.

"Accept early on, John, that you will not always be right. You can only try your best. Being right is important but perhaps not the most important thing. Thomas Edison was asked if he were sorry to have tried a thousand ways to make a light bulb before finding one that worked. His answer was, no, he discovered a thousand things he didn't know before. His chronic probing and that of all responsible thinkers drove him, as it may drive you, toward consideration of alternatives. Others without your curiosity and the understanding it enables will be defenseless in the face of convenient answers." Miss Pancake knelt eye to eye with the boy. "Mistakes can be valuable, John. When Thomas Edison died, every light bulb across three thousand miles of this continent was turned off in unison to salute his life. Millions of people for one gallant soul. The more mistakes you make with honest effort and a sharp mind, the further you will go. Greatness courts failure. Stick your neck out, and learn as you live.

"Now for truth. It is not born whole, John. With continued search, you will build upon it step by step. Answers may not be obvious, but they are available. The more you know, the more you will realize there is to know. OK?"

John paused. He nodded.

She grabbed his shoulders and pulled him close. "Of all I have ever said to you, remember this: the exploration and discovery, the questions they answer and generate, give your life purpose. But, *it is the struggle for truth that gives life meaning.* And *that* is the experience of being alive. It's an adventure, John. Enjoy the quest."

John studied Miss Pancake, fearing to leave her face would dim the imprint on his heart and mind of what he felt and knew were true.

Miss Pancake stood. She turned John and swatted his behind. "Now, off you go. You have a friend waiting."

The crunch, crunch sound over frosty ground became a pitter-patter of steps away from the old schoolhouse. Positioned in the faded warmth of a level sun, Bubbles sat in his spot by the tall red maple.

Mister Stevens waved. "Well, howdy there, Miss Pancake! Fancy seeing you here. Just look at it! How can anyone ask for a prettier day?" Miss Pancake smiled. "Did you hear the good news, Miss Pancake? Even after Ford put out the workforce and the banks went under, in New York City, they built a building one hundred two stories high! Out west, they're building a forty-two-hundred-foot suspension bridge. A golden bridge. Good times are coming, Miss Pancake. Exciting times!"

John crammed papers and the stub of a pencil in his pocket. He brushed Bubbles' head as they passed the tall red maple for home. Tree limbs of a wood perimeter made sunlight flicker on John's boots like thoughts in his mind. Trotting by his side, Bubbles looked up at his master.

"Ah, shoot, boy, I'm sorry."

John crouched to hug Bubbles.

"I didn't greet you proper, did I? Just got a lot on my mind, that's all." He scratched the dog's head. He looked back at the schoolhouse through almost leafless trees. "Miss Pancake said I won't have time to learn everything, though I can't for the life of me figure why. If I don't learn what I need to be an independent man, we could go hungry, and I could lose you. But I can never lose you, Bubs. You're my best friend.

"Pa says salvation is food in the belly, but one thing I know already is there's no bigger salvation than friendship." He kissed Bubbles' muzzle and rubbed his face.

On his way home alone, Kevin Crownauer could hear the conversation between Miss Pancake and Mister Stevens wane with distance. He opened his slip of paper given earlier that day and read it. "Two negatives make a positive. Such as, 'ain't neither.' Furthermore, 'ain't' is not a word. You know that."

He smiled. He coughed and kept coughing.

\*\*\*

Farmers streamed into Marion, a city of thirty thousand. They looked like clones of one another—frayed overalls, stained straw hats, worn leather boots. They gawked at sparks that jumped from wires above trolley cars rumbling over uneven rails. Buildings made of brick advertised everything from furs to five and dime. Men employed by the WPA swept streets and doorways.

Outside Iowa Meat Packers, vehicles and horses arrived from miles around. Trucks bore banners that read "Fair Prices!" "Honest Pay!" and "Hungry Yet? You Will Be!"

With a thump, men rolled spiked telegraph poles off flatbeds at the Meat Packers' entrance. Men cheered. Rake and hoe handles swung in the air. One after another, trucks with cattle for sale arrived at the main gate and were turned away by a crowd of farmers.

Wendel slapped Joseph on the back. "This is where we draw the line, Joseph. Time for some citizen training. Our time. Like Grozier's penny auction, we're together now. The bank sold all he owned to neighbors for two dollars. Then neighbors sold Grozier's place back to Grozier for two bucks, and he went back to work his own place. That's what happens when farmers stick together.

Worked there, it'll work here too."

Mister von Schiller grabbed Joseph by the arm. "See them beef boys on the phone up there in the window?"

"I see 'em," Joseph said.

"Callin' reinforcements is what they're doing. But don't you worry, brother, no damn city boy pass the test a farmer give 'im."

Mister von Schiller cupped hands around his mouth to shout, "Farmer's Holiday Association is holdin' a holiday!"

Joseph watched police lean against squad cars. They chewed toothpicks. They tapped nightsticks against a stripe on their slacks.

Farmers repeated, "Eat your gold! Eat your gold!"

Wendel laughed. "What do you think, Joseph?"

"I think it's quite a sight, Wendel. Just not sure what kinda sight it is, heaven or hell?"

"Betwixt the two, Joseph. 'Fore day's out, it goes our way. Get the price we deserve. They won't break us down to wage slavers for them monopolies. We won't lay down for them bankers. No more high and mighty words turned into laws used against the man that feeds the rest. No, sir."

Joseph felt preposterous and exhilarated. He could feel his heart pound faster, aware of something he was not.

A bolt of energy charged up his spine. A teeming of grievous voices spun him about to see what he heard.

A wall of deputies fell into the crowd. The quick rhythm of nightsticks met with hoe handles. Blood squirted from faces. Gunfire erupted from one corner of the battle to set off a succession of gunpowder pops in response and reinforcement.

## 5. What the World Is Made Of

John, his brother Thomas, and Bubbles crossed fields and valleys, nearing a wall of trees that looked like a mountain range. Their father's twelve-gauge shotgun, almost as long as John was tall, tucked under John's arm.

"Because Pa's ma and baby sister died of starvation in '95 from the Panic of '93, Thomas. That's why Pa worries so. But with the Castle Patch and lowlands to feed us, we'll never go hungry. And while we bring home the game, Pa, Uncle Wendel, and the neighbors are meeting with Iowa Meat Packers to get a better price for pigs and cattle. Food and cash money—good times coming, brother."

"How's a place get a name like Castle Patch, John?"

"They say a man from New York City passed through here on his way to California's 1849 gold rush. Found he needed wilderness for his soul more than towns for his brain and the money to live in 'em, so he stayed. Claimed his parcel under the Homestead Act and built a home with his own two hands. After a hunnert years by himself, he got lonely and—"

"A hundred? John, you sure it was a hundred?"

"Maybe not. Maybe fifty, I don't know. Anyway, he got so lonely he decided to free himself of earthly worries and go to Heaven. A survivor of those Irish gang wars, he was opposed to bloodshed. So, rather than shoot himself, one night he went to bed and held his breath, which made him faint but far from dead. He tried to stop his heart, which only made him mad. Try as he might, he couldn't die. Then all of a sudden, in the middle of the night, the man heard bluebirds sing. He stepped outside and whistled up at them birds. Down came a toot from the trees. Up went a whistle and a stomp on the ground from the man. Pretty soon, they all sang the same tune. A popular big band song the birds heard on a radio someplace. Lots of trumpets, wind instruments, a bit a percussion, they say."

"They got radios back then, John?"

"Guess so. Finally, the man yelled, 'This is my castle! This is my patch!' And so the name, Castle Patch."

"What happened to the man, John?"

"Folks say he never could die. Became part of the forest, hid along dark ways never ventured by men before. Paths in the wood most pure and black as anger. Ways protected by his dragon."

They stopped before the wood barrier. Wide-eyed, they looked at each other. John pointed at a dark cavity. "Like that one!"

In they ran. The deeper they went, the darker it got. The place was permeated with a chatter only the forest seemed to understand.

Rising from a valley, they came upon open grassland crowned by a giant structure of what must have been the castle. A porch swing swayed in the breeze to pivot on a board broken off at one end of its seat. A rocker stripped of finish creaked forward and back. Windowless frames looked like entries to a cave in the dead mansion.

Thomas pondered the size of it. "Great golly…There really is a castle. Maybe there's really a dragon."

"There's a dragon all right, and we're gonna tame him, Thomas. Get all the game he's got. But gotta hurry, folks are hungry. They're counting on us."

"Why do dragons have all that game, John?"

"Treasure. Like city folks who surround themselves with things they don't need. So they don't have to pay attention to living, Pa says. Same for dragons."

Thomas grimaced. "I don't know about this…"

John held up the twelve-gauge. "What's the worst that can happen? Can't even kill us. Not for long, because God takes all good men to Heaven. Grandmama says the dead aren't really dead, they've been freed. I've got it all figured: we'll be honored by the respect of men or freed by the glory of God. Remember your Gospel—God freed Jesus."

Beyond the Castle, they approached a fence line, halting now and again to look back at the place. Bubbles mirrored their movements.

"Grass been eaten just this side of the fence, John. How's that you figure?"

"Dragon's been reaching over for food, Thomas."

"Dragons eat grass?"

"Sure thing."

Bubbles sniffed strands of tan horse hair hooked to barbed wire. Thomas picked a thin bundle of it from the fence and placed it in his pocket. John pulled up on the wire, his foot on a lower line, spread for passage. They scuttled up the grade to a hillcrest. Behind them, chimney smoke wafted from the castle.

At the summit, John pointed. "There he is, Tommy, our dragon."

Thomas squinted. "Why...that ain't no dragon, John. That's a horse!"

"Shhhh...That's no horse, *silly*. That's the holy grail, center of the world, gold at the end of the rainbow. *That* is what the world is made of. Mister Stevens said life's special if you let it be. Let it be, Thomas." John rolled on his back, twelve-gauge close to his chest. "That's no horse. That's a dragon. *Our* dragon. Remember how Ma said Pa gained honor as a doughboy in the Great War? Got his glory at the Battle of Argonne under General Liggett. Well, I'm the general here, and this here's our battle for the dragon. Tame that dragon, and we get more than just food on the table, we get known for character and courage."

Thomas considered what he heard. "That's a dragon, all right. Are there others, John?"

"Lots of 'em."

Thomas ran ahead. "Gonna get that dragon, Johnny!"

"Can't just get 'im! Gotta have a plan, Tommy!"

Thomas stopped. "A plan?"

"Yesssss. You're all cattywampus. Get back here...Now listen, I'll point at the beast and draw a slow circle with my finger to hypnotize him. Heard you can do that with chickens. The dragon will find himself bewitched. Now, to take the forward position demands bravery and daring. That's me. But you get the glory part. When I give the signal, you leap from behind the brute. Ride 'im till he's broke, tame, and friendly. Brains over brawn, brother. Let's go!"

In their positions, John stepped closer to the animal. He traced a spiral in the air. To flood its senses, he accompanied movements with loud breathing.

A voice bellowed from the hillcrest, "Hey! What a ya doin'?"

John fell from his trance to see who it was.

Bubbles barked.

Thomas sprang for the horse as the animal bucked with a convulsion, rippled from its neck to the tip of his hooves to kick anything nearby.

\*\*\*

Miss Pancake and Mister Stevens approached the schoolhouse two miles distant, Kevin Crownauer's farm behind them. A strong evening breeze worked against them.

"Mister Stevens, I have a question. Look around, tell me what you see."

"Just a road, Miss Pancake. Leaves still on a few trees over that way."

"More than that."

"I see a darkened sky with lights that twinkle, just barely. A faded rainbow of colors still over there on the horizon."

"Yes. More."

Mister Stevens cleared his throat. "Well…I see moonlit trim on clouds, traced out by a full-faced moon smiling so wide all we can see are his teeth. Off that way, I see wispy clouds high in the sky like brush strokes left by an artist in a world I'm surprised to find is real."

"What do you see, Miss Pancake?"

"A world—even in hard times—so magnificent, I too am amazed to find it real. While not far behind, in a house down the way, a boy lies dying of consumption." Miss Pancake shook her head. "Kevin was becoming such a fine gentleman; a citizen. A boy who might see the world the way you do, Mister Stevens—twinkling lights, and wispy clouds. And so I ask you, how can both be true? How can there be such beauty and anguish? Which is real and true and what the world is made of?" She glanced at fields infringed on the road. "I feel something I must have to live has left the air I breathe."

Mister Stevens fumbled for a handkerchief. For the first time in three years of knowing her, he held her hand. "What you need is here, Miss Pancake."

He looked to the road ahead as they walked. He checked the stars above. "I remember after my ma died, my pa was so lost he couldn't find his way. One day he told me six months apart was long enough, and he passed too. But my pa had a grand life, Miss Pancake. Grand because he had someone to share it with. And not just with Ma, but with God, right here all around us. Now I believe this is so because somebody...somebody told me, Miss Pancake. But not just anybody." Mister Stevens hesitated and glanced either side of the road ahead. "You see, something happened to me when I was a boy about Kevin's age. I fell out of a tree at the house, pretty near on top of my ma hanging up clothes. Soon as I hit the ground I was helped up by this fellow, I swear I was. The most wise, the most kind...man. He told me to be careful, and we talked for the longest time. I asked him, 'If I had died when I fell from that tree, would I wake up in the Kingdom, freed, like they say?' And do you know what he told me, Miss Pancake? He said, 'The Kingdom of the Father is upon the land, and men do not see it.'

"Now, my ma said I could not have met such a man, that I lay next to her while she called for Pa. But whatever really happened that day, I found something I didn't know I already had. The days and the nights, folks like you to share 'em with, I never take 'em for granted no more. It's true that hard times like these make people ask, Is there salvation to come? Well, here it is." He motioned toward their enclosure of earth and cosmic guardians. "We can decide to see the Kingdom or not. For me, that's easy. That don't mean this living always makes sense. It often don't seem to, but nobody told me it would."

Mister Stevens shrugged. "I dunno, Miss Pancake. I'm not a wise man or scholar. I live by the seat of my pants like most folks. I guess I figure we should share the tears, pray when we should, smile when we feel like it, and help others smile if only just a little whenever we can. You see, when a man's said and done, he hopes he had that chance to say—"

Like nervous nails in a coffee can, noise from a Stovebolt Six engine in a Chevy truck raced by from behind them. A Ford Model AA followed, its flatbed crowded with wounded farmers.

Miss Pancake covered her mouth. "Mister Stevens, is that Lou Cannon lying on that truck? And Andy Manson and— Why, they look...they look dead."

\*\*\*

Uncle Wendel seized Joseph's arm. "You can't leave the fight, Joseph. Would you want farmers to quit if they'd shot you out there today? It's what the world is made of now. Power versus those without it."

Grandmama stood with her Bible. Aunt Arlene entered with wet rags heated in the kitchen.

Joseph held a moist towel against his temple. "Wendel, I will stand by my neighbors, but I will not follow the mob. That today was shameful."

"What's shameful, Joseph was we didn't have more there to support us."

"Wendel, of all places when sticking together is needed for survival, Americans are killing Americans in the Heartland. That was nothing but lawless."

"Lawless on both sides, Joseph! Law is used against us now! Those bureaucrats and lawyers have forced us into the streets. You gonna lie down for it?"

Outside in the dark, John and Thomas neared home on a horse, Bubbles trotting by their side. A hemispheric glow hugged windows about the house. The horse kneeled, left his cargo, and turned for home. Thomas was groggy but awake, helped inside by John. Both were greeted by a burst of questions.

Claire hugged John. "What made you do such a fool thing?"

John dithered. "Well...how do you mean, Ma?"

"What persuaded you to chase that man's horse?"

"We...had to measure our character, Ma. Boy's gotta gain glory to be a man. Way Pa did in the Great War."

Joseph checked the blood on his cloth. "Not a thing glorious about that war, boy." Joseph's eyes met Claire's. "But a simple fact of nature is that a boy's gotta test danger. You've been trying to make a girl out of him since he was born."

Joseph lifted the shirt Thomas wore. He felt his ribs, a pair of bruises and a crease of dried blood in the shape of a horseshoe on his swollen chest. He opened the boy's mouth and looked in his throat for signs of bleeding. He lifted Thomas upside down. Still dizzy, the boy grumbled, but nothing ran out of his mouth. Joseph put him down. He smelled barrels of the twelve-gauge. "Get any game, John?"

John looked down. "No, Pa."

"No...no you didn't. Happens plenty. You win or you lose. So what do we eat tonight, son? Gotta save chickens for eggs 'fore there ain't no chickens left." John watched the floor. Joseph towered above him. "That's right, John. You don't know. I expect a few nights without meat will make a more determined hunter outta you."

Joseph pressed the cloth to his forehead. "If it ain't a war with foreigners, it's a war with the land," he said. "If it ain't a war with the land, it's a war with our own country. If it ain't a war with our own country, it's a war with that old woman's God! After all we've been through, what else can you call this life we got but a war each and every day? If we don't give life meaning, it ain't got none."

Wendel pointed toward town. "That's right, Whitaker. Life's a fight. You win or you lose. Make it mean something. You'll fight to keep a roof over your head, won't you?"

***

The windmill creaked a metronome beat in the night. Joseph entered the children's bedroom. Next to John, Bubbles raised his head to watch the man. Joseph nudged John. "Psst...Let's take a walk."

John massaged his eyes. He glanced out windows into blackness. "Where to, Pa?"

"Gonna get that game you missed 'fore we find ourselves without a place to live. Double-quick, before Wendel gets to morning chores."

On a swift walk, an hour from home, not a word spoken.

Bluebirds woke. Owls and raccoons went to bed. Joseph shifted his twelve-gauge from one arm to the other. "Everybody depends on everybody else to get by out here, John. You fail too many times, and somebody could die without enough food on the table. That somebody could be you, or your friend maybe."

John reached down to Bubbles, motioned closer. "I'll work harder, Pa. I'll do my part."

"Only reason that dog sleeps with you is because I told Wendel he keeps you calm, free of that breathing problem you got."

John checked his father's expression but admitted nothing.

"Don't want Wendel putting that dog back outside at night, John. Pretty soon he's gone missin', you follow?"

"Bubbles makes a good hunter, Pa. Smells out grouse and pheasants."

Joseph grunted. "Ain't seen it."

"You got a pretty stout knot on the noggin there, Pa." John smiled. "Guess you could use a stiff drink."

"Never touch the stuff."

"But your flask is always handy."

"Purposes other than drink, John.

"So, tell me, son, did you tame him?"

"Tame who, Pa?"

"Who do you think?"

"Yes, sir, we tamed him. Once Bubbles got him corralled and kept him on the straight and narrow, he did what we wanted. Thanks to Bubbles."

"So you made the dragon your ride, that right, son?"

John looked up at his father. "You call him the dragon too, Pa?"

"Everybody calls him that. Least early on. Funny thing is, dragons have magic powers until we're older. Like God, they depend on us, our perception of them."

Farmers could be seen in the distance, leaving their barns for fieldwork. Joseph quickened their pace. When they emerged from forest cover, the mansion was in view.

"There's the castle, son."

"You been to the castle, Pa?"

"Not this one." Joseph stopped. He shook his head. "Don't have time for this, but in we go. Quick."

Inside the house was little different from outside, a space vast and empty. Dust layered everything like sediment at the bottom of an air ocean. John ran over floorboards to a table next to a fireplace. "Right here's the table, Pa." Bubbles sniffed the spot.

Joseph stooped to flick a finger full of powder off an old iron grate. "Hasn't held a fire in years. Another fireplace in here?"

"I don't know, Pa. But this here's the spot. The man sat Thomas on this table, next to a big fire. Thomas came to now and again, maybe he'll remember."

Joseph whisked an even layer of dust from the tabletop. "Windy last night. Coulda covered the place in dirt, I suppose. This man you saw, John, was he a skinny sort a fella?"

"Skinny and wrinkly and hairless, like a stick figure brought to life. You seen the Castle Patch Man, Pa?"

"What makes you think this skinny fella and the Castle Patch Man are one and the same, John?"

"I think he said so."

"Did he now? He spoke to you?"

"Sure thing, Pa. Face to face. Said Thomas would live but not like it for a while. He talks to animals too. He cupped his ear like he was listening to somebody not there, then whispered in the dragon's ear to take us home, and off we went—led by Bubbles, I mean. Why you so interested in the man, Pa?"

"Folks say he has answers to the most important questions. By now, I know what questions to ask."

"Have you've seen him, Pa?"

"Not lately." Joseph looked about the place.

"What's the matter, Pa?"

"Something like this happened to me all those years ago. Came upon the man too soon, I guess. But I balanced the books. Paid for whatever it was kept me outta the grave early.

"Something's gonna happen, John. Something bad."

## 6. Bubbles

"In-laws are in the fields," Helen said. "Ma and Pa are leaving for town. Me and Rachel will have our swim and chores done before Pa gets back and you get your stupid fence holes dug, Little John."

John carried a shovel over his shoulder. "Forget these silly girls. Come on, Tommy…Bubs!"

On the porch, Joseph closed the door behind him. By his side, Claire whispered, "Joseph, what happened to Roy and Clara's boy, Thaddeus?"

"Shirtsleeve caught in the power take-off. Driveshaft sticks out back of the tractor, powers towed equipment. Probably reached over it for something."

She shook her head. "Thank God they're not here to see it."

Grandmama barked from inside. "Learn from Thaddeus, Joseph. A Christian man, home with the Lord."

Joseph stepped for the door. He pressed it open. "Read your Bible. Don't look like no word a no Lord I ever heard of." He pulled the door shut.

Muffled, Grandmama hollered, "God's truth helps us sleep at night!"

Joseph opened the door. "Truth so twisted round in those murderous stories of yours, can't figure nobody'd get no sleep."

He pulled his flask from an overalls pocket. He shook it at her, closed the door, and left the porch with Claire.

"Temperance, sinner!"

"Prohibition's over!" he said.

"If Carrie Nation could see you now!"

"She's dead!"

Grandmama kept shouting, but Joseph ignored her. He called to the children. "I want you kids to know, John shot the deer we're gonna butcher."

John nodded. "Bubbles pointed him out, Pa. I wouldn't have seen that deer if it weren't for Bubbles."

Joseph looked at Helen. "Makes the boy a man. Don't call him Little John no more. Now to the bunch of ya, stay out of that haymow and horse tank. Uncle Wendel wants chores done now, not next week. Them chores keep a roof over your head and food in your belly."

The children watched their Desoto drive away. Both girls ran for the horse tank in a nubby field chewed barren by a few slender cattle and ox team.

"Hey!" John shouted. "Can't go in there!"

John bit his lip and looked toward an unfinished fence row. He and Thomas watched the girls laugh and dance their way to the tank.

John and Thomas ran to catch up. Bubbles growled and crisscrossed their path.

Supplied by a windmill pump, the tank lay just beyond barbed wire. Asymmetric blades of the windmill turned with a recurrent squeak. With shirts and socks scattered, the boys slipped underwater. "In and out quick," John said.

Girls folded stockings then jumped in. Bubbles lapped refreshment from the tank. The children floated on their backs.

John took a quick bite of water, hesitant. "Don't nobody pee in here. This ain't the creek."

"Why?" Helen asked.

"It's drinking water, that's why."

Helen began to laugh. "Drink some, Little John?"

Bubbles barked and kept barking.

Disgusted, others started to leave the tank when Rachel screamed, "Cleveland!"

From the hilltop, Cleveland was on a full run for his property. The children splashed water to cool his fury. Bubbles bit at hooves that could have crushed him as Cleveland delivered a shock that lifted his intruders on a wave.

Horns burst holes through the thin tin barrier.

Cleveland slipped in fresh mud.

38

Angered, he slammed their perimeter.

Children shouted routes of escape as metal caved in about them.

Cleveland hammered the tank again, changed position, and hit it again as the barrier collapsed around them.

An explosion was heard with no assistant tremor from the tank.

A groan and exhale emerged from the animal.

Cleveland slumped against the container. Hooves dug for traction.

Another blast as the children twitched in unison, and Cleveland spun sideways. On his knees, he grappled with slippery earth and fell flat.

Joseph broke the gun's spine. Blue smoke slid from both barrels. Ejected shells bounced off his boot. He stepped over barbed wire on a march for the tank, fresh slugs inserted.

Joseph bent down next to Cleveland and his heaving chest.

The children peered over their deformed vessel. Cleveland's eyes, red with rage, met theirs to feed his strength.

The animal turned his snout toward the man. Joseph winced when Cleveland snorted a scarlet aerosol over Joseph's face. Joseph stood and snapped the barrels shut.

The girls turned to hide their eyes as both muzzles flashed. The boys' staring pupils contracted in response to light.

Cleveland's skull shattered as life left the animal in a seizure of heat, one last signature of existence racing away at the speed of light. His eyes dilated, turquoise reflected from their gaze.

Joseph walked through mud, around the ox, toward the house. Beyond the fence stood Claire, hands over her mouth; Grandmama on the porch with her Bible.

John gripped the metal wall above a pencil-thin fountain of water splattering Cleveland's face. "We're sorry, Pa! We were just playing when—"

Joseph spun back. "What did I say about the tank? Don't expect we're any closer to keeping that roof over our head, are you?"

"We figured we'd get more time for chores, Pa, and—"

"Figured wrong!" Joseph turned back for the house.

John pleaded, "We were just playing when he came on. We're good to old Cleveland. Never did him no har—"

"What made Cleveland a capital worker made him an

39

unstoppable fighter," Joseph said and kept walking.

"But couldn't you done something else to stop 'im, Pa? Couldn't you done something—"

Joseph twisted toward John. His brain overcome by the Roosevelt Recession, years in another man's house, his dissolving body forcing him from land that gave it life. He *had* been "doing something." When he faced John, he looked like someone else. He dropped the twelve-gauge. He lunged for John to yank him from the tank. Drops of water fanned off the boy's head. Joseph slapped him first with his palm, then back of his hand, from left, from right. "Thinking the world's gonna treat you fair 'cause you're a good person is like expectin' the ox not to charge 'cause you don't eat meat!"

Bubbles barked at the man.

Claire begged.

John's throat squealed for oxygen, his body wilting.

Joseph stilled his son long enough to strike with each heartbeat, then hit him again. "It don't make sense! No one said it would! Stop thinkin' living is supposed to be good! That's for young'uns! You're a goddamn man!"

Bubbles bit Joseph to rip skin on his leg. Joseph kicked the animal away.

Joseph dumped John like a basket against the ground. "You dishonor this family again or leave the bunch of us hungry without a place to live, you're on your own!" He paused over the boy. He turned for the house.

Piled in a heap of tears, there was no holding back this time. John looked to see his father recede, then hid his face and wheezed for air.

Silent, each child left the tank, got dressed, and walked by Cleveland's dead body and John. Bubbles snarled and braced for battle as the others passed.

\*\*\*

John sharpened his pencil with his pocket knife, scratched numbers on a page, and checked each value. He nodded. "Yes, Mister McCormick. Add these column totals on this side, subtract this opposite side, and you get this final number. At fifteen cents a pound for hogs and forty-three cents a bushel for corn, minus interest for the bank, supplies, and feed for draft horses, you come out with minus…minus three hunnert ninety-three dollars and…and twenty-five cents, sir."

Mister McCormick sat an arms' length away around a wooden table. He rubbed whiskers on his face. "And twenty-five cents, ya say."

"Neighbors run a tab, sir. Pay when they can. It's not charity. We're neighbors in the same boat."

"You're not telling folks my status are you, son?"

"Oh, no, sir! I didn't mean—I never share private business, sir. I said so first day, and I stand by—"

"OK, OK, your Pa don't raise no liars." The man walked to a kitchen drawer to withdraw a cloth pouch. "Before them no-good bankers get it, I figure those that do fair work deserve fair pay." He dropped twenty-five cents in John's hand. "Full day's salary."

John stared at the coins like they were food to a starving man. "So you'll call me back when things turn around, will you, sir?"

"Sure thing, John. But before you go—" Mister McCormick leaned over the paper and pointed. "Cross out that number. Write out, three hundred ninety-three dollars, and *no* cents.

"Now run along, John. I expect your furry buddy is waiting on you."

Arctic air pierced coat buttons to chill John's heart. Beneath a depressing gray sky, he pulled tight his wool cap, wrapped a scarf around his neck, and searched empty space. "Bubbles! Here, Bubs!"

Intermittent snow built up against the north ridge of everything. The annual burial commenced. Snowflakes dampened sound.

John appraised the distance. "Bubbles!"

John entered home to find his mother over the sink, her apron of bright red flowers about her waist. He removed his hat and coat. "Have you seen Bubbles, Ma? When I came out of the McCormick place, he was gone."

"Lowlands, with Uncle Wendel. Quail hunt."

John bolted out the back door. He dashed across fields, over fences, through brush. "Bubbles!"

John crested a hill. He saw Wendel walk through marsh grass, his body layered in clothing. Ahead, a white and russet mane hopped over growth. A covey of quail scattered in all directions. John could hear Wendel curse. John whistled as he ran. "Bubbles!" he shouted.

Bubbles' head popped up. "Bubs!" John called.

Under, around, and over obstacles, Bubbles doubled the speed of their approach.

"Uncle Wendel!"

Wendel stopped but did not turn. Quail flew ahead of the dog. They reversed course toward Wendel, too fast to track. He dropped his gun level to the earth. Another pair of quail broke free.

John strained to run faster. "Lay down, Bubbles! Stay!"

Brush and twigs moved to trace Bubbles' path until one last obstruction forced him to jump.

Recoil surged through the man. Light and smoke blossomed from the gun barrel as the blast expanded in a spherical sound wave on its way past John. In midair, Bubbles contorted and vanished in tall grass.

No sound could be heard. No cry from Bubbles. No screams from John. Not the crunch of icy earth beneath his feet as he ran.

When John arrived, Bubbles tried to stand but could not. He flopped about, soundless. Life sprayed from him like a hose.

John crouched on his knees to clutch their bodies close. Echoes from outside found their way into his brain. He pressed his face against Bubbles. "No, dear God! Please, God, don't—" He met both hands round the animal, clasped in prayer. Air squeezed in and out of John's throat. "Your paws between my palms. Pray, Bubs. Pray!"

Clumsy, frantic, John fought to coordinate Bubbles and himself to keep them together as his hands slipped off the wet animal. "Please, God!" he said.

John held Bubbles tight. He made promises. He reviewed actions deserving punishment. He struggled to breathe and kept praying. "Of all times I ever need a miracle, dear Lord, answer my prayer. I know you will, I know you will."

He rocked back and forth with the animal to still convulsions that shook them both.

Bubbles released a sound he could not have made and soaked the boy in a syrup of clots dripped from John's eyebrows, lips, and elbows.

Radial arms of sunshine broke in and out of cloud cover. John combed Bubbles' mane with his fingers. "See those rays from Heaven? The power of God's love heals all, Bubs. We're gonna see the world together. Lots more to see."

He held the dog's head still to look into his soul, but there was no movement of Bubbles' eyes, no permanent smile. Leaving the world as he entered, tiny bubbles formed and broke in a red liquid filling the animal's mouth.

A chickadee bent the limb of a sapling it landed on. It watched the scene. It tilted its head, one side, then another.

White flakes stood out against blood then disappeared into it. Already a rim of frosty white collected on Bubbles' neck.

Bubbles' head sagged from John's shoulder.

John sank his face into Bubbles' fur. "Is it true, Bubs? Is it true what they say? Have you been freed?"

\*\*\*

The end of another year, and Christmas break for students at the old schoolhouse. Buttoned and scarfed, children scattered for home. Rachel shook a pleat on Miss Pancake's dress. Eyes shaded from a grazing sun, the girl waited for permission to speak.

"Yes, Rachel?"

Rachel scanned their schoolyard. "Where's Mister Thaddeus Stevens?"

"I'm afraid Mister Stevens isn't here today, child."

"Will he be here tomorrow?"

"No, darling."

"Did you have a fight?"

"Oh no, no, we could never fight, sweetheart. You see...I loved Mister Stevens, Rachel."

By now, Rachel knew enough about English to recognize a sentence in past tense. "You don't love him no more?"

"Oh, I will always love Thaddeus Stevens, sweetheart. And—" Miss Pancake looked over grass stubble and patches of snow. "And I believe he will always love me too." She shook her head as the scene before her dissolved.

Rachel reached up to hold Miss Pancake's hand. "Did he die,

like Kevin Crownauer?"

Miss Pancake kept shaking her head.

Rachel waited, stroking Miss Pancake's hand, then stepped off the stairway to catch up with others.

Miss Pancake turned to go inside. She faced John standing in the aisle. "Oh, John…I am so sorry."

John nodded. "I guess we both lost our salvation."

She walked to John. She kneeled down to hold him close.

Miss Pancake watched him walk away, rounding the tall red maple for home.

She turned back to consider an empty spot beneath trees where Mister Stevens waited nightly. "My garden is already tilled," she said. "Keen for flowers in the spring. I will plant them for you, Mister Stevens."

Leaned against the rail, she folded her arms. "What would I do without my gardens, my children, and you? I so look forward to that day when we will be together again.

"Watch over this place with my father and brother, won't you? I suppose you three make quite a trio by now."

She turned for the doorway, then looked back to say, "You were wrong about one thing, you know. Of all the men past and present, you, Mister Stevens, are among the wisest."

As Miss Pancake entered the old schoolhouse, she heard a voice leave the schoolyard, "Wish upon a star tonight, Miss Pancake! Wish for another day just like this one!"

\*\*\*

Rachel sat next to Grandmama in a darkened room near the radio. Grandmama dug at her eye. Edward R. Murrow reported, "And on this day in 1938, Japan pounds Manchuria, as American, Soviet and German aid flows in to help the Chinese people."

Joseph arrived with possessions in a crate. "Grandmama, Rachel, pack your property at the double-quick. Today we move."

Grandmama puzzled. "Move?"

"That is what I said. If you would prefer to—"

"Where?"

"To town. I'm a railroad man now. Western Weighing and

Inspection Bureau."

"You can't turn your back on a way a life, Joseph."

"Can. Did. Pack. Two hours to gather what little junk we got before Wendel's home. We'll voice our appreciation in person, loaded up, ready to go. Take nothing that ain't ours. Leave it clean."

Both went upstairs. Grandmama pulled herself up with one hand and rubbed her eye with the other.

Footsteps crossed the kitchen floor. "Work ain't finished, Whitaker."

Joseph stopped. "Wendel, I thank you for your generosity."

"Owe me your word. Said you'd do the work I got."

"Paid you square with the work we done."

"No railroad work support the bunch you got."

"Railroad pay is honest pay, Wendel."

"You're a free tradesman. Wage labor don't make citizens." Wendel leaned into Joseph. "Wouldn't be irate 'cause I rid the world of one bad huntin' dog, would ya?"

Joseph dropped his crate to grab John as he blasted through the door.

John twisted to escape. "Pa! Why you helping him?"

Joseph pinned John to the wall. "I'll knock you down if you keep on. We're here by this man's charity. He's your elder. Do not dishonor your family. Pack your belongings."

John yanked free. His eyes bored through his father. He ran upstairs.

Joseph met Wendel face to face. "You got a cruel streak, Wendel. I seen you shoot the dog, nothin' to it. Tired of a dog flushin' birds you can't hit." Wendel's eyes flashed aside. "Know what else?" Joseph said. "I seen you shoot that deputy in the back at Iowa Meat Packers. Ashamed I didn't turn you in. But tell you one thing sure, if I had a mean upbringing, I'd of sent you to hell both times."

Joseph paused on Wendel's eyes. He picked up his crate. He walked out the door to his rusted Desoto.

Wendel trembled. "You, Whitaker, shoulda not shot my ox! Eye for an eye, I say! Dog ain't worth no working ox! Life will get even with you, you hear me?"

## 7. Glory, Glory, Hallelujah

John and Candace Jane Spaulding walked to the county fair, both now seniors at Marion High School. Lavender light of a low-lying autumn sun tinted their faces. Beyond railroad tracks, calls to take a chance for a penny could be heard over bells and buzzers.

"That's right, Candace Jane; I'm gonna be a soldier in the war. I'll impress you like nobody can. Sure, it'll be hard, all the training and drills and fighting, sometimes hand to hand, I bet. But we get paid cash dollar I'll send home, and I'll return a hero, you just wait.

"Until then, Miss Spaulding, I figure you and me better have all the fun we can. Today the county fair, tomorrow we fish the Wapsipinicon River. No matter what, we'll catch fish because I keep a secret charm in my split-willow basket creel. A genuine ventilated counterbalanced Shakespeare spindle. I'm a fly fisherman. When I walk that fly on water, no fish can resist."

"Why do you like to fish so much, John?"

"Because that's where your friends are, Candace. Birds sing you a song, squirrels cuss you out, mayflies pop from waters for a life of just one day. And always smiling is that happy moon above. Hard to imagine a place so friendly, or pretty as that."

"Where else have you been?"

"Illinois."

"Nice there?"

"Sure is. Lot like this."

Candace squinted at cornfields in every direction to the horizon. "There are mountains out West, John. Oceans further on. My grandfather saw glaciers on volcanoes out in Washington State. It's a big country. I want to see those places, and I expect I will. Don't you want to see those places? Wouldn't you want to live there too?"

"Sure, I wanna see those places, after I do my duty and graduate from college. Miss Pancake used to say I have what it takes for college. But this is my home, Candace. Home is where you're raised. If I had my druthers, I'd fish that Wapsi for a month of Sundays. No matter where I get to or how I get there, I guess I'll always make my way back here somehow or other, even if it takes a miracle."

"What if I moved somewhere else, John? Would you move there too?"

John frowned. "You're moving?"

"I don't want to live on a farm, John. You moved a couple times pretty easy."

"Because our crops failed out east, then my pa got a job as inspector for the railroad. Are you moving?"

"What's he inspect?"

"I don't know what Pa does anymore. Candace, are you moving?"

Candace looked toward people riding skyward on a giant wheel invented in Illinois. "I have something to tell you, John." Both stopped. "I suppose you know my father drinks some," she said. "Reason it affects him so is because he's half Cherokee. Some people think that makes me Indian. Only reason you don't know is because the girls made a pact never to tell, and you live outside of town a good measure from neighbors."

John released lungs full of air. "That's it? You're not leaving?"

Toots from a distant train interrupted. John ran for the railroad tracks, ear to rail. "Come on, Candace Jane! Have a listen."

Candace pressed her ear to cold steel. "I can hear him coming down the line, John."

John laid a penny on the rail. "Watch this."

A Burlington engine chug-chugged round the bend, pulling twenty cars and a caboose.

"Do this, Candace!" John spotted the train's engineer and "pulled the chain."

The engineer blasted steam through a collapsed column of black smoke to make the train's whistle scream and John hoot.

47

Legs dangled in the air from open doors of one empty car with unpaid passengers, smoking cigarettes. A man could be seen reading a book in the caboose as it passed. Fire confined by a lantern swung from the handrail of this last orange-red carriage.

The couple dashed for the tracks. Candace snooped about railroad ties. "I hope we didn't lose Mister Lincoln again," she said.

"Patience, Candace." John followed his reference several steps along oil-stained gravel. On a tar-tinctured tie was a loop of baling wire. John lifted it to feel a base slime on its fragrant surface. It was a toy to run with, dipped in soapy water to create bubbles on the wind. "Bubbles," he whispered. The animal convulsed in his mind.

"What, John?"

"Over there, Candace. See him shine?" John grabbed the penny. He polished its surface. "Look how big he got. 'Bout an inch and a half wide, but you can still see the president and his monument."

"Well, would you look at that? How will you spend your penny, John?"

"Oh, it's more than money now, Candace. It's a memory maker." John handed her the copper disk. "Hold this penny tight, close your eyes, and no matter where you are or when you'll find yourself back here with me in this very spot."

Candace hesitated. "I could never take money from anyone."

"It's not money, silly. Been transformed by God's gravity and man's steel. Take it, and let's get to that fair!"

The train's taillight curved out of sight. Above a turquoise horizon, Venus spun earthward to chase the train.

Along the fair's midway, strangers talked to locals as if they knew them. To locals, it seemed to be what big cities must be like. Next to a giant ear of corn built from ears of corn, a man shouted at passing people. With greasy hair covered in bows, he pointed at John. "Step right up, sonny! Get any of this corn in that basket and win your little lady a bow!"

Candace searched. "Have any blue ones?"

"I got a blue one." He pulled an aqua bow from the back of his head. "Three throws, one penny."

"Here's your penny then." John took aim and bounced his first and second ear of dry corn off the basket base. He shook his head. "You got a spring or something under that basket, mister?"

48

"Wouldn't cheat no Iowonians, sonny."

John lobbed the last ear. It recoiled from the basket as if it had been thrown out.

The man held out his hand. John looked him in the eye and handed over another penny. "You said any corn, Mister. Well, here's some." John stripped the cob and threw a hand full of kernels in the basket. "I'll take the blue one."

"Not how the game's played, sonny. Wouldn't be fair if you played 'er by different rules."

"Game's rigged, mister. Unethical. Rules aren't as advertised."

Curious farmers joined a group of others to watch the local boy confront an outsider. "That right, sir?" asked one man. "You cheating folks here?"

"No, sir. I'm a God-fearin' man and don't cheat, nor steal, nor convert my neighbor's wife."

"Guess we can take a look-see at your basket then. Happy to prove yourself before God above and Iowans present. That so?"

The carnival man turned to Candace. "Here's your bow, little lady. Run along now. Step right up! Three pitches for a penny!"

John and Candace walked away and laughed each time they turned to see the number of straw hats and overalls swell about the corn toss.

"How 'bout some sweets, Candace Jane? Cotton candy's a favorite of all good Americans."

"You're spending too much money on me."

"And I'll spend as I see fit."

"Your mother doesn't need another reason to dislike me, John. I came to spend your time, not your money."

"Well, Miss Spaulding, aren't you swell. And I agree, time is more valuable than money. Hope I get all I want."

"Scared?"

"Me? Heck no. God chose Americans to right the world. What will become of this country if I don't do my part in that plan? Other boys fight the good fight, and me not do my duty? No, ma'am."

"But, John, think what could happen."

"Don't think I don't. Those Sullivan brothers from up in Waterloo, all five killed on the same ship at Guadalcanal. But did you know the Sullivans' last child, their daughter, Genevieve, she joined the navy? Courage like that makes you strong, Candace, like you want to do your share. Plus, this war's bigger than the Great War. I'd have more honor and glory than my pa. I'd be a hero. We'd all be heroes when we come back."

"What if you don't come back?"

***

John was part of the 738<sup>th</sup> Military Police Battalion, dispatched on the seven-thousand-island archipelago of The Philippines, in Manila. The second-most devastated city of World War II, after Warsaw, Poland. John had new friends in Levantino, Skeeter, and Roy, all military police.

Levantino negotiated mosquito nets to hand out letters from home. He handed one to John. "Here's yours, farmboy. Usually, you get 'em in twos. Who's it this time? Mom or the girl?"

"Mom," John said.

John read, "You are courageous just for being there, son. Do not volunteer for dangerous duty. Let lesser boys do that."

One page into a two-page letter John reread lines. "Don't be surprised if things change while you're away. Girls come and go."

Remarks from Grandmama ended the second page. "I could see it when you were born, John. Do God's work. Mind your *p*s and *q*s."

"Mind yours," he said.

John stamped and sealed shut a letter to Candace. He wrapped blank paper around cash, placed it in a stamped envelope for home and flicked two letters in a corner for pickup. "Levi, you sure there's not another letter for me?"

Roy lit a cigarette. "I've decided to name our group The Pure Breeds."

Levantino tapped a cigarette ash in Roy's direction. "How 'bout The Purbs for short?"

John sorted through letters in a pile. He said, "Inside a day, we'll be known as The Turds by every patrol on base."

Levantino laughed. "I like it! But if they call me a turd to my face, I'll bean 'em one. Bronx guys ain't afraid a nobody. Not God or J.P. Morgan."

50

Roy smiled. "What about Skeeter? You're afraid of him, aren't you, Levi?"

"Skeeter? Hell no." Levantino bumped Skeeter. "Stand up, Skeet, and put the knife down. Let me show The Turds I ain't afraid of no Wyoming mountain man who spent his life on horseys chasing pigs like old farmboy over here."

"Doggies," Skeeter said.

Levi cringed. "Dogs? You people really are crude out there. Off your ass, soldier!"

"They're cows. We call 'em doggies, city boy." Skeeter stood. He spit tobacco with meteoric splatter against Levantino's boots.

Levantino watched the man rise. He tilted back until he nearly fell over. "Ain't no way you could ride a horse. Other way around maybe."

The MPs laughed. Skeeter sat on his cot to whittle again and spit tobacco on the floor.

Levantino poked Skeeter. "That's right, you know who's boss. Big men come in tight packages, like me."

John grabbed his boots to polish. "Anger Skeeter, you'll be a tighter package than you are, Levi."

"Watch da mouth, farmboy!"

Manila was the kind of town few Americans had seen. Black market everything, rampant bribery, chronic murders, organized and unorganized crime everywhere. All was for sale, from drugs and girls to jeeps and ammunition stolen from the US Army. It was jeep thefts the MPs focused on this month. While MP duties appeared endless on paper, most of their time was spent looking for something to do. It was night. Manila was coming to life.

Roy blew smoke overhead. "First day off in a month. Chase tail, fellas?"

John applied polish to leather. "Have fun, Roy."

Roy slapped the side of John's head. "You have too much respect for honor, Whitaker. What's the skinny on this girl back home?" John said nothing. "Then let's shave sissies, Whitaker. Hell, even Skeet will do that." John breathed on the toe of his boot to fog a patch for buffing. "Stupid grunts don't know it's a man dressed up like a woman," Roy said. "Up to us to expose 'em, if you know what

51

I mean." He waved his cigarette in John's face. "Gonna wear a hole in those government issues?" John smiled and glossed his boot.

Levantino kicked Roy's behind. "Leave the farmer alone, beach boy. Whitty the farmer, and the Brawny Bronx Man—that's me— are gonna break heads tonight. Just one night left before the rat record stands for all time, and it's gonna be mine. You and the redneck hick go chase homos, but don't go pokin' any."

With Skeeter, Roy walked away and shouted, "I should be the one giving advice, Levi! I could have been your daddy, you know, but the guy in front of me had exact change!" Roy roared with laughter and disappeared into a murky Manila. "Hey, Levi! My pappy's a preacher! Bring your folks by when we get back to the States. He'll marry 'em!"

"Yeah, yeah, keep walking, beach bum!" Levantino slapped John's face, pointing an accusing finger at his nose. "Let's get 'em, Whitty. If I crack the record, we split the pool so you can send more money home to Mommy. And who knows? Maybe we'll stumble on Matros, and his big dollar dog fights again, so you can play hero and free puppies."

John nodded. "Well, it is true that Matros is a rat," he said.

"And there ain't no rat too big and bad for me. You know what they say. I ain't afraid of—"

"God or J.P. Morgan," John said. "Congratulations. John Pierpoint's been dead since 1913."

"Yeah, but he got a son named J.P. too."

"Did. Died two years ago."

"How do you know all that shit, Whitty?"

"I can read. Can you? Apparently not."

"Watch da mouth, pig poker!"

As the two approached their jeep, other MPs bellowed, "Is that you? The Turds? On another date, I see! She's a pretty one!"

Levantino saluted with an obscene gesture. "In your ear, sergeant shit-ass! My date's better looking than that dog you got!"

"Better shear that one, Levi!"

Levantino threw a clod of dirt. "I did already! Just not his face yet, lieutenant major asshole!"

In downtown Manila, alley trashcans contained the foul stench of rotted food, sometimes human bodies or their parts. Rodents came from miles around. MPs made a sport of killing them, tallied on Monday mornings outside enlisted mess hall.

John clamped a trashcan lid, hit the sides with his baton, and lifted its cover. Levi slammed away to cripple then crush heads of fleeing three and four-pound rats.

After hours of breaking heads, John wiped his face with sweat-drenched shirt sleeves. "I'm tired of this. Let's go, Levi."

"What are you tired of, hillbilly? You ain't hit a single rat!"

"Watching you and this flesh and bones mess you made and this sweltering humidity and these dead black alleys and the rancid stench of this place and your constant grunts and groans and giggles."

Levantino folded his arms. "Anything else?"

John started to speak.

"Shut up! Listen, Whitty, it's one a them nights when history is made. Gimme backup. One more and I'm breakin' the record." Levantino fixed his stained nightstick to John's nose, oscillating the handle. "With me?"

John cuffed the nightstick away from his face. He rubbed blood off his nose.

Lights from open windows extruded a shimmering hallway into every alley. Haunting sounds of the illegal emanated from surroundings—cheers from brutal cockfights, moans from opium houses, bedrooms, rooftops.

John sat against a trashcan, shoulders slumped, nightstick pinned against his knees. "More Americans have died in the last six months of this war than in the first three years, Levi. Thousands of caskets shipped home from Saipan, Okinawa, Iwo Jima. Civilizations rise and fall, and here we sit on the sidelines. Where's the honor, the glory?"

"Honor's in doing what you're told, plowboy. Told to be an MP, you're an MP. That's more than honor, that's luck. Glory's in staying outta them caskets and beatin' the rat record."

"I thought you wanted to climb the beach at Honshū? Capture the paper palace on your own?"

"Devil Divers changed my mind, Whitty. I saw the face of one a them guys headed for the water, damn near hit us. They're nuts. You know they got guns?"

"I put in for a transfer, Levi. I'm going to the front. Honor and glor—"

"You're a dumbass hick! See your buddy's head blown off, splash your shiny boots with his brains, you'll lose them stupid Midwestern morals. By then it's too late, you're eatin' bullets on the beach. Besides, you'd never leave me here by myself."

"There's a war on, Levi!"

"They lost Saipan, Okinawa, Iwo Jima, dipshit."

"And they won Lingling and Kweilin. China can't stop them, Levi."

"It's almost over. Trust me, hayseed. You're stayin' with me."

"And you'd rather be here, banging on rats in a trashcan?"

Levantino nodded. "That's right. And I like namin' 'em. Gives each a personal flair, don't ya think? Like Squallin' for Stalin, Moosey Dung for Mao Zedong." He chuckled. "How 'bout Shitler for Hitler!" He bent over laughing. He whispered, "I like names that rhyme with excrement. Skeeter taught me that—excrement. It means shit. Bet you didn't know that, did ya, Whitty."

"Sun's coming up, Levi. I need sleep."

A door opened to the alley, two buildings away. Two men and a woman stumbled out. John locked on sounds that entered the alley with them.

"Hear that, farmboy?"

John nodded.

"Don't look, Whitty, but we got spies. Above the door them drunks and whore come out of."

"Just hold on, Levi."

John shook a Lucky Strike from its carton, pressed it into Levantino's mouth, and lit the cigarette. Levantino drew hard on tobacco, a gleam on his face from the burn.

Another man exited the door. He dragged his dog by a choke chain as it limped, barely able to walk. He cursed and kicked the animal. He yanked it down the alley away from John and Levi.

"Dog fights, Whitaker. Matros is killing puppies again."

Levantino walked to the jeep. He slid a Thompson submachine gun from behind the front seat and held it behind his back. From the jeep and its pile of rats, John lifted a large rodent by the tail.

"What are you doing, Whitaker?"

"I said Matros is a rat. Somebody else said you are what you eat. Let's feed the rat a rat."

Levantino grinned, cigarette hung from his lips. "But the guys aren't gonna believe I tied the record if you stuff that rat into Matros."

"I'll say I fed him two."

"Two?" Levantino bit his fist, eyes clenched. "Yessss...I beat the record! Grunts will believe you. You're the only guy on base who ain't a liar...Least till now."

Rat in hand, John marched toward dog pits beyond a building they called The House of Ill Repute. Heads in windows above disappeared. Both MPs sprinted for the building.

Already tense, they jumped when screams and three quick gunshots escaped The House. A crash of glass and two flashes of sailor white dove out a window ahead of them

Levantino pursued. "Halt! MPs!"

John stowed his nightstick. Trailing Levantino, he drew his Colt .45, rat still in hand.

The escapees ducked into a back entrance toward the dog fights, followed by Levantino. Two mushrooms of flame cleared windows from The House of Ill Repute and knocked John to the ground, his rat lost on a forward spiral. John heard shouts and the agitated loading mechanism of Levantino's Thompson submachine gun as it pounded five rounds into a brick wall. John stood, ran, and tumbled in the back door they entered. Flattened a second time, this time by a stampede, John struggled to rise. "MPs! This is a—" Knocked down again. "Raid!"

His dog on a leash, Matros trampled over John on his way out.

"Bang, bang, you devil!" John yelled. "I'll get you, Matros!"

John rose to follow Levantino in hot pursuit of gamblers running upstairs. John scampered over piles of dead and dying dogs as the last of bettors fled in every direction, Filipino and American. Three steps at a time up dilapidated stairs in the dark, he could not see rotted holes in planks underfoot.

The MPs reached roof access together. They huffed and panted.

"You shoot somebody, Levi?"

"What now, Whitty?"

"Did you shoot somebody?"

"I tripped!"

John cringed and closed his eyes.

Levantino jabbed John with his gun butt. "Stop bitin' my ass. Go or no, which is it?"

"Who are we chasing, Levi?"

"Matros."

"He's gone, Levi."

"*Shit*. Then hell if I know."

"I thought you were after the sailors."

"If they're just taxi drivers for the marines, so what, Whitaker? They shot some Pino whores, so what? Sex is messy. We leave now, them and us be stateside inside a year, nothin' to it."

"We don't know they're sailors, Levi. Could be Pinos in black-market navy bellbottoms."

Levantino jerked his head back, the Thompson pulled close to his torso. "You're right. Stay low. You first."

John busted through the tin door, its doorstop snapped off a fetid roof. Levantino spun out to face empty whiskey and beer bottles.

Brown smoke heaved in surges from The House of Ill Repute. Flickers pranced through a putrid haze.

Levantino shrugged. "Better flush rooms downstairs."

John walked to the roof's edge. "Forget it, Levi. They're gone. And this place could light any second. We gotta get out of here."

Levantino pointed toward the roof next door, soon to be tinder dry. On it, a man watched luminous faces of people gather below. He was thin, wrinkled, and hairless, like a stick figure brought to life. "Hey, mister!" Levantino said. "Get the hell off that building!"

John studied the man. "It's you!" he shouted.

"Whitty, you know that guy?"

John holstered his .45. He ran downstairs.

"Whitaker!"

Through a shower of embers, two Filipinos drove John's jeep past him as he ran for The House of Ill Repute.

Levantino emerged on the alley. He turned ten steps for the jeep already distant. "Stop, or I'll shoot!" He stopped, arched his back, raised his machine gun, and yelled. "Goddamn it!" He reversed course for John. "I shoulda shot you bastards! They got my rats, Whitaker!"

John shouldered doors ablaze to the touch. Nails popped, timber cracked, tar on the building blistered. The man on the rooftop above followed John step for step.

Levantino dropped his Thompson and grabbed John by his belt. "What the hell, man, he's a goner!"

John broke free. Levantino yanked him back from a rain of cinders with the help of two other MPs. Together they dragged John far from the building and dumped him on the ground, wheezing.

"Holy shit-oly, Whitaker!" Levantino kicked John's behind. "What the hell do you think you're doing, and who was that?"

On hands and knees, sweat ran off John's face, clothes pasted to his body. "It was—" He gasped, breathless, shaking his head.

Levantino bowed down next to John. "Well, who'd you think it was, you dumbass bastard? You were pretty near toast. And what's wrong with you? You gonna die?"

John squeaked, "Don't tell. Bust me back to the States, and a shrink."

Levantino hesitated. He nodded. "Asthma. Gotcha." He stood to face gathering MPs. "All right, all right, what are you lookin' at? I made him run three miles, pulling my jeep. Just so happens, he misplaced it. Back to your stations. Nothing but a fire here. Move along, ladies."

John stood to watch flames heave from windows, one room after another, one floor to the next. Through a wall of heat so immense the world beyond distorted in wavering densities, John could see the man above return his gaze. The man then looked to one side, cupped his ear, listened to someone not there, and disappeared in an eruption of flame. Gawking crowds trampled each other in retreat.

"Look at that, Whitaker. Why is fire so fascinating to watch?"

With all firefighting equipment stolen or destroyed by Japan in retreat, the structure and twenty others, large and small, were consumed before cesspools, open sewer ditches, and bombed-out buildings halted the fire's advance.

Walking back to base, Levantino nudged John. "Already late in the morning, Whitty. You can cipher good. What time is it in Nip country?"

John checked his wristwatch and added an hour. "Eight fifteen a.m.. August six, in the year of our Lord, nineteen hunnert and forty-five."

Fifteen hundred miles away, a free-falling package called Little Boy triggered at a hypocenter eighteen hundred feet above ground. One particle of uranium 235 fired into another inside a torpedo-shaped metal case scribbled with notes for the Emperor and a pin-up of Rita Hayworth. When the event began, one intangible neutron begat two, two begat four, four became eight…

Seismic shivers of fission energy splashed across the populated basin and proximate hills. A transparent pressure veil moved outward over Hiroshima and American prisoners known by military intelligence to be there.

*** 

Without Japanese submission, threats of up to one million casualties from a beach invasion of Japan, and memories of Pearl Harbor still fresh, a second atomic bomb was dropped on Nagasaki. After a failed coup designed to destroy Emperor Hirohito's recorded announcement of surrender, it was broadcast on NHK radio. It was the first time the public heard his voice. It was Japan's first defeat in over two thousand five hundred years. Admiral Halsey withdrew air missions launched from carriers with orders to shoot down all snoopers, as he said, "Not vindictively but in a friendly sort of way." Seamen kept guns at the ready as they watched Admiral Ugaki's last kamikazes accept orders to plunge themselves into the sea. Admiral Halsey congratulated his men and added, "The use of insulting epithets in association with the Japanese as a race or individuals does not now become officers of the United States Navy."

John, Levantino, and MPs on base gathered around loudspeakers to hear voices broadcast from Tokyo Bay. By way of politics, Army General Douglas MacArthur led the ceremony for what was a naval victory. Navy Admiral Nimitz was granted rights to sign surrender documents after he voiced disdain over the appearance of MacArthur winning the Pacific.

Above President Truman's favored *USS Missouri* quarterdeck bulkhead, the Stars and Stripes, flown by Admiral Perry's 1853 flagship, flapped in the wind. Girdling the battleship, over 260 warships swarmed so thick the ocean seemed too small to hold them. The upper works of the *Missouri* were crammed with sailors. A multitude of uniforms from each Allied power maneuvered for position as General Umezu, Japan's feeble Mamoru Shigemitsu, and their entourage came aboard. They were not saluted.

"It is my earnest hope, and indeed the hope of all mankind," said MacArthur, "that from this solemn occasion a better world shall emerge out of blood and carnage of the past. A world dedicated to the dignity of man and fulfillment of his most cherished wish for freedom, tolerance, and justice."

At that moment, a rising curtain of 1,900 Allied aircraft vibrated Earth from one horizon to the other. Saluted off deck, the Japanese delegation, no longer adversaries, were provided coffee and cigarettes by order of Admiral Nimitz. Decks of each armada member exploded in song and dance.

MPs cheered. Levantino swung at the air. "Homeward bound!"

John shouted, "That's it? It's over?"

"Bet they're jitterbugging the streets in Manhattan, farmboy!"

Hitler succeeded in suicide. General Tojo did not. He was cared for and recovered in time to be executed.

This conflict was second only to the Civil War in the number of Americans killed. Only 6000 of the 90,000 German prisoners taken by Soviets at Stalingrad would survive, the last returning to Germany in 1955. The last Japanese soldier to relinquish his jungle hideout would do so on Lubang Island in 1974. Between the Atlantic and Pacific theaters, service and civilian, Allied and Axis, World War II buried over sixty-five million people—so many, a final number would never be known.

On this day, VJ-Day, Victory over Japan Day, September 2, 1945, a man named Ho Chi Minh formed what he called a Democratic Republic in a place called Vietnam.

# 8. Together Forever

John stopped at the door and whispered to Candace, "Sometimes a man has to choose between the family he came from and the one he's about to make. It's time my mother learned I don't belong to her."

John opened the door, his plans interrupted by Doctor Riley.

"Congratulations," the doctor said. "Home from the war and for a wedding to boot." He escorted the newlyweds to a room populated with John's family. The doctor addressed them all. "Grandmama wants to impart some wisdom on you, Joseph," the doctor said. "You too, John. You're the reason she's hanging on."

John hesitated. "Why me? What's wrong with her?"

Rachel straightened. "What about me?"

Joseph strode past the doctor. "Wisdom is it?"

Doctor Riley grabbed his arm. "You might be surprised."

"Might not." Joseph pulled away and entered Grandmama's room.

Grandmama lay on a couch. She looked Joseph up and down. A cloth held against one eye and the side of her face. "You win, Joseph."

"Win what?"

"My Bible."

"Just one?"

"My name's crossed out. Yours in its place."

"How could I accept such a...gift?"

"This way, you won't have to sneak a peek at it when you think no one's watching. Consider it your reward for keeping a roof over the family and food in their belly." Grandmama squinted at him, waiting. "And here you thought I was gonna stir things up. Instead, I give you my prized Bible and a compliment." Grandmama chuckled.

Joseph had never seen her smile. His baffled expression turned her chuckle into laughter.

Outside the room, Rachel looked at Helen, aghast. Claire shook her head. "The old woman's sobbing," Thomas said.

Sounds in the room subsided. Joseph emerged with Grandmama's Bible. He motioned John toward Grandmama's room without eye contact and sat on a chair.

John entered. She peered through one eye at John. "You never liked me, did you, boy?"

"Not for a long time."

"From the first day I checked you out full, I've loved you, John."

"Odd way of showing it."

"There's something you don't know, son. Saw it the day you was born. Then God answered my prayers to understand. My dying duty is to reveal the gift God gave you."

"You're not making sense, Grandmama."

"Oh, I will, John. You'll see."

"You don't have much time. Better speak your peace."

"You'll know I'm right, John. In that last tiny instant alive on this earth, you'll know."

"Know that you arranged for Uncle Wendel to take Bubbles from the McCormick place on a quail hunt? I already know that."

She struggled to her elbows. The cloth fell away. Mad flesh engorged her eye, appearing as though it were about to engulf her face and slide off onto the floor. John stepped back. She hissed, "All part a the plan! Most don't get the chance you got, boy."

"Plan is you lost your mind years ago when you lost your girls, your boy, and husband," John said. "You let rage dominate your life and gave it as freely as a kind person gives love."

"I didn't lose nobody, John."

"If anyone had something they cared for, you wanted it taken away so they could feel what you feel for what you did, Grandmama. For abandoning Orville Clem, when he begged you not to send him off to fight the Spanish. You lied about his age, and everybody knows it."

"For the glory of God, John! To repel the Catholics!"

"The chance I got is to bury my hatred for you at your grave. Hurry along, Grandmama. I'm a married man with a family on the way. I've got a life to live. I got a future. Yours is over. Stop wasting my time." John spun about-face and departed.

"Don't go, John! I have to tell you! See what I saw!"

John returned to the family with an air about him they'd never seen. "Ma," he said, "as soon as I left the States, you tried to pull Candace and me apart with your fabrications. Every letter was like the last. You and Pa couldn't even attend the justice of the peace. Well, we're together now and forever, whether you approve or you don't." John caught the flare of his father's eye. "And you won't have to trouble yourself with hungry offspring, Pa. Least not this one."

Joseph slid the Bible sideward off his lap, about to stand.

John stepped in front of him. "Not this time, Pa. I'm not that little boy swimming in the tank."

"Shoulda stayed a farmer, John. Instead, you're nothing but a floor sweeper."

"No labor, no matter how humble, is ever demeaning, right, Pa? And what's the difference whether I work in a factory or for the railroad?"

"You're nothing but a wage earner."

"Like you, Pa."

"I had to leave on account of my health."

"And I left on account of my future. Life is lived through a department store now, not off the land. That's what America became, one big city of buyers and sellers." John bent down, level with his father's face. "You should have never sided with Uncle Wendel."

"I didn't shoot that dog."

"You may as well have. You could have been strong, but you weren't. Salvation isn't food in the belly, that's survival. Salvation is family *and* friend. You dishonored both."

John straightened and turned for the exit.

Joseph's features relaxed, watching his son.

Claire intercepted John. She hugged him, then faced Candace. "I suppose I should congratulate you too," then did not, and turned for the window to turn skin on her hands. "I hope those twins on the way are OK," she said.

John stepped toward her. "What did you say, Mother?"

"You know what they say. Babies born from the wrong side of the tracks are slow learners. She's part Injun, you know."

Joseph's eyes lifted to Claire's profiled face. Newlyweds left out the exit with a slam of the door.

Claire knotted her kitchen apron, its red flowers faded and torn. She whispered to the windowpane, "He's *my* boy. I told him that, first day."

**PART TWO: HOLY IN THE MEMORY**

# 9. Free Will

Inside 213 Swathmore Street, a radio advertised Walt Disney's 1964 film hit *Marry Poppins* in theaters. John entered the kitchen. He turned off the radio. "So, little lady, when are you going to tell me what the kindergarten teacher said about our youngest son?"

Candace pulled a pie from the oven. "*Your* youngest had another fight in school on Friday, just after the fight he had on Thursday."

"I thought you went to find out what he likes in school?"

"I did—fighting. He's terribly strong-willed, often for the wrong thing. She said it's up to us to direct him. I hope the counselor helps with his problem. Maybe this fighting has something to do with it. And of course, Opal works in the principal's office. Wish we lived across town from that mean old woman, not across the street. She told Morgan he'd be nothing but a ditch digger." Candace sat her pie on the stovetop. "Oh, and Morgan's other favorite things are art and science, and he loves animals."

In the living room, Morgan sat in his rocking chair. He strained to sound out words in his *How and Why Book of Dinosaurs*, learning how ants survived dinosaurs to remain among us still. He tore open a mound of Play-Doh. He rolled antennae from its material merged with a round head to sculpt an ant of his own.

"Morgan," John said, "remember when you wanted honor and glory like soldiers in that World War Two movie? You'll get all you want if you catch the first fish. You'll be a famous fisherman, like those guys in my magazine. Your brothers are going."

Morgan ran for his father's fishing gear. He stood by the car, a fishing pole in his hand, his Twin Cities ball cap askance.

John stepped outside. "We'll stop by Bill's Bait Shop for

minnows, then catch some bass with 'em *after* church, Morgan."

Morgan slumped. "I want to be a famous fisherman."

"Hour of church won't hurt. Might help. Besides, your mom's taking her best apple pie for coffee afterwards. Get ready."

Inside, John slapped aftershave on his face. He clasped a fifteen-year Marion Manufacturing pin to his tie. He zipped up the back of Candace's dress. "Let's go, crew!" He pushed Junior and Elder out the door.

Stationed by the car with his rod and reel stood Morgan. His father's shadow approached until the boy was eclipsed by it. "Morgan, I told you to get ready!" John swatted Morgan's behind. Morgan hopped and covered his posterior with one hand but moved no further. "We're gonna be late because of you," John said.

Morgan stared at the ground.

John pointed. "In the house."

John pinched his ear. Morgan twisted free, stood at attention, and pulled tight his hat.

John leaned into the boy's face. "Do you really think your will is superior to mine? It's not. Now give me that." John clenched the fishing pole. He pried free one finger at a time. He lifted the boy and handed his stiff body to Candace. "Dress up this little devil. We'll clean his soul at church."

At Marion Christian Church, a silver communion plate traveled down the pew. A dirge oozed from the organ. A man coughed. Morgan heard it echo from above. He looked up at an arced ceiling, corrugated by titanic wood beams like ribs in a whale.

Candace interrupted prayer to grip short hairs on the back of Morgan's head, pushing it forward. "Pray," she whispered.

"For what?" Morgan's voice echoed from above.

Candace pulled Morgan's ear. She hissed, "In silence. Pray for salvation, for The Promised Land."

"But, Mommy, The Promised Land sounds like a crummy place."

She murmured, "The Promised Land is right here where we live, in Marion. That's what we believe."

Morgan listened to the minister pray aloud at his podium beneath a cross hanging from the ceiling. The man quoted scripture in an unintelligible mixture of love and slaughter. Morgan coughed and listened. He coughed again.

John leaned forward to look past Candace at Morgan.

Head bowed, eyes closed, Morgan waited for that skull-cracking thump from his father's middle finger.

\*\*\*

An old man limped past a tractor toward John and his sons. "Whitaker! What are you doing on my property?"

Morgan looked up to his father, who seemed not threatened by Mister von Schiller's greeting. Elder and Junior laughed.

"You old coot," John said, "I'm here to show you how to harvest. Same reason I come every spring."

Time-carved gullies in Mister von Schiller's face caused Morgan to stare as though witness to a deformity for the first time, gruesome but intriguing. He wore OshKosh overalls and a hat to match. Shirtless, the man's chestnut arms and neck bordered skin so white it looked painted.

Mister von Schiller shook John's hand. "How the hell are ya, John? How's your pappy doing? I told the old bastard if he'd come out here we'd catch some fine bass. But he's afraid of youngsters like me—he's got five months on me, ya know." The man's body jiggled with laughter. "And how's your ma?"

"Trouble with her back. Slowing down some."

"Hell, John, they'd not have all them ailments if they stayed outta them goddamn cities. I know a lot a good farmers and not a one of 'em lives in the city." He held his back with one hand. He chuckled and rotated a finger in an empty tooth socket. "Hell's pitutty, in the city you can't even build a fence if somebody on the far side of town happens to think it obstructs their right to see something or other. In the country you mind your own; the other fella, he mind his. We all pitch in when help's needed. Don't need no war on poverty to help each other out."

"But Johnson says mobilize government to beat poverty, way we beat Germany and Japan," John said.

"Bull crap. Another unconstitutional, undeclared war. Screw up like the one we got going on now. Gulf of Tonkin, my ass." Looking down at Morgan, the man growled. "Nation's going to hell, boy.

Decline of civilization right before your eyes. Like Rome. Ever hear of Rome?" Morgan shook his head. "Rome was a big country, kiddo, like this one. Powerful, militaristic, and rich. Gone. Gone to hell. Where do you think this country's gonna be by the time you're my age?" Morgan shrugged. "Gone!" Mister von Schiller snapped. "Gone to hell."

The man refocused on John. "Lost our civic virtue, what's proper, what ain't. It's human nature to be lazy about a thing. Takes extra effort to do right. In the city, you get lost in the crowd. Nobody knows ya, and you don't know nobody. So you measure up strangers with fashions, big cars, and gemstones." Mister von Schiller spit to the side. "Phooey! When you lose virtue in the city, you lose virtue in the nation, because that's where everybody lives now." He looked to the barn, shed, and fields, all works of his own. "But when you see things shinnied up against the yardstick God gave ya out here, why hell, all that other don't mean a hill a shit."

He motioned over trees in the distance and one lone gravestone enclosed by a crisp white picket fence. "Not a richer place on earth than right here in the middle a nowhere. All of it, the land, the people come and gone, the memories—

"Holy," he said.

He bent down over Morgan. "How can you feel special when there's so many of ya? Lost in the mass of folks, hidden by buildings, swallowed up by them roads, signs, and restaurants. How do you find meaning there?"

John patted Morgan on the head. "Be a while before the boy asks questions like that," he said.

"Ain't asking him to ask. Asking him to answer." The old man looked at Morgan. "Gonna be somebody? Or do you even need to be?" Mister von Schiller straightened, smiled, and pulled suspenders with his thumbs, an expression of country arrogance.

John squeezed Morgan's shoulder. "I teach my three to be responsible. You're right about getting lost in the crowd, but it's easier on the wife, and I've got a good job supporting them in town."

"Just because it's easy, don't make it better, John. And what the hell? Coulda had it good supporting 'em out here." He patted John on the shoulder. "But shit, John, I know you're a good man, and you

70

do what's right."

Mister von Schiller wiped sweat off his face with his forearm. He lifted his hat to feel the even surface of his bald scalp. He shook a bony finger at the forest and took a snippet of air between his tongue and tight-pressed lips. "What the hell," he said. "Tell your pa to get his scrawny ass out here to fish now, ya hear?" He fitted his hat and walked up an incline toward his tractor. "And show me them fish you steal before you steal 'em. Not that you'd know a fish from a kumquat. Maybe you'll share some. And I don't mean kumquats!" He chuckled and spit to the side.

John tapped Morgan on the shoulder. He pointed toward the forest.

On their way, Morgan glimpsed up at Junior's sun-framed face. "Junior, why does Mister von Schiller cuss so much?"

Junior laughed. "I think he's funny."

"He's just a good-spirited man," John said. "But don't you start talking like he does, Morgan."

Down the path, Morgan turned to watch the old man recede. "Dad, what'd Mister von Schiller mean when he said I'd have to find meaning? Do famous fishermen mean a lot?"

"Just look at this," John said. "Tommy and I used to play in this forest. What's left of it."

At the Wapsipinicon River, Morgan dug in his father's tackle box. "Dad says I'm gonna be in *Field and Stream* magazine."

Junior shoved him. "Get out of there. Bass won't bite on jigs today."

"Says who?"

"Get a minnow, Morgan. Hook it inside the bottom lip."

Morgan winced.

"How do you think you're gonna get it on your line, sissy Morgan?"

"Does it hurt?" Morgan asked.

"It's just a fish." Junior snatched Morgan's pole. He seized a minnow. He plunged the sharp point of a hook through its lip.

Morgan swung at Junior. "I saw what you did!"

Elder growled. "We're gonna do the same to you if you don't catch a fish."

"Shut up, Elder, or I'll give you a bloody nose."

Elder stretched for Morgan. "Why, you little runt! Do that again and—"

Junior laughed and pushed them apart. "I suggest you stop picking fights with people thrice your size, Morgan. And stop bellyaching about fish. They can't feel anything."

Morgan slapped his arm away. "How do you know?"

"They don't have a brain, stupid. They can't feel pain." Junior handed Morgan the pole and turned toward John. "Elder and me are going downstream, Dad. I'll whistle when the first fish finds us. After we catch our limit."

John smiled. "You do that," he said. John hurled his martyr to the stream. "He's quite an outdoorsman that Junior. Maybe in eleven years when you're sixteen, you can be the outdoorsman he is, Morgan."

John and Morgan sat on a tree-shaded sandbar. Morgan watched patterns of the stream prance. They seemed random yet repetitious. "Dad, why do you call Mark and Mathew, Junior and Elder?"

"One was born before the other."

"But, they're twins."

John hesitated. "Throw your minnow out there, son."

Morgan's minnow lay beneath shallow water inches deep. It fishtailed on a sandy bottom, circled about the heavy hook in its mouth. Morgan watched it.

"Throw that minnow out there where bass can get at it, son."

"I think my hook's too heavy, Dad. My minnow can't carry it."

"That's right, takes him down to where the bass are."

"But he doesn't seem to like it. His eyes are wide open and he keeps gasping for air."

John grabbed Morgan's pole. The minnow soared like a stone. "Here. Fish. Pretend you're Junior."

No longer able to watch over his minnow, Morgan worried. Water spun round a fallen tree, swallowed by a whirlpool. Morgan tied his shoelace. "Dad, will bass eat my minnow?"

"Of course. You know what to do when that happens, right?"

Morgan dusted sand from his palms.

"You're gonna set the hook, Morgan."

Morgan cringed.

"This is important, Morgan. You want the first fish. The one who shows others the way."

Morgan watched clouds overhead.

"The first fish gives himself willingly, Morgan, so we can live another day. Jesus was a fisher of men to save their souls. You're a fisher of fish, to save your life. Be the one to catch the first fish, and you'll show your brothers the way."

"I don't want bass to eat my minnow."

"Living things live by eating living things, Morgan. We harvest nature; we don't savage it."

Morgan shrugged.

"Bass eat minnows, Morgan. We eat bass."

"I don't wanna eat bass."

"See those cows over there? We kill cows to make hamburgers, way we kill fish to eat fish."

On a hill in the distance, tails of grazing cattle swung.

John shook his head. "Now don't throw up because you just found out where hamburger comes from."

"I'm not gonna eat hamburger anymore."

"What will you eat?"

Morgan waited. "Pork chops," he said.

"Comes from pigs."

"Ham."

"Pigs, Morgan."

"Sausage."

"Sausage comes from pigs, Morgan."

The boy's eyes traced stream currents. "Popcorn," he said.

"Little boys can't grow up to be like Junior if they don't eat meat."

"I don't wanna kill things."

"I thought you wanted to be a famous fisherman."

Morgan shook his head.

John turned away. "Good grief...I've got a girl for a son. Facts of life, Morgan. Sooner you get used to 'em, the sooner..."

Each time John looked away complaining, Morgan drew in his line until he could see his minnow in shallow water. Pondering what the first fish must be like caused Morgan's brain to wander. Time passed. The sun climbed higher.

"Dad, do you think the country is going down like Mister von

Schiller said?"

"No. He doesn't either. He says that because he's old. Old men get cranky when they see how different things are compared to when they were your age. This is the greatest country to grace the globe. You and I, we're lucky to be born in such a place."

"When you're old, will you think this country is like…whatever he said?"

"Rome. Probably."

"Will you be wrong?"

"Probably." John tied a feathery fly, yellow and black, to his second line. He pointed his fishing rod at the stream. "Right there." Back and forth, the fishing line flowed, a dancing partner with air.

"I heard there's a new kind of radio coming out on some late-model autos," John said. "Has a two-letter name, like AM. FM, I think. News won't be different, just sound better. Wonder if it will make crazy Khrushchev sound better, or news about that dang birth control pill. They say FM goes right through the sky, past the moon."

Though an icon of night, Morgan spotted the moon in daylight. "Dad, who made the moon?"

"God made it. To see by at night. God's like our parent. He provides everything we need."

"What does God give us to see at night when there's no moon?"

John squinted. "Flashlights," he said.

"Dad, the minister said God kills people he's mad at. Is God cranky because he's so old?"

"See all this beauty? Look like something an angry God could make?"

The buzz of a fly silenced to land on Morgan's reel. He counted its legs. Great zot…I've got only two, he thought.

John began to whistle a tune.

"Dad, why is that grass over there so tall?"

"Wetland. Grass likes water much as you do. Water makes things grow."

Morgan untied his shoes and tied them again. He watched clouds move.

"Morgan, do you have a bite?"

With a one-shouldered shrug, Morgan said, "No."

"How can you tell? You're not watching your line. You didn't want to go to church because you wanted to be a great fisherman. We're here to fish. So fish."

"I wanna go see the tall grass."

"And if you get a bite?"

"I'll come back."

John grumbled. "Morgan, why do you feel duty-bound to test my will? You should be like your brother." He shook his head to impose a delay, knowing he would surrender. "Don't go where I can't see you," he said.

Morgan set off to investigate. Insects scurried about grass taller than he was. Morgan touched the antenna of an ant tending aphids. It zigzagged on a leaf, like a soldier dodging bullets in no man's land. He touched another. It behaved like a copy of the last. Under moist rocks were roly polys up and around every contour.

He crouched close to a ladybug. "Here, lady, get on this finger. Going up...Now you got a real launchpad." Wings extended from beneath wings to set sail. Its bulky body, sideways in the breeze, swayed back and forth, gliding away. "Have a nice trip."

Lavish with activity, Morgan kneeled low to identify what he could. He jumped back from a high-pitched squeak underfoot. Beneath fallen grass and last year's leaves, he found something tiny and alive. He uncovered the creature. Its leg twitched. It panted in sharp breaths. He gasped, "Get a drink, little bunny. Water makes plants and people grow."

Morgan carried it two paces to the stream. He touched its mouth to eddies of water. A thread of red unraveled from the animal to mix with currents it was made of. Morgan ladled liquid into its mouth with wet fingers. It did not drink. Its eyes darted about. A pink drop of water fell from its nose like a tear.

John saw motion rifle through tall grass. "Morgan!" He dropped his pole. He ran.

Morgan's legs fanned through puddles, one hand clasped over another. Uncoordinated, hands together, he fell to his knees in the shallows.

John lifted him by the shoulders. "Snakebite?"

Morgan extended his arms, the rabbit nearly thrust in his father's face. Staring into space, the animal was motionless, short fur about its mouth wet and matted.

"What happened, Morgan?"

The boy shook his head.

"Let me see it." John took the baby rabbit.

Morgan's lip quivered. "Can you fix him?"

"No."

"You are my parent, you have to fix him!"

"I can't."

"Can God fix him?"

"No."

"Why?"

"I don't know."

John returned the corpse and followed the boy, who seemed to know where he was going. At the spot where they met, Morgan dug a hole. John kneeled to help.

Morgan laid down the rabbit. "Is God mad at me?"

"No."

"Was God mad at the bunny?"

"No."

They covered the rabbit with dirt. John placed a twig in the ground. He tied a blade of grass about its axis to form a cross. "It's OK, Morgan, he's been freed. We bury the dead, so they can find salvation, as God's best friend. The way we bury seeds. They grow new in another season, a better place."

Morgan watched the grave. He expected something.

"I know you love animals, Morgan. You're young, it's OK to cry."

Morgan sank and covered his face. "Does he not have a brain neither, Dad? Did he not feel the pain?"

# 10. I Saw It in a Dream on Route 66. Then Came 1968.

Hot wind sped by the Whitaker's maroon Pontiac Catalina, a half day's ride from Grand Canyon, destination California. Historic wonders of the Oregon Trail lay behind them. Air pounded open windows. Two round vertical pairs of headlights bounded an inverted triangular emblem to lead the way west. Their environment looked like an Albert Bierstadt painting. Tons of rock lunged skyward, falling back in slow motion called erosion.

John swerved. "Look out!"

Morgan turned in the back seat to see out the window. "We didn't hit a animal did we, Dad?"

"Would of hit a tumbleweed if the wind hadn't jerked it away like that. I didn't work all that overtime just to get my new-used car scratched by an import of Russian thistle from those Communists."

A radio voice cleared static. "Egypt's president Nasser demands Jewish settlers return the homes taken from seven hundred thousand Palestinians, as Egyptian, Jordanian, and Syrian planes fall from the sky."

Candace adjusted radio knobs with noise the dominant sound. "Wish there was some music," she said.

Morgan obliged with his rendition of Otis Redding's "Sittin' on the Dock of the Bay." Junior and Elder complained. Candace asked for an encore. Morgan delivered and imagined his future. From the emptiness of arid plains they now drove on to crowds and their approval on a scale wider than elfin confines of a Pontiac Catalina. Gotta be somebody, he decided. Like Mister von Schiller said.

Junior and Elder drifted in and out of sleep. Alert, Morgan anticipated his life. Mom says Batman and Green Hornet are actors, he thought. Actors tell stories, and people go to theaters to see those stories. Like going to church, except they want to go to theaters.

Morgan reached over the front seat to press his father's shoulder. "Dad, I know what I'm gonna be when I grow up—an actor."

Junior rolled his eyes. "Only famous people are actors. You're not famous."

"Remember when you wanted to find dinosaur bones on distant planets?" John asked. "We decided that might be an unlikely profession."

Morgan shrugged. "Then I'll hunt bones in Marion and be an actor and a sculptor." Laughter bracketed both sides of Morgan.

Candace smiled. "Oh, Morgan, my boy, it's only a dream."

Morgan focused on a mirage over pavement dead ahead and just above the dashboard. In it, he could see the future.

John smiled. "An American family on the American road, in their 1963 Catalina," he said. "Don't know if it gets better than this, Candace." She patted John on the knee and nodded agreement. "These vehicles that carry us," he said, "this one of metal and these of flesh and blood—they're time machines, you know. Soon we'll wonder how things could be so different. Trying to remember that time we were on Route 66 in 1967."

At attention, rock monuments passed in a succession of pillars like a lost tributary of the Silk Road. The car's dusty wake dissolved behind them. It receded over a flat horizon.

***

A black Burlington Northern engine approached Marion Terminal. Whitakers waited.

Morgan longed for sweets from the ice cream and soda shop across the street. He could see Civil War hero and Medal of Honor recipient Andrew W. Tibbets in marble, still on duty at a distance from Marion Christian Church & Memorial. In the cemetery, yellow leaves could be seen to fall from a ginkgo tree. A circular area about its trunk glowed with the color of solar fusion, one graveyard within another.

Morgan watched a black-and-white television report news in the train station. A reporter said, "In Chicago, Mayor Daley commands police to shoot, kill, maim, and cripple looters, arsonists, or anarchists of any kind. The Tet Offensive, assassinations of Martin Luther King and RFK, and now machine guns atop the US Senate. Some fear America has finally—"

Controlled collisions of a dozen train cars brought passengers to a halt. Candace and John stood rigid in the presence of hometown witnesses. John wore his department-store suit purchased on sale. Candace wore imitation orange pearls. Her dress, updated from past fashion, now ended just above the knee.

John squeezed Morgan's shoulder. "There's nothing more important than family, Morgan. Junior's here for his big send-off, so behave, look sharp, don't slouch."

Off the train bounced Junior, in military-issue hat and tan uniform. He maintained composure with even statelier control than other Midwesterners not prone to expressions of emotion. He hugged his mother mechanically and shook hands with his father. He rustled Morgan's hair. "How are you, kiddo?"

Morgan ducked. "What happened to your hands?"

Junior glanced at his knuckles. "Coral beach preparation."

"What happened to your hair?"

"They cut it off. What'd you think happened to it?"

"How come you're so big?"

People at the train station smiled at Junior. Men tipped their hats.

John motioned toward the car. "Well, Marine, ready to surprise your brother? You two have never been apart this long. Maybe you'll find some recruits at the university."

When they arrived in Iowa City, others noticed Junior in his uniform. He stiffened.

Elder emerged from Quadrangle dormitory with long hair, beads, and bellbottom jeans. He ran for his twin brother to hug him openly in sight of strangers. Both checked the other's clothing.

"Let's get a move on," John said. "Highlander's got surf and turf for the bunch of us." John glimpsed a grimace on his wife's face. "I know, five dollars a plate. Special occasion, honey."

Stilted dinner conversation gave way to silence. Metal forks clinked against china. Candace looked up from her plate. "Elder, you look like a girl."

"Don't start, Mom."

"People are laughing at you."

"No, they're not."

"Who are they laughing at if they aren't laughing at you and that silly hair? It looks—"

"They laugh at him, Mom." Elder pointed at Junior and looked back at his food.

"I saw them." Junior poked his own chest. "I'm about to leave Saigon for the field, to defend these kids so they can burn down campus, and they call me a baby killer. You didn't see it, Mom, but one of those draft-dodging longhairs spit at me. If you hadn't been there, I'd of given him a course worth having."

"Oh, Junior, don't be silly," Candice said.

"You don't send hippies to defend America," Junior said, and glared at Elder. "You send men courageous enough to risk death, strong enough to kill. While students back home get inflated grades from professors who decided courses in the classics aren't important but keeping their students from defending this country is."

Elder pushed his hair back from his face. "What makes you think you're defending America, Junior? You're about to fight a civil war in another country so politicians can funnel cash to defense contractors to buy their votes."

"Outside your gullible campus, Elder, nations fall to communism, one by one, closer to home. Stop it there, keep it there, away from home. That's how you defend this country while fighting in another. Just look at Walter Cronkite's NVA, and VC body counts. We're winning."

"Awful lot of dead people for such a small country, Junior."

Candace stuck her steak with a fork. "So help me to kingdom come, Elder, I find you're on a march, the money stops. And one more thing while I'm giving advice: don't even think about sleeping with a girl. That is for marriage."

Elder snarled, "Where did that come from?"

"I called your dorm room, and a girl answered. Don't think I don't pay attention. I'm just reminding you of what the rules are."

"You and Dad didn't wait for marriage."

Candace stuttered. "No, but we did not live together."

"So I can screw whoever I want as long as we do it on the street?"

"You are not so old I won't wash your mouth out with soap! Your father and I are grateful for you two, but we suffered for our transgression."

John's head sunk between his shoulders.

Elder smirked. "What transgression, Mom?"

"For...you-know-what, before marriage. We were judged harshly by friends and family."

"For being in love, Mom?"

"For our actions, not our feelings. We broke the rules."

"Mom, we're not confined by oppressive social chains anymore."

"You should be. Your father and I paid for our mistake in the eyes of others. A force that keeps people together called *community*. Today there is no cost for bad behavior and no reward for good. Restrictions on you-know-what before marriage is just one of a hundred leashes your generation wants to cut."

John looked at nearby tables. "Can we talk about this another time?"

Elder dropped his fork on his plate. "You act like sex is some dirty little secret, Dad. Everybody knows about it, but nobody talks about it."

John whispered, "Some things are kept private, Elder. We don't belittle them by making them public. By speaking about them like some gutter conversation between sailors."

"Today, we know love is an illusion, Dad, mere animal reproduction, pure biology. We're open-minded now. We speak out against all forms of authoritarianism."

"Indeed, as your generation demeans speech by revering it less. Your brother is right. In the Second World War, we accepted our roles. We defeated the Nazis, fascists, Imperial Japan, in their countries, not ours. It was right then. Why isn't it right now?"

"Because rules that applied to World War Two don't fit Vietnam, Dad. There is no clear enemy or reason to be there."

Junior stabbed his lobster. "Communism is reason enough!"

John pointed. "Son, voice down."

Junior leaned into Elder, whispering, "We aren't dying over there for nothing, Elder."

"You're right," Elder said, "*we*, as a country, are dying for less

81

than nothing. Dying for someone else's arrogance, their blustering, their talent of stirring American passions with lies told enough times we think it's the truth."

"Elder, freedom is not free," John said.

"It's not free of rules of how we get and keep it either, Dad."

"So there *are* rules you respect. The war is a moral matter, but sex before marriage is not. What will become of America if we don't fight for it?"

"What will become of America when corruption by powers that own us render nothing worth fighting for, Dad?"

"The cause may be more abstract, Elder, but results are the same. Nation after nation has fallen to the Reds—China, the Poles, Czechs, Hungary, Romania, North Korea. If we're the last free nation standing, will we have what it takes to protect our own borders? Junior is right, stop it there before it moves home. The cost could be much higher if we don't."

"Higher than losing your son?"

John nodded. "To the country, yes."

"How 'bout two sons?" Elder speared Morgan's shoulder. "If we're still in this war for as long as we've been there now, you'll be dead too, Morgan."

Morgan spoke, his mouth full. "I wanna be somebody, but not a solider."

Elder crowded him. "You'll be a dead soldier. Dream about that. But don't fret. People will salute your lifeless corpse, drape a flag over your coffin, and shove you in a grave just before they run off to the mall for the next big sale at Christmas."

John watched Morgan. "Don't believe him. I was a soldier. I survived."

"And forty thousand Americans in Vietnam so far haven't, Dad." Elder turned back to Morgan. "Ever heard of them? They wanted to be somebody too. Instead, they filled a hole in the ground."

John nodded. "And you're free because of them, Elder. We honor them still."

"Really, Dad? What are their names?"

Morgan ate nothing. He watched one face and the next.

## 11. Toynbee's Proof

John, Candace, and Morgan sat at the table for breakfast. John tapped the table. "Morgan, put those down, please. Prayer time."

Morgan tucked Stanislavski's *An Actor Prepares* and a copy of *Popular Science* under his seat.

All heads bowed, Morgan clasped his hands and spoke mechanically. "Dear God, thank you for this food, and thank you for these people, and thank you for this country, amen."

John opened one eye at Morgan. "And?"

Morgan closed his eyes tighter. "And don't let what happened to *Apollo One* happen to *Apollo Eleven* when all those guys got killed. Amen."

John slid bacon on his plate. "Hurry up, Whitakers. Launch waits for no man. This is history, gang. July 16, 1969. What happens over these next few weeks will be recalled till the end of time.

"Remember, Morgan, when Mister von Schiller asked how to give meaning to life? This is how. By the time you're my age, you might be up there on the moon. To work or take vacations to see Earth from space." John held up his empty glass. "Mars is next. One planet after another. What an adventure."

Candace filled his glass with milk.

"There's three thousand million people on this planet," John said. "They call that three billion. One-fifth of them will watch liftoff on TV. And did you know that Saturn Five launcher they're gonna watch was designed by the same guy who worked with Van Allen to launch America's first satellite? How 'bout that?"

Candace placed her hand on Morgan's head, rotated toward his plate. "Eat," she said.

"Who's Van Allen, Dad?"

"Who's Van Allen? Iowa's favorite son, Morgan, down at Elder's university." John frowned. "You should know that. And did you know, it took a couple days just to get that spaceship three miles up that crawlerway to the launch pad? Most important three miles I know. Has to hold the rocket, launcher, and crawler all at the same time. *Twenty-four million* pounds all told. How they gonna get that thing off the ground? They used some of our equipment to build that crawlerway. Rock crushers, pavers. Means I had a part in this thing too."

"Dad, you helped send men to the moon?"

"And I'm honored to fill my role. I figure an American can do anything anybody else can do, and do it better. That includes showing the Russians just because they're first in space doesn't mean they're best. Our astronauts are gonna prove it."

"What do you gotta do to be an astronaut, Dad?"

"Be smart. Know science, math."

Morgan watched his food.

"Don't be afraid of math, Morgan. Persistence matters more than brains. Neil Armstrong makes *thirty thousand dollars a year*. Aldrin and Collins make almost eighteen. They know math. Way it ought to be. Reward achievers."

After breakfast, in the living room, John moved a wire back and forth behind the television attached to their new roof antenna. He checked the image. Lampshades cast cones of light over the wall and a wood-framed Jesus in prayer to heaven.

John sat on the edge of the couch. "Look at that. Thirty-six stories tall and going to the moon," he said.

A camera panned Firing Room One at Launch Control, where a hundred men watched data monitors. Signs could be seen about the room, reading Boeing, Rockwell, MacDonald Douglas—one company for each stage they built.

Reporter Walter Cronkite remarked that ice could be seen on the craft thanks to -420° hydrogen stored inside. "The moon at liftoff will be two hundred eighteen thousand miles away," he said. "We've passed the two-minute mark."

Ex-astronaut and Cronkite's technical companion Wally Schirra added, "Power transfer complete. All second-stage tanks pressurized."

John stood to pace. Candice and Morgan stared at the television.

"T-minus fifteen seconds," Schirra said. "Guidance is internal."

Cronkite counted. "Ten, nine…Ignition sequence started."

The support tower, taller than a skyscraper, shook with its umbilical of electrical channels to feed a machine come to life. The Whitakers watched service arms retract.

Cronkite's voice cracked. "Two, one, zero…All engines running!"

Four twenty-ton hold-down posts fought to keep the vehicle in place. A flame trench bigger than a house deflected seven million pounds of thrust away from the launch pad. Its volcanic ash surface vaporized by the most common element in the universe. Fifty-eight thousand gallons of water per minute drowned the platform.

John kneeled before the television. "*My God…*"

Hold-down posts exploded. *Apollo* quaked. A hail of ice showered from its surface, sacrificed by *Apollo*'s furious engines. Tiny astronauts inside rattled like riders on a wood roller coaster.

Cronkite shouted, "Liftoff! We have liftoff thirty-two minutes past the hour!"

Six million pounds of twentieth-century pyramid rose with a continuous thunder. Fifteen tons of fuel per second poured from General Dynamics F-1 engines. Even over television speakers, they could be mistaken for the deep-throated roar of a thousand men an arm's length away. Applause erupted from Houston Launch Control.

Almost in tears, Schirra said, "Four billion years after its creation, the moon is about to greet its first visitors. And along for the ride, just sixty-six years after its flight, are two pieces of the Wright Flyer."

John's voice trembled. "When I was a boy at work in the fields, my father and I decided such things were impossible. And it will take just three days longer than it took Lindbergh to cross the Atlantic. I've never been so happy to be so wrong in all my life. I've never been so proud. So proud to be an American."

John walked outside to look for the moon. Neighbors on their porches considered the sky. House to house they looked at one another.

Morgan stood next to his father. "Where's the moon, Dad?"

John searched.

"Do you think Junior sees it—the moon?" Candace said.

John smiled. "I think so...No, I know so."

He looked to Candace. "Do you?"

\*\*\*

John pulled from a closet the hat and coat he wore to church. "Look smart, Morgan. Show respect to the soldiers, and do so at the double-quick. They're giving us one hour to get everything moved."

"What if I want to wear what *I* want, an expression of the real me?"

"You venerate others by how you present yourself. A demonstration of deference. Get dressed and get in the car."

"What if I don't want to get in the car?"

"Don't test my will, Morgan!"

Morgan turned for the washroom. "Don't test mine," he said.

The university was thirty miles away. It seemed a continent was crossed to get there. Traffic to Iowa City was channeled and stopped by the National Guard. Standing outside their cars, the drivers, all men, were copies of John with formal hat and sport coat. Soldiers held mirrors on poles under the Catalina. Like I'm back in Manila, in reverse, John thought.

Led and followed by military vehicles, they toured campus like a funeral procession. Headlights designated their group. Personnel carriers lined every street. Campus green spaces were cluttered with broken bottles centered on torched patches of ground. Wisps of smoke escaped a stone pile that had been a four-story building. Scuffles between students and guards drifted by.

Finally, out of their cars, each driver turned over his license. "You're here for? Full name, sir."

John rubbed his forehead. "Elder...I mean, Mathew. Mathew..."

"Alan," Candace said.

John nodded. "Mathew Alan Whitaker."

On the dormitory's third floor, two additional soldiers met John, led to Elder's room.

John's eyes slashed his son. "What's going on, Elder?"

"Weathermen, sir," replied a soldier. "Intelligence detected bomb manufacture."

Elder thundered, "Weathermen are not at the U!"

John smacked the back of Elder's head. "Get downstairs and shut up!"

"Don't shout at me! It's the patriarchs of My Lai!"

"I'm not shouting! Move!"

John threw bags of tie-dye shirts and bellbottom jeans in the trunk of the car. Candace left the front seat, Morgan emerged from the back.

Elder glanced toward campus. "Mom, some buildings burned down—"

"Buildings don't just burn down," John said. "If you were in on this, Elder, I will—"

"Send me to war, like your son?"

John slapped Elder's face. Elder slapped him back. Morgan flinched. Candace pressed them apart. "Stop, you two!"

Elder yelled, "I can't let this go on like you, Dad! They shoot students now! They tear-gassed our dorms, they closed the U, they killed your son! If you don't fight them, he's next!" Elder thrust his finger in Morgan's face. Morgan stumbled back against the car.

"This is war, Elder, not a game," John said.

"It *is* a game, Dad! America lost one of its pieces, that's all! Aren't you ready to question them yet? Are you Job? Must you give away everyone to prove your allegiance?"

John wiped sweat from his brow. He looked as though he were about to vomit. "He did his duty, Elder. He fought for America, not for politicians. He was a brave man. A good soldier."

Candace hugged John, her voice trembling. "Elder's wrong. America would never send its sons to die for nothing."

"Junior has been freed," John said.

Elder covered his face, sobbing. Morgan bolted. John reached for him. Morgan spun free.

"Morgan!" Candace shouted.

Mute, John watched Morgan run away.

## 12. Work Is Hell

A burned-out light bulb on the ceiling made the kitchen dim. John tossed his newspaper on the counter, its headline: Nixon Says Peace at Hand. Folded over on the back page was a story about a break-in at the Watergate Apartments in Washington, DC.

"We're having a sit-down breakfast this morning," Candace said. "Like old times, Morgan. Isn't that nice?"

Morgan rubbed his eyes. "Not really," he grumbled.

"You always liked pancakes."

Morgan groaned, "Tired."

"You can sleep more tomorrow," John said. "Say grace, son."

Morgan folded hands and bowed his head. Others waited. He looked up. "Not today, Father."

"You've been saying grace for years now."

"So?"

"Pray, son."

Morgan looked at the floor.

Silence.

"For what?" Morgan said. "To who, and what's the difference?"

"Don't flex your personality with me, Morgan. Say grace."

Morgan punched his own chest. "I know my individual rights! I've got no duty to you, or God, or any other invented authority! I fill the role *I* want!" He lifted his fist high. "*Free choice!*"

John simmered. "Put your hand down. And who told you that?"

Morgan said nothing. John bowed his head and recited a prayer. Like an anthropologist, Morgan watched his father pray aloud.

John began to eat. Candace watched her plate. The only sound was John chewing his food.

John said, "We'll get some good fishing and hunting in this year. We can spend twice as much time together as we used to, Morgan."

Morgan shrugged.

John nodded. "We've got lots of time. We'll make it a good year. There's nothing more important than family."

\*\*\*

Windowed buildings of Marion Manufacturing sparkled with electric arcs. Sounds of hydraulic hammers battered eardrums of third-shift workers. Before John was out of his car, Hal from inventory met John in the parking lot. He shook a piece of paper as they approached the factory. "John, got a problem," he said. "Are those two-cent screws from Japan part of inventory, supplies, or evaluation? Dick wants to know and pronto. He's gotta have cost and budget on his desk by seven a.m., and trust me, John, you don't want to get on Dick's bad side."

"It's almost seven now, Hal. And what makes Japanese screws better than US screws we already use?"

"Not better screws, boss, cheaper screws."

"Cheaper for who? Not my neighbor, the screw maker."

"Business is about the dollar, boss, not the flag. It's the American way."

"I have multi-million-dollar rock crushers to build. The deadline is last month and upstairs wants a layoff. Few things less important to me than which sheet of paper two-cent screws go on."

"Dick's real sticky about balance sheets, John. Don't piss him off."

"He's also new around here, Hal. He's a big shot from a toilet-roll company. Let him decide which sheet to wipe his screws on."

"They say it doesn't matter whether he was in toilet rolls or skyscrapers, John, he can manage and count beans."

John reached the entrance. "Ask me about his screw problem later—after retirement."

Opening the door to Building 36 felt like entering a hurricane. Fifty-ton cranes circled overhead. Men shouted to be heard within feet of each other. Hot metal sparks jumped from welders.

John hunched over budgets and part costs in his office on the factory floor. He could hear one tone among the din was absent. He left for the paint booth.

Troy handed a paint sprayer to John. "Can't do my part till Harley and Dusty do theirs, Mister Whitaker. They say I work too hard. Against union rules. That true, sir?"

"No, Troy."

Harley smiled and tracked a trail of cigarette smoke from his fingers. "Sprayer's broke," he said.

"Can't do no work wrong," Dusty added, his saucer-shaped eyes on a square face.

John turned to Harley. "Put that cigarette out. You know you can't smoke in here."

Harley's eyes fixed on John. Harley squashed the tobacco on his wristwatch band.

John tested the tool. "Seems fine. Here, Harley, try it."

Harley held the sprayer, rotating it. "How 'bout that? Guess it ain't broke no more."

"Test the sprayer, Harley."

Hal entered the paint booth. "It's seven a.m., John. Cost and budget?"

Harley faced John. He raised the spray gun above his head, about to follow John's request.

"On metal, Harley," John said.

With years of familiarity, the gripped sprayer in free fall, Harley tripped the trigger. A snap of level paint shot across a metal sheet. "Imagine that? Works fine."

"How do you know if you don't look at the strip you laid?"

Harley smiled. "Can hear it. Don't need to look."

"Good. Any further troubles, come see me."

Harley bowed. "Yes, Master."

John left. Upstairs he slammed the office door. "Sorry, Mabel. I need to see Jed about personnel."

"Go right in. He's busy doing nothing, per usual."

John entered Jed's office, closed the door, and sat down. "Jed, have you found a way I can split up those two brothers in the paint booth?"

"Lots of union under their belt, John."

"Men should do an honest day for honest pay, Jed."

"These aren't the good old days, John, it's 1973. Even the president's a crook."

Jed's office door opened. "Well, well, glad to finally find you, John."

John nodded. "Dick."

Dick turned to close the door. He paused, facing the entrance. "We have some sterling news. Sit down, John."

"I am sitting."

Dick spun about. He slapped a notebook in his grip. "I'm proud to report my management theories have paid dividends! We're making bigger profits than ever. Even in a recession, people build roads."

"A hometown boy heads the Department of Transportation, Dick."

Jed grimaced. He shook his head at John.

Dick smiled, then frowned. "I'll get right to it. We're going to properly size our operations. Leverage assets to meet market demands. Our employees are our most valuable asset, John."

"You're going to furlough my men."

Dick narrowed eyes on his notebook. "View it as though we've been giving them a job they would not otherwise have up to now. To put them out there with fresh paychecks, back on the search after a rest."

"I'm sure the men will appreciate that," John said.

"We'll have to cull the youngest, most inexperienced ones, of course."

"You'll get rid of the best workers we have, Dick."

"Actually, I won't be the one to deliver pink slips, John. You will."

Layoff notices were in hand on a late Friday afternoon. The whistle blew. Troy stood in John's office. "I beat every other fella on production, Mister Whitaker. What have I done wrong, sir? I'll fix it, promise I will."

"It's just economics, Troy. We hope things turn around so we can get you back."

"But the new boss said we're making progress. It must be something I done wrong."

"Economics isn't about right and wrong or ethical—" John

stopped himself, Miss Pancake in his mind's eye. "Troy, you're one of the best workers we have. I wish we had more like you."

"I got the wife and boy, Mister Whitaker. You'll call me back soon as you can, right, sir?"

\*\*\*

"It's not all Dick's fault," Jed said. "Our economy's in the pail and getting worse, John. Arabs got an embargo on us, and despite Dick's theories, today's profits are from last year's orders. I keep telling you, kiss ass or Dick will put you out on the street with the rest of 'em."

"They blame me, Jed. I'm the heavy out there. And I'm expected to support this as though there's no moral component to the bottom line. Like it's all just part of doing business."

"It *is* just part of doing business, John. People are mere commodities now. We all are."

"Jed, I remember not long ago, in the fifties, when companies could count on their men and men could count on their companies. These men are like pawns in a game to—" John sat up straight.

"What, John?"

John shook his head. "It's a game like Elder said. Managers of business, managers of government. We simply move pieces around. Fire them or bury them…Jed, did you know that North Vietnam's leader, Ho Chi Minh, was an OSS agent supported by the US in World War Two? I just learned this. Since this nation's founding, we've had forty-eight wars, including one with ourselves. Two years of war for every three years of peace. Are we a nation of laws, Jed, or a nation of wars?"

"Welcome to the human race, John."

The door to Jed's office opened. "Well, well, hello, John. Fully execute your plan?"

"Wasn't my plan, Dick. But yes, sir, they're all gone."

Dick sulked. He sat in front of Jed on Jed's desk. The desk groaned. Jed leaned left, looking past Dick's abundance for John.

Dick gripped the desk's front edge. He looked down. "It must have been hard on you, John."

Silence.

Dick stood and approached the wall. He studied a calendar with pictures of asphalt pavers on a long blacktop road. "Well, I have more sad news. Sit down, John."

"I am sitting."

Dick reeled about, striking fist to palm. "We've got to properly size our operations! Leverage assets to meet market demands!" Dick resumed his seat on Jed's desk. Jed leaned left. Dick looked down and said, "We all have to bend a bit just to hang on, John."

Jed leaned right to disappear behind Dick's back.

Dick looked as though he might cry. "We really want to keep you, John."

"When is my last day, Dick?"

Dick grinned. "Oh no! We don't want to lose you!" He stood. He saluted. "We want you as part of the team! Play along, be a good soldier for business, profit, the bottom line." Dick approached the door then turned to face John, one hand over his heart. "Keep America strong, John. God bless America." Dick turned and departed.

John watched the door close. "Am I out on the street or not, Jed?"

"We're in a recession, John. You've got twenty-six years invested, a pension, a family, and you're not union. You're handcuffed, my friend, like the rest of us. Take whatever he gives you."

"And what is that, Jed?"

\*\*\*

John pushed his broom past the paint booth in a hurry, careful to make the area clean in one pass. Breathing hard, he wiped sweat from his forehead.

Behind John, leaned against a rail, Harley scratched his crotch with one hand, cigarettes fed in his mouth with the other. He grunted, "Hey, Master! Missed a spot!"

In his mind, John saw a tan horse he once imagined as a dragon, Bubbles happy by his side. The world was different then, he decided. When no work was demeaning. What virtues serve me now? What connection is there between this place and my family, or even this country, beyond a paper dollar? If I'd only gone to college. I meant to go to college.

Dusty slithered back in the paint booth, his face wadded in giggles. "He said, missed a spot, ya stupid!"

John looked back. He saw a paper sack upright on a pile of metal shavings strewn across the floor. He returned to pick up the bag. Its moist bottom failed and dropped human feces. John cleaned the area as fast as he could. Sounds of office managers approached. Air squeaked in and out of John's throat.

Harley bellowed as smoke shot from his nose and mouth. "Hee-haw, hee-haw! Clean that shit up, jackass!" Harley ducked in the paint booth as management arrived.

Dick and upper-office managers rounded a stack of steel. They walked by John, waste in his gloved hand. He tried to control his wheezing, made eye contact, and nodded once to acknowledge their existence. They looked away, engrossed in time-motion studies and organization charts in a three-ring binder.

John leaned over his broom. He pushed piles of dust. Factory work is not like working the land, he thought. City people are not like people of the earth. America is a nation of cities now. A nation of strangers.

***

Morgan sat in the basement. Having graduated from Play-Doh as a child, he sculpted a piece of stone with a chisel.

John called downstairs. "Morgan, I'm off to look for deer signs at the reservoir. Want to go?"

"Not so you can kill animals, I don't."

"Harvest, Morgan. If you change your mind, let me know." John left.

Morgan stood. He fixed his Twin Cities ball cap, ran upstairs and out the door. Transistor radio pressed to his ear at full volume, he walked across the yard and sang "Do It 'Til Your Satisfied" by B.T. Express.

Leaving his driveway, John stopped the car. He turned down the volume on Leo Greco's polite polka party. "Hey, kiddo, changed your mind?"

"Nope," Morgan said and continued up the street.

"You sure? Where you off to?"

"Just off!" Morgan walked uphill.

"All I asked is where you're going?"

"Away! OK? Don't worry about it."

Events flooded John's brain—Vietnam, riots, the Black Panthers, Nixon, Jane Fonda, a financial arrangement he volunteered for that forced him to keep a job he could not pay bills without. He slammed the car into park. He lunged at Morgan and shook him, the radio sent free.

Morgan shouted, "Lay off!"

The man slapped the boy first with his palm then the back of his hand, from left, from right. "It's my place to worry! I'm the man of the household! I sweep up other people's crap! I grin and bear it! Life wasn't meant to be a bed of roses!"

Tears in his eyes, Morgan threw a punch, seized by his father's grip. In John's mind, he could see his father recede, Bubbles his only defense. What could have been a blow delivered by John's superior size turned into a hug as John's arms wrapped around his son. John wheezed, "I'm sorry, Morgan."

Morgan twisted and escaped. "You may be stronger, but you can't defeat my will! I'll win!"

"Win what?"

Morgan grabbed his radio and ran up the street. "You think I want to help you kill defenseless animals, like what the Viet Cong did to Junior? I'm nothing like you! You're nothing but a janitor! I'm gonna be somebody!"

# 13. July 12, 1978

Morgan shoveled gravel. He looked over parched plains near Scottsbluff, Nebraska. A lane of fresh rock dumped over wagon-wheel ruts converged on a rock monument and migration marker in the distance. He squeegeed sweat off his face. In America, we pave over the past, he thought. Even the Oregon Trail's not safe.

Or maybe it's best to forget history, he decided as he recalled his one and only semester in college. Standing before his class, a six-inch-high "F minus" carved in red marker on his paper, rattled by his professor in Morgan's face.

That was the most exciting period in my life, he thought. So many girls. Three dates in a single day. Rafting the river, cafeteria food fights, beer. I was more popular than I ever dreamed. An achievement crowned with a one-point GPA on a four-point scale.

He shook his head. He whispered, "Digging ditches like she said."

Trucks arrived, lined up and backed in for dumping. Morgan watched them navigate one another. Little mattered except lunch. It provided something for his brain to think about. He could feel breakfast still in his stomach.

A hired driver, whom they called Driver, stood next to Morgan. Driver faced Morgan and crouched, his fists in boxing posture. He feigned a strike at Morgan's chin.

Morgan nodded. "Driver," he said.

Driver relaxed. "Morgan." He motioned toward the asphalt paver. "Better get 'er goin', eh?"

Morgan scratched his neck. "Yeah."

Driver looked beneath the machine. "Yeaaah," he said.

Morgan responded, "Yup."

Driver replied, "Yupper."

Neither looked at the other. They set up the paver, sprayed oil on rollers, and continued this one-word dialogue until fearing it may never end Morgan reached up to turn the ignition. With a thud, its motor howled. Parts shook like an old tractor. Little could be heard beyond two feet. Driver gauged the flat gravel surface, talking to himself. "Yup, yup. Yes-sir-ree."

Driver took his seat on the machine. He leaned sideways and looked down, mesmerized by a pebbled earth. The two owners of this five-man paving company hurried about their equipment to oil gears. One shouted at Morgan, "We got a schedule to meet, college kid! Get that shovel outta your ass and get after it!"

Morgan scooped gravel. The men about him seemed like children that had only grown larger. "And most of you people have reproduced," Morgan said out loud, though he could not be heard. "You've become parents with less training than how to put on your pants."

Morgan saw one of the drivers idling in his cab, watching Morgan from a rearview mirror. Morgan wiped nothing from the sides of his mouth. To think you people can vote, he thought. No wonder America's so screwed up.

The first truck bed rose to pour 400° asphalt into the paver hopper. Morgan climbed the truck. He placed one foot atop a swinging tailgate, his other high in the bed. He broke a sticky substance with his shovel. Material fell, dump truck to hopper. Chemical miasmas rose from bitumen. Morgan's nose bled again.

"Having your period, kid?" one shouted. Others laughed. Morgan had no option but to scoop.

With their left lane laid, one of the owners—a white-haired, sun-weathered man—drove over the route with a Hyster Hypac made of two large rolling drums. "Watch yourself, college kid!" he said. "Hate to swerve at you like I do them damn joggers." He scowled at the ground. "Goddamn joggers…"

The second owner met Morgan. "Eh!" He pointed down at a bump on the gravel road. "Eh! Eh!"

Morgan pointed at the spot. He repeated this guttural note, "Eh?"

The man nodded, "Eh!"

Morgan raked rocks flat. He raised his head to grunts in the distance. The man pointed down and shouted, "Eh!"

Morgan waved. Their noisy paver neared. "He does speak English," Morgan said. "I heard him once. Not only am I afraid to utter complete sentences around you people, but complete words probably won't make sense either."

The man made a more emphatic sound.

"All right, all right!" Morgan said. He shoveled and talked to the stones. "Early hominid prick with a one-sound vocabulary."

\*\*\*

Each day was a replica of the last. Gravel shoveled among primitive syllabic fragments, heat, and humidity. Crew and trucks were gone for another load.

Morgan scooped rocks and watched a point on the sky's margin formed by the road and perspective. This is not what old man von Schiller meant, he thought. I have not distinguished myself from these others. I work for them.

A tributary of the North Platte River flowed nearby. He stepped down into a ditch toward the stream, minnows near its surface. "Are any of you the first fish?" he asked.

A shift and grind of gears came up behind him. Morgan walked up from ditch to road. He stretched his back, tugged up his belt. He shoveled stones. He knew he'd been seen.

The crew parked and left their trucks, gathered one by one around the paver. "What do you think you're doing, college kid? Ain't break time. Got a schedule to meet."

"I saw the boy zip his pants. Takin' a crap, kid?" asked another. The men laughed.

"Nope," Morgan said and leveled uneven topography.

"Come on, college kid." One man put his arm around Morgan. "I won't tell the men. I know how it is when you're a boy, boy. You humped the girl rocks, I hope. You're not one of them faggots, are ya?"

Men bellowed. Morgan forced a smile. One man took a rake and placed its handle between Morgan's legs from behind. He raised it to Morgan's crotch and pushed it forward. "That how it grow? Long and hard? Cipher that in centimeters, college kid!" The men cheered.

Morgan snatched the rake. He walked to the lead dump truck in line for transfer. "Don't we have work to do?"

"Well, well, our young scholar might grow up to be a man after all. Get his hands dirty. Use his back like an honest man."

Morgan shrugged. "What else is there to use around here? Quite apparently there's no surplus gray matter."

"What's gray matter, kid?"

The truck bed rose with a shriek. Morgan straddled space, teetering between the tailgate and layers of hardened asphalt. Engulfed in hot fumes, he tried to break free tarred and sticky pebbles.

"Watch out, fellas, the girl's bleedin' again!"

Perched on the truck bed's risen angle, Morgan tried to wipe blood off his face. Balance lost, he fell in and rolled down to the paver hopper where he cracked a cooling outer crust of black.

"Pave 'im! That's what I call a queer matte!" shouted one and hit the kill switch.

Morgan climbed out, staked his shovel, and brushed steaming nuggets from his clothes. Sweat beaded from every inch of him. He spit blood running over his lips. "I deserve better than this shit," he said.

"What else you gonna do, go back to college? Face it, kid, you'll be nothin' but a ditch digger, like the rest of us."

Morgan nodded, remembering, his eyes fixed on the man. "Well, maybe I'm not at the end of the road just yet." He pulled his shovel from the ground. "A dead-end like you people."

"Watch the mouth, kid! This is real work, not some ivory tower bullshit. You're just like us, or will be once we get you in shape."

A burst of wind blew Morgan's Twin Cities ball cap toward Scottsbluff. Morgan stepped forward, picked it up, and kept walking. "I'm nothing like you assholes."

"Watch it, kid. You work for us."

"Yeah, that's the problem," Morgan said.

"Where you goin', kid? Ain't break time. Can't you tell time?"

Morgan cinched tight his salt-rimmed cap. He did not turn back. He checked his wristwatch and talked to himself. "And the time is, two thirty-two, Wednesday, July 12, 1978."

"That shovel's our property, kid! You walk off with it, we'll get you for theft!"

Morgan squinted at the frontier. He whispered, "Let's see...Three miles per hour, twelve miles. Four hours, no problem. And let this be a lesson. *Never* tell humans your failures or your dreams. You've only given them a neck to hang."

Morgan wiped his brow on sweat-laden wrists. He lifted the shovel, an extension of him now, vertically balanced on his outstretched arm straight overhead. In a parabolic arc, he launched it high and into the ditch.

One leather work glove flew up and into the stream. He blew his bloody nose inside the other and sailed it up and behind him. "Now what do I do?" he asked.

***

Morgan trotted up Iowa Avenue under mercury streetlights, past university buildings in the dark. He looked at the clock tower. "She's gonna kill me," he said.

He glimpsed snippets of inlaid bronze quotes from literature along Iowa City's version of the Walk of Fame. Under a hanging lantern, surrounded by students, a boy played ragtime like a paid professional at one of several outdoor pianos placed for public performance. Morgan watched the boy as he passed. They don't call this Athens on the Prairie for nothing, he thought. And next week the Spartans meet Athens in the Michigan State game.

He hustled past people lined up at the Free Listening Booth. There, a psychology student listened for hours to talking strangers. He passed a series of shops, one named Ruby's Pearl with a large sign in the window no one seemed to notice. "Hate Men!" it said.

Suddenly, Morgan found himself between two protest groups. One group, all male, named themselves The God Squad. The other, a group of women wearing t-shirts that read, "Nobody Knows I'm a Lesbian." He pried himself between them.

He emerged into a nest of bushes to startle a squirrel onto the street. He jumped in front of traffic. "Stop!" he shouted.

Tires squealed as a student's head poked out his car window. "Hey, ass wipe!"

Hands still in the air, Morgan watched the squirrel cross to safety. "You were gonna hit him," Morgan said.

"It's a friggin' squirrel!"

"Bite me," Morgan said and flipped an obscene gesture.

The student driver motioned behind, "If this guy rear-ended my new car, I'd kick your ass!" he said.

Morgan stamped a flat-footed dirt pattern on the boy's front fender. "Doesn't look new to me," he said and sprinted through hundreds of students headed for bars downtown.

From grassy green space about Schaeffer Hall stood Roscoe taunting students, his Bible held high. Roscoe fell to his knees. "See those hordes?" he shouted. "Whoremongers running for whores! Back, ye evil one! Cast ye out of these wicked little bastards!"

Morgan checked once behind as he crossed the Pentacrest, crowned by five university structures, including Iowa's original 1842 capitol. Its gold leaf dome reflected starlight back to where gold is made. He heard bagpipes drift up the river valley from outside the music complex. He could see couples stroll by the stream. If aliens visit this place, they'll think humans come in pairs, he thought.

Melody sat on a wooden bench-back beneath weeping willows. An iron footbridge spanned the river with an aqua hue, accented by incandescent canisters marking the way from science to arts.

"Hey. Sorry I'm late, Melody. Ready for the lab?"

Melody gazed at the crescent moon. Her shoulder-length hair separated across her face. "Morgan, I can almost see the full moon. Even though it's not lit by the sun. Is it real?"

"It is." Morgan sat next to her. "That pinkish glow is earthshine. Sun shines directly on the white crescent, but clouds from earth reflect sunlight back on the moon's dark side. Earthshine. Even people reflect some. See 'em?" He pointed.

Melody smirked. "I don't see anyone."

"See that faint patch of light over there? Andromeda galaxy. Furthest object visible to the naked eye. Made of billions of stars over two million light-years away. That's twelve million trillion miles—give or take. Just think, light waves from that galaxy, right here, right now, started their journey two million years ago. About the time Australopithecus scooted across the savannas of Africa.

And while those light waves sailed through space, humans foraged their way across the Bering Strait, agriculture was invented, cities appeared and disappeared on the Tigris. Egypt, Rome, Spain rose and fell, and here they are, those light waves free for the taking. But maybe the most amazing thing is the mathematics that describes those light waves also describes sound waves—" He pointed skyward. "And airwaves coming off that plane, and waves that ride that river. The universe, its infused with some kind of improbable unity." He shook his head in disbelief. "We're one with the stars, Melody—for real. What you sit on, all that you see, and the eyes that see it, every atom was forged in the heart of a star. A star that died, seeding our region of the galaxy to give us life."

Melody shrugged and smiled. "Neat. Have you told that story before?"

"Sort of. When I was a little kid, my parents and I used to eat popcorn, watch the stars, and tell stories about them."

Melody pointed at his pocket. "Don't lose your letter. Writing other girls, are you?"

"My dad."

"So you're going to patch things up with him?"

He pressed the envelope in his pocket. "The poor college life is almost over, Melody. I'm about to be a big, stinking, filthy-rich success. Off to find the Promised Land, because it's not in Marion." Morgan hesitated. He looked for listeners. "But only if I graduate."

"What does that mean?" She held his hand.

Morgan checked for listeners. "Quantum mechanics has cooked my goose. It's the most non-intuitive thing. As though reality depends on faith in something you can't see, hold, or stand on. And Dr. Van Allen's my instructor, head of the physics department, king of the cosmos. He's also my advisor. I don't know if that helps or hurts me. But I have dreams of a big red F on my final exam. And the clock ticks. I have mere weeks to decipher the most complex physics in the universe. Saved at the bell or saddled with past performance, a permanent nobody."

"Morgan, are you serious?"

"As a heart attack…When I was a kid, a neighbor lady used to say I'd be nothing but a ditch digger. Years later, a guy on a road crew repeated it. What if they're right?"

## 14. Portentous

Morgan and Roxanne drove home to the outskirts of Boston after a late show. Roxanne spoiled the silence. "I saw the previews. I thought it was supposed to be a happy love story, not some sappy show about baseball. You'd think by 1989 they could make movies that make sense…And drive a little faster. I want to go to bed."

Morgan accelerated. "Message seemed clear to me," he said.

"And what would that be?"

"To resist the norm, listen to your heart, follow your dreams."

"There wasn't a thing in that movie about dreams, Morgan."

"Odd title then, don't you think? *Field of Dreams*."

"Why couldn't they have made a movie about something happier?"

"Happier than proof there really is a heaven?"

"Blasphemy!"

"Blasphemy…Roxanne, where do you get these ideas?"

"Doctor Chakra, that's where, Mister Scientist."

"Fine. I thought it might be interesting to see how Costner handled this role, Roxy." He knew she hated the name Roxy. "That's why I chose it. It was my turn to pick a movie."

"Oh, that's right, *the role*. Tell me again, why does a scientist, sometimes sculptor, study acting?"

"I've been interested in it since I was a kid."

"That's it? Just a childhood dream?"

"Odd as it sounds to you, Rox, I never felt more like myself than on stage when I played somebody else."

"*Somebody else?*" She laughed. "What are you going to be, famous? You're just another bookworm, like all those other nerds

103

you work with."

Roxanne kept talking. Morgan glanced out his window. I gave her a neck to hang, he thought.

"Does that work for you, Morgan?"

He hesitated. "Fine."

"*Fine?* Fine for who?"

"Roxanne, I'm already exhausted from a normal day's work. I don't relish a normal day's battle with my wife. Let's just remain silent like we usually do and enjoy a little peace."

"Kiss my ass."

A rise on Interstate 93 approached, cars braked at its crest. Construction shut four lanes down to one.

Roxanne clenched her fist. "I…want…to go to bed! Why in the hell would they do such a thing at this hour? Can't you do something?"

"What would you have me do?"

"Try thinking once in a while."

"Thinking."

"Of a better route, Morgan. Shoulda never let you drive my car."

"This is the quickest way home."

"I can see that," she said.

Morgan sighed, "Usually, dear."

"Don't *dear* me."

"Would you rather upon our exit from the movie I said, 'Roxanne, let's go home the long way tonight. There might be construction on the fast route.' It happens. I'm sorry. It's not my fault."

Roxanne mumbled out her passenger window.

Morgan tilted his ear toward her. "Excuse me?"

She sneered. "I should excuse you."

"See how you treat your husband, Roxanne? How do you treat your enemies?"

Roxanne snarled to bare her threat-face. "What makes you think they're not one and the same? Remember, I've had practice filing divorce papers, Morgan. It's not hard. Better try to stay on my good side."

Morgan wavered. "Your good side?"

Roxanne inflated.

Morgan seized the moment Roxanne required to build her mental list of offenses before delivery all in one breath and furnished his own, long since prepared. "Don't forget all the times I sided with you against some new scoundrel, Rox. The latest vendor to cheat you; the latest employee not to properly kiss your feet; the latest ex-friend who forgot their obligations to you for all those gifts you bought them. I thought I could be a sounding board for your rage, Roxy. I didn't know it was infinite. But as the German adage says, better an end in horror than a horror without end."

Morgan had two-thirds of a mile to stop. He closed the space between gas pedal and floor, one rigid line from shoulder to toe.

Roxanne was quiet for the longest second, her list on hold.

A tempest, she fanned her nails like talons across his face. "Stop this car before you piss me off!"

Morgan tasted a seam of blood on his lip. He swerved by cars. "So, Roxy, the real you has emerged from beneath that brittle shell of oppressive rage. Forged in that fusion of hate you claim to be a victim of. Who's in control now, love of my life?"

All claws, Roxanne clove Morgan's hand in her attempt to steal keys firmly guarded. "You stop this car or there'll be no fucking for you!"

Morgan laughed, "What a change that would be!"

Autos at rest ahead appeared to leap back at them. Their car tipped nose first beneath five vehicles in front of it as it augured into concrete to carve a trench through the freeway. Pieces of energy were carried away into space as sparks, metal, and flesh spread in a fountain from the impact.

Shockwaves rippled from the event like the circular spread of a percussion bomb dropped on a jungle enemy when Morgan sprang up from his bed, gasping in the dark.

A border of light could be seen about curtained windows. Roxanne was gone, early for the office as she always was.

Morgan absorbed his setting. Wow…How liberating, he thought.

***

Inside the house, Morgan navigated for the bathroom by outside streetlight through curtainless windows. Periodic flashlight

105

illumination bridged the darkest places made unfamiliar by now absent furnishings. He scooped water from the bathtub with a bucket, caught purposely from this morning's shower.

Outside in the dark, he checked up and down the street for onlookers. Over his garden, he spilled water on dry flowers. This house is all I have to show, he thought. This is my step up the ladder. I'm not stepping down.

By an open window, Morgan sat cross-legged on the floor with his book angled toward the streetlight. A jet-black kitten with golden eyes jumped on his lap. "Hello, Hawkeye. You sweet little girl." He rubbed her neck.

Hawkeye's unrelated snow-white brother, Sammy, zigzagged across the floor. "Sammy, you hippie longhair, can you go plop for me?"

Sammy fell on his back to expose a hairless belly, shaved to keep him cool on these hot nights.

Morgan paused on the book cover of *The Technique of Acting*, by Stella Adler. "Can you guys believe I paid money for this?" he said. "But the soul needs food. Been starving this one for a hundred twenty-nine weeks. That's nine-hundred days. And would you like to know what nourishment I found for the soul? When the scene clicks on stage, or the chisel reveals life in stone, or equations lift to fly from the page, it's the same sense of awe. The only difference; a scene is shared. The others—solitary loves. But each is food for the soul. At least acting is free. All it costs is time spent at the theater. And I don't need sanction from the tyrant for rehearsals."

He looked out through the screen. "My first lead role starts in two weeks, guys. My character is married to a woman he fights with incessantly. Who needs rehearsals?"

Morgan opened the text to its bookmark, a still-undelivered letter to his father.

Cats scattered from a knock at the door. A spotlight jerked over walls through a glass frame about the entrance. Morgan cracked open the heavy wood slab. His face blocked a strong beam of light.

"Hey, sorry, Morgan. Thought there was a burglar in here."

"Just me and the cats, Mac."

Mac's light explored over Morgan's shoulder. "I'll say. Where is everything?"

"Don't have a lot of clutter, Mac."

"Did last month. Full house."

"Decided to simplify."

"Yeah, I see you even ditched those mad scientist awards. So why—"

"Mac, can we not resuscitate this loony argument about whether scientific findings are political inventions? Science simply tells us what nature is and how it works. Science is why you have a flashlight, a truck, a TV, and a stint in that heart of yours. All working just as science designed them to. Trust me, science could not care less about Republicans and Democrats."

"I was going to ask, Why are your lights off?"

"Oh…Sorry. Power's out."

"For two weeks? Need help fixing them? My brother's an electrician. He—"

"Nope. Thanks, Mac." Morgan shut the door. What does he mean I don't have anything? he thought. Roxanne left me a used bar of soap for my personality and a half roll of toilet paper for my ass…Or is that the other way around?

Morgan snuck next to a window. He whispered to Mac walking across the street, "Well, I've got something, Mac. Chicago brick, a twenty-by-twenty master bathroom, heated pool to swim in that icy Boston wintertime, and four fireplaces to dry out with. Are you blind? Your wife and everybody else on the block seemed to have eyes enough for that eighteen-wheeler that pulled out of here while I was at work…Of course, they fear Roxy as much as I do."

He stared at interior blackness. All I want are my carvings and books back, he decided. Those sculptures were my children, which is of course why she took them. By now, they bless the bottom of a landfill. And those books were my best friends. What are you doing with all my books, Rox? You don't read.

He kneeled to pull carpet fibers matted by legs of a lost table. He headed for the open window. He felt nail holes in the walls as he walked.

I know what you're doing with my books, he thought. Starting your client's fireplace, while his wife enjoys a European tour with the kids. Sleeping in his mansion is the only reason you didn't want this place. You expect to get his.

Morgan sat back against the window sill. He whistled. Sammy pounced on an empty spot, lit by streetlight. Hawkeye attacked Sammy, then sprang behind Morgan.

He stared at the price stamped on his book. He calculated disposable income in his head. A mortgage almost as large as his salary made the answer easy.

"Guys, why on Earth did I build a house with four fireplaces?" he said. "Who the hell needs four fireplaces? I wonder, could I sell a couple?"

***

Morgan inched forward in line. He pulled the sides of his beard and long hair. He counted over two hundred people snaking out of Middlesex County divorce court. Morgan's lawyer wore a fedora, commando boots, and tight, black leather clothes. With divorce in threes, Morgan was accompanied by two women, receiving the full attention of his lawyer with Jersey accent and diamond rings on all but his thumbs. The lawyer's back and ponytail were perpetually in Morgan's face.

Morgan tapped him on the shoulder once, then again. "I'm not sure I want to go through with this," Morgan said. "I think I need time to assimilate."

The lawyer tickled the chin of one of his clients. "Morton, you been—"

"Morgan."

"Mormon, do you want to get divorced or not? You been on the Exodus for months. You're within eye-shot of The Promised Land."

Morgan deliberated, "So that's The Promised Land...I don't mean I don't want to get divorced," he said. "I mean, just not today. Maybe when there are fewer people."

"Sonny, this is a slow day."

Morgan looked toward others in line. Look at them, he thought, cruising for their next ex. Some euphoric, others catatonic, like this is their first time too.

One man in line assessed Morgan as a competitor. He wrapped his find with one arm and poked a candy in her mouth.

Morgan elbowed his lawyer. "See that guy? Biologists call that *male guarding*. Practiced from insects to primates."

Morgan watched another man wearing sunglasses inside, an unlit cigarette stuck on his lip. The man counted folded hundred-dollar bills. Females broke out of line to initiate conversation with him. Elsewhere, women with unnaturally high centers of gravity and low-cut knit tops found themselves drawing males like bees hovered about a hive.

Morgan whispered, "My personal experience with symptoms of a massive national meltdown. Rise and fall, civilizations, the fate of America." He returned to face his lawyer's back. "That's what I mean when I say I need time to assimilate. This event is too big to fathom in just one day…Week…Lifetime. Well suited for historians maybe, but not for me. I see here every sense of human senti—"

A crack from the gavel startled Morgan. A silver-haired woman in a black gown, replete with splattered mustard, looked down over bifocals from her podium. She asked Morgan a list of questions in legalese.

Morgan stared up at her.

The lawyer bumped him. "Say, yes."

"To what?"

"To what she said."

"What'd she say?"

"Just say, yes. You're holding up the trail of tears, Mike."

"But how can I know what I agree to if—"

Morgan's lawyer turned to the judge. "Yes, your honor."

Snap went the gavel. "Next!"

Morgan ducked, palms forward. "What happened?"

"Congratulations, kid, you're divorced."

The lawyer faced Morgan and put his hand on Morgan's shoulder. "Let today be your lesson. Marriage is like dating. Dates you lose, the memories you keep." The lawyer and two of his clients departed.

Morgan watched the line of people. Every human sentiment but two are present, he thought. Peace and certainty.

Morgan left the courthouse for its parking lot. He reached in his trunk for his used bar of soap and a roll of string. He grumbled to himself. "I feel like I've just been born again, confused as I am. Maybe that's what I felt the first time?"

Trailed by ten beer cans on two strings, Morgan's car quavered down the street. His back window read in cursive soap, Just Divorced!

He shouted out his window, "I untied the slipknot! Happily unmarried!"

Morgan nodded. Now that's the kind of marriage that can last, he thought. But what about the bank?

***

Morgan stood by his car at the curb in front of his house. Hawkeye and Sammy stared at him from the front seat.

Morgan felt his shaven face. He looked over his property, a patchwork of dead grass, cremated flowers, and shrubs. He could see through windows to the backyard. Light reflected off white walls, glaring over nail holes he knew were there.

He took one step toward the entrance. "They picked the wrong color," he whispered. "Looks like road construction or Halloween. You don't put a fat orange lock on a dark wood door like that. That door cost six thousand dollars."

He looked at neighboring homes. Curtains moved to fill gaps. He looked at his rusted car. Trim flexed from a cracked windshield. Despite weekly refills, one tire was perpetually flat. Can life get more humiliating? he wondered. And yet, despite it all, she taught me how dead I could be and still be alive. A lesson worth every penny.

He started the car. Plastic rattled on the grill. The tailpipe belched oil smoke. He turned to the cats. "Here we go."

## 15. For Those Who Don't Surrender

Two years after he left Boston with debts, freedom, and his two furry friends, Morgan flourished in Research Triangle Park, North Carolina. His employer, The Center, was known for its innovations and its architecture. Pillars crowned by Corinthian capitals, ceilings painted with frescos of great discovery. Center projects included wetware development of computer chips made from living neurons; DNA-sorting technology for the Human Genome Project; magnetic magic for an atom smasher called the Superconducting Super Collider destined for a tunnel in Texas. Morgan's division engaged in remote sensing, listening to light waves whisper of where they had been. Around The Center was a forest as dense as it was tall.

Morgan left his office to go outside. Light through his window one story above smoldered in the night. He approached wooden sentinels of the void. Tree trunks melted into a ground-hugging Raleigh-Durham fog. He spoke to the darkness. "Finally, things are going well. I cannot jeopardize this."

He folded a yellowed envelope, "Dad" printed on its surface, slid into his pocket. He recalled a story about how the mere utterance of sins committed frees the heart from its mosaic of grisly burdens. It does not, he thought. He headed for the airport.

Three days later, Morgan loitered outside Marion Christian Church during visitation. He searched for the steady traffic of fishermen at Bill's Bait Shop, pursued now by an army of none. The ice cream and soda stand with its bar stools and meeting room was now a fast-food drive-through owned by a corporation in Rhode Island. The train station lost its tracks. An arm was absent from the statue of Andrew W. Tibbets. Morgan went inside the church.

111

There, John's white-haired brother, Thomas, stood between Helen and Rachel, their arms around him. Thomas looked down into John's casket. "Who could have known we would end up so far from each other?" Thomas asked. "But we took our chance when we had it. Keep riding that dragon, Johnny." He pulled a loop of tan horsehair from his billfold. He slipped it in John's suit pocket. "I'm not far behind you, brother."

"I always said you boys were plain as a dry field," Helen remarked. "I'm sorry for that now."

Thomas handed her a handkerchief. "We knew you didn't mean it."

"But I did," she chuckled.

"Well...plain isn't so bad."

Rachel looked up at her brother. "He's with Grandmama now, don't you think?"

Thomas thought for a moment. "I doubt he's happy about it."

People left the visitation room. Morgan remained. He placed his hand on his father's chest. The man's hands were like plastic, covered with makeup, including his fingernails. His hair parted on the wrong side.

"Can't even check the photo we gave them," Morgan grumbled, raking fingers through his father's hair. "Why didn't somebody fix this already? Midwesterners afraid to break a rule."

Wood walls rich with varnish framed windows to a black night, mirrors on the interior scene. Scent from flowers filled the room, not yet aware they had been cut from root.

Morgan held his sealed envelope, "Dad" printed on its surface. A letter years in the making, he thought. Added to. Subtracted from. About why I am the way I am. To end our— My obstructions. Never occurred to me I should hurry to finish it.

Morgan pressed the letter into John's suit. I won, he thought. My will prevailed. I knew it would.

But what did I win?

He watched for a sign.

He thought he saw his father swallow.

He stared and waited.

*** 

Tuesday, September 7, 1993. At John's gravesite, the minister spoke about how Helen taught John as a boy to count in order, the way one breath follows another. How proud John was to hunt for the family in hard times. His service to the country in World War Two. All of it eluded Morgan's ears as sermons had years before. Preferring the solid ground of reason over the immediate relief of faith, I find myself with neither, he decided.

A Veteran of Foreign Wars held a microphone next to a cassette player. "Taps" and static played over loudspeakers. The old man fumbled for another tape. For a twenty-one gun salute, he played the blast of seven rifles fired three times. Candace jerked in her seat at the retort of recorded sounds. One aged veteran was sent to give a speech but was barely able to stand for the length of John's service.

The coffin was freed of its flag. A stout, uniformed, and resolute VFW representative, stood at attention before Candace, then bowed to hand her the folded Stars and Stripes. "Mrs. Whitaker," he said, "we will remember always an forever that your husband, an men like him, gave us all da freedoms we have. John achieved honor an glory in The Philippines. He saved me more than once from those many hazards of enforcing law in a dangerous country destroyed by war. You see, I was his comrade. He was my friend. He used to call me Levi. I can tell you from experience he was da finest soldier I ever knew. More. He was da finest man."

*** 

Morgan lay on the bed he slept on as a boy. Hawkeye and Sammy in their places. One cat pressed against his back, the second draped over his knee. Again the click and hum of a mercury streetlight.

Morgan felt his chest. My heart's not the problem, he thought. Thankfully, I'm heartless. Problem's my brain. It won't stop running.

A photo of his family hung against the wall. His father smiled from the image. There he is, crisp as ever, Morgan thought. Pictures of people should fade when they die.

He placed a vinyl record on his old stereo. It crackled with dust on the needle.

I cannot linger here, he decided. If I don't get back to work soon, I could lose my program. If I lose my program, I could lose my job and— Imagine that. Death doesn't recognize schedule and budget.

"How did all this happen?" he whispered. "The big and the small. From Dad to me, from the rise of a civilization to its descent, from God's certain presence to his absence."

He jumped up to open his closet and pulled free a book from dozens on the shelf. He blew dust off its edge. He hugged it. "Saved from inferno by neglect," he said.

He grabbed others. He kissed them. "You live because I forgot you. I won't forget you again."

He flipped pages. "Surely someone has solved this problem. I'm not the first to pose the Great Question."

For days, piles of books replaced piles of others about his room. He read Aristotle, Greek tragedies, the Old Testament and New, Rousseau, Goethe, Aquinas and Augustine, Voltaire and Pascal, Spengler, and Nietzsche. As a physicist, I'm not new to this kind of inquiry, he thought. Lots of practice with confusion. All I need is some spare adrenalin. Lest I sleep to meet that dream in reruns, syndicated to my brainstem...Or is my subconscious trying to tell me something?

He sat on the floor with a notepad and detailed the dream. Nighttime, he wrote. I have a puppy. I stand on a balcony open to views of the city. River, twenty stories down. I love that dog in my arms more than anything. It occurs to me I am complete master of this creature. I extend my arms, its body beyond the railing. Mouth open, its tongue flaps, happy to be in my grasp. I know the smallest of motions will change everything. After that act, nothing can return him to me. I cannot cushion his fall or reverse gravity or turn back time. With exertion as insignificant as freeing a spoon, I release him. I study the look on his face, immediately one of curiosity—he never felt weightless before. He slips away.

Morgan rolled on his back. Scattered papers crinkled beneath him. A head between two black paws watched him from the bed above. The symphonic dread of "Cantus In Memoriam Benjamin Britten For Strings And Bell" bled from stereo speakers.

"Kitty, what is the point of all this?" he asked Hawkeye. "Just a stupid dream." He fell asleep.

He lurched for the dog as it slid through the air. His arms crisscrossed as Morgan paddled the wind and nearly went over. Desperate to explain himself, vein-splitting pressure produced utter silence. Hair on the animal's body flittered in an artificial storm. It pawed the air in an attempt to climb skyward as it accelerated away. Eyes bulged and weaved, its mouth opened wide then closed, but never did its gaze leave the cause of its destruction.

The puppy smacked water as though liquid were concrete. The sound hit Morgan with such authority he felt it on his face. In a sheen of sweat, he whirled away from what he'd done and woke up. He rolled over to write questions to himself, diagrams, categories to investigate.

Candace knocked and opened the door. "Are you hungry, Morg— Morgan, what a mess." She pushed in to see pillars of books in a shallow sea of papers and kneeled to gather them.

Morgan jumped at her. "Don't touch it! Just—" He smiled. "I know it looks like hell, but I know where every piece is. I have to put it together in a certain order, that's all. Only looks crazy."

"Oh, Morgan…Elder has a friend who's a doctor who—"

"Keep that hypocrite out of this! Can't even be true to his counterculture."

"Morgan, he's your brother. He loves you."

"I suppose he loves Dad now too."

"He always cared for your father. We all did."

"So much he slapped Dad in front of the whole fucking National Guard in Iowa…City." Morgan gazed out his window. "Sorry, Mom…No F word…"

"Morgan, that was years ago. Those were hard times."

Morgan stared at a lamppost. "F word…Cursing…Dad never swore. I can't speak without it." He ticked off a count, whispering, "Values, norms, habits, decline…Individuals, their speech, behavior, actions—all symptoms of civilization's illness. I'm just a reflection of a larger social disease. That absence of peace and certainty. Small scale, holding up the large."

"Elder just wants to help, Morgan. What about your job?"

Morgan watched the floor. "Invisible foundations of the visible," he said. "Values, norms…What else did I say? Mom, did you hear what I— Habits! Habits and decline, that's what I said. Like habits of virtue—Aristotle said that—or their absence, like today."

Morgan sat on the bed to write on a slip of paper. "OK, that sounds good, Mom. I have a lot of work to do."

Candace left with handfuls of apple cores and banana peels.

Morgan rose later each day. The dog in his dreams had become a small bunny, pink drops leaked from its mouth. Nightly it transformed—a cat, a bleeding ox, an infant boy that began to cry just as it hit the river. The infant got older, finally able to accuse Morgan with language only a genius or messiah could deliver. When Morgan woke, he wondered if others already knew these things about him.

He suspected not only prose but lyrics might harbor pieces of what was missing. He lay next to an almost silent stereo speaker as Chris Rea's desolating *Road to Hell* was played and played, nearly free of its groves.

He stood. He squeezed his chin. "Elder slapped him," he whispered. "But I punched the man. I'm no more to be trusted than the rest of these humans. And that makes me wonder, does God really punish generations of innocents for the sins of their fathers? Is death of the fathers that punishment? Not of the fathers, but of the sons. The sons remain prisoners, of their thoughts."

He leaned against the window frame. Eyelids sagged from abuse. He looked to the side as though he'd heard something. He grabbed a pen to write on paper flat against glass. The world narrowed through a hole punched in the sheet, holding a star. He peered through two other holes meant for a binder—no star.

"Ooo…" He looked at the cats. "Just one," he said. "After all that, there really is proof. The Great Question is answered. I'll be damned. And maybe I will be. Who wants free-thinking heretics?" He leaned in against arms that straddled window space. "Thousands of books, centuries of study, millions of pages, and it's just a *one-word* adjustment. I had to be tired enough to stop thinking about it. The problem has always been not that it's too complex, but that it's too simple. The proof is contained in *one word*. It's not what God does *for* us that proves his existence. It's what God does *to* us."

He looked at the star. "You can't help it either. It's the way we

116

are. We're a team, you and me. Me in your image."

Morgan studied the dark night. Even now, keeping safe the dead of Egyptian Pharaohs, the Big Dipper hauled its neighbors about Polaris in that region of ever-present night, free from Earth's hungry horizon. Molecules of fog, stars by the million, rose from the teapot of Sagittarius. Scorpio's sting still poised, ready to defend the vault of heaven.

Celsus was right, he thought. There's no need for a devil to assign evil, all to save my precious vision of God. It is that evil in perfect infinity no devil could match that confirms God as real. And so there is salvation in this world. It's peace of mind. The peace that comes with knowing this. Even if God will do evil, *he exists*.

Morgan fell back on his bed, his feet on the floor. Hawkeye and Sammy settled in their places. Peace, he thought. At long last, peace. All I want is peace.

Stars turned outside Morgan's window without notice. Million-dollar projects screamed for Morgan's attention in Raleigh-Durham. Morgan's eyes closed in sleep. With a motion as insignificant as freeing a spoon, Morgan dropped his father from his balcony twenty stories above the river. He reached for the man. Desperate to explain, vein-splitting pressure produced utter silence when a giant of a beast appeared before Morgan. It crashed through the railing to break a cane in Morgan's grip and sliced him to pieces with it. Guards hammered his attacker with rifle butts. A wail from humanity filled the world, horrified by the utmost of fears.

\*\*\*

Candace, Morgan, and clean-shaven Elder in his suit and tie listened to John's doctor describe the heart and how it works. There had been no autopsy. No desire for doctors to saw the man's lifeless body as he lay there staring into blackness, shoved, rolled, and lifted involuntarily like a sack of peat.

The doctor pointed at a color image. "Probably in John's case, the anterior interventricular branch of the left coronary artery was blocked," he said. "When this happens, time is of the essence."

Morgan held the picture. "What my mother hopes— What we hope you'll say is that no matter what she could have done, it would have made no difference. As if it were destiny. To give us peace of mind. To free us from blaming ourselves."

The doctor hesitated. "Of course, sooner to hospital the better, but—" He nodded. "At the same time, yes, it was destiny. Everything happens for a reason. God never gives you more than you can deal with."

Morgan leaned to his left, tilted his head, and dropped the image from his grasp.

Waving an index finger, the doctor addressed Morgan. "It is God's way, son. Accept it and go on about your duty for the Lord. *He has a plan.*"

Morgan pinched shut his eyes hard enough to hurt. He sat straight.

"There is pain now, son, only because your faith is not staunch. Let this strengthen your love for God. God works in marvelous ways. But make no mistake, *He works.*"

Morgan nodded. "I completely agree. God works evil like nobody can. But I don't think Mom knows that yet." He patted Candace on the shoulder. "Everything's fine, Mom. It's God's will. You OK with that?" Morgan shrugged. "I'm OK with that." He pressed his index finger to chin. "Hmm…Or maybe I'm not. When people murder people or fail to assist those in desperate need, we reject them or put them in prison, doctor. What do we do when God does that?"

"It's not murder or neglect, son. Your father's gone to a better place. All part of the plan. Lessons for those with the wit to learn."

"Well, I'm not sure I have that wit, but let's see…Murderers have performed a service. They've sent their victims to heaven early. Let's write a book to honor them and call it scripture." Morgan leaned close toward the man's face. "My father was still in there. *You* failed to let him out, claiming your incompetence as God's will. '*God* never gives us more than we can deal with.' Have you heard of newspapers, radio? Infants fail bone-marrow transplants; children hit by cars while they play; women stabbed to death in Central Park; men ripped to chunks just doing their job in another war politicians got some votes with. Just think of all those people who never got more than they could deal with. Sixty thousand dead in Lisbon, on All Saints Day no less. At least they didn't have far to go. They all died in church! What were they guilty of, doctor? Not embracing a God that gave them free will to choose him, unless they didn't, then condemned them to hell? But what a marvelous lesson in God's love they got. And I just got my own. My love for God grows with each dead body I stand on." Morgan slapped the man's back. The doctor flinched. "How 'bout you, doc?"

The doctor looked like a statue.

Morgan leaned in. "I asked you a question!"

The doctor pressed back in his chair.

"When people suffer loss, doctor, the last thing they need is a preacher like you. *Never* tell survivors they deserve what they get, their pain is for someone else's sins, or it's all part of a *plan*. Near East mythology to keep your house of cards in order."

The doctor stood. He nodded to Candace and Elder. "This is all I can do. I'm sorry." Then to Morgan, "This conversation is over." He turned down a hallway.

"Of course it's over," Morgan said. "There's nothing left to give...No, stop!" Morgan jumped from his seat to follow the man. "Wanna work on me, Doc?"

Morgan yanked open his own shirt. Stripped buttons rifled against the wall. He poked his bare chest. "Another example for some lucky learner. Gather the faithful. Spread the gospel. And when you're finished, chalk up another dead man for God!"

The doctor opened his office door and spun on Morgan. "Don't blame my God. He gives us choices. Plaque results from poor diet, kid. Your father is to blame for his death, not God." He slammed the door behind him.

Morgan dove for the doorknob as it locked. He pounded its wood surface. "Free will was a penalty, not a gift!" He kicked the door with all his force, then kicked it again and again, fully intending to go through it. "God gave humans free will only to find them guilty!"

Panting, Morgan turned to see Elder, embarrassed, his arm around their mother. Candace covered her face as tears squeezed from her eyes.

# 16. Challenge the Myth

Outdoors at the Research Park, the same incandescent glow that cast down on Morgan months ago in the middle of night did so again. Other illuminated offices at The Center made sight past the pine perimeter possible.

A shine from Kip's cigarette lit his face. "This is our fifth hustle this year, Morgan. I spend four nights per week sleeping on a cot in my office to save commute time, lengthen my workday. When I last probed the secrets of nature, I cannot remember. But I've done a lot of proposals, schedules, and budgets. I slaved for my doctorate with hopes of expanding human knowledge; to count myself among the heroes of science, not profit. If I'm to be a salesman, I want to get paid like one.

"But this is about more than contracts, Morgan. The very essence of our careers is at stake. Fundamental science is under siege in America. From this economic system we made, from this nation's absence of science education, from liberals and conservatives with their political agendas. What will become of America when we lose it? I've got a dozen years on you; you don't feel it as acutely as I do. The core of our careers has become an imitation, as it has for all Americans, whatever their pursuits. Everything is marketing now."

Morgan patted Kip on the back. "Kip, Kip...On this very campus, brain neurons are turned into computers. Next door, Hans is probably still working on his quadrapole magnet."

"Really? The Super Collider was *canceled*, Morgan. Where have you been? Working all night? Hans' magnet is a multimillion-dollar paperweight, while Europe presses forward on their Large

Hadron Collider." Kip shouted toward the Magnet Science building, "Last out of Collider tunnel, fill in hole!

"Despite our *peace dividend*, Morgan, the Super Collider didn't have manufacturing vendors with jobs in districts of powerful politicians. Thus it didn't have the votes. Mark my words, they'll shut down the Tevitron accelerator at Fermilab, NASA, NSF. All to be more practical, efficient, in *service to the people*. The celebrated discoveries will come from Europe or someplace else, as America's innovation culture fades.

"Morgan, what we spend in one month on warfare pays for the entire Super Collider, but science doesn't rank nearly so high as protecting oil in another country. Contrary to political claims, it's not about jobs, jobs, jobs." Kip drew hard on his cigarette and drained his lungs of smoke.

"Morgan, did you know Aristotle's contemporary, Epicurus, wrote over three hundred books?"

"No, and what's that got to do with anything?"

"Aristotle's views were unique. We cherish them still. So too, Epicurus, with ideas no one thought of before him, or probably since. Do you know how many of his books survived? *None*—only letters, and what others said about him. Ever wonder what his mind discovered that will never be known, lost forever?

"Time, perishable documents, the burning of Alexandria's library—accidents of history, Morgan. In the modern era, we abort the future intentionally. The Super Collider was lost because it appeared to have no *immediate practical* use. But James Maxwell's unification of electricity, magnetism, and light had no use either—in 1873. Yet his discoveries gave us radio, television, computers, radar, satellite communications. The Super Collider was an extension of Maxwell's path. What would its discoveries have led to?"

Kip spoke between clenched teeth pinching his cigarette. "Something as monumental as The Collider was lost with barely a notice. Why? Because of the way Americans view the world and themselves in it. The Collider's rise and fall were thanks to that wonderful flowering of philosophy, the Enlightenment. Enlightenment science is what gave birth to The Collider. And Enlightenment economy is what killed it. When Enlightenment made self-interest a virtue not a vice, it not only redefined virtue but changed the essence of man. What was to be avoided was now to be sought. Hence, we pursue personal interests, and a free-market economy becomes the rational order of society. Good. However, not only does economics become paramount but, over time, exclusive. Today, things merit knowing only if they make a dollar. Eventually, everybody thinks this way. *We don't challenge the myth.* With primacy of the practical, we jettison philosophical inquiry. And with that go answers to the human condition. We've reversed Aristotle's claim that things worth knowing are worth knowing for their own sake.

"I'm not claiming the pursuit of utility is wrong, Morgan. But our aperture is so distorted now that economic utilitarianism squelches options that once opened the door to undreamed-of possibilities. Muir said it: 'Nothing dollarable is safe.' But it's not just the physical world at risk; we've clear-cut our intellectual and spiritual soul. Consequences are traceable. Our economic machine naturally leads to a utilitarian educational system, which leads to scientific illiteracy, which leads to political dogma, which leads to an inability to acknowledge problems we create, much less solve them. Even an adolescent defiance of environmental ruin on a planet-wide scale if it might cost somebody a dollar. Ruin that directly affects the human race. See the cycle? Our attitude, pushed outward, folds back on us.

"Now, I'm not suggesting, Morgan, that we stop using nature for our advantage. If a yew tree might save someone from cancer, please, explore, cut it down. But sacrificed because I want toothpicks? Leave the forest alone. If human heart transplants advance through experimentation on animals, then proceed, with humane conduct. But destroying animals for cosmetics? Forget it, I'd rather see my girlfriend natural."

Morgan laughed. "Funny. But I'm not sure I can agree with your idea extended to animals. I'm not sure humans are worth it."

"Including your father?" Morgan stiffened. "Forgive me, Morgan, but your father was given clot busters in an attempt to save his life, right? Didn't come to the pharmacy untested…See the difference? To the merchant, toothpicks make money just as green as clot busters. Without scientific training to challenge our myths, these are choices without a distinction."

"And what bureaucracy will dictate that people should save the forest, Kip?"

"The people themselves, Morgan, *if* they had science in their blood."

Kip ejected his cigarette and shook another from his pack. Flint sparks flashed on his face. "What is the primary commonality between all species, Morgan, no matter what?"

"Sex."

"No; bacteria clone. They don't have sex unless the environment becomes harsh, to mix up genes in hopes of a survivor. Consumption, Morgan. Consumption, consumers, markets. Be it bacteria in the agar dish or humans in the world, the command is to consume. Everything. See? Utility is *instinctive*. Ways to dominate and control for consumption—this is our articulation of what those bacteria express when they sack their world in the agar dish and themselves with it. We call that behavior useful, productive, profitable. Whatever name we give it, we'll eventually convert every last stick to our uses. We'll build a machine planet and terminate the most important machine of all—natural wilderness and its inhabitants—upon which we are utterly dependent for the proper operation of everything else.

"The answer must come from the people, Morgan, those who consume. But actions contrary to instinct must come from the head, not the gut or gonads. We can only override instinctive habits if informed by the brain.

"*Science*, Morgan, *and the reason* it engenders. Not *motivated reason* in which we persuade ourselves of the answer we want, ignoring all that refutes it. But these habits and their supporting myths march on because this is not an intellectual's country. It's a businessman's country with the primacy of finance, equities, property, and its legalities. Hence, we advance property rights as sanction for devastating natural environments comprising our property. Wholly ignorant that Locke's rights—which spurred creation of this nation—did not begin and end with property rights. He started with a natural right to life. But an argument for rights to life with the same authority as property gives the natural world a value it did not appear to have. Populations are now ravaged by floods because razed forests hold no water. But somebody had rights to those forests; they made a dollar.

"Morgan, the only options in America now are either-or, all black or all white, no gray. Environment or jobs; government control or individual rights. Busy Americans are wary of intellectually extravagant solutions. We want facile generalizations, like candy, a quick-fix sound bite for ideological brawlers.

"To suggest preservation of anything—a species, tradition, a forest, virtue—the response is, Must we stop living; create a police state; end production; retreat to a cave? But a bit of theoretical plumbing finds that *reason* demands a flexibility of thought. The solution is a bit of both property and life, but this escapes us because it's gray. Our Founders' rights have become narrowed *because there are now so many of us.* The latitude rights once garnered becomes restricted when our population is ten times what it was in their day."

"Humans have always impacted their environment, Kip."

"But we didn't always have five and one-half billion eating mouths and counting, Morgan. The difference is not one of *kind* but of *scale.* At some point, a threshold is reached. And just like the electrical circuits we work with, the natural world is chock-full of feedback systems—self-reinforcing amplifications that make things worse faster. If we force Earth's planetary systems into nonlinear behavior with a runaway response, take cover; the bad news won't be about the spotted owl.

"Now it's true, environmentalists have claimed an end of the world since the sixties. Because they didn't grasp the extent to which technology would increase the burden Mother Earth can shoulder. But like the physical limit of transistors on a computer chip, there's a limit to the number of bushels per acre. Eventually, what saved us—our instinctive utility—will be what defeats us. What we now do to other species we will do to ourselves. We'll be the latest cause for mass extinction, finding ourselves among the fossil record." Kip appraised his fingers spread wide. "Wonder how I'll look as a fossil?"

"You're already a fossil, Kip."

Kip slapped Morgan on the back and pointed at him. "Remember, I said the economic system is not alone in this assault on science. There's a growing hostility to science from Left and Right, with identical tactics. Compare with the Right one of the

Left's pillars of virtue: gender theorists, also known as feminist theorists, which are to feminism as the Taliban is to democracy. These are the people directing our university Women's Studies courses that claim Newton's *Principia Mathematica* is a rape manual. They demand that science conform to political, social, and gender-based perspectives of feminist theory. While Creationists on the Right demand science abandon its description of nature to make us feel better. To feminist theorists, science is racist, sexist, classist. To Creationists, Darwin is socialist, communist, atheist. While masculinity in science is evil, feminism in science is not. While science in religion is evil, religion in science is not. See the parallel?

"Anti-science has been expressed before, Morgan. They called it Proletarian Science in the USSR and China. Massive crop failures resulted, with the largest starvation in history between 1958 and 1962, costing between twenty and forty million lives. Mao called it The Great Leap Forward.

"Now I ask you, Morgan, how can both political sides in this country be so much the same?"

Morgan concentrated. "No scientific training?"

Kip held arms vertically, signal of a touchdown. "Ironically, we reached this end by way of scientists—the Founders. They saw religion as essential for moral instruction, but the method they employed to defang it—relegating religion from fact to opinion—is applied now to all things; truth, morality, even science if it might detract from profits on the Right or offend someone's sensibilities on the Left. To Americans, science is just another opinion. Reason planted this seed of unreason.

"We as a people are now so bereft of reasoned thought, Morgan, that the most absurd notions are given credence. Not only by the public but by university academia—once the light of rational inquiry—now wardens at trade schools. It's a downhill process. As evidenced by the Dark Ages, it's very easy to let reason roll downhill; very hard to push it up.

"Where is the valley floor, Morgan? I'll tell you where. Once we reach a rainforest minimum, for the production of soybeans or gold or diamonds or charcoal. Once ocean temperatures cross that phytoplankton thermal limit, killing our last most vital source of oxygen. That's the bottom. That's when the worldwide clash for

125

scarce resources exceeds even God's wrath. One last heroic stand for a desire to breathe.

"Imagine—" Kip's cigarette-bearing hand swept over darkness. "Tattered tribes in the tens of millions maraud one continent to the next. Landscapes stripped. Competitors trampled, human, bird, and bee. The high priest stands tall on a rock outcrop, his robe and gray beard lifted by an easy breeze. Surrounded by blue skies, bone-dry streambeds, endless dunes of a Missouri desert." Kip lifted both hands. "'*Pray*,' he commands. 'For forgiveness! For salvation!' His flock falls to their knees for miles like an army of dominos. 'All in holy heaven above, do not let mankind perish form this earth, we beg of you!'"

Kip whispered, "And in the midst of dread, Morgan. Above...Up there...See it? An answer to their prayer. A light. A stern and angry light flickers at them at about...oh, let's say Mach six, eight maybe. All turn skyward, and in a flash, they see the one true God. A Lord of such brilliance they could have never imagined.

"In an instant too pithy to measure, he arrives to punch the ground with a deafening thunderclap, home after so many millennia of exile.

"They howl at the beautiful image of his grace. They cover their eyes as he rises like a mushroom cloud high in the sky above them. Pitiless, he bellows outward with such rage the air cannot contain his magnificence. So very bright it's painful.

"Then, suddenly, his tender warmth covers them all to become an intense heat with an impact of such glory flesh melts from bone. Torn away in hunks of neutron-laden radiance by a supersonic nuclear wind. Their grief and suffering dragged away, once and—in a millisecond—for all. Their last judgment. Justice served. Ransom paid in full. Payment from a world no longer able to support them. Payment from others who want those resources too."

Morgan fixed on a waltzing star. He looked down from the hemisphere of night. He waited.

"It's happened before, Morgan. The Permian extinction suffocated ninety-six percent of all life on Earth. It can happen again, and this time we'll know why: because we didn't challenge instinctive urge. Because we abandoned science and the thinking it incubates that can stand up to that urge."

Morgan nodded, seemingly looking toward the back of his brain.

"Morgan, do you see how this entire system is a self-perpetuating process? I salute commercial success that finances those legendary projects like the genome, the Super Collider now dead, and Apollo long ago abandoned. Look at communist East and capitalist West Berlin, a virtual lab experiment. One side prospered, the other built a wall to keep people in. The capitalistic ideal is *correct* in its concept, it fits human nature, but *wrong* in the limits to which we have taken it. We all feel a sense of discomfort in this system, but deny a way out because that would oppose this mechanism so successful in addressing common needs with material results."

Morgan grimaced. "Could you say that again?"

Kip nodded. His eyes turned red with a pull on burned tobacco. He paused. "No. Ha! I can't remember what I said! Damn, I think it was good, though." He rummaged for a pen and paper in pockets.

Smoke emerged from Kip's mouth in puffs as he spoke. "Morgan, did you ever hear of the *Principle of Voluntary Simplicity*? Richard Gregg wrote a little-known pamphlet by that title in nineteen thirty-something. Find it. He was a Quaker and a communist, but you needn't be either to recognize the truth of voluntary simplicity. It's about an avoidance of exterior clutter, an invitation to shun possessions irrelevant to the chief purpose of life. Not asceticism, not monasticism, but partial restraint in some directions for greater abundance in others. While our contemporary world emphasizes quantitative assessments, the essence of human life lies in *qualitative* existence, Morgan. Simplicity understands this. It's not the cost of the car, the square feet of a home, it's our moral, ethical, emotional substance that matters most. Yet how do we measure happiness? Quantitatively—more, bigger, faster. Our GDP measures everything except what grants life most meaning."

Morgan grinned, shaking his head. He was enthralled by a mind he could remotely keep pace with. He tried to memorize it all so he could repeat it to himself.

"America was founded by scientists, Morgan. Thomas Jefferson: naturalist and inventor. Franklin: founder of electrical physics. Hamilton, Madison, and Jay appeal to scientific metaphors in describing the best system for society in their Federalist Papers.

So, how is a civilization founded by those practicing the methods of science supposed to survive without it? Civilizations rise and fall in a blink now. Rome, in altered states, lasted a thousand years. The USSR—a world superpower—ended after just seven decades. For our republic to survive, I argue science must flourish among *the populous*. Not for the findings of science, but for its method of thinking in all quarters of their lives. Problem is, that way is not for the TV generation, Creationists, or graduates of feminist theory. It won't come in talk radio sound bites or pop-culture self-help books.

"I wish I had time to address these matters, Morgan, but I'm behind on budgets. Someday, I hope a moral artist steeped in the rigors of scientific thinking will see clear of our times—a savior to save us."

Occasional bats occluded stars in acceleration for insects overwhelmed by sonar and speed. Perpetually moist brick walls in a subtropical North Carolina climate smelled of mildew.

Morgan sat down on steps to face the forest. He pulled a blade of grass. Kip sat five steps up, leaned against a pillar.

Morgan tried to laugh and sounded like it. "My mother told me something when I was home," he said. "That thirty years ago, my kindergarten teacher said I was interested in two things: art and science. I won't be that savior you seek, but I know what you mean. Humans do art and science better than anything. Civilizations...maybe we don't do that so well. At least not for long."

Kip watched Morgan. A red-yellow ring climbed up the cylinder drooped from his mouth.

"Compared to you, Kip, my perceptions are primitive, and they'll remain that way as long as I chase titles and paper money. But I graduated with an elevated capacity to consume, what else could I do? The template was pretty clear. I accepted the myth and didn't know it. Pretty soon, like some peacock, I had enough money to buy the car and house as display items to lure females looking for financial security."

Kip chuckled. "Did you see the Sexual Selection series on PBS? Showed how males of all species fight to the death for resources, so they can display it to females. She seeks resources for the kids, and he knows it. He seeks youthful females to bear his genes. Biologists call it *the handicap principle*. Translation? Rich old men with young, hot gold diggers. See how primal urge is a match for free-market individualism?"

"Kip, I embraced that arrangement and ended up married alive. Been trying to dig myself out ever since. That's some handicap."

"Married alive? I love it! I was married alive too! Where's my pen?" Kip scribbled on a slip of paper. "Men are taught to grin and bear it, Morgan. Shoulder to the wheel, nose to the grindstone. There's no war to fight, we need something to do. You had something to do—give away your money."

"Maybe we could accept the grind if we had family," Morgan said. "I'm not talking about lunatics like the one I married. Someone out there must be normal."

"You have no evidence of that."

A pinecone struck a branch with a click and soft landing in last year's elongated solar cells. An early-morning airliner ascended above the Research Park. Morgan followed its lights blink out of sight.

"Kip, do you know not long ago I made a realization that should have been obvious? That I won't have another chance with my father. Isn't that odd? That I just came to grasp that, I mean. This universe will disappear into eternity, and our paths—his and mine—will never cross again. I had my chance. I didn't know it was a chance. I wish there were a God to give me that chance again. My internal battles would be resolved with one simple act—belief. I thought I proved God's existence and already I'm not sure. But I am sure of hell. Hell is realization, Kip. In Boston I learned we aren't who we thought we were, others aren't who we thought they were, our country isn't what we thought it was—love, marriage, life, none of it's what we thought it was.

"Is life what you thought it would be, Kip? I don't mean the job; I mean life, fulfillments of truth, good, right. Those unquestioned idealizations of our youth. That what we *should* be about is what we *would* be about. That's what I thought when I was a kid. One of the earliest things I learned was that adults were of the highest in every regard. They were admirable people, truth seekers, and I'd be one too someday. 'Respect your elders,' my parents said." Morgan shook his head. "But adults are little more than larger children with added power to ruin. Do adults have more sense than a child? Of course—'Stay out of the street, kid.' That's not what I mean. As adults we refined our duplicity as liars, to ourselves. That discovery was a big disappointment for me.

"The only trust deserved in this world belongs to nature, Kip. Not men, not institutions, not society. Nature and the animals in it, they're the authentic ones. Even the killers. I try to find solace in that, in nature—and art. But I'd avoid all these disappointments if only I believed in God."

"You're the kind of man who would read the Bible, Morgan. You wouldn't simply swear by it without intense study of what your beliefs were based on. You'd never tolerate its countless self-contradictions and intermediate morality. You'd never accept applying reason everywhere except the Bible."

"I wouldn't have to believe in the Bible to believe in God, Kip. I wish I believed, don't you?"

"Did. Altar boy, remember? Only person in my parish to memorize New Testament, chapter and verse—age eight. I was a party favor on Wednesday nights."

Kip looked at the sky, then back to Morgan. He squinted one eye intercepting strings of hot carbon. "What's made for the masses is not made for the artist, the poet, nor the true intellectual, Morgan. But such types are rare, and so societies are built for the masses, not for the gifted. Nor *should* societies be built for the gifted, for to do so makes them sterile, non-communal, irreligious. The masses need belonging. The gifted, they never belong. You'll never belong. I'll never belong."

A florescent-green Luna moth glided by Morgan. Its wings scattered upstairs light. Too large to fly, it bounced up with a single stroke, coasted down, followed by another aerodynamic pump. Morgan studied it. And what will lift me up? he thought. I thought it would be science.

Morgan slapped his knee. "But I still have my program," he said. "This is important work. Meaningful work. And this dot-com boom will heal my finances, pronto. I can still be a success. In a few years, maybe ten, I could run this place...No, I could run a bigger place with more people, a larger budget. People would look up to me for...*Me.*"

Kip held his cigarette vertically, rolled between fingers. He watched it burn. "What happened to you out there in Iowa, Morgan?"

"Not much."

"Don't think so."

"Had a deep wallow in self-pity, that's all."

"Something's different, Morgan. I don't mean what you say. You still talk the talk. I mean your voice. You *sound* different— tone, tempo, cadence. You sound…misplaced. What changed?"

Morgan hesitated. "I feel it's all been done before, Kip. All of it forgettable. I seem to have—" Morgan smiled. "Misplaced something…Maybe. I dunno.

"Do humans invent meaning, Kip? You get divorced with a strike of the gavel. You see your father's stuff—a simple fishing lure, priceless to him—sold at a garage sale for a dime. All those things that make us who we are, the car, the house—vapor. We made them mean something to make ourselves feel a certain way, to invent ourselves. We can just as easily uninvent it all. Thing is, once you know what you're up to, you can never pretend again. That's the utility of a god, is it not? If God provides meaning—even if we concocted God then forgot we did—our worth is not up to us…Maybe." Morgan shook his head. He stood. "Of course, it's all baloney. Same shit, different day."

He hurried for the building. "I'll never be somebody sitting here psychoanalyzing myself with you."

# 17. Farewell Colonies

Morgan, with his cats in his car and all his possessions, approached eastern boundaries of the North American prairie with the smell of distance in it. Made of mountaintop soil spread west by trade winds over sixty million years, it stretched one thousand miles east from the Rockies; eighteen hundred miles south from the North Saskatchewan River nearly to the Rio Grande.

Morgan's parting from The Center was fresh in his mind. He could still hear Kip say, "Was it something I said, or the death of your father?" With one hard down-stroke, Brian shook Kip's hand and walked away.

As Morgan drove, he watched metal horses seesaw atop oil wells behind a sign to Cherokee National Forest. Beyond that, mountain tops were inverted ditches for coal mining.

"Kitties, would you look at that sign," Morgan said. "My great-grandmother got a forest named after her people for that long death march President Son of a Bitch made them take. Isn't that's nice?"

Morgan rolled to a stop before the bridge over Watagua Lake, no traffic in either direction. He checked two pharmaceutically relaxed felines on the floorboard. He inserted a cassette tape for the occasion. Elton John sang "I'm Still Standing."

Morgan rummaged about the glove box. "Watch this, guys. Time to leave a mark in this world."

Outside the car, Morgan dug a hole with the toe of his boot and lifted a cloud of dust next to the road. In the depression, he placed the cardboard core from a toilet roll and a sliver of soap. He stomped the roll flat. He scooped soil sideways, buried both items, and twisted on his heel to seal the grave. "My father claimed the dead are freed," he said. "Just be buried. Don't be freed." He dusted jeans and turned for the car.

Driving across the bridge, he slowed to look back. "Adios, colonies. I'm off to find the Promised Land." He looked at the cats. "Tall grass ahead, kitties. The most immense transformation of our natural world by mankind anywhere on earth. Three hundred million acres, once natural habitat, now three hundred million acres of biodiversity desert. North America's Serengeti—gone. Lost in the length of one lifetime. Factory floor of an agri-planet. But who would not salute those rugged pioneers? When natives in harmony with nature met dreams of invaders who dominated it. I'm here because of them. Both of them. And I'm free."

Morgan's next selection played Johnny Nash, "I Can See Clearly Now." He scratched Hawkeye's head. He rubbed Sammy's belly. He accelerated uphill.

From the lake, Morgan could be heard singing. The past slipped down in his rearview mirror. The rest of America rose to take its place.

*** 

From the kitchen at 213 Swathmore Street, Hawkeye and Sammy watched a goldfinch on the deck John built years ago.

Seated in the dining nook beside the deck, Candace asked, "What about you, Morgan? You should have children. There's nothing more important than family."

"Mom, do you remember when Elder said you were oppressed and didn't know it? That Dad left you here with your screaming kids, while Dad enjoyed his 'interesting' work, pushing a broom. Is it the family you thought it was?"

"Oh, he didn't mean all that. Elder was strong-willed, that's all. Like you."

"He's nothing like me, Mom."

"You should have a family, Morgan."

"It's the 1990s, Mom, not the 1940s. Though I wish it were the forties. Wish so hard there are times I feel I've gone back in time. In my imagination, I can even see the stone that buildings were made from, without every square inch turned into a hustle. Well-kept homes with porches where people could actually see their neighbors.

"I can't speak for the old South or big cities, Mom, but in your place and time, in the Midwest, life was hard and honest. People mattered more than things. It was all so...respectful. Of others, I mean. Not the imitation of respect out of external politically correct coercion, but internal public duty. A sense of humility, modesty, not entitlement. Very odd."

"Doesn't seem odd to me, Morgan. I did see it. Today seems odd to me."

"It's those quiet signs that are most telling of a civilization, Mom. The soft parts, the small parts, the parts you can't see, like imperceptible atoms that hold up the sun.

"It wasn't the Vandals, Visigoths, Huns—they didn't vanquish Rome, Mom. Those are the parts we can see. It's the unseen attitudes that matter most."

Morgan watched the goldfinch. It appeared spellbound by humans inside. Its head tilted one way then the other.

"So what will you do, Morgan?"

"It won't be office politics, paper-pushing, or material display. Humans are irretrievably nuts if they think that's normal. I, however, am going to be somebody. Just not sure what body it's gonna be."

Candace sighed. "Oh, Morgan, my boy, it's only a dream."

Morgan smiled. "You know what, Mom? It is. And it started a long time ago on Route 66."

***

Outside Marion Manufacturing, Morgan looked through a chain-link fence enclosing the site. Abandoned by mergers and economic upheavals, garbage piled in corners about gray buildings. Rusted roof supports were visible through broken windows. A plastic bag rattled, pinned against chain-link by the wind.

Locals sold control to some faraway corporation because money meant more than neighbors, he thought. Neighbors—another word for people we don't know. But at least somebody made a dollar. Can't argue with that, right?

I wonder what he did in there? Which building was his?

134

At Marion Memorial, Morgan faced his father's grave. He watched a backhoe break bricks from the train station. A crane lifted the head and torso of Andrew W. Tibbets, hung by a chain over legs attacked by a sledgehammer. Earthmovers gouged the land of ten-ton lesions. Black smoke from their engines obscured the sign for a truck stop and adult video store under construction only a half-mile from the freeway. A hawk perched on the sign. It stared at bulldozers. Morgan whispered, "Wonder where you're next mouse comes from?"

He stepped around John's grave, his back to the truck stop. This is not the same America, he decided. But I can't change that trajectory, only my own.

He looked at his car to review the list of things packed in his mind. Glad I found Dad's old camera, he thought. Like the dog he had, we'll compare what we see, his camera and mine…Did he have a dog? I thought he had a dog. Maybe not.

Can't wait to see what's on that other half roll he shot, still in there. Shoot some at the Grand Canyon, like when we were kids.

Morgan looked about for others. He crouched to touch his father's name in stone. I have guilt enough for a hundred men, he thought.

A bluebird sang. It swooped down, chased by English sparrows toward an October sun. Morgan stood with a nod and turned to follow the bluebird. He felt a wave of solar photons end their eight-minute flight on his face. To the west, the TV tower, crowned by a red beacon, waxed and waned to tick off time.

At the car, Morgan scratched Hawkeye's head. "We came home to visit my past, Miss Kitty, only to find it paved. The world won't be born new again, but through this adventure it seems young, if only for a moment."

He looked over the graveyard. He watched flags and trees respond to the same force of motion. "I guess home will always be in Iowa. And home is as close as my memory. Old von Schiller said it: In that memory is something holy."

He petted Sammy. He started his car. It lurched and burped smoke. Eyes squeezed shut, Morgan shook his head. He looked to the cats. "Here we go."

# PART THREE: RELATIVITY

## 18. Revelation

Dyersville, Iowa, was a seventy-mile drive from Marion. A cold front crowded the sky with clouds. Morgan could see John Deere combines flicker through billows of chaff. He played a CD of 1930s and 40s music. Johnny Mercer's "Ac-Cent-Tchu-Ate The Positive," the Andrew Sisters' "Choo'n Gum."

"Kitties, would you listen to that," he said. "What you hear is a song about chewing gum. Rather different from rap music about how to murder and rape your mother in that order."

He reduced speed through a village on a gravel road. He saw a restaurant called the Oaky Doky. Beside it a gas station. Its *Standard Oil Ethyl* sign squeaked in the breeze.

Skies cleared, and Judy Garland's "The Trolley Song" played from Morgan's stereo as he pulled into the station and saw gas pumps topped with glass bottles.

A clean-cut man in a white jacket, black slacks, and black polished shoes tipped his hat to Morgan. "Fill 'er up, sir?"

Out of his car, Morgan examined the man and appeared about to guess his weight. Morgan nodded. "Sure," he said.

With profuse appreciation, the man set to boil a tower of gasoline. Its level dropped past volume marks on a transparent cylinder.

Morgan whispered, "Why pump gas from a glass container?"

"Certifies we sell only the cleanest of brands, sir."

"I was expecting dirty gasoline?"

"Not here, sir."

Morgan pointed at the man before him. "Where's the camera?"

"Sir?"

139

"You know, *Candid Camera*. This place is too…traditional, and you're too polite to be from my era. That show's still on cable, right?"

The man cleaned windows, headlights, taillights. He checked oil, belts, and reached into the car for items of trash to throw away. He scratched Hawkeye on the forehead. "Hello, pretty girl," he said.

"How'd you know she's a she?" Morgan asked, then stared, mute even to questions asked by his attendant, which the man answered himself as if Morgan were not there.

"OK, forty-four PSI in the tires. Yes, sir," the man said.

The man finished, anchored the pump spout, and turned to Morgan. "That will do ya, sir, at just a dollar eighty-seven."

"For?"

"Gasoline, sir."

Morgan chuckled. "Guess I needed less than I thought."

"Oh, she was right thirsty, sir." The attendant pivoted toward the station, pointing to an old man inside. "Now, you just pay that young fella right inside there."

He turned back to Morgan, shook his hand, thanked him, and bowed. He skipped to assist customers tending an antique car with a trailer of possessions.

Morgan looked for a price sign and calculated the usual cost per gallon times a near-empty tank in his head. He pinched himself. "I'm awake," he said.

On his way inside, Morgan passed the antique car's driver. In straw hat and work overalls, the man assisted an old woman to shade beside the gas station. Must be his mother, Morgan decided. But why tow a trailer with a classic car like that? Worth a fortune.

Morgan paid and left the station, mumbling, "These people are running a sale or something. That's why I got the special on gas."

Back on highway 136, capricious Iowa weather returned back to overcast skies. Near Dyersville, signs pointed the way, reading, "Movie Site."

At the site, a white house with a wrap-around porch and swing sat behind home plate. No one occupied the field. Morgan rented a bat for a dollar from the souvenir shop. He walked to home plate with his own baseball. He saw the grass where Shoeless Joe Jackson played, the bleacher where Ray Kinsella sat, and where Moonlight

Graham saved Ray's daughter from choking on a hot dog in his favorite movie, *Field of Dreams*.

Morgan stood at home plate. Two farmers appeared from cornrows; one scraped mud off his boots. Morgan tossed up the ball, tried to kill it, and spun himself to the ground.

He stood and dusted jeans. He lofted the leather sphere. His swing, slightly late, drove it into dirt.

Thrown higher, the ball's lace rotated like features of a planet. A crack echoed off the house. Bat over shoulder as if he'd swung at the sun, Morgan watched the ball sail into corn stalks.

He flipped the bat free, laughing all the way to first. Appearing from the cornfield, a farmer threw Morgan's ball to home plate. From left field came the sound of one man clapping.

When Morgan rounded second, he tipped his Twin Cities ball cap on his way to third. In his mind, he was in a loud stadium filled with applause. Finally, he was somebody.

The white farmhouse bounced up and down in his view. He slammed home plate with his boot.

He took photographs of the house, bleachers, and ladies at the souvenir stand. He bought a baseball cap with the film logo. He sat in his car, watched the field, and waited for something to happen. "Did you see that, kitties? A home run!" he said. "Without steroids!"

He drove away, retelling his game-winning hit to the cats. Leaving the nearby village on a gravel road, a smiling attendant appeared in his mind. He looked back for the Oaky Doky and gas station but had gone too far to see either. Ahead lay Interstate 80, parallel with the old Lincoln Highway.

Two days later, west of Denver on Interstate 70, Morgan crept up a steep Rocky Mountain range. He gripped tight the steering wheel, his accelerator pinned to the floor. "You can do it, girl," he said. Coming downhill toward him were eastbound trucks, their brakes ablaze with the transfer of elevation into the radiance of heat.

Morgan inserted an audiotape, Copeland's "Appalachian Spring," about a different mountain range, older and in another season, but the right mood. Peaks came into view with each crescendo.

In Utah, he traced Highway 128, hugging the Colorado River. He stopped the car. He left it to absorb what he could and photographed the rest. Small trees crowded the bank with leaves so thin, dense, and blonde they seemed covered with hair. Carrot-colored cliff walls, like wilderness skyscrapers, allowed only a slice of sky above. Devoured by the stream, red rock spires consoled one another side by side. In a sweeping corridor, they framed avalanche-laden heights of the La Sal Mountains thirty miles distant.

There it is, he thought. The Truth. Cleared of clutter, these rocks are the skeleton that hold up the world.

Patches of snow hid in nearby shade. He packed a snowball. He made a wish on its collective crystals and sailed it into a muddy Colorado. Bobbing on the surface, it mixed with molecules on yet another amble in the water cycle. He wondered, Will my dreams reach the Pacific before I do?

A day later, on Grand Canyon's South Rim, Morgan mounted his father's camera to a tripod, half its film roll already shot. Morgan set the timer and ran for his spot in its frame overlooking the gorge. He waited for a click.

Nothing.

He checked the camera and pressed its shutter button again. He ran for his mark and listened for sound. Old and faulty, he finally convinced the camera to cooperate and pressed on.

On I-40 in Arizona, Morgan saw a sign to "Seligman and Historic Route 66." Another sign read, "66, Decommissioned in 1983." He followed the warning.

Occasional buildings appeared along the route, desolate and abandoned. The 66 Tap, Burrow of Indian Affairs, and Chiefs Motel, a vacancy notice its last remnant. "Vacant...I'll say," he muttered. A cafeteria at Grand Caverns Inn had seated perhaps one hundred people when he last met this place as an eight-year-old boy conjuring his future. A lone old woman sat at a table in the empty room. The lazy angle from her elbow ended in the grip of a cigarette next to her face. Her back defied a wall of plate-glass windows between her, the highway, and its outside world.

Morgan looked at her and looked again as he drove by. "Like the rest of us," he said. "Deserted by redirections in civilization...Or is it the other way around? You deserted civilization."

Near a place called Peach Springs, which had neither peaches nor springs, the fossilized remains of a lonely 1937 Plymouth Coupe sat as a testament to this layer of life buried by time. Its flat and brittle tires among car and truck parts blasted by nature's elements.

Wind whistled through open gaps in Morgan's windows. Diesel exhaust from coal trains one hundred twenty cars long mixed with a musty smell of limestone. The scent merged with air pounding his ears and acted as a memory trigger to pull the past forward. I'm a twin in Einstein's paradox, he thought. I've traveled three decades at the speed of light with no chance for reflection.

He crested a slope to see the road reach a point on the horizon, not a car in sight. Barbed-wire fences galloped either side of the highway. Driven by gusts and occasional dust devils, tumbleweeds freed by fences jetted across his path. Radio static stronger than music divulged a familiar song among the noise.

"Otis Redding," he said. "Still 'Sittin' on the Dock of the Bay.' Can you guys believe that? Continuous play for twenty-seven years."

The song faded. Two colors dominated now: honey-colored earth and blue-white sky. White dashes on pavement blinked past, a single lane in each direction.

From backseat speakers, Morgan heard a voice. "I know what—" A Phoenix radio station barely pierced the passive barrier of range. Radio volume seesawed as he drove through a complex FM interference pattern blanketed over arid terrain. He deciphered reports of battle between Israel and Egypt. He whispered, "No way. They can't be fighting with all the money we give them not to."

He searched what he could see of floorboards packed with minor possessions and cats. "Have you guys seen my water bottle? If I had a working AC, I wouldn't be so flippin' hot. Course, you guys love it."

Train tracks beside Route 66 detained a railroad crew in orange safety vests, yellow hardhats, and blue shirts, lit against jet-black volcanic dikes, once lesions on a bleeding earth. Hammers in succession struck two to a spike, a dozen ties long. "Poor bastards," Morgan said. "Nice workspace, though. Every time I look up from my speedometer, it's like a different planet."

Rising heat led Morgan to open windows further. The only sound louder than blasts of air was a bang from Morgan's rear tire. Its flap-flapping eased as he rolled to a stop.

He got out and opened the trunk. "Shit…My spare's under all that."

Rumbles from the west sounded like the approach of a truck. He looked down the road ahead. "Where did that come from? Kitties, you should see this. One lone, black, ugly damn thundercloud in the desert, headed right for us. Imagine the headline: Changing Tire, Flash Flood Kills Iowa Man.

"Speaking of water, where's my water bottle?" He kicked the tattered tire.

Possessions lay strewn about the roadside. Fighting lug nuts put on with an air hammer produced paragraphs of four-letter words. Sweat fanned off his head and contortions of his torso.

He heard the voice again, that of a child. "I know what I—"

He hopped up to look in his trunk and car for no good reason. He pulled a transistor radio from the backseat, held to his ear—silence. He turned it on, off.

One foot braced against the tire, the other against the wheel well, he cranked lug nuts. "You…rotten—" The first nut broke. His back hit gravel to pierce t-shirt and skin. He lay there, heaving for oxygen. "That's uno. You won't defeat my will. Three to go."

Muffled inside the car, the voice, "I know what I want—" trailed by echoes as though leaching signals from another dimension.

Morgan sprang up. "Who said that?"

He searched. He found his empty water bottle instead. He peeked inside the clear container. He twisted tight its cap with the full rotation of his body. Rifled against pavement, the bottle recoiled to hit him in the face. Morgan scampered after the bottle in a zigzag path. He arrested it, threw it down, and watched it flip end over end to chip paint off his car by its hard top.

He squatted to squint at the mark. "Only spot without rust," he murmured.

With gritted teeth, he turned on the bottle. Punctuated by primate grunts, he jumped up and down to flatten the source of his rage. Towering over the wrinkled form, he pointed at it. "Go ahead, bounce!" It did not move.

Morgan grabbed the cat's near-empty water jug. He filled their bowl. He held the bottle to his lips. He stopped. "No. Vet said cats dare not dehydrate. They can't run out of water out here."

He returned the bottle and attacked the tire, mounted the spare, and stood to shade his head under the open trunk. Patterns of salt laced about his shirt.

From the west on Route 66 came a crack of lightning followed by a modulated hum of spinning tires. So, somebody else is on this road besides me, he thought.

He stood straight, arms at his side. Soaked to the bone, he felt water leave his body in two percent humidity. Tilting his head, he studied an audio composition only one car could play. He stepped from behind his car and toward the pavement.

Another flicker of electricity wiggled itself into the ground beyond a shallow rise to the west. Streaks of windshield budded from a concrete mirage. The hood appeared, bound either side by two vertical pairs of round headlights. Its grill centered by an inverted triangular emblem. It was a maroon 1963 Pontiac Catalina.

Lightning flashed the car's driver and front-seat passenger, both approximately Morgan's current age. Three boys were in the back seat. That familiar Otis Redding song sung by a boy overlaid complaints from two others.

Morgan stared for the longest time, then sprinted down white stripes toward the Pontiac, arms waved overhead. Gusts pressed him sideward. "It won't turn out the way you think! Nothing is what you think it is!"

Morgan was forced to change course by a racing tumbleweed. Its thistles speared his leg as it zipped by him and the car as the driver veered past in a blast of hot air. A boy in the back seat said clearly, "Dad, I know what I'm gonna be when I grow up."

Spun about, arms above his head, gasping for air, Morgan watched the vehicle disappear. Barely discernible, the woman in the Catalina said, "It's only a dream."

He limped to his car to start the engine. Rocks peppered discharged possessions. He swerved eastward on the highway. Blue clouds popped from the tailpipe. His goal sank over a gentle grade.

Nearing the crest's peak, a spasm rocked him and the cats. Puffs of smoke filled his rearview mirror. Coasting to a halt, out of the car, he gimped for the peak. Breathless, he squinted at a stretch of Route 66 as long and abandoned as any so far. He watched for motion. He listened. He looked back, forward, above. He waited for something to happen.

Back in the car, he stomped the accelerator. Over and over, the "row-row" sound of his starter faded with his battery.

He stopped. He pressed his forehead against the steering wheel. "*Shiiit...*"

Stalled halfway into the wrong lane, west of the crest, he waited to greet a westbound vehicle in a collision. Should I put the cats out? he wondered. Unload the rest of my stuff? He hesitated. His mouth formed words but made no sound. He held his breath, turned the ignition, and started his engine, gagging on a cloud of smoke.

Up and down a three-mile length, he drove. He looked for fresh tracks on side roads to nowhere. He stood on the hood to see an expanse of nothing.

Morgan returned to his flat tire. He hobbled over possessions. Between shoulders of the Mother Road, he folded hands on his head. He looked one direction and the other. A lizard darted behind a rock. Why were they driving east? he wondered. We took Route 66 west, to California. We didn't return this way.

Morgan opened the trunk. He sat on his back bumper, biting lips cracked and paper dry. There is a theory in physics, he thought. That if something can happen, it does, on different lifelines, each a new and freshly minted cosmos.

Thunder clapped behind him.

My mind is a victim of that water bottle, he decided. I can barely hold myself up. He rubbed his face with both hands.

"So is my father sending a message across the void?" he asked. "Which would mean what? That there is a heaven. Meaning that there is a who? A God."

He chuckled. He sagged, watching his feet. An ant snooped about a box of books. "You won't steal those like whatshername, will you?"

The sun ducked beneath Morgan's private cloud, no longer blocked it baked the car. The cats meowed.

Morgan bent down. He touched the antenna of one ant. It faced Morgan, mandibles splayed. "Were I to discover you on another planet it would be an astounding discovery unparalleled in science. I'd be famous. Instead, we humans see you on a kitchen counter and squish you without so much as a thought of what a miracle you are.

But this human can do better."

From an empty bag, he sprinkled breadcrumbs on the ground. More ants arrived to lift crumbs as large as themselves high over rough topography. Several joined the first to tug its crumb home. Morgan spoke to them. "Without argument or contest of rights, entitlements, or union rules, you simply join in the act of living. We should learn from you."

He certified a spot free of life forms. He dropped cross-legged on pebbles, shielded from the sun by his car. He watched the ants. "I can honestly say I have seen things no one else ever will—you. Without this occasion, you would have passed unobserved. Like countless trillions of others…Like me."

Sparse raindrops hit ground from the black spot above him.

"Are there thousands of us out there?" Morgan asked. "In other universes with other worlds? Like these ants that no one knows about, yet crawling beneath the very air we breathe. Is one of those places where all the right things happen? Is that heaven?"

Morgan opened his mouth skyward to catch drops of rain. Flashes of white created shadows in broad daylight. He held hands forward, palms down, trembling from fingers to elbow. "I need water," he said. "Soon…Yesterday."

Drops picked up their pace and grew in size.

He rubbed his wounded leg. He watched shade inch away over sand in front of him as it had every afternoon for the thirty billion afternoons since this place became dry. He looked for a rainbow. "I'm done," he said. "I want to be mummified. Right here…And I will be if I don't get moving."

Robotically, Morgan commanded limbs in sequence to stand. He looked back to where the Catalina went. "Wrong way," he said. "I'm headed west."

He packed and closed the trunk as the sky opened in a deluge. He centered himself on the highway. He looked above, arms extended, his body in the form of a cross. "I dare you," he said. "Strike me."

He waited. Water ran off his face and into his mouth.

Ants and their crumbs tumbled on waves of water over stone.

The air split with a crack of lightning.

## 19. Dirt Roads Aren't Made for Fast Travel

After a four-day drive to California, Morgan stood between the parallel routes of east-west Sunset and Hollywood Boulevards, north-south Martel and Vista. Just blocks from Grauman's Chinese Theater and its famous celebrity handprints. Outside his apartment building, Sammy in his arms, Morgan pointed. "See that? Your new home."

Morgan turned to look up the street on a steep incline. Above was the Hollywood Hills, their vast views of ocean, blanketed by racks of multi-million-dollar houses on stilts. He looked down the street. "Great zot…Hope we don't get hit with some giant, kick-ass, monster quake. We'll end up downhill with the poor folk. Padding for the wealthy. I need to succeed. Soon, so we can move up there."

Inside he unrolled a foam pad. With blankets provided by his mother, a bedroom was ready in sixty seconds. He unpacked a spoon, fork, knife, and two plates—one for the cats. And two plastic cups, once home to milkshakes from Iowa City's Hamburg Inn Number 2.

Through the door, he heaved a block of marble, partially sculpted. He stood back to look at it. "Come out of there. You may be, at long last, *the* perfect work. If you don't fall through that floor first."

He appraised the almost empty room. "Wonder if this satisfies Gregg's *Principle of Voluntary Simplicity?*"

By car, Morgan toured the city at night. Knotted lanes of automobiles immersed in caustic fog slid round one another like snakes in a mating frenzy. At a stoplight, Morgan watched a man hold a leash. The man shouted at his pet for urinating on the crosswalk, despite the fact there was no pet. Along Santa Monica Boulevard, multiple billboards of the same pale, large-breasted, barely clothed woman, presented only a phone number. Signs advertised telepathic therapy at doggy daycare, and traffic reports every six minutes on local radio in a place where cars never appeared to move. Spiked lavender hairdos were more common than a haircut. Morgan groused, "Tocqueville predicted this. Americans prize their sameness."

He saw a promising designation, "The Miracle Mile." He pressed on to find it.

Morgan discovered the miracle declared by a sign at Rodeo and Wilshire. He drove down Rodeo and back, past its many shoppers. "First of all, it's not a mile," he said. "They should call it The Miracle Quarter-Mile. Lesson one: things in Southern California are four times less than advertised.

"Actually, that applies nationwide."

He parked the car and proceeded on foot.

The sound of Morgan's boots shadowed an impeccably dressed elderly man with shoulder-length white hair. A young, beautiful female walked at his side, her fingers weighted with gems. They quickened their pace. Bags with large logos flopped beside them. Like bells on a goat, Morgan decided. Cereal-box tops; proof of purchase.

Morgan stopped to gawk at the woman's legs. *Judas*, he thought. It's pretty clear what keeps him in orbit. The handicap principle in spades, man. I better never find a woman with legs like that. I'd give it all away. Both plates and all the silverware.

Morgan cupped hands around his mouth and shouted. "Ladies! Coal is a better friend than diamonds! It will keep you warm!" Hands on his hips, he thought out loud, "Laden with mercury and arsenic, it can't be clean coal. But at least it's worth something, versus the contrivance of diamond cartels."

Morgan stepped toward another couple. "Excuse me, ma'am." They hurried away. "I just want to ask you a question," he said.

A tanned man with glittering earrings and cashmere suit put his arm around her and left Morgan behind. The man growled over his shoulder, "Fuck off, buddy."

"As your buddy, I just want to ask if you know those minks on

149

your girl's shoulder are dead?"

"I said fuck off!" the man responded, and extended a middle finger overhead.

Morgan turned to speak to a cascade of storefronts. "Two hundred fifty thousand years ago, Homo heidelbergensis made a twenty-inch long, twenty-five-pound hand ax. But a useful ax was less than a pound. So what good was such an unwieldy object? Good for nothing. Other than an object of display—a status symbol. Deep down, nothing's changed. Nevertheless, I am astonished to find that *things* advertised with a promise of status, bestow status. They weren't lying; it is a miracle. And what's doubly miraculous is that an entire civilization can run on this. It's not only those road-working Neanderthals I pushed rocks for. The top side of this economic ladder is as twisted as the bottom. This country's more screwed up than I thought. And I want to be part of this?"

At his apartment, Morgan was greeted by Sammy. Hawkeye pawed the countertop in excitement to see him home. He scratched their heads. "Guys, we're on another planet. And just the planet I can manage. Doesn't take a rocket scientist to work this system."

He poured a plate of cereal. He made a plate of cat food for the cats. He looked in the drawer for a spoon and found one. Cross-legged on the floor next to his bed, he felt milk drip from his lips. "At thirty-five years old," he mumbled, "there is something either very wrong with a man who once owned the most beautiful custom home in his neighborhood and lost it, or something very right with a man who can still appreciate simple pleasures."

Sammy's belly splayed at the ceiling. Hawkeye meowed her time-to-go-to-bed meow.

Morgan gazed out his window at the wall of a building next door so close he could touch it. "What a grand day," he said. "And there's another tomorrow. I have no deadlines. I don't have a job. I don't have a boss. No office. No politics. No bullshit but the kind I tell myself.

"Damn…This is living."

***

Now, as a Screen Actors Guild union member, Morgan never

missed their seminars as another opportunity to network. He made connections through auditions, acting classes, and improvisational workshops. Like everyone else, he volunteered for anyone for anything related to the movie business in hopes of discovery. He read hundreds of screenplays for his talent agent's literary branch, where he learned how and how not to write scripts. He attended colloquiums and clinics with major filmmakers via IFP. Independent Feature Project was a cooperative of four thousand yearning-to-be producers, directors, and writers. At IFP, he learned filmmaking's most critical components: finance and legal. He also learned how film is a business that eats money. A single Panavision film camera—never sold, only rented—cost $5000 per week.

After two years knocking on the actor's entrance guarded by casting agents, Morgan sought control of his life. He set out to make his own movie, a path worn by thousands of failures before him. Despite the micro-budget nature of his film, with Morgan as primary financier, he made himself nearly penniless, a skill practiced in Boston. He functioned as co-producer, director, occasional key grip, and bit actor. Due to site availability, scenes from the middle of his film were to be shot first at a mansion in Beverly Hills. Sunlight painted oak shadows on another day.

He stood before his crew, all contacts made at IFP. Next to him was the breakdown board—a detailed schedule of locations, scenes, and who was in them. Morgan watched the script shake in his hand. He tipped his *Field of Dreams* cap. "OK, gang," he said. "Pre-production complete. It's day one of production. Don't be frightened just because I've never done this before." His voice cracked. "Morale is of utmost importance if we're to meet this schedule. We do this not for the money— Sorry, there is no money. Yet! But there might be!" Morgan slapped the back of his frowning DP—Director of Photography. "It's not the money, it's the message.

"For most of you, it's been a while since we talked, so a quick refresher. As we approach our new millennium, a few people have emerged with fervent desires to know how we as a nation became so polarized, so dogmatic. Their central question is, What will become of America? With our deepest foundations for knowing abandoned, we find among them a hero…A rich artist. An actor."

People laughed. "Story has to be plausible, Morgan!"

Morgan motioned to surroundings. "All this luxury comes to be seen by our hero as an ointment, soothing the burn of having lost his way. He feels a sense of doom but doesn't know why. He has been raised on two things: money is paramount, and truth is relative. But how can he know money is paramount if there is no truth? Because these are two of America's myths, absorbed without challenge. But our hero has a problem, he asks questions.

"Upon ascension, he finds a world that was supposed to be at its best, instead its abject worst. He climbed the ladder only to find nothing there. In order to see, he blinds himself; literally, peepers gouged from his head."

The lighting assistant rolled her eyes, laughing.

Morgan pointed at her. "Cindy, you know the difference between a good film and a bad one is a matter of execution. Mostly."

He turned back to the crew. "Later, our hero is taken by a female friend to Europe. Through her, our hero feels the place in his bones. Not pop culture, not cash culture, but high culture, real art. He sets out to study the great philosophers, the ancients. He formulates a set of fundamental principles; returns to the States; becomes fiercely impassioned; and uses his massive wealth—all of it—to push his message.

"As an itinerant blind man, preaching from one street corner to the next, his influence grows. Person by person, a sightless man makes them see. He revives meaningful relations between men, women, and the natural world. So provocative, he unintentionally breeds a revolution. And, he discovers love."

Tom, the key grip, spoke up. "So, Morgan, you mean to say our hero initiates a movement in which men and women love each other? Like the old days?"

Morgan hesitated. "This is not based on a true story, Tom."

The crew laughed and cheered. Groups of men tossed bean bags used to anchor light stands at groups of women.

"Men. Always in need of women to give them life!" shouted the makeup artist.

"You mean money!" shouted a crewman.

"I make more than you!"

"You got a free lunch?"

Morgan waved. "Hang the battle armor, kids, the gender theorists are on vacation. On this set, we're all starving artists.

"Now, as things go beyond our hero's control, all he wants to recover is the woman he cares for, his European guide, lost in the chaos. Of course, instead of finding her, our lead must die. So, no, this film does not have a happy ending because life doesn't have a happy ending. This film serves notice that there are right ways to live. And a warning of the dehumanizing potential of this system we made. Kapeesh?"

Morgan nodded and clapped once. The crew moved sound equipment, lights, props. Morgan huddled with his DP, checked angles, shadow, and framed the picture. Neighbors barely noticed another film shot in their midst.

The lead actor approached. "Hey, Mister Whitaker. Like, I got issues with the hospital scene, dude."

"What's that, Rick?"

"Well, like, I don't know. It's like…you know?"

"No, I don't. Tell me."

"Well, like, I lay there after I just, like, blinded myself with this smile on my face, and I say, like…" Rick flipped pages of his script. "Wait…Like, I don't say anything. But like, how can I like, smile if I just, like, blinded myself, dude?"

"You didn't blind yourself, Rick. Your character did. He smiles because finally there is something inherently precious—not contrived—that he must recover. He has presented himself an obstacle, and a reason to engage all he can to surmount it. He had everything, was given everything, pampered by everyone, loved by everyone—so long as he brought in the box office. Yet none of it held meaning for him. Blindness has given him *insight* into that solid-rock core of truth by clearing away the clutter—the marketing, the packaging, the massification of everything. Your character realizes the wreck he made of his life and others along the way. He'll do anything—" Morgan looked away. He appeared confused. "He'll do anything to make it right—" Morgan squinted as though trying to recall something.

The DP nudged him. "What's wrong?"

Morgan shook his head. "And the only act big enough to atone for his sin is what, Rick? It's to save the world from itself. Instead of striving to *be somebody*—" Morgan's eyes found what they were looking for. "He becomes *about* something vital. You see? The question is not, What do you want to be when you grow up. It's, What do you want to be about?"

Rick nodded. "Sure, dude. Like, he's got this history, man. Then he's like, afflicted with blindness and—"

"No, Rick, he's not afflicted like catching a cold. He did it to himself."

"Right. Cool. He smiles because he's, like, not forced to see the world around him." Rick scratched his head. "But, dude, what's it all mean?"

Morgan panned the sky. He folded his arms. "It's about the irrationality of our times, Rick. Irrationality shared by Left and Right. Their *blindness* is the same, and these are people with eyes. They believe without question, they don't challenge the myths. Like moral relativity is the new high ground, and material displays really do place you higher than your fellow man. Well, the notion that anything goes is wrong, Rick. And all that shit you can buy down on Rodeo doesn't make you more. In this picture, we confront these myths for the lies they are and the lies they cover up.

"But, Rick, my question for you is, Are you set for the scene we're about to shoot, *right now?*" Morgan placed his hand on Rick's shoulder. "We'll talk later. We're about to roll camera." Morgan pointed toward the set. Rick left for his mark, a Duck-taped X on the ground.

Shooting completed in six weeks. Post-production repair of scenes that should have been correct in production cost another three months and money—audio booms bobbed into frame, power lines dashed across corners of a set, license plates released after the date of a scene. Voice dubbing almost compensated for peculiarities of mishandled microphones.

Morgan approached a list of independent distributors to finance prints and circulate the film with no advertising, only word of mouth. One agreed to limited distribution through a handful of specialty theaters in the US and Europe. Box office returns were small, but Morgan was able to pay his crew pennies on the dollar they would have made from substantial films. To each, Morgan delivered a check in person with a script for his second project.

Despite his film's caution against being consumed by the system, Morgan was a prisoner of it. When not assisting in edit, he rewrote scenes or arranged elements of the next project. Every other waking moment was a hustle for money or dealing with lawyers.

With so much invested in books by dead philosophers, Morgan was well equipped with thoughtful material, in a town where the number-one complaint was a lack of scripts with substance. But the substance of his work was neither easy nor pleasing.

After his second film, critics said Morgan's work required thinking, while cinema was a place Americans least wanted to do such a thing. Editorials in Hollywood trades labeled him a racist, as his leads were always white, both times. Single-paragraph reviews in corporate journals claimed he was another frustrated America-hater. His films had too little violence and too much dialogue to sell in the Far East, but France and Germany read subtitles with interest.

Late on his rent, he and his cats on a diet, studio to studio he went, a starving salesman, not an artist, desperate for cash.

\*\*\*

Seated in a plush office, Morgan faced a team of accountants, lawyers, and financiers scattered about a teak wood room. Morgan gushed with enthusiasm. He laughed at every mundane remark.

"But we want to rarify your message, Morgan. We'd prefer you direct a chick flick first, one of our studio favorites in the lead role."

Morgan laughed. "I thought you were 'enchanted' by my script?"

"We are. But we have this splendid opportunity for you. From this piece you can extend your name. Command projects bigger than the four you did. And in just fourteen years, twice the average pace."

"*Rarify*," Morgan chuckled. "Define that."

"Rarify, smarify, you know what rarify means, Morgan, come on."

"I know what it means to me. I also know what profit means to me, but it's not what profit means to you."

One man cleared his throat. "Morgan, we've rounded up seven million from a domestic distributor, four million for foreign rights, and four more abducted from our period-piece division to make a

155

movie. Show some gratitude."

Morgan's face faded. "That's fifteen mil—"

"Morgan, Costner did *Dances with Wolves* for eighteen. We're offering you a package deal for fifteen."

"And *Wolves* was eons ago," Morgan said. "Wait—you mean fifteen includes prints and ads?" The man nodded. Morgan recoiled. "P and A for *Wolves* was probably another twenty-five million. So you'll make one copy, run that reel around the country on horseback, one theater at a time with a printed ad on the horse?"

"Hungry producers, directors, and wannabe actors find fifteen million a lot of money, Morgan."

"And you have my sincerest appreciation. Truly you do. But not exactly big money in Movie Town. And let's face it, you want to hand over probably five million dollars for a B-list guy, one person—I don't know why, maybe you owe him a favor—who then gets portions of the gross. That leaves eight million for me and my crew to scrape by for filmmaking and a couple mil for prints. I can already do better than that on my own. I asked for the money I asked for to make the film I believe in."

A well-dressed man spoke. "*Rarify*. It means no radical, left-wing message people won't part with cash to see. Cash, Morgan—it walks, it talks, it gets movies made in this town. Volume matters. Message? Sell it at the Democrat Convention."

Another man spoke. "Left-wing? I thought his films were Right-wing."

The well-dressed man sat on the edge of his desk. "What do you expect from your films, Morgan? *Hope and change*?"

"My films are an invitation," Morgan said.

"To who, Greenpeace and Earth First?"

"An invitation to fundamentalist liberals who disregard reason because only political retribution matters. An invitation to fundamentalist conservatives who disregard reason because only God's retribution matters. See? I didn't forget anybody."

"Your films forgot the audience, Morgan."

"Then fund me for the big picture show that covers all the bases. Let my film confront our myths because True Believers deserve challenge!"

The well-dressed man folded his arms. "And you, Morgan

Whitaker, unknown filmmaker, are about to redirect the very arc of civilization. If Caesar only had you."

"Why not me? Maybe I'm that moral artist steeped in scientific thinking to see clear of our times."

"Ha! Morgan Whitaker, the savior."

Morgan steadied himself. "Seven hundred scripts per week in your period shop alone, while you bitch about an absence of scripts with meat. I gave you a script with meat."

"Uncooked, and a bit raw. Now you listen to me, Morgan. You're a talented guy. You have the touch. You just need to touch the right thing. You're not going to change the world with a movie."

"It's been changed by a book, why not a movie?"

"Name one such book."

"*The Bible*, Montesquieu's *Spirit of the Laws*, Rousseau's *Social Contract*, *The Federalist Papers*, Adam Smith's *Wealth of Nations*—"

"Alright, alright, Morgan, enough."

"Philosophy is a risky venture, gentleman. I make philosophical films. Of course, it takes time for the message to brew…early on."

"As you know, Morgan, ninety-ten rule: opening week we get ninety percent of box office, theater gets ten. Our percentage drops ten percent per week. Brew? Bankrupt."

The room moved. One man caught a falling vase. Items rattled on the desk. Morgan ducked, hands overhead.

"Morgan, what are you doing?"

Morgan hesitated. "Involuntary response," he said. "No matter how many tremors—I hope to stop the roof from hitting my head."

"I don't think it works like that, Morgan."

Morgan looked at the ceiling. "My goal is to answer those questions of why we are the way we are. Why—"

"Morgan, put your hands down."

Morgan knit his fingers in front of his chest. He glanced above. "Why that most precious of human characteristics—love of *truth*, love between men and women, and of fellow man—is flagging. See? My pictures are love stories."

"Ancillary. We want it in their face. Consider what you just said. You want sixty million. Truth be told, you think you're worth blockbuster funding of a hundred or more. But you just heard it:

audience dismisses the first weekend, we risk the studio."

"You're asking me to direct what's not mine. Did you try this with Spielberg or Howard?"

"Morgan, they don't need our money. Play along, don't bite." He patted Morgan on the head. "God works in mysterious ways, but He works, Morgan. When I came to this town, I wore the same kind of rags you wear now, but look at me—diamond-studded Rolex, Gucci coat, Mercedes in the lot. Politics does not matter, Morgan. Ideals do not matter. Whether or not this nation falls into the trash heap of history does not matter. Money matters. Money is why me and my liberal friends don't kill each other. Just as your Federalists wanted." He winked. "So face facts, Morgan. You're a fact-oriented guy, I hear."

The man opened his ledger to scribble a note. He put a period to his reminder. He leaned down, level with Morgan's nose, rotating his watch-bound wrist in Morgan's face. He tapped Morgan on the forehead, blessed him, and walked to a high-backed leather chair. Seated, he cleaned his fingernails. "Be a success, Morgan."

Morgan's jaw nearly split teeth. "Depends how you define success—what you want to be, or what you want to be about. Maybe you wore your diamond-encrusted 3D bullshit glasses to my films and missed the point." One man signaled surrender, but Morgan insisted no bridge remain untorched. "So I too can wreck the planet for display items, like you. To enhance probabilities for a quick fuck, or adulation from strangers who think you matter when you don't. All to elevate your fragile ego while you take up space in style. After all, it's God's work."

Morgan leaned elbow against knee, prepared to leap. "Just one question, doctor. When liberals convince us there is no truth, does that make it easier for conservatives to start another war? Was the last one for apple pie and the *American Way*, or was that God's will? And if it was, what do we do with God?"

The man snapped shut his ledger. He stood. "You can insult me, but not God. Out you go!" The man grabbed Morgan and pulled him for the entrance. "Conversation over."

Morgan pushed back. "Of course it's over. What else can you do to me?"

Another man grabbed Morgan and another. "This was a favor to one of your old crew who moved up the food chain, Whitaker. I lied; I never liked any of your shit."

Morgan slapped the man's face. "Why not offer me a soap opera?"

Wrestled toward the door, Morgan grabbed a handful of the rich man's hair to pull his face in close enough to spit in it and shout, "Reality TV, would that be in-your-face enough?"

Shoved out the door, Morgan's opportunity closed behind him with a slam. He leaped for the doorknob as it locked. He banged the wood surface with his shoulder. "I changed my mind! I'll film your porn scripts! You can make a buck and a fuck at the same time!"

Morgan dropped to the floor. He shouted under a gap beneath the door. "You can't match wills with me! I don't need your money! I don't need anybody! They're all looking up to me now! *Me!*"

He stood, panting. He kicked the door. He poked his chest. "Me!"

He watched the doorknob.

He swiped sweat off his brow. His eyes traced a tight seam between the door and its frame. No one's looking up to me, he thought.

## 20. Jericho

Morgan stood on his sun deck, Sammy on his shoulder, Hawkeye at his feet. He eyed passenger jets sweep over San Gorgonio Mountain, sixteen lined up in eight pairs for landing. A lacework of power lines, antennas, and billboards cluttered his vision. A view punctuated by ragged palm trees shedding last year's growth and accumulation of airborne grime. A recorded church bell played over loudspeakers.

"How ironic," he said. He looked down at Hawkeye. "Imagine, Hollyweird has churches."

Daylight worshipers could be seen dotting nearby roofs. Houses on Hollywood Hills balanced above like bricks on a stick. Downhill, rooftops and street lights stretched to the horizon, all coated in decades of pigeon visits.

Morgan covered Sammy's face. "Don't look. This whole place is made for cars and buildings. Not humans—or cats."

Beyond a tangle of phone, and cable connections, Morgan watched passenger jets touch down at LAX in front of a low-lying sun. "Hollywood is a factory town," he said. "A movie-factory town. And life is a maze. I was so certain…once."

Morgan searched the coast and recent history in his mind. In the words of a businessman, I am not well-capitalized, he thought. I can't save this picture. Insignificant financial horsepower to hang on over the long haul. There's a box-office ceiling I can't break, and the investors know it. Living hand to mouth like a monk, I'm no closer to taking charge of my future than…four and a half films and fifteen years ago. He cringed. And in a town that worships youth. I'd hate to get old here. Older than sixteen.

This filmmaking is barely controlled chaos, he thought. A business riskier than oil wells. Which makes it exciting. A gamble on being known, or making a difference. But not for long, even if you win.

He looked down at the apartment's front yard, a ten-foot width of asphalt, spray-painted green. A ground-to-rooftop sign pasted on the side of a Sunset Boulevard building beckoned him to visit ancient history in the Yucatan. Another painted with one large word, "LOVE," its letters diced by occasional windows.

What's that supposed to mean? he thought. Love someone, love something? He looked through smog toward the ocean. I haven't been in love since— He hesitated. Since college, he remembered. The word love means no more to me now than the word plastic.

The sun glistened through nitrous oxides off Pacific waves unseen. He spoke to the coastline. "Mister Otis Redding, I'm not exactly on the dock of the bay, but I can see the bay...sort of."

Three youths with chains in hand chased a fourth on the ground below. Without sirens, a police car slid sideways around the street corner at Sunset, up Martel. It accelerated so fast Morgan could hear its carburetor inhale. He watched them pass.

"That Pontiac was going the wrong way on Route 66," he muttered. "Why was that, Sammy? Was that hallucination trying to warn me of all this?

"Tribal leaders told boy warriors not to go north in those Native American myths. So they went north, conquered dangerous forces, and became heroes. Could be said I satisfied the first part of that story, albeit westward. But the conquest and hero part...not so much."

Morgan could see a sliver of the 101 Hollywood freeway, its traffic gridlocked for the Hollywood Bowl, Santa Barbara, Mammoth Mountain. Thousands of headlights in unbroken columns like crazed eyes open and blind to the world.

"I'm so citified I'm solidified," he said. "Desperate need of wilderness. Someday I'll use those European flight miles gathered at The Center, travel that fifteen-hundred-mile Ruta Maya—the Mayan Road—until my money runs out." He pulled nickels and dimes from his pocket. He showed Sammy. "Will that cover it? But since when did I let a lack of security mitigate my thirst for risk?"

Billboards along Sunset made celebrities of news anchors, real estate agents, auto mechanics. One presented a desert image; a trickle of water vanished into sand. It counseled conservation as sources like the Colorado River were already gone.

Morgan's eyes strained to read its blurb—the river exhausted by farms and cities decades ago. His face relaxed. "My wish…it never reached the ocean." His eyes wide, fixed on the billboard. "It died in the desert," he whispered.

A television helicopter swooped overhead to film the LAPD for the Southland's daily dose of police-chase coverage. Air conditioners rattled, jackhammers broke concrete in a half dozen places. The screech of tires and pulse of car horns could be heard with such persistence they combined for one continuous, fluctuating hum.

"Sammy, when I was young, all I wanted was to be somebody. Which turned out to mean having my worth determined by others. Then I tried to be that one who shows others the way, like the first fish. And to atone for my sins. Like every character in my films. But either the world didn't want to be saved, or I didn't show the world it needed to be."

He exhaled a long-drawn breath. "Perhaps diplomacy requires as much effort as art and science. Not a talent I've developed with much alacrity."

Hawkeye meowed. Morgan looked down. "Thank you, kitty. I always believed I could be a great man.

"But I wasn't."

He reached up to scratch Sammy's head. "I wanted to find meaning in science and art, but neither would give it to me. Both are pointing away. But where?"

Morgan studied what he could see of Paramount Studios. He bit his lower lip, calculating. He shook his head. "No…It's over."

He watched Los Angeles, wondering if he would see it again. He slapped the railing with both hands in resignation, and said, "I honored my dream. My dream did not honor me. So it goes.

"I have no career, no friends, no family of my own. I don't know a single human soul except my mother

"But I know you, sweetie." He reached down to pick up Hawkeye, Sammy's claws needling his shoulder. "And I love you

162

both dearly. You are my friends." He rubbed Hawkeye's head. "You're getting tired aren't you, old girl."

He faced the boulevard. He studied Yucatan's offer. "No matter what happens, there's always one thing I have to look forward to: leaving wherever I am. What do you think, guys, another adventure?"

He stood at attention. He saluted Hollywood, a childhood dream conceived on Route 66, and turned for the exit.

***

Morgan's plane landed in the state of Quintana Roo. He made his way to the ancient Mayan city of Chichén Itzá on a two-dollar bus filled with locals and their handheld livestock.

At the site, he sat on the ground to watch a line of people up and down stairs of Chichén Itzá's central pyramid, known as The Castle. Imagine sitting in this spot sixteen hundred years ago, he thought. A culture with the zeal of shared beliefs, common goals—cutting people's hearts out. Lost to foliage for a thousand years. As mysterious as what's happening to America.

Finally, no one remained to scale the pyramid. Morgan ascended. From its peak, green extended beyond a 360° horizon. Mounds of plant life still covered ruins, saved by archeologists for advanced excavation techniques in the future. Above the canopy, an observatory gazed over the same night sky. Morgan sat high on someone else's center of the world. "So this was The Promised Land," he said.

Morgan left the ancient ruins and followed a dirt road to Pieste, a village of cinder-block buildings and thatch-roofed houses. Light bulbs hung in series from a solitary wire, drooped from one tree or building to the next. Open-air restaurants and foosball tables summoned people in groups. Old told stories to young. The young listened with interest. Mothers with babies rimmed a public square to watch scarf-blinded children swing at a treasure-laden piñata. A group of boys played Latin music.

Morgan watched them. A rich poor town, he thought. People here openly enjoy the fellowship of others. But no luxuries? How can these people be happy? In America, we call this deplorable.

Pavement was uneven and potted, no billboards, no flashing lights. Morgan looked end to end at the only street in town; not a single car. This place isn't screaming at me like everything in the States, he decided. I can't stand it. I think I'm about to relax.

He pivoted about a point. "They have nothing to compare," he said. "I remember a move to higher social ground after college, where a rise in possessions brought a decline in camaraderie. This explains it. Once on the material track, people strive for more to fill in for less."

A marauding gang of eight-year-olds with dilapidated bicycles circled Morgan. "Gringo!" they said, and pointed to the piñata. Morgan shook his head no. They kept shouting. Adults noticed.

An old man approached and reached high to put a wrinkled hand on Morgan's shoulder. The man said something in Spanish and gestured toward the center space.

Morgan declined. "No, no. That means no in Spanish."

A courtyard full of people stared at the American.

"Oh my…" he murmured. He stepped forward. They applauded. "What if I hit somebody? Might be me hanging, not the paper pony."

The old man pushed Morgan and swatted his behind at center stage. A drum roll played. Blindfolded, clasping a stick, Morgan was spun about. He probed the air, swung, and missed. People sighed.

Time and again, he wandered toward the courtyard's edge. Shoved back in, his head bumped a package. He beat the horse with rapid blows. Children stormed the scene. Morgan threw his blindfold. "The gringo delivered!"

Cheers and applause sounded from the natives. Adults retold the scene just witnessed. A girl in a white lacy dress tugged at Morgan's pants. He looked down to see her with a doll from the piñata. Made of a corn cob, it wore a cowboy hat from a gourd over a face drawn with a pen. He accepted and thanked her. She smiled, shrugged, and ran through a crowd of well-wishers.

Morgan reenacted his blind wandering. People laughed.

Morgan looked skyward, then to an old man over a foot shorter than he was. "Did you hear that?"

The man shrugged. People dispersed.

Morgan considered the sky. "Did I hear that?"

\*\*\*

The Ruta Maya was richer with distance. Uxmal's Pyramid of the Magician towered one hundred twenty feet over Morgan, but it looked to be a thousand. He sat on the forest floor in a breeze given life by density of plants shading ground. Hung by vines having strangled their host, jungle tree branches like arms pulled from a man, swayed bodiless in the air. He watched one lone couple disappear beyond the temple. Some things never change, he thought. If aliens visit this planet, they'll think humans come in pairs.

He read from his travel guide, "Uxmal was on a trade route with that Mother Culture and forerunner of all Central American civilizations, the Olmecs, who emerged from obscurity by 1200 BCE."

So, he thought, the Olmecs and Hebrews came out of the woods at the same time. With the fall of Troy in Anatolia came the transient rise of Mycenae in Greece, while a decline of Egypt's New Kingdom allowed Hebrews to form their state. And on the opposite side of the world appear the Olmecs…right here.

He drove his index finger into soil, drilling back and forth. He pinched earth from ground held close to squinted eyes. He smelled it. He rubbed fingers together to touch what he could of the past. He spoke to the pyramid, "This world, it's a boneyard."

Morgan flinched when a woman spoke English behind him. "Xiu legend claims this pyramid was built in a single night, by a single man," she said. "So in love with the moon, he finished before the sun could betray his vision with daylight."

Intrigued by the lilt of her dialect, Morgan turned to see a woman focused on the summit and was stunned by the sight of her. Hiking boots protected thick hiking socks; shorts secured a loose-fitting t-shirt; strands of dark curls across her face. Morgan's typically single-second assessment stretched. He checked one feature after another, hoping for flaws, terrified by their absence.

In a biological riot, chemical transmitters in Morgan's brain battled to bridge nonconductive gaps not roused by electricity in decades. Her face, so beautiful he could hear it. Her hands, perfect—

165

meaning she had equivalent feet with delicate toes, satisfying his foot fetish without having seen them. Obsidian eyes cleaved light into a rainbow as fervent as any crystal-blue or green-eyed woman he'd ever known. She matched a template in his brain he dreamed about then forgot and never saw before. So this is how Newton felt when he saw the apple, he thought.

Gravity turned Morgan's face toward the most beautiful female legs alive—tanned, fit, young. Wherever relics of attraction still lurked in his chromosomes, they had never been in such full blossom. He commanded his head to turn away as it battled to stare.

She continued her appraisal. "It's believed this very sight was power central for the Xiu clan. When Xiu attacked the Cocom at Maypan in 1441, it was a massacre that divided the Mayan population and impoverished them all. Then faraway ice sheets changed ocean currents, and with those currents went worldwide average temperature. With that, Mayan civilization entered a tailspin." She smiled at Morgan as he watched the pyramid. "That's a long run for a civilization. About two and one-half millennia in one form or another." She studied the monument. "In that time they refined a calendar inherited from the Olmecs, independently invented agriculture in the Americas, and discovered the number zero. Must have been an amazing era."

Still, Morgan looked away. "You know a good deal about this place," he said.

"I've been on several digs here."

"You're an archeologist?"

"Used to be. Scientist turned author."

Semi-recovered, Morgan looked back to ask, "Really? Books, articles?"

She dropped her backpack and sat cross-legged beside him. A solar glow cast off their tower of stone. Behind the Magician, a magnified full moon rose, dwarfed by their monolithic manmade mountain.

She tied loose laces. "I used to write love stories, then travel guides. Now I get an occasional feature in *National Geographic*, and I'm writing love stories again. I found that's what discovery really is, a romance. Now that I know that, my travel tales are juicier, more alive."

"Sounds like an exciting profession," he said.

She nodded. "Was trapped for a bit in Rwanda during one of their civil wars. Since I had a computer, locals concluded I must know medicine. They were so desperate, you could practice as a physician if all you could do was spell *medicine*. Discovered some critical essentials thanks to a nifty satellite modem and doctors back home."

The Magician pitched its spell. Morgan looked away. Intelligent, artistic, and a French accent to boot, he thought. He smiled, watching the temple. "The arts are a hard row to hoe in a business country," he said.

"If not for business, my creativity would have no outlet. And what would pay for my travel?"

Morgan shrugged.

She pointed to his chest. "I like your t-shirt. It's a famous story down here."

"I bought it for the colors. Bartered it for five bucks worth of freeze-dried food. What's the story?"

"That's Itzamna," she said, "fatally wounded beneath the seven stars of heaven. This is the Moon Goddess, Ixchel."

"Looks like a jaguar to me," Morgan said.

"She's only in the form of a jaguar."

"Ah, a fairy tale."

"A mythical metaphor," she said. "Like God in the form of a dove."

Morgan nodded. "You mean like religion, it's a lie."

"No."

Morgan said, "It can only be true or false, right?" He tapped his shirt. "Seven stars. Why do we see this same number in ancient stories, no matter where you go? *Seven*, from Gilgamesh in ancient Iraq; two thousand years later in the Old Testament as the time it takes to create the universe and get a bit of rest; and again, two thousand years after that for the Maya. Why? Because seven heavenly bodies move against a stationary sky. Mercury, Venus, Mars, Jupiter, Saturn, the sun, and the moon—seven. Ditto for the number three. The moon dies in darkness during new moon, *resurrected* in new light after three nights. Sound familiar? Civilizations absorbed these ideas through diffusion from others or discovered them independently. After all, Sumerians, Israelites, and Mayans all saw the same sky."

She smiled. "Impressive."

Morgan bowed. "That doesn't mean numerology is true. Numbers are just numbers. If there were eleven visible planets, God creates the world in eleven days."

"But they're not just numbers from the sky," she said. "They're numbers from the sky with meaning. When strange things happen in a story—contradictory natural events, or intersections of different times in history—these are cues to read between the lines, to use your heart, not your head. You interpret myths factually."

Morgan frowned. "What other interpretation could there be?"

"They don't describe scientific truths," she said. "But rather truths about us as humans, like music." She motioned about their surroundings. "You could never communicate to others your experience in this forest before this spectacle unless you mythologized it. The ancients mythologized their experience with miracles, and every listener gets it. 'Aha,' they'd say. 'Wonderful. Of course, I feel what you feel.' This experience, this sense we have in communion with the world, it's impossible to describe. That's why myths are able to tell it."

Morgan's eyes widened. "Whoa…You must have been educated in Europe."

"Born and raised in a small town south of Seattle. Moved with my family to San Francisco when I was in high school. Only child. Live in Southern California now."

"*No* kidding. So do I. Where?" Morgan asked.

"Redondo Beach."

He turned away. "Sure you do." He laughed. "This is all a dream I'm having." He faced her. "Hi, my name's Morgan." He shook her hand. "Morgan Whitaker. What's your name?" He felt her skin. He scrutinized delicate fingers. Seems real, he thought.

"Ne Shoul De Roue. That's nee shoal dee rue…Pleased to meet you. Ne Shoul is my first name, and my father is French—De Roue."

"Ah, that slight accent. Love it."

She fluttered black eyelashes. "My middle name is Cheron. My mother wanted to name me after the satellite moon of Pluto, but she misspelled it. Thank goodness she did. Charon—Pluto's moon—is a mythic ferryman in the underworld; escorts dead souls across the river Styx. Who wants a name like that?"

Morgan frowned. "Hmm…I happen to know when Pluto's moon was named."

She paused. "Oh, how sweet." She tapped his arm as about to divulge neighborhood gossip. "You're guessing my age. I'm thirty-one."

Morgan smiled, mumbling, "Under half my age, plus *seven*."

"Really? I would have guessed you at least ten years younger."

"Way to go! Points for you."

"So you're a seasoned citizen," she said.

"Watch it."

She chuckled. "Honest questions, always welcomed."

"Excellent. What a name, Ne Shoul Cheron De Roue."

"Ne Shoul's native for pale moon," she said. "Grandmother on my mother's side was a Nez Perce Indian. Chief Joseph's tribe. She liked to tell of how he defeated US troops at Big Hole River."

Morgan nodded. "Quite an accomplishment. Stone Age beats steel. And my great-grandmother was Cherokee, while my great-great-grandmother was Blackfoot."

Faded facets of a million stone reflections warmed them. New World monkeys flurried in and out of view on vines to snatch a glimpse of relatives below.

Ne Shoul wrapped arms around knees pulled tight to her chest. "So, here's an honest question: How would you describe yourself, Morgan Whitaker? In a word."

"Just one?…Dreams—my central force and principle."

"*Entelechy*. What you said is called entelechy. A vital force and principle directing growth and life."

"Really…Entelechy. You're not making this up, trying to impress me?"

"No."

"Just no? Not no, and yes?"

Ne Shoul looked down a row of temples still claimed by jungle cover. "Where's your travel companion?"

Morgan held up his camera. "This is my travel mate. Tolerant of no-frills trekking and patient enough to let me focus on the story I want to tell. I use this as fodder for sculpture."

"You're a sculptor?"

"Of animals. Tried to sculpt living people, but they always want to look younger, thinner. So I switched to wildlife; they never complain."

"My, my. What's your goal as a sculptor?"

"Inspiration. And long after I'm dead. Like the creations of cave painters in France thirty thousand years dead, still an inspiration. But that can only happen if my work survives modernity when lacquered excrement is called sculpture; when screaming until unable to speak is called performance art; when colors spattered on a canvas is called painting. Snake oil as a substitute for talent."

"What is it you hope to inspire?"

"Motivation to turn away from the world we made. To feel what I feel—like you said about myths." Morgan squeezed his chin with index and thumb. "Never thought of that. Art, like myths." He hesitated. "You see, I wonder if the *cause of awe* is the *soul of things*. True art reveals that soul, built from ourselves and from all the world. Our ancient and slaughtered ancestors, yours and mine, they knew that, and we call them primitive. If I could just release those souls from stone—the perfect work—nothing else could matter more. The Promised Land is everywhere, Ne Shoul. If we can just free it from what we made."

She nodded. "Nice. That you know what you want. That you have the courage to be alone." Ne Shoul halted, about to say something.

"I'm always alone," he said. "Maybe I always will be, but I'm never lonely. There are times—"

"Do you nurture your independence on the world's disapproval?"

A word froze on Morgan's lips. "It's an abundant source," he said.

Ne Shoul touched his arm. She looked from beneath disarming eyelashes. "Go on, 'there are times'—there are times what?"

Morgan rattled his head. "Yes, where was I? There are times I'd like to share my experience. To see Van Allen's radiation belts trap those dazzling auroras on some backcountry hike. To see Neanderthal, eighty thousand years dead, buried in fetal position, facing east and the reborn sun of another day in Iraq. Does sharing confer joy beyond the solitary journey? I don't know the answer to that. But I'm willing to try it."

Ne Shoul rested her head on arms still wrapped about knees.

Morgan laid back, arrogant, hands behind his head. "What? Say it."

Unseen creatures called for answers in the jungle. Heaven pierced the sun's dominion in a thousand places overhead.

***

After a week together, Ne Shoul and Morgan sat side by side on a white sandy coast. Their legs extended into a warm splash of marine atmosphere. A waning moon glittered over water, stoic and more permanent than tombs of Mayan Pharaohs. But for bursts from deckside arc welders, ships were barely visible. Had they looked, no one could be seen along the entire length of their beach.

"My father used to remind me this show plays every night," Morgan said. "Every night it's new, and it's pretty much free."

Ne Shoul pushed a strand of hair from her face. "Pretty much?"

"Takes time to look. Good trade, though, you think?"

She agreed. "My grandmother said, Do not offend the sun by failing to praise it at dawn and wishing it goodnight."

"Lovely...What do you love, Ne Shoul?"

Waves washed over her feet. "Music. Words. History not yet made."

Morgan waited. "Wish I could do that," he said. "Be brief, I mean."

When Morgan turned toward her, they were within inches of one another. She studied lineaments of his face, battle records written in skin. "Morgan, at Uxmal, you said you might always be alone. Could you do that?"

"I received a degree in physics when others told me I'd be nothing but a ditch digger; survived psychological warfare in the same house with my assailant; my father's death was shattering, but here I am. Not exactly tested by world war, but I guess I can do anything. Except convince Hollywood bankers to give me their money. Maybe the question is—much as I hesitate to say—can love survive in our modern world? When radical individualism vilifies mutual dependence, need, and the complementary nature that once united healthy relations."

"What matters is if these errors inhibit *us*," she said. "We can't put the world together again. Rich, tropical islands do exist in hostile oceans, Morgan." She drew an equation in the sand: $1 + 1 = 2$. "To you, the fate of love is a transpired reality. You are very pragmatic, Mister Whitaker. You have all the facts and stats and figures. But the sober approach to love is not the perfection of maturity. Shakespeare's Romeo left room for the heart. It's crazy, but what can you do? On this issue of love, you dictate existence with your head, not your heart. There is survival value in that. But humans are not described by equations." She wiped flat the sand. "I cherish the empire of reason as well, applied where appropriate, but the poet in me feels there is more to us than machinery. Is it risky? Yes. You want to live life, Morgan? Live it all."

"Ever been divorced?"

"No," she said.

"Try it. See if it doesn't leave an indelible mark."

"So you've gone some painful miles. That made you meek about love?"

"Try it."

"Why not wrestle with it as you do the other big ideas? For you, Morgan, the road less traveled is the one that opens your heart. Open your heart and find it really does make all the difference. You fear that you will fall hard. So fall hard."

"As Romeo fell hard? Today he'd be labeled a stalker and Juliet would call the cops."

Ne Shoul rolled her eyes. "So your solution is isolation? Yes, you will avoid the players, the duplicity, an era of vulgar humanity, and all the rest of your fluent indictments. But will your reward of peace through disassociation outweigh the cost? Take that path to the side. The one you've never been on, or not for so long you can't find it. You've got a chance, Morgan. They don't come often."

His eyes seized hers. He tracked curves of her torso to the sand. "A chance," he whispered. "I didn't know it was a chance."

Beyond ships no longer seen, stars flashed warnings to stellar relatives about to be grabbed by an equatorial ocean. Tidewater slipped below their ankles.

Morgan leaned close. "Could you repeat that?"

She bit her lip. "Yes," she whispered.

"Yes what?"

"Yes," she said.

Morgan moved a curl from her face. "We're alone. Why are we whispering?"

"So as not to startle the universe. We are in a precarious place, you and I."

"We are the universe, No Shoul. Nothing exists but you and me."

Like the contact point of a battery, Morgan bristled with static charge. Every cell of his body was in frantic communication with every other as each strained to find out what was taking place outside. When their lips touched, current surged with a pathway established. Now the cells knew, and they were happy.

Throughout their travels amid dreams in the dark, Morgan thought he heard trumpets in the jungle, faint but stronger by the day. Now, fully awake, their sound was so loud he could feel them against his chest. On a dangerous margin, his world felt in peril for feelings he could neither elude nor endure.

Ne Shoul ran fingers through Morgan's hair. "Trust is the foundation of all things great. Do you trust me, Morgan?"

He studied her eyes. She smiled. She touched his cheek. "Did you know," she said, "that after World War Two the HMS *Queen Mary* was called the Ship of Beginnings? It brought GIs and their ten thousand brides home to the States."

Morgan shook his head. He began to speak. She touched her index finger to his lips. "Morgan, I go overseas for another story next week. I'll be there for *seven* weeks. After a quick stop in San Francisco, I'll be home on May Day. May first, Morgan. The Ship of Beginnings is a lovely place to meet. I will be on it. Will you?"

# 21. Seismic History

Through anteroom windows to the observatory, people watched Morgan move under the dome. He positioned a nine-ton, two-hundred-inch-long Carl Zeiss telescope as though it were binoculars. He engaged eighty-year-old German gears that made the telescope a clock. It incremented position with time. A squeal from motors turned a fourteen-ton copper hemisphere overhead. Its shutter divided, open to the sky. With a clap, the dome and shutter halted to frame the telescope on a corridor to infinity.

Before opening to the public, Morgan sat on a movable staircase to the eyepiece. He texted Ne Shoul in a manner lost to practice, pencil and paper in hand. I'm writing software for a small company in Burbank, he wrote. It's also my opening night solo as pitchman for order and numbers in the heavens at Griffith Observatory.

He slipped the letter in a pocket full of newspaper articles. Time to make Professor Van Allen proud, he thought. Dousing white incandescent bulbs, red lights cast an eerie tinge.

He directed the first sixty patrons, filed against the circular wall. "Come see the stars!" he said. "Real stars, not fifteen-minute celebrities. And later tonight, the comet!"

One boy climbed stairs to examine the view. "So, like, when we gonna see the comet?"

"It rises at nine. Come back then. It's free. Where else can you find something for free in Los Angeles?"

"Dude, rather pay than stand in line."

Morgan held up his hand. "Does everyone know what we're viewing tonight?" No one spoke. "Except for the sun, it holds most of the mass in our solar system!"

174

Yawning, a girl pointed at a glass case signed "Tonight's Viewing."

Morgan punched the air. "Yes! Jupiter! That's what you'll see through that eyepiece!"

A boy squinted into the lens. "Doesn't look that way to me. Fuzzy."

Morgan shrugged. "Heat rises from the city," he said. "Makes the image waver like it's over hot pavement—improves as the city cools down."

"Lotta good that does me," the boy said. He left the dome.

Morgan turned to the audience to pronounce, "Jupiter is eleven Earths wide and almost a star!"

Silence.

He pointed to the sky. "We sent two spaceships there in 1977!"

More silence.

One after another saw Jupiter without remark. Morgan searched a book for facts. Sweat beads grew on his forehead. He solicited questions. Each in the dome was staring at something different, and it wasn't Morgan. "I thought making movies was hard," he muttered.

Finally, someone spoke. Morgan listened. "Sorry, the dome plays tricks with sound," he said. "Did someone say something?" He waited.

He began to speak. The same voice interrupted, but from outside. Morgan looked out the shutter above. He hurried out the exit. Throngs covered the observation deck and Griffith Park. Lovers stood hand in hand overlooking a grid pattern of sodium lights crisscrossing Los Angeles to a coastal curvature of blackness. Hundreds of children with parents crossed the grassy mall, headed for the observatory, or the Hollywood sign high on a hill beyond.

He examined Griffith's Monument. "Copernicus, Kepler, Herschel, you didn't say that, did you?"

Night air was clear, no smog, no marine layer. A sparkling column drifted skyward from Dodger Stadium like a flashlight dropped in a dusty bucket. Straddling Griffith's 1400 elevation perched the Greek Theater, where Neil Young could be heard to sing "Old Man."

Aha. I get it, Morgan thought. Power of suggestion. Heard that song in the background and didn't know it.

He looked toward Jupiter huddled close to the constellation Sagittarius, gateway to the galactic center. I'm not twenty-four anymore, Neil, but I'm like my old man. And I want those misplaced things returned. At least a connection to them. Like some precious coin from another age.

Morgan pulled a photo from his billfold and drew it close to his nose. He shook his head. "Impossible," he whispered. "I heard the old man at Pieste too. 'Show others the way. Like the first fish.' But which way? I can't even determine my own direction."

Morgan went back inside. He sat on a barstool beside a clear box. Inside this case, gears could be seen to drive the telescope. He pressed his index finger against his temple, talking to himself. "This machine focuses the image of Jupiter on my eye..." He traced a line to the back of his skull. "Down this optic nerve, splashed on the back of my brain, where I save what I will." He tapped his forehead. "From visible light to electrical signals that trek highways in my head, to thoughts about them, to heat rising off my scalp." Still seated, he faced the shutter. "Radiated back to Jupiter, to Sagittarius, and the Great Attractor, whatever that is. As it drags our massive Milky Way and local cluster of galaxies—" He pointed above. "That way. Maybe the ancients were right. It's where the loved ones lie, calling us."

The dome's concave interior amplified whispers, shuffling feet, the hum of motors turning their telescope.

Morgan watched the sky. "People," he said, "you can never destroy energy, only change its kind. Does that make you wonder if we die, or merely change form?"

A boy and his father checked each other as though Morgan might be a threat. A small girl with braided hair walked up to Morgan. "Mister Astronomer?"

Startled into the present, Morgan looked down. "You have a question?"

"Are there people on Jupiter?" she asked.

"A question— A first-rate question!" Morgan spun on his barstool and pointed at the girl in orbit about him. "This young scientist asked if there are people on Jupiter. Well done! Astronomers have studied Jupiter since Galileo discovered the four moons you're about to see. So far, no people."

A boy asked if a comet hit Jupiter, would it add enough weight to make Jupiter a black hole. A girl asked how old were the planets and why they were round. Another if there really were crash-landed aliens stored in the basement. Morgan ricocheted about the dome from one probing mind to the next. For a people overdosed on diversion, neurons fired with such swiftness he could barely keep pace.

The space filled with chuckles, laughter, and continuous conversations until a small boy raised his hand to say, "I know something about astronomy."

Morgan held his arms high. "Wait! Ladies and gentlemen, this little man has something to say." Hands behind his back, Morgan leaned forward, hovering over the boy. "Let's hear it."

The boy spoke with perfect enunciation, but so tenderly, people in the dome fell mute to listen. "I know there are galaxies far away that eat each other. There are stars that blow up so hard they fall down. I know a thing called a...a neutron star where a little bit weighs..." He paused, index finger held up in mid description. "Tons," he said. He looked up, smiling at Morgan.

Morgan turned to the audience. "I have been outdone by a five-year-old."

"Five and one-half," the boy said.

"Ah...Five and one-half it is then." Morgan stepped to the center and pointed at the floor beside his feet. "Come."

The boy obeyed. "Am I going to be your helper?" he asked.

"No. You stay here. I'll stand in line with your mom." Morgan walked to the perimeter. "You're the astronomer. This is show town. This is your show. Take it away."

The boy scanned a long line of people, many much larger than he.

Folding his arms, Morgan shrugged. "We just want to know what you know. Go."

Arms at his side, the boy continued his story. Patrons huddled about him as though sustained by heat of some cosmic campfire. German engineering tracked the sky. The two-hundred-inch container scooped light from faraway worlds, spilled on the floor with no eyes to catch them.

177

When the boy finished, he walked without hesitation to his mother's side. He held her hand for his turn up the stairs. After a moment's pause, an old woman began to applaud. Her solitary clap echoed off the spherical ceiling before others responded in kind.

Morgan whispered through their ovation, "I have been enthralled by Davis Gaines' voice in *Phantom of the Opera*. I felt nature's wizardry in my bones at Big Bend National Park. I touched artwork in stone by men three thousand years dead in Greece, but *never* have I seen such a thing as this. It's not what you show, *it's what you know*."

When the braided little girl descended the stairs from her turn, Morgan approached. He looked to the audience. "Is anyone here a lawyer?" No one responded. "All I'm going to do is shake her hand—and I have witnesses."

He leaned down to her. "All these questions are wonderful, but yours was the first. You started it all. You showed the way." He extended his hand. She shook it and performed a quick curtsy. "Little girl, you're the first fish."

She cringed. "First, what?"

"Fish. I know, we'd rather it be the first gemstone, magic sword, or golden ring, but those are fiction, this is real. Where I come from the first fish is the one most brave. That one who gives itself completely. And for what? Not for men and their souls, but for *ideas*."

She shrugged. "Thank you," she said and took her father's hand as they turned for the exit. "Daddy, do you know about the first fish?"

Morgan bowed to her and held his position of respect as she departed. Those in line hailed another of the night's many marvels. The girl waved like a prom queen as her image disappeared behind stainless steel spring-loaded doors.

People streamed in, furious with questions. Connected by an unseen thread, those who missed initial events were alive by it anyway. Descriptions of gravity and the Big Bang, the fate of our universe, and where atoms come from climbed in enthusiasm with each description.

Morgan pointed at the machine. "Ladies and gentlemen, adults and those too soon to be, this is your telescope. That is your sky.

Through it and the poisons we inhale, see the universe from where you are. Tonight we go to Jupiter! Only a half-billion miles away, what you see now happened forty-five minutes ago. You are literally staring into the past because light takes time to travel. At 186,000 miles per second, light that scatters off your nose and mine is a million miles away in the time it took me to speak this sentence." Oohs and aahs dotted the audience. "Astronomers describe distance just as we do in LA," Morgan said. "Santa Monica may be a half-hour away or two hours, depending on traffic." People groaned and nodded. "But the speed of light never slows for construction, car wrecks, or road rage. While you may think Jupiter is far away, it's in your back pocket. Now, to paraphrase John Dobson, no question you ask here will lead to a life of sorrow. Maybe out there." Morgan pointed to the city. "Not here. Now, more questions!"

Hands in the observatory rose in salutes to curiosity. People outside pressed to get in. Those inside didn't want out. Their minds were full of wonder and had been since the day they were born.

"How old is the universe?"

"How long would it take to walk to Jupiter?"

"Is there intelligent life elsewhere in the heavens?"

Having survived its encounter with the sun came the comet, rising with Orion. Its ion tail—now some forty million miles long—pointed away from our local star to lead the comet, like a headlight. Its uncharged tail of dust trailed behind, undriven by electric solar gales.

Morgan repositioned the telescope. "That ion tail is sixty times longer than a full moon is wide," he said. "Spectacular comets are seen only two or three times per century. The last gifts of this caliber were called Hyakutake and Hale-Bopp. This is one of those guys."

He squinted one eye to line up the machine of steel and glass with that of plasma and vacuum. "If you eat right, mind your parents, and stop watching television," he said, "you might see this one return...in five thousand years!" People applauded. Some swore never again to watch television. "Imagine what it saw on its last transit," Morgan said. "A civilization in Mesopotamia inventing the written word, the wheel, the calendar, and cities. Ancients believed comets were an omen, a sign of great things to come. Well, here's your comet. Who else could it belong to?"

179

Morgan stepped from his eyepiece. Lively owners of the sky squeezed upstairs in what seemed like the only party in Los Angeles.

As crowds cleared from Griffith Mountain at closing, sporadic laughter and voices entered the open shutter into an empty observatory. Motors rumbled. The dome turned away from a racing comet. Morgan's eye kept pace with his telescope as it tracked Sagittarius down. "I am looking into the heart of my galaxy, thirty thousand years distant," he whispered. "I just can't see it very well."

Lights on the ceiling flickered with interruption of power to the planetarium downstairs. Keys clinked against the stainless steel exit. A female staff member opened double doors. She fought to release her key from the lock. "Gonna hang out for a while, Morgan?"

"Think so," he said.

"Enjoy. I'll padlock the gate downstairs—if I ever get this key out...Hey, people liked you. An elderly lady said you're a natural."

"Naturally excited, I guess."

"Either way, we're glad to have you, Morgan."

He eyeballed the tube's collection of forever. "It's a fun place to be."

"Are you on next week?"

"No. Even though I'm new here, and broke, the boss let me take some time off for personal business."

"You mean you'd forgo that big LA Parks and Recreation money, voluntarily?"

Morgan laughed. "I know. But choosing life's practicalities—like paying my rent on time—is the coward's part. Besides, my landlord, Belva—isn't that an interesting name? I think she's Russian. She said I'm cute. There's a lot you can get away with if an old lady thinks you're cute. Not that I want to find her limit, but so far, my tardy payments have not exceeded her pleasant nature."

"Must be pretty important personal business."

"The only important business between here and..." He looked through the eyepiece. "And about two hundred thousand trillion miles from here." He focused on the girl. "I'm going to the *Queen Mary*! I've dreamed about this trip since I returned from the Yucatan."

"Dreams about the *Queen Mary*? Surely there's more to the

story than that," she said. "But the *Queen Mary*'s in Long Beach. You make it sound like some faraway place."

"When I get there, it will be the farthest I've ever been from where I am."

Freeing her key from the door, she turned to leave. "After your visit, bring her by sometime—the girl, not the ship. We'd all like to meet her." Doors closed with a thunk.

Crawling up a shallow canyon, up eucalyptus trees, and in the shutter wafted vocal companions of a harmonica. Morgan hummed along with Neal Young and his "Harvest Moon."

Through the eyepiece, Morgan cruised depths of interstellar space. "This is seismic," he whispered. "Historic. I've been waiting for this all my years and didn't even know it."

He capped the eyepiece, closed shutters, and shut off the lights. "Here we go."

\*\*\*

Candace woke throughout the night. Beside her, Bagit growled at every move. From nearby trees outside came the voice of a dove.

In her dream, Candace saw John sit close. He looked at the floor where he fell that last day. Asleep, Candace sat up and straightened a lock of hair on his forehead. "Wouldn't it be nice to have our morning coffee together?" she said. "You could tell me another one of your stories, you sweet old man."

John turned to her. "Who you calling old?"

Candace covered her mouth. She poked him. She squeezed his arm. "You spoke— John, did you hear it too?"

John looked at himself in the mirror. "Yes, I did. Can you see me?"

"Of course, I can see you!" Candace hugged him and began to cry. "I am so happy to hear you finally say something! Why didn't you do this years ago?"

"Can't say I know the answer to that. Quite a thing to speak and be heard."

Bagit barked.

"Hello, puppy. Miss me?" John scratched Bagit's head. "It's a fine night outside, Candace. Now that you can hear me, let's have that coffee, go outside and tell stories about the stars."

Candace pulled him close. "But is this a dream? Are you real? Are you here to stay?"

"Just take a deep breath and follow me."

"Am I dead, John? Are you taking me to heaven?"

"For crying out loud, Candice. I said we're going to the deck. But we're not going anywhere until you let go of me. Come on. Don't have much time."

Holding his shirt, Candace followed. Bagit trailed single-file. John switched on the radio to a station that played music from the 1930s, and 40s.

"John, I didn't know there was a channel like that in town."

"It's not in town." He spun Candace around, dancing past her. She turned, while her eyes fixed on him.

From the backyard deck, coffee in hand, John inspected his yard. "What happened to my pine trees?"

"Cut down, to fit in more houses," Candace said.

"And my apple tree?"

"Some kind of disease. I don't know. Ask your youngest."

"Boy, he's doing well. Got a girl, you know."

"I didn't know that."

"He's in love, Candace. Hit him like a ton of bricks. He doesn't want to tell you about her until he's sure. He's afraid you'll think he found another crackpot."

Candace shrugged. "He never loved that one. He was desperate, that's all. Stumbled over her at a bad time in life."

"He hasn't been so full of it since he was in college," John said. "Even more now. Doesn't rush a thing, does he?"

"Not enough for me. I want another grandchild before I'm over the hill. The problem is, I'm afraid he's over the hill. So what about this girl?"

"That's the good part. I said it hit him like a ton of bricks." John leaned forward. "Same for her. He's got a live one this time. One with some depth, substance, promise. Big on life, full of life. And hear this, Candace: she's an artist *and* a scientist. Believe that? If ever a match were made in heaven, this is it."

"So when will I meet her?"

"Can't believe they cut down my trees," John said. "If there weren't so many humans, wouldn't need so many houses."

"Forget the trees, John. I can see what you're up to for the umpteenth time, but I won't drop the subject of this girl."

Bagit barked.

John scowled. "Quiet, dog, you'll wake the neighbors." He sat on the bench. He patted his knee. "Come here, girl."

Bagit jumped on his lap. Candace watched, witness to an epiphany.

"Good girl. Missed me, didn't you. Boy, she looks great. Must be about a hunnert in dog years."

"Are you real, John?"

"Does it matter?"

"Of course, it matters. I want to know this is not some crazy dream. I want to know you're still alive. I want to know I will be too."

"People put too much emphasis on just plain facts, Candice. There's another link, a forgotten one, between material and divine...And there's the funnies. I miss the funnies."

"Fine. Then you are real."

John smiled at Bagit. "Never lacked persistence, has she, girl?"

"Well, answer me, are you real?"

John put the dog down. He studied his wife's face, her white hair. "I didn't leave just because I'm dead, Candace. I needn't travel to the bounds of our universe to reach heaven. It's all right here in dimensions you can sense but never see, hear, or touch. Until, like me, you die and never leave."

"What does that mean, John?"

"Remember when I told you about that fellow on a burning building in Manila? Remember why I was heck-bent to reach him?"

Candace chuckled. "Heck-bent...Because you thought he was the Castle Patch Man, and you knew the most important question to ask: if what they say is true. That Bubbles had been freed. That we'd all be freed."

John pointed at her. "You have an unmatched memory, do you know that?"

"Why ask me this question?"

He tapped his chest. "I meet Bubbles by the tall red maple every day I leave school."

"You mean the happy past has been restored?"

"No."

"Then what school, John?"

"It's the same day I met you, the same day we got married, that day the twins were born, the day I left this place. It's all there. Mine united with all the others."

"What others?"

"Candace, all that separates us is the finest of membranes between this universe and another. You've just gotta be able to listen to dimensions you can't hear, see what's not there, feel. The Kingdom of the Father *is upon the land*, Candace. Mister Thaddeus Stevens told me that on my way home from school when I was a kid. Now, every day, he waits for class to end so he can talk to Miss Pancake, and remind me once again. He gave me that gift, Candace. And do you know who gave it to Mister Stevens?"

"Who, John?"

John watched her.

"Who, John?"

John released his gaze and looked away.

"Oh, John, it doesn't matter if you can't remember. All I want is to meet this way every morning. I want to greet the sun with coffee and my husband. I want—"

"Too much wantin' sounds to me."

"So?"

"Pa says, 'Some things we think we need, we need. Some things we think we need, we don't.' 'Sides, you wouldn't want it anyway."

"I most certainly would!"

"Nope."

"Why not?"

"Cause it wouldn't be real. Not the way you mean."

"You just said you were real."

"I did not, you did."

Candace sunk in her chair. "So this is a dream."

"I didn't say that."

Candace started to speak. John interrupted. "Just hush. Accept this moment as it is. Don't categorize it. Just hold my hand and tell me a story. I like stories. It can be a true story, or…or it can be a lie that tells the truth, like me."

The two talked and laughed for hours. Curtain waves of particle emissions energized by an absent sun skipped overhead. Auroras streaked ephemeral blues and greens.

John slapped his knee. "Time for me to go."

"Where?"

"You need your sleep."

"I'm not tired."

"I'll tuck you in."

"John, I'm old enough to stay up without permission."

"But I'm not."

"Where will you go? Will you come back? Come back tomorrow. We'll do this again."

A dove rustled on a limb over the house. John looked up at it. "It's a gift, Candace. A fabulous gift. That lost connection between material and divine, right here and all around us. So long as we don't destroy the last of it, we can bring it back."

"Bring what back, John?"

He shook his head. "I'm still trying to figure all this out. Each day I know more and— How 'bout that, Candace? Learning is sacred *and* eternal. I always knew it was sacred.

"Candice, I learned a word once when I was a kid after I rode a dragon, and that word was *transcend*. What I can tell you, limited by words, beautiful as they are, falls so short of reality we can't tell it, or write it, though try we must. Truth *transcends* anything we can say, but not anything we can do. Among the living, the way to transcendence is salvation of that gracious gift." He looked up at the dove. "Before we lose it. So you see, I can't tell you because it can't be told."

She smiled. "That I understand. I'll wait."

"I once said I'd make my way back here, even it took a miracle," he said.

"I remember."

They left the deck.

"Now you get on your side of the bed, ma'am. But what I need is a pillow. What happened to my pillow?"

"Here, take this one. Bagit threw up on the other one."

John yanked the pillow from her grasp. "Cripes...I leave, and the place goes to pot—trees cut down, dog pukes on my favorite pillow, my only pillow."

Bagit jumped on the bed, nestled between them. John snapped his fingers. "To the foot of the bed, dog." John rolled toward Candace's side. "If you need me, I'll be right— Wait...The radio. Hear that? Andy Williams, 'Happy Heart.' I couldn't have said it better. He's part of it too, Candace. Every day he sings, and every time it's like the first time you ever heard him."

John left to turn off the radio. Candace sat up. She watched the doorway. She waited.

When Candace woke, she called for John. She searched the house inside and out. It was 8:00 a.m. in Iowa. She dialed California.

After a third series of rings, Morgan struggled from his bed to see the phone's LED message, "Mom." With a voice like nails on a blackboard, not words from a man, he answered, "Mom, do you know it's the middle of the night?"

"It's eight in the morning."

"Six on the West Coast, Mom."

"I have to tell you something. I had a dream last night. But it wasn't a dream."

"You're paying to push electrons two thousand miles to tell me you had a dream?"

"Stop your bellyaching and listen to me. It wasn't a dream. It was your dad! He came here last night, and *he talked*. We talked for hours, on the deck. I rarely remember what happens in my dreams or whether or not I had any. But I remember every word, every look...Morgan, do you think it was Dad?"

He hesitated. "Maybe so, Mom."

"Well, a person just doesn't really know, now do they? You just never know."

Morgan waited.

"Dad said it was real, Morgan. I remember plainly. He said it was real. I've never had a dream where the dream said it was real before, have you? Even Bagit saw him. Now that says it right there. It must have been real. I think it was real. I know it was."

"What do you mean, Bagit saw him?"

"He called her, and she jumped on his lap. He petted her, and she lay next to us just like she always did. Dad made her move. She hasn't laid in her spot like that since he left."

"That's really nice, Mom."

"You don't believe me. But I'll tell you what, Dad said you met a girl. A special one. Did you?"

Morgan studied empty space. "Dreams are often speculative, Mom. You want me to meet a woman, that's all."

"He said she's an artist and a scientist, like you. Is that true?"

Morgan pressed the phone tight to his ear. Dreams…are speculative. Mom, who have you been talking to?"

\*\*\*

With daylight in Los Angeles, the perpetual rush hour peaked. Children crowded schools, office buildings filled with people. Hasty and troubled, Morgan stuffed his daypack with snacks and water for his visit to the *Queen Mary*. A popular Hollywood interview program played out its recipe routine on Morgan's new seven-inch television, rescued with other outdated electronics from refuse of another vanquished actor.

He leaned down to Hawkeye. "Sweetie," he said, "for years I have believed no person could be trusted, least of all one's spouse. Because in the daily dealings of everyday life, in such close proximity, the only possible outcome is a kind of disgrace at the inadequacies of being human. Disgust *must* grow over time, rooted in reflections of ourselves in the other, to kill anything alive between us and ourselves with it. How could the result be anything but hatred, divorce, and financial ruin?"

He stood up. "I am weaponized," he said. "Can I disarm?"

His hands trembled. "But look at me now, with little more than a kiss."

He zipped bag compartments. I've had experiences that were illuminating, he thought. Some inspired me. Some disturbed me. Rarely were they life-changing. But never all four at once. She brings out the me in me.

He looked at Sammy, hesitant. "Will she be there?" he asked.

One arm through a strap on his backpack, he fitted his *Field of Dreams* cap, thread-bare but washed for the first time. He inserted earphones. Sensing another departure, Sammy meowed. Morgan reached to turn off the television, but Hawkeye hopped on the counter in front of it, positioned for petting per Sammy's notice.

He rubbed her nose. "That's right. I'm about to take a trip. Because I'm a lucky man. I'm *the* lucky man." Morgan cradled Sammy in one arm as Hawkeye pawed the counter.

He scratched Sammy's head with a corner of his new-old iPod. He examined its playlist. "Ooh...Perfect. Cliché even." Morgan scooped Hawkeye from the counter, one cat per arm, and waltzed to an orchestra of violins as Etta James sang "At Last" in his ears. "If you guys could hear what I hear."

He sang. Sammy purred and watched Morgan's lips move. Wide-eyed, Hawkeye watched Sammy.

"It's true, my loneliness really is over at—" He froze, legs flexed. Grazing the underside bill of his baseball cap, his eyes fixed on a puff of dust in free fall from the ceiling.

On Morgan's television, celebrity guests told unremarkable stories to hosts with remarkable overreaction as furniture, hosts, and their guests sprang from the floor. One host forced a joke about his "moving" program as catwalks jumped from their anchored fixtures to crush him. Clear skies of an ideal climate beaconed chaos through a hole in the roof. The TV image flashed, went black, then flashed again. The only sound heard was like that of a freight train run through Studio 29 as its video was lost to random electrical noise.

Crustal folds of the San Andreas Fault unraveled. Pent-up power released chain reactions in multiple quakes, any of which would have been devastating on its own. The concentration of energy released, so immense, even shock reflections from hidden bedrock were enough to flatten multistory dwellings. The Elysian Park fault muscled up against Dodger Stadium and downtown to perform a bump and grind in a natural effort to seek stability, like shaking beans in a jar. Hollywood fault—the length of a football field from once Grauman's now TCL's Chinese theater—was pried and kicked like a door stuck in a car crash.

Aircraft about to touch down veered off as LAX slid into the Pacific like wet spaghetti off a hot plate. Jets taking off but still connected to earth were flung sideways; their fuel tanks as onboard bombs. Pilots above lacked range for direct contact to operative airports to record their disbelief with Long Beach, Orange County,

Burbank all under siege.

Overhead, satellites recorded it all in multiple bands. Radio cries flowed skyward by the terabyte. Infrared bursts glowed from Long Beach oil refineries. Chain-reaction failures of entire urban areas released pops of air-conditioned cold into a hot basin. Overpasses leaped off the ground as though they were thrown. Gas lines lunged from landscape like worms fleeing a buried monster. Skyscrapers thought too flexible to fall swung with such authority, antennas on their roofs could be heard to crack the whip until rifled through structures four blocks away. Buildings ground past each other, ionized local atmosphere, and prickled with lightning, as meshworks of kilowatt temples to capitalism surrendered to nature's indifference. Southern California Edison's lattice shrank ever tighter into regions not yet collapsed.

Swells bounced across LA's basin, amplified or attenuated at intersections with different waves to create freakish outposts of damaged but standing square blocks among endless ruin. Dotted again with square block regions of such utter eradication, the place seemed atomized.

Reminiscent of Boston during the 1811 quake at New Madrid, Missouri, an angry Earth rang bells in Seattle nine hundred miles distant. Not since the 9.2 quake in Alaska flowed land like jelly into Prince William Sound was such force experienced by humans.

To erase the last remnant and bury it all, raging flames gasped for cubic miles of air to breathe. Dust storms poured in from bone-dry mountain valleys like supersonic Santa Ana winds. Boats of every kind spilled from every inlet. Billowing smoke on land looked like the eruption of a sixty-mile-wide volcano. Small aircraft disappeared in blackness of the rising column, boiled skyward in rocket-hot turbulence with such ferocity they splintered into countless slivers of aluminum, flesh, and bone.

The world's omnipresent network had a hole like a finger punched through a spider web. Some lines contorted their way into LA, but none responded. No electrical handshakes, no binary traffic, no returns from operating systems could be found. As spacecraft spied Earth below, a media thunderstorm was brewing, about to soak the world.

## 22. On the Wings of a Photon

A stream of gravel peppered cuts in Morgan's face. He pushed a flap of skin away from his left eye. "Hawkeye? Sammy!" he called.

Morgan heard a muffled voice of someone beneath him. He felt surroundings. One arm was fastened to a shoulder strap pinched under stone. He yanked back and forth, found the buckle, and released his arm. "Sammy? Hawkeye? Kitty, kitty!"

Diagonal columns of light shimmered in air replete with debris. Morgan pushed rocks from his feet. He stood and rapped his skull against something solid. Crouched, he gripped his head, "Talk to me, Sammy!"

A faint meow came from behind a vertical floor. Morgan burrowed. He ripped carpet backing knotted with concrete pebbles. Water ran through his fingers, making it hard to grasp anything.

Hands wiped on his shirt, he saw dark patches smear across dusty white. Turned toward a scattering of light from thirty feet away, he found his palms lacerated in a dozen directions. He tore his shirt in half, wrapped hands, and dug. "It's OK, Sammy, Daddy's here!"

A woman's voice rose through fissures underfoot. "Help me!"

His path to Sammy was blocked. Hands waved over surfaces mostly in the dark, Morgan felt for a passage. He coughed a chalky paste. Sammy sounded an arm's length away.

Morgan hung from something unseen and kicked a slab of drywall. Two-by-four supports cracked. Wood broke free to release a barrel of rubble over Morgan's ankles. Sammy's voice was closer.

The woman below threw something. "Help me!"

The building rumbled and shifted. Sammy screeched. Morgan

fell against a panel charged with nails. Gaps above closed, others opened, more dust filled the air. He pressed a solid surface above his head as though he could hold it from crushing him.

A shower of nuggets ceased. He spit mud from his mouth. He unraveled cloth from one hand and placed it over his face. Breathing through the material made it fizz like the sound of a respirator as tiny blood bubbles fractured in crosshatched spaces it was made of.

Artificial winds shrieked through fissures, lured by the temper of a prancing yellow light outside. "Don't suffocate me!" he shouted.

It got harder to breathe despite less airborne filth. He knelt down to inhale from a breeze pulled up through spaces in the building. His eyes burned, insistent he keep them shut. "Hawkeye? Sammy? Talk to Daddy!"

Sammy howled.

Morgan's previous route was closed or moved someplace else. His foot secured to something with such permanence it seemed to have grown there. He heaved. He twisted. He drew free his foot from his shoe and attached flesh. He tunneled.

The woman pleaded. "I'm not far from you!"

"You're a human!" he shouted. "You have a brain. Use it!"

"Please, I'm old! Like your mother!"

Morgan captured a curling tendril of haze with his eyes. He recognized her voice. He was two floors down, on top of his landlord, Belva. He calculated, he wagered, he turned for her.

He worked blocks attached by wire mesh side to side until snapped free. Sammy meowed. Morgan mined his way down.

His support broke to dump him down an incline. Under splayed legs of her kitchen table, she praised Morgan like the arrival of God.

Crawling toward her, he reacted as though he touched a hot stove, his palm laid open by shattered edges of a porcelain toilet sharper than a scalpel. He pinched his hand shut and shouted up the passage, "Daddy's coming, Sammy!"

He reached the woman. "Can you move?" She said nothing.

Half standing, Morgan towed her to the armrest of a vertical couch, a scant trail of red behind her.

"Easy! That's not my couch," she said.

Morgan appeared about to drag her back under the table. He ripped a strip of curtain, tied his hand shut, and turned up the hole.

191

"Where are you going?"

*"To get…my cats!"*

"You can't leave!"

"You're fine!"

"But can't you hear them?"

"Who?"

"The others! Can't you hear them?"

Morgan's eyes flitted off corners of darkness. He squeezed fists, dripping blood. "What do you think I'm gonna do, reassemble the building?"

He climbed. Faster he quarried for Sammy. Sounds of Morgan's breathing dampened those of helpless humans distributed in a sphere around him. Squirming through impossible convolutions, Morgan was almost there.

Sammy's torso emerged from shadow, his hindquarters beneath a steel support. Sammy's barely open eyes leaked mire. Sammy moved his mouth to meow but made no sound.

"It's OK, daddy's here, Sammy." Morgan lay flat so the cat could see him in frail light. He pushed the flap of his own face away from his eye. He split blood running from his face into his mouth. "Maybe there's a gap to make room for the rest of you under there. Nine lives, Sammy."

A badger digging his pit, Morgan thrust trash between his knees. Electrical wires, pipes still running water, internals of a television, all sheathed in a concrete mix as though fresh from the bag.

Crouched, Morgan tugged on Sammy's torso. He plucked rocks and tugged again, sliding Sammy closer. Morgan sat cross-legged in their cramped space and lifted the cat to his chest. Sammy twitched. A meow froze on Sammy's mouth as internal organs drained into Morgan's lap. Morgan gasped, caught them, and slowly pushed uncorked bowels into the cavity they came from. Sammy's body jerked. Morgan stopped to hold what he could. "Oh no…Sammy…"

Sammy breathed once, followed by the longest pause. Morgan rubbed the animal's forehead. "It's OK, we're together, Sammy. Daddy's here. Daddy loves you, Sammy." Shaking his head, Morgan repeated reassurance like a sermon at a funeral.

Sammy arched, squealed, and vented a cup of liquid on Morgan's face. "It's OK, Sammy, you're not in trouble, it's OK."

He scratched Sammy's forehead, a drip, drip of fluid from Morgan's chin.

Like trying to hold up a string, the release of tension in Sammy's body announced surrender. His head leaned on Morgan's chest.

Morgan knew human minds can run for minutes once starved of oxygen. He kept talking. "Such a good, good boy, Sammy. You're the best boy I've ever known. Daddy loves you, Sammy."

Morgan petted the animal, asking if he remembered the day they met. He told him he was sorry to have scolded him all those years ago. He confessed he should have never come to California to satisfy vanity and childhood dreams. "I am so sorry, Sammy...I'm so sorry I did this to you!"

\*\*\*

After days of chaos, fire, and aftershocks, satellite communications were established for rationed use. Morgan stood outside, a FEMA cell phone in his hand, a plastic bag over his shoulder. He searched beneath slabs of suspended concrete, hung by arthritic fingers of reinforcing rod. "Hawkeye? Kitty, kitty!"

Shirtless, Morgan's body was sculpted by stone in a hundred places. A bandage held a flap of his face against his head. A filthy beach towel protected his neck and shoulders from sun. His hands bound in bloodless sections of someone else's t-shirt. He coughed a film of concrete slurry on his lips.

He sat on a vertical chunk of Sunset Boulevard. He stared at Palos Verdes peninsula, hypnotic, its ember hills wavering. He punched numbers on the phone. A computer voice spoke.

Morgan shouted into the mouthpiece, "No, the number *I* have is no longer in service!" He poked numbers again as if to press harder and longer would matter. A phone rang in Iowa.

"Thank goodness it's you, Morgan."

"Elder?"

"It's about time the government helped you, Morgan. We've watched people on TV plead for aid for days."

"Because people here prefer to impersonate New Orleans after Katrina, not Sendai after the tsunami. No need for TVs and jewelry when there's no food or water. First—control yourself. Second—

don't sit on your ass waiting for the State."

Elder hesitated. "You'd think this nation could do something."

"Liberals should be happy, we're all equal again. Get Mom on the phone, Elder. I've got five minutes per call per day."

"What about your apartment, Morgan?"

"Gone, downhill. Don't even have a chair to sit on. But I never had a chair to sit on."

"It's the only thing on the news, Morgan. Stock markets around the world have plunged, and now Taiwan. People are frightened to death, even here."

"What about Taiwan?"

"China's taken advantage of US distractions from global affairs. They've claimed Taiwan, the South China Sea, and Japan's Senkaku Islands as their own. Japan's called for us to uphold treaties and step in with force. But China knows our condition. They know the quake is more than we can handle. They've jammed surveillance and shot down every aircraft they see, claiming they're Taiwanese kamikazes. Only thing we know comes from seismic readings emanating from the island, but China says they're LA aftershocks."

Morgan erupted, "Like hell they are! Suddenly seismologists can't pinpoint a source? With all the practice China's got 'accidentally' shooting down our satellites and stealing our tech, they've freely cleansed Taiwan with that massive military machine we paid for, importing their junk. Tibet all over again. They know we can't afford combat with the most powerful nation on Earth."

"The cats, Morgan, are they all right?"

"Hawkeye's here somewhere. I'll find her. Sammy's with me. I'll have him cremated and bury us together. Get Mom on the phone, I've about one minute left."

"Morgan...Mom died."

Air drained from Morgan's chest. He leaned back against an upright piece of street.

"Died in her sleep," Elder said. "Must of had a bad night because the coffee pot was just barely warm early this morning when we found her. There were two cups of coffee on the deck table—probably confused again. One full, the other half empty. Not sure what she died of, loneliness maybe. Next to Mom on the bed was a piece of copper, beaten by a hammer or something. I don't remember that from anything, do you?

"Hello? Morgan?"

"Two cups?" Morgan asked. "Why would she make two cups?"

With a loud click, a computer voice announced, "Su tiempo de unión asignado ha estado satisfecho."

Morgan stood. He looked toward the sky. Not again, he thought. They brought me into this world. And I wasn't there when they left.

He dialed Ne Shoul again—nothing. He looked over an expanse to the ocean. Thousands of people huddled near clefts in horizontal walls to reassure loved ones they'd be freed. What if she's lying in a hospital someplace, waiting for me? he thought. But what hospital? Where would she be? Redondo or the *Queen*?

He dropped the phone in his pocket and walked away.

From behind, "Sir!"

Morgan stopped. He reached in his pocket and lifted the phone behind his head. A National Guardsman grabbed it.

Morgan draped the bag holding Sammy over his shoulder. He trundled eastward through wreckage. He coughed paste and limped on a dead man's shoe that didn't fit. "Hawkeye! Kitty, kitty!"

\*\*\*

Morgan's odyssey found America as though attacked by foreign enemies. US flags flew from office buildings, trucks, fast-food coffee cups. Merchant signs read, "Save LA, Spend Money!"

Mangy and wounded, Morgan stood before a shop in Show Low, Arizona, TVs on in the window. Muffled by glass, reports said factions had been drawn. Liberal television hosts claimed The Quake was a product of Ronald Reagan's Star Wars satellite ray-gun. As a white male concept, it was meant to kill only Hispanics, blacks, and women but malfunctioned to kill everybody. Talk radio conservatives told their TV comrades the blow was delivered by God for the sins of liberals. "Now that *everything* has changed, it's no time to question the will of Gawd!" said one host. "Unite against intellectual elites! Fly the flag! Lock and load!"

Morgan sneered. "What happened to plate tectonics?"

Through glass came his answer. "The Joe Creed Show says plate tectonics is another left-wing myth pushed by environmentalist wackos back-tracking on the satellite hoax."

"Media echo-chambers and their liars," Morgan muttered. "This way, both sides can remain perpetually pissed about things that aren't even true. What a surprise…So everything hasn't changed."

Anxious for filler in twenty-four-hour coverage, cable channels discovered Morgan. From the air, he could be seen to thumb for a ride among moonscapes scorched by drought and fires spanning the Rocky Mountains along I-70. Television networks agreed to avoid assistance, instead to follow him step for step along his route, a green decision not to interfere with nature.

Morgan flipped an obscene gesture to helicopters overhead, "I'm not Forest Gump!"

Truckers provided Morgan transport and safety through one of the West's five-hundred-year dust storms that struck every five years. Discharged in Iowa, Morgan was mobbed by local reporters feverish for connections to national stories. TV news elaborated his odyssey for *Escape from The Quake*, Morgan portrayed as the sole survivor.

Days later, at Marion Christian Church, people filled pews and stood about the perimeter. Television trucks crowed its small parking lot outside.

In her will, Candice asked her remaining children to make a statement about their family.

Gray-haired, Elder stood at the podium under a cross suspended from wires. Completing his written statement, he said, "And so she is with Dad in heaven. As real as this place. As real as you and me."

Elder left the podium and took his seat.

Arriving at the podium, Morgan examined an unfolded paper. He returned it to his pocket. "Sorry, Mom," he whispered. He looked at wood grain stagger across his lectern. "It would seem," he said to the audience, "that the God-is-dead generation has found their claims not quite so fulfilling as when tormenting their parents."

He glanced at Bible stories in stained glass. Jesus held his hand upon a woman in need; loaves and fishes appeared before stunned disciples. Silhouettes pressed against windows trying to see in. Morgan looked to the mourners. "I see you grieve, but I wonder why?" he said. "I mourn too because once every atom of my parents has dispersed, that is just the beginning of an eternal span over which I will never see, hear, or meet them again." Strain swept across faces in the pews. Some shook their heads. "But you are believers," he said. "With certainty that my mother lives; that you too will defeat death. So what's to grieve? God is good.

"Unless you're not certain.

"So do you cry for my mother or yourselves?"

He studied those staring back at him. "Truly, I do wish I believed in your God. I've tried.

"It would give me someone to blame."

At the gravesite, people began to leave. Seated in a folding chair, Morgan considered three headstones. Elder placed his hand on Morgan's shoulder. Morgan did not respond. Elder walked away.

Alone, Morgan watched workmen lower the casket with ropes and a portable pulley device. One scooped dirt while three others leaned on shovels, talked, laughed, and lit a cigarette.

Now one workman remained. He patted sod with his shovel.

"Three managers, one worker," Morgan said. "Must be state-regulated...Gravedigging, I mean."

The man tipped his hat, turned, and stabbed his shovel into unused ground. He stacked three pristine spades and wrapped a rope about them. He picked up a cigarette butt, tucked in his pocket. With another rope wound over his shoulder, he hoisted the three bound shovels, pulled his from the ground, and receded into evening. The sound of his heels faded with range.

Morgan reflected on the man. Young, muscular, patient. Seems content, he thought.

A remnant of tranquility protected Marion Memorial, shadowed by billboards, and the stench of fast-food grease. An irksome ditty nagged from what was the adult video store, now a strip club. Morgan looked at food wrappers collected against headstones. "We hollowed out the land as we hollowed out our souls," he whispered. "And by the same means."

He felt scabs and sutures on his head. He tugged at gauze about his hands. He loosened the tie on his neck. Years ago, I sat in church and saw my father dead in a casket before me, he remembered. For just a moment, I understood for the first time the meaning of God the Father. And the promise of life after death. In that instant, I felt my father continued elsewhere, and we would meet again.

Comfort and certainty, he thought. But comfort and certainty didn't make it true.

He watched a red light wax and wane on the TV tower. Nor false, he decided.

A dove called out from a ginkgo tree. He spoke to it. "Is there a universe out there where my father and mother live together still? And I'm there too?

"Problem is, that place is not this place."

There seemed a one-dimensional impression about Morgan's environment. A link twined through noise of his five senses hidden by its thinness to a sensation of remoteness that spanned forever. But for one remarkable woman, the only people he knew dissolved into an empty void.

Morgan pulled a circular piece of flattened copper from his pocket. He divined a pattern on its surface. "Lincoln," he whispered. He flipped it over to trace curves of wheat bounding smeared words, *One Cent*. "It's a penny."

***

Waiting for his ride among crowds of volunteers, residents, and relations, Morgan looked up at C-5 cargo planes over San Diego. North they flew with supplies for Los Angeles. In a location thought to be warm, people there were freezing to death at night in sixty-degree temperatures while Congress dawdled. How to coordinate recovery was as partisan and stalled as a budget agreement. Nevada BLM land received dead Los Angelinos, dug up and delivered by the trainload.

A ride from San Diego to Hollywood could cost thousands, usually paid by lawyers from back East in search of claimants for class-action lawsuits. Morgan made use of a less expensive cottage industry in private vans once loaded with illegal immigrants.

Morgan felt a tap on his shoulder. "Hey, buddy, share some food," the man said.

"What makes you think I have any food?"

"Pretty pack ya got. And you're too clean to be from LA."

"I was there when it happened. Been away for a while."

"Why'd you come back?"

"To find someone."

The man nodded. "Should have stayed where you were. City's gone. Firestorms swept through."

"I left after the fires."

"Buddy, they've had seven-point aftershocks up there. Shakes flammables free for the next fire. Can't keep fires from starting and no way to get to those that do. Last one in Anaheim burned for three days. People say it got so hot, metal and glass turned liquid, then cooled like frozen waterfalls. Melted hydrants sent geysers sixty feet in places—where they had pressure, which is almost nowhere. People thought they could survive there, cooled by the water. Didn't. Fires sucked out all the oxygen. So they say. Hear a lot that ain't true and some that shouldn't be but is."

Morgan turned to find his place in line.

On the road, inside the van, Morgan could hear the driver and his assistant navigate roadblocks, impromptu bribery, and off-road byways. While claims of National Guard control were frequent, freed passengers walked wherever they were going without guidance. They formed groups among themselves for protection. Seen as a threat to liberty, government regulation was wholly dependent on the personality of commanders on site. A patchwork of control or none at all.

Morgan read a pair of signs beside each other with arrows in opposite directions. The left sign noted that documented residents were allowed entry if their address was deemed to possess portable items. The right sign warned of shoot-on-sight permissions.

"So the government's in charge," he said. "Should be able to do whatever I damn well please." He reread the second sign. "However, that's a little disconcerting."

Near his old home, a robotic all-terrain vehicle, bound by two armed military guards, rambled toward Morgan. Fully loaded, it towed a long cart. Morgan grimaced at the stench from their trailer.

A soldier motioned his rifle in Morgan's direction. "State your business, sir."

"Headed for Long Beach."

"Long way to go," the man said.

Morgan shrugged. "This is where they dropped me. Plus I used to live here. I'm looking for my cat. They can go weeks without food, ya know."

"What's the pipe sticking out of your pack for, sir?"

Morgan hesitated. "Walking stick."

"Walking stick in your backpack? No weapons allowed on any but the Guard, sir."

Morgan reached back to grab it. He pivoted the pipe's point on the ground. "See? Walking stick."

"Recovery's being done in sections, sir. No one's allowed here. Shelter is forty blocks northeast."

"Define blocks."

"Four miles northeast, sir."

Morgan loitered. "I'm in a really big hurry, guys, do you mind?"

"Sir?" The man pointed northeast.

"Just once, bend the rules, boys. I'm trying to find someone."

"Sir, so is everyone else."

"And what if she's waiting for me, and I don't make it in time because of you?"

"Sir, I don't know you from Adam. If there's really a girl and she's alive, she'll be found. Go. We'll follow you."

Morgan cursed and grumbled but acquiesced.

A preference for areas already burned and fears of wave-ravaged lowlands led to shelter high in Griffith Park, capped by Griffith Observatory, split and quartered. Tents covered this shallow range above the city. Like scenes from the Civil War, amputated body parts lay in piles near surgical tents.

A boy in a uniform two sizes too big stopped Morgan as the guards and their ATV continued uphill. "ID, sir?" the boy said.

Morgan leaned, hands on his knees, panting. He watched the guards leave. "That's a climb," he said.

Morgan held his license nearly against the boy's nose. "Any news on Long Beach? Does the *Queen Mary* still float?"

"*Queen Mary*'s a hospital ship, sir. Aground." He pointed and recorded Morgan's ID on a handheld device.

Morgan's eyes expanded. He turned. "Son of a bitch…There it is. Clear as a bell."

Morgan smacked his lips, tasting air. "No wonder I got this far without choking."

The atmosphere was free of smog. Canyons on Catalina Island

appeared as though across the street. Multiple lines of people could be mistaken for beetles in the distance, stones handed one to the next. Skyscrapers looked like petals fanned from a flower. All else looked like a twice-bombed Hiroshima.

"Great zot," Morgan said. "It's almost featureless out there. Except for a handful of places that look like nothing happened—relatively speaking."

"Nobody knows why that is, sir, but they're management centers for the reconstruction now."

"Management? Last thing this place needs is managers; it's already wrecked." Morgan turned to the boy. "Sell your compass?"

"Sir, I don't have a compass."

"What kind of idiot doesn't have a compass in this mess?"

Morgan shaded his eyes toward the coast. "Did you say it's a hospital? Bet they accept volunteers if all they can do is spell *medicine*."

"City's closed to wanderers, sir. You'll have to stay here. Soon as my commander sees you, you're enlisted."

Morgan descended downhill.

"Sir, you can't go that way."

Morgan calculated. Fifteen miles to Santa Monica. Stay on the coast to Redondo, check there. That's another fifteen. Then fifteen to Long Beach and the *Queen*. Forty-five miles. But it won't be a straight line. Some camouflage coat will grab me. Unless FEMA runs the show in that direction. In that case, I'm home free.

In a swivet, hands on hips, the boy hunted for higher authority.

Straight to Redondo, twenty-five miles, then Long Beach, Morgan decided. Forty total. Damn…Out of a car, you don't realize the expanse of this place. This will be like mountain hiking. Three days to the *Queen*. Four with bad luck, which is a certainty. Better hustle. With a couple days' food and water, do I have enough? The answer is yes, even if I don't. I busted an air-hammered wheel off a car in the desert without water, I ought to be able to cross this dump.

Man, this is gonna hurt.

The boy shouted, "The signs say, don't go that way! I'm gonna report you!"

Morgan ran away.

201

## 23. On the Frontier

Explosives followed by graders flattened areas of Los Angeles once congested with traffic. Heavy lift helicopters suspended spans of steel toward recycle centers on the islands. Cargo ships hauled millions of steel tons per stopover.

Air came to life with a putrid breeze emitted by decomposed bodies brewed in pools of sun-warmed water. An eruption of rats were so dense they bumped into Morgan's feet.

At night Morgan visited abandoned people in one compound after another. Each surrounded itself by a ring of ignited shingles and tires to repel aggressive rats and diseased dogs. Warmed by a fire, Morgan crouched among the twenty nearest people. He released his pack. "Is this Redondo Beach?" he asked.

Seated on a steel wheel and covered in soot, a man spoke between bites gnawed from bone. "This is Redondo. I oughta know. These are my streets" The man grinned to expose missing teeth.

"So you're a street person," Morgan said.

"You're a home person?"

"OK, you're a person."

The man held his fist high. "I am *a person!*"

"Promise, I'll take sensitivity training after the city's rebuilt," Morgan said.

"Who's sensitive? I'm just funny. Now that all the professors are dead, I figure they might hire me back. Damn near had tenure until a little meth with my students got me the boot.

"Did you know, Home Person, there's a sporty debate in the humanities department over whether The Quake really happened?"

Morgan ignored him. He scratched the corner of his eye. He

watched people at other fires.

"Oh yes, Home Person. Followers of London's School of Economics' Karl Popper say if The Quake did occur, no one could know for sure, as tracing knowledge step by step backward in time would eventually lead to a place where the definition of knowing must be questioned. Intellectual disciples of MIT's Thomas Kuhn insist whatever we believe about The Quake will eventually be replaced by another paradigm. So there's no point thinking what we know today will be what we know tomorrow. While university postmodernists maintain that since we're imprisoned by cultural structures confining our outlook, Americans will be forced to believe there's been a quake because it's true for their structure. Those who died in The Quake died only because American cultural structures made us think they had. Other cultural structures—merely social preferences—will determine those people alive and well, which will also be true, but only for those with that structure."

Morgan grimaced. "What?"

The man smiled and said, "Of course, what's not written or said is more important than physical facts. And since professor Foucault has shown all interpretations are fictions, results will be endlessly analyzed with fresh doctorates generated. One of 'em's mine. After all, I am *a person!*"

Morgan rolled his eyes and looked away. "Has anyone seen or heard of a woman by the name of Ne Shoul De Roue? She's a beautiful thirty-one-year-old with obsidian eyes and long, dark hair. Five-foot seven, hundred fifteen pounds."

No one spoke. The man chomped on his roasted creature. He inhaled black clouds from the fire. "Ahh…Tar smoke," he said. "Keeps you safe from Satan's touch."

Morgan waved air from his face. "Satan's what?"

"Tar smoke kills whatever it is that makes all those people rot before they're dead, and rot pronto. Couple days, it's adiós."

"So, you're a medical doctor as well."

The man nodded. "I've considered a career in gynecology."

Morgan watched others eat rats.

"Don't worry, Home Person, they're tasty. Besides, these buggers are the most plentiful source we got. It's them, somebody's pet, or one of those birds. They got in the air when it all came down, and for some reason, they aren't dying."

The man shoved a mostly furless rat torso at Morgan's face. "Rats eat people. People eat rats. Keeps it even," he said.

Morgan turned toward adjacent campfires to call out, "I'm looking for a woman! Her name is Ne Shoul De Roue! A name like that you can't forget! She lives in Redondo, somebody should know her," he said.

The man picked meat, and mumbled, "This is America, home person. Nobody knows nobody."

A woman cradling a child nodded her head. Morgan left his pack, hopped over smoldering shingles, and knelt beside her. "Ma'am, do you know her?"

She nodded, rocked the boy, and whispered in his ear.

"Ma'am, I can't hear you. Have you heard her name? Ne Shoul De—" Patches of dry mud checkered the boy's face and naked body. The image of Michelangelo's *Pieta* flashed through Morgan's brain.

Sounds came from Morgan's pack as children stole water and protein bars. Morgan vaulted for them. "You little shits!"

He picked up strewn items. He counted what remained.

From one flame to the next, he went. "Her name is Ne Shoul De Roue!"

\*\*\*

After a full day's walk, Morgan tracked the moon until it sat beneath a ruined earth then forgot where it was. He stood, thinking, never has this place been so dark. No stars on the horizon that way, blocked by mountains. He turned. And stars on the horizon that way—beach—boat.

For another day, Morgan found no compound and effectively navigated pockets of government authority. He found little difference between beach cities and Hollywood, except an average elevation of nine feet had left beach cities washed by surging seas. Mosquitoes and flies—rarely seen in the basin—were so thick they looked like a dim fog in the night.

Morgan leaned against his walking stick beside a canted wall in the dark. Rodent feet sounded like a necklace of teeth pulled over pebbles. Supported by his walking stick, he tilted his head, listened for waves, and dug wounds on his face. He tried to sleep standing up.

Yanked backward, Morgan's body hit the ground.

A shadow blacker than sky met his skull to sound like a morning newspaper hit the sidewalk.

"You stole my pack!" a man shouted, and ripped it free to fly a half dozen yards. Its contents skipped over skeletons of a building.

Morgan held tight his pipe with both hands and rammed it into the man as both wrestled for it.

The man latched his teeth into Morgan's throat. Like a dog trying to snap the spine of its prey, he shook his head.

Morgan bit off a hunk of the man's scalp. He grabbed a handful of groin to crush tissue with a twist as the man wailed.

In charge of his weapon, Morgan wound up as though back at the *Field of Dreams*. From high, the pipe sank and swung forward like trying to hit a ball in the dirt. It ticked a stone at his feet to rise with full velocity. On impact, the man's chin lifted his body, teeth emancipated from his mouth.

Morgan followed steel around for another cycle and shattered the man's skull.

Pipe overhead, Morgan gasped, one eye wide and panicked. He squinted at a pile of man, motionless but for a periodic mist spurt from his head. "It's my bag!" Morgan said.

Morgan stumbled back. He dropped to his seat, legs stretched before him. He spit hair from his mouth.

Morgan grabbed his throat, bleeding, though not pumping from an artery. He cringed, wiping filth from the injury.

Overhead another cargo craft glided earthward. Wingtip lights sparked in unison. Flocks of helicopters from Vandenberg airbase flew in medicines for plagues of cholera and typhoid. Rodents nipped at Morgan's feet.

He found a stretch of muscle uncovered by skin still attached to his neck. "Water," he said. "Clean it."

He crawled for his pack. He felt inside. "Oh no…"

Frantic, he reached through gaps in concrete for food and water.

\*\*\*

Plants imported from around the world with microbial stowaways, dead humans, and household pets by the tens of thousands lay about seawater puddles. Germs plugged into higher energy outlets of a hotter world, rich in raw materials. The only conditions similar to this existed in Southeast Asia and tropical Africa; breeding grounds for flu and Ebola.

Morgan consumed a hefty daily dose of ultraviolet, aiding fungus factories established in lesions about his cooked skin. Fungus digested collagen, the superstructure of his cells, his skin progressively paper-thin. Strenuous movement alone could crack this permeable fortification to an exterior jurisdiction stalking carbon concentrations like him. Tendrils of infection appeared to stitch his head to his shoulders, enraged with whatever bacteria his human attacker's mouth left behind.

Morgan stopped next to a quakeproof helix of reinforcing rod, unfettered by its concrete cloak and bridge it once supported. He coughed and cursed the hot sun made hotter by countless tons of stone like bricks in an oven. "Rest," he said.

He looked down to a dead man whose extremities appeared human while the core of him slid in a goop even rats and flies avoided. Morgan kept walking.

***

Several people gathered under fragments of an overpass to shadow them from daylight. Each lay in stages of decline unique to their affliction. Morgan squinted one eye open. He held one end of the pipe against his chest. He pressed the opposite end against a man's torso supporting a pillar. The body fell over. He stole the man's shade, narrowly able to hold himself up.

He picked at caked formations on his eyelids. Rivulets drained from corners of his mouth. Infection staggered down past his elbow. He felt his swollen throat with one hand and tried to flex fingers of the other. "That mad dog son of a bitch disabled my arm," he slurred.

Morgan's head bowed. He dropped to his knees, braced by the pipe. He looked for the sun for direction. He leaned back, fell on his side, and stuttered indecipherable sounds.

He heard footsteps approach. Eyes nearly fused shut, Morgan swept the metal pipe like a broken branch on a tree in the wind. "It's my bag," he hissed.

A man spoke. "My name's Father O'Connor. What's your name?" The man held Morgan's hand. "God will save us," he said.

Morgan's forehead lay against his arm, his chin nuzzled in dirt. He mumbled like a man suffering from alcohol.

The man recited a prayer. Morgan rolled on his back. Dirt ridges dammed threads of saliva ambling down his face. Unable to open encrusted eyes, he studied the man with his ears. Mud chipped off Morgan's mouth as he spoke. "Pray to ease God's sorrow, Father."

"For what, son?"

"His impotence."

"Don't talk that way. You're sick."

"I'm resting."

"I have the fungus too, son. Like sin, we share the same fate."

Morgan labored to open his eyes. One cracked, bleeding tears.

The man placed a hand on Morgan's chest. "Pray. Pray, son."

"For what? To who, and what's the difference?"

Morgan rolled over. He quaked on hands and knees. His head hung like a metal nozzle on an empty fire hose.

The man leaned closer. "Will you build another temple? In three magical days, start over again amidst the ruin? Will you deny your death and fail to be saved from it?"

The man ran to chase thieves stealing dying people's billfolds. He knelt to pray by their victims.

Morgan's teeth clattered. He pressed body from ground. "I remember the temple, Father. It is magic."

Pushed against the pipe, Morgan stood. "She'll be there," he murmured. "The *Queen Mary*. But what if I don't make it in time?"

He lost his support. Spun round by the pipe, it ripped his cheek from lip to jaw joint. Face down, he stammered through splatters of blood to a priest not there.

Blind, he reached to grab a handful of earth he thought was the man. "Her name is Ne Shoul De Roue. A woman like that you can't forget."

## 24. Blessed

Hospitals filled with patients, doctors, nurses, and the largest group of volunteers ever assembled in peacetime anywhere. Quake victims spilled over from São Paulo, Brazil, to Anchorage, Alaska, and east to Bangor.

Three hundred miles north of Los Angeles, the San Andreas Fault reentered an ocean under continuous touchdowns of cargo aircraft unloading sick and injured in San Francisco. Patients were placed in wards of Virus, Bacterial, Fungus, and Unidentified. Each held bracelets for identification in a vast database and to correlate effects of various treatments. Without personal identification or capacity for speech, many were listed as numerically incremented Jane or John Doe.

Of virus victims, an extreme 60% perished, only 30% less virulent than Earth's most lethal pathogen. Some unidentified agents were overactive, killing their host before passage to others. For bacterial victims, boosted immune systems could terminate sixteen million offspring of a single bacterium every hour for what should have been nearly 100% of the time but wasn't because of short supplies, stretched facilities, and antibiotic resistance. Fungus victims, though fewest in number, were in mysterious jeopardy, with no cream, ointment, salve, soap, or solvent so far known to have any effect.

Parked against a wall, Morgan felt his body nearly slide off a stainless steel cart. Muffled sounds echoed in his ears. He tried to open his eyes, bonded by settlements that looked like colonies of coral. He thought he recognized a female voice.

"We'll have you up and about in no time, sir," the masked

woman said as she looked at another nurse and crossed her fingers. "Your ID and belongings are under radiated fumigation. Once data entry gets that government software fixed, we'll update your bracelet and get you in the database. For now, you're John Doe 237F." With protective gloves, she patted his shoulder hidden by a sheet and opened cracks in his skin. She walked away.

\*\*\*

A female TV reporter stood with a microphone in front of Morgan's bed as he slept. A clear visor revealed her face, her body in what looked like a hazmat suit. In her most compassionate tone, she told of those who were acclaimed and those who were not. "Sadly," she said, "in this ward are fungal victims, with slim hope of survival. Behind me is a patient known as John Doe 237F. This reporter, Angela Famous," she rattled her nametag, "has found this victim to be Morgan Whitaker, a low-budget independent filmmaker for rogue groups of radical conservatives. Contrary as it sounds, critics claimed his films showed him to be a tree-hugging, anti-corporate socialist."

Morgan's life grew exponentially as the reporter spoke. A group of physicians and nurses rushed behind glass doors and the reporter.

"As you can see," she said. "Heroines abound as they strive to save those that can be. Each victim has a story. Most, we'll never know."

The camera zoomed in. A tear staggered down her face. She motioned to the cameraman. "That's a wrap. Did you get that?"

The cameraman gave a thumbs up.

"I mean the tear. Did you get the tear?"

"Got it," he said.

"Are you sure you got the tear? How'd it look?"

Her masked cameraman—neither bagged nor gloved—stood at the foot of Morgan's bed. "His movies were outstanding. Did you ever see one?"

"Who has but a group of wackos in Montana and Texas?"

"You just said he was a great filmmaker."

"No, I didn't. And besides—" She pointed at the camera. "This is television, kid. I tell, they believe."

209

The cameraman said, "I liked his stuff. I wish he were still alive."

"He's not exactly dead yet. Maybe by eleven—" She paused and whispered, "Maybe he'll die on camera."

***

In the viral ward nurse's station, coffee, colas, and sugared treats covered tables. Cots were scattered about, half of them occupied. On the wall, a television droned over small talk. "Behind me is a patient known as John Doe 237F…"

A nurse sneered at the TV. "This isn't a concentration camp. We know most of their names," he said.

Another laughed. "And check out the body bag she's wearing. I know it sells airtime, but if she doesn't touch the guy, a mask will do."

A woman reached for the television remote. "Let's watch reality TV on the Hick Channel," she said. "I want to see humans destroy nature, even the score a little—Wait! Did you see that? We just ran behind that reporter. Now everybody in Fungal knows we got off on the wrong floor."

Leaned against a wall, donut in hand, one volunteer moved a curl of dark hair from her face with her wrist. She approached the broadcast. She stared at the screen.

A nurse spoke to the woman with a donut. "Bad pastry, darling?"

Double doors blew open as a nurse followed the woman running through it and shouted, "Ne Shoul, is that him? So who's watching the database?"

***

Corporate friends of the current administration were paid monumental sums for quake recovery without knowing for what. Negative remarks about how The Quake was handled were viewed as unpatriotic and disrespectful to the victims. The Treasury extended debt limits with a Congressional nod and the Federal Reserve printed dollars with abandon. The President called for

210

foreign support and investment in America. If Greece, Italy, Spain, Ireland, Iceland, Portugal, and every other country could be saved by someone else, why not America? But US war debts, corporate giveaways, and social welfare scams could no longer be concealed off-book, all far worse than previously known. With global debt at seven times annual worldwide GDP, there was no cover for seven hundred trillion dollars in derivatives, collateral debt obligations, and credit default swaps never tamed by regulation. World financial markets sank and kept sinking.

Children began to disappear from schools, especially in mixed-race neighborhoods, despite America's post-racial era. Farmers defended their land with firearms against cities claiming eminent domain. All was paid for with the Chinese yuan or precious metals in stratospheric sums.

Grocery stores, ammunition retailers, garden-seed sellers emptied across the continent. Mosques closed, churches bulged, synagogues hired security. Apocalyptic speech dominated airways as The Quake had been predicted by Revelation and Nostradamus.

Doctors were flooded with false claims of sickness for antibiotics. With the last antibiotics manufacturer in the US closed in 2004, America was wholly dependent on foreign supplies, not infrequently found to be inert placebos. Police and the National Guard protected drug shipments; several guards shot stealing for themselves. Outbreaks of common bacterial infections, easily halted by modern drugs, swept Asia and Africa's Sahel with every pharmaceutical on Earth selling to the world's highest bidder in California. Third World nations were forced to rely on their own healthcare, most of which had none. No Doctors Without Borders, no roaming mobile clinics, no nurses on loan.

US world-aid of every kind ceased. In ways not fully grasped, the United States had helped, placated, corrupted, or constrained the global human mind in ways as mysterious as mental illness. As one of the smallest nations on Earth with America's biggest bankroll, Israel found its loans forgiven as standard practice, now demanded paid in full, despite immense pressure from the country's most powerful lobby.

America had been financially busted for decades. Finally, America believed it. Even illegal foreigners in the US, favored over

American citizens with in-state tuition and rent assistance, were forced to go without, spawning cries of racism, followed by claims that genocide was imminent.

With desperate need for economic activity, the US government lifted all rules and oversight on resource extraction and harvest limits. Companies commenced to savage one-sixth of Alaska, from the North Slope to Bristol Bay. Expanded operations led the world's last salmon fishery to begin its exit thanks to mine tailings. Grizzly bears were escorted the way of Great Plains buffalo as a matter of labor safety.

Charities dependent on prosperity to save vanishing species from the effects of prosperity withered without cash, as Japan and Norway led whales in the Antarctic Whale Sanctuary to oblivion. Without funds to protect elephants, poachers slaughtered remaining populations, their ivory smuggled out of Africa on official Chinese Communist Party aircraft for religious iconography in Asia. The only elephants remaining were those evolving under the selective pressure of ivory hunters; elephants born with a mutation that made them tuskless. But their respite was brief, as elephants, along with Dian Fossey's last four hundred highland gorillas, were razed for bushmeat. Earth's last tigers, sea turtles, harp seals, were driven into extinction because Asian myths alleged their bones magically cured any ailment, sold most per ounce within California's City of Angels.

After years of tense European toleration, thousands of Islamists set ablaze their host cities of Paris, Amsterdam, Berlin. The Netherlands and Australia deported them all, radical and innocent, dumped on desert coasts of Arab nations, fully intending they starve there. France expelled Ghanaians as threats to French jobs. Germany expunged the country of Turks. Greece and Turkey fired weapons over Cyprus again. Having tried to sterilize Tibetans decades ago, allowing Chinese parents more than one child only in Tibet, Chinese authorities rounded up hidden pockets of natives and shot them all. To show solidarity, China dispatched one ship of food and used clothing for the port of Long Beach, as its navy engaged in harmless naval exercises off the coast of California.

***

Ne Shoul held Morgan's belt as he leaned over the tall ship's bow. Sails cracked in the wind. White tops exploded against the hull in San Francisco Bay. The slender, white Transamerica Pyramid signaled a periodic red light above the fog on land.

Morgan shouted, "There's a crack in the earth down there! Under such strain, it thrusts one-time seafloor three miles into the sky a hundred miles away! Same crack that ruined Southern California."

Morgan faced Ne Shoul. "I won't ply the waters of Europa," he said. "I can't change the destiny of eight billion humans or bring Amur leopards back to life. But if you and I are the answer to that celebrated split by the gods, then our union will fix the universe. You are the agent of my salvation, Ne Shoul, not God."

"And a brilliant team of doctors, Morgan."

Morgan felt disfigurements on his face. To port, though misty distance, he could see deckside sailors on a naval vessel. "Look at that," he said. "Troop carrier. World War Two vintage…And there are others. This is a commemoration of something big."

A sailor's arms outstretched. He held Japan's rising sun aflutter in the airstream. Sailors lifted arms in the shape of a V.

Morgan turned to them. He raised both hands. "Yes! Victory!" He stood at attention. He saluted the ships. "Like Independence Day, it comes every year on September second," he said. "And my father died on that day, VJ Day, Victory over Japan Day. A choice day to die for a man who served in the Pacific…Except they're early. VJ Day is in September, It's August, right?"

"Morgan, it's October second."

"It is? Then they're late."

Rows of sailors in white stood by their railings. The gray ships steamed through vapor to join it and vanish from sight.

"Ne Shoul, look at that. They look like ghosts."

"Look pretty real to me," she said.

"In *Field of Dreams*, Ray's wife could see the ghosts he saw on the baseball diamond. I wonder if anybody else can see them?"

Ne Shoul tapped Morgan on the shoulder. "Morgan, what did you—" She bent over.

"Ne Shoul, what's wrong?"

She held her stomach and giggled, "Growing pains?"

"You're fully grown, Ne Shoul. Where does it hurt?"

"It doesn't." She began to laugh.

"What's so funny? And stand up, please."

She straightened, rubbing her abdomen. "Actually..." She giggled again. "Actually, it felt...pretty good." She bent over laughing. "Maybe these ships are sent from heaven," she said. "A representation of something else. Like Zeus in the form of an eagle in his flight over Semele. Nothing happens, and yet she becomes pregnant." Ne Shoul squeaked, "Maybe that's what this is—immaculate conception!"

"You won't need that. But just in case...Nine months will put you in labor on or about...late June. Summer solstice. But what would that mean, I wonder?"

Laughing now hysterically, Ne Shoul tried to breathe, barely able to stand.

Morgan patted her back and gazed into the mist. "Let's see...Summer solstice. Maximum light, maximum good? Or a return to darkness? Remember, winter solstice is the birth of light from darkness, resurrection of a new day, a new way, that birthdate assigned by the Church to baby Jesus. So what would summer solstice be? Jesus returns early? Jesus late? Anti-Jesus?"

Morgan pulled her up. "I have a question. But you have to stop laughing." He waited. Ne Shoul tried to compose herself. "About this conception topic," he said. "When might we consider some experimentation in that direction? Practice drills. Certification all the parts are in order. I'm a little rusty."

She stroked Morgan's hair. "Dear honey bunny, nature demands you pursue what you must. I, on the other hand, am the civilizing force. I've got to ensure you're authentic."

"I am authentic."

"You are sincere and quite genuine. Your genes want in my jeans, they aren't lying." Ne Shoul chuckled. "But once your lust has been quenched, will love grow?"

"You didn't hear my bit on Europa and leopards and—"

"Yes, bravo! Wonderful and quite romantic. Truly. But only if love thrives beyond immediate urge is consummation of it justified. You see, sex is an ingredient of love, Morgan. Not, as present fads preach, apart from love. Not a primal act, a divine union."

Morgan stared at her. "Wow...Sounds like something I'd say. Not that I believe it entirely."

She shrugged. "See?"

"I was joking."

"Sex is not mere animal nature, spoken of in clinical terms, my sweet," she said. "It's not about power or dominance."

She pressed her palm against his chest. "You must realize, Morgan, if we move forward, there is no possibility for separation, for if that option exists, we are already separate. No free choice. No me. Only us. The family."

"OK, all right already, we're on the same page. Let's get after it."

She touched her finger to Morgan's shirt. She flicked his chin. "Yearning, said Augustine, makes the heart grow deep."

"Ooh, I like that too. Part of me likes it...OK, I'll wait."

She whispered in his ear, "Do you think you can?" She kissed his cheek.

He winced. "Ouch. Careful, missy. Morgan's law: the success of love hinges on the chemistry of conversation. Keep talking like that, and I'll build the manger. But a kiss doesn't hurt. Just be careful where you kiss."

Morgan turned to look for ships through fog. Ne Shoul wrapped arms about his chest as they met a barely visible future. Pylons of a shadowy Golden Gate passed overhead to punctuate the moment and disappeared in moisture they were born from.

Morgan clamped his fists and yelled at the sky hard enough to pierce the damp. "See this? You missed me!

"What man can lay claim to birth a third time?" he said.

Generated by a moderate jolt on land and beneath their feet, a shock rippled across the water. Unseen ships answered in howls about the bay like whales calling over the scale of a sea. One by one, church bells pealed seven times from the hills of San Francisco.

Morgan turned to Ne Shoul. "Hear that? Seven bells. What's that supposed to mean?"

## 25. Dancing With Oblivion

Morgan raked grass in his backyard on the slopes of San Francisco Bay with his son, John, named after Morgan's father.

"Remember our camp at Lassen Peak, John? You were particularly interested in my lecture on DNA. That's the part of humanity you should stick to. These ideas of yours are completely abnormal. You're a thirteen-year-old. Go play with model airplanes, wonder if girls don't have cooties. You're at least two years from idealistic notions of saving the world."

Morgan pointed. "Grass." He pointed at a bag. "Bag." He pointed at John. "Work." He chuckled.

"I dunno, Dad. You assign me all these books to read, half of them I can't understand. I guess it just seems right to talk about these things."

"I assign. You read. I tell you what to think. Who needs discussion?" Morgan snickered.

"So you know all the answers?"

"That's right. I know all the answers...almost. A friend of mine at The Center where I used to work, he knew all the answers. His name was Kip."

"I want to know what other people think," John said.

"No, you don't."

"My teacher said when someone has all the answers with no debate, you should worry."

"Liberals and conservatives killed debate before you were born, John. You didn't support the troops if you disagreed with this country's impulse to go on another crusade. You were a bigot if you didn't kiss the feet of anyone who could define themselves as a victim of something. We all knew what we were *supposed* to say at our monthly diversity training. Then, as now, our indignation industry required a steady diet of burnt offerings. What a joke." John frowned. Morgan waved him off. "Well, it's true. Today, disagreement is hate speech. Cross the administration, you're a terrorist. Tell the truth, that's political. You say moral depravity is a cause of our decline? Why, you holier-than-thou Christian fundamentalist. You see the natural world is in tatters? You hippie tree hugger. Americans don't *debate* to find *truth*, John, they *argue to win*. And for any argument, what Americans want is conquest— who won the fistfight, not truth, not reason. Never forget that."

"People disagree, Dad."

"The battle now is over conformist recitals of this or that creed, John. While we wear ourselves out in some socioeconomic crevice to learn ever more about ever less. You don't see it because after mere years of awareness on this orb, you have nothing to compare with. I recognize decline when I see it. I've lived the comparison."

"Why is America now so different from any other time?"

"For the same reason Rome is no longer with us," Morgan said. He pointed the rake handle at his son. "And what is that reason? I mean for great civilizations that can't be destroyed by others, only by themselves. It's the disease of mutating norms, John. As illness is silently communicated among concentrated numbers, so too, norms are concealed person to person, most rapidly in cities. Of course, improvements occur in norms, as with any human venture. But the positive advance of slavery's abolition and women's suffrage get wrapped up with distorted assessments of Kinsey's human sexuality and some frustrated gender theorist's definition of marriage as the torture of women.

"Mutation does not only happen to living things, John. Look how the Supreme Court transformed a right to privacy, which kept personal matters from public view, into a right to make free choices, into a right to abortion. When my father was a child, the Bill of Rights was a safeguard for states against federal intrusion. By the time I arrived, the Bill of Rights was used to *justify* federal intrusion. An interpretation originally envisioned in 1938 over a case involving *adulterated milk!*" Morgan cracked the rake handle against a shallow stone wall between his yard and the bay downhill.

217

"People naturally push the boundaries of acceptable behavior, John, just as they press technology. We call it innovation. It's what humans do, with everything. But social norms come in bundles, and we're no longer able to separate them because society has omitted the filter of truthfulness. Hence, our capacity for reason is in shambles. As Kip said, all we have now is *motivated reason*— accepting evidence only if it supports what we want to believe, rejecting all else. In other words, lying to ourselves. We're a nation of liars now.

"Notice that in science, John, nature judges your hypothesis true or false. While everywhere else, one may offer any notion of cause and effect, no matter how outlandish, with impunity. This leads to an abandonment of all standards, including truthfulness. So, perspectives are ever more perverted, until thresholds are crossed, and our collective immune system no longer sustains the body of society. Add consequences of The Quake—not least of which is that Southern California is now a third world country in our own borders—and we see clearly that one event was America's last straw in a slow-motion decline.

"But there's one weighty difference about this stumble, John. Deep down, *no one cared.* I don't mean no one cared about The Quake and its aftermath. I mean, no Americans cared about our ensuing demise. The rest of the world seemed to almost expect our indifference. After the flags and bumper stickers, the entire event quietly submerged all but a sense that we deserved it. Liberal intellectuals yearning to punish America for its crimes had groomed this terrain for decades. The religious Right could smell the Left had pilfered our purpose, sensing opportunities for redemption. But neither could steer the outcome because once a threshold is crossed, it doesn't matter what political party you pick."

"Dad, I don't think I get all this."

"Give me that sweeper. I need something to shake when I talk, and this rake is too heavy." Morgan grabbed the broom. "All the way back in 1835, John, Tocqueville—he's on your booklist too—predicted this would happen. Americans have freedom of speech, he said, not freedom of mind. Our loop of allowable thought centers on just two extremes now as the noose gets tighter. Our population numbers are too expansive, our senses compressed by too much societal complexity. Whipsawed from one outrage to the next, *we must become inflexible* to compensate for this constant uncertainty we've created. Our dogmas and creeds are the answer. We stake our turf. We claim control when we know we have none. Frantic for faith and trigger happy about every issue, whether it's to hang the Duke lacrosse team or invade another country."

"Duke who?"

"Duke, a University. Lacrosse. It's a sport. The team was pilloried nationwide for something they never did back around 2010. I suppose you don't remember that."

John laughed. "Dad, I wasn't born yet."

"As Benjamin Franklin said, John, the more corrupt people become, the more need they have of masters. As Jefferson said, an industrial economy would school the people in corruption. And so it has. We created what was once a commercial powerhouse able to fend off foreign invasion, and while we did, we debased our souls.

"Remember, John, it was Hamilton, Madison, and Jay's Federalists who dismissed moral teaching in favor of systems, processes, and institutions to offset the fact you can't make everybody virtuous. But that doesn't mean we shouldn't have tried. We should have tried, for those few who would have learned the moral lessons. But we decided virtue would hinder indulgence, slow economic growth, and demand standards. So America disconnected *the Good* and our founding morals from practice and perceptions while embracing every foreign value system. Open to other ways, closed to our own, we call this *open-mindedness* and *multiculturalism*. This has unstitched social fibers in the most dangerous way. A people rife with contempt, superstitious about everything, and eager for a savior. Just as an exhausted Rome was eager when Jesus came on the scene.

"What matters most to societies are the soft parts, John, the small parts, the parts you can't see, like imperceptible atoms that hold up the sun."

Morgan scanned the bay. "And how do we put all these genies back in the bottle? Answer: it can't be done. Because this is what civilizations do, John. If you think American history was extraordinary in the past, and it was, you just wait, kiddo. Rocky Mountain passes will bear massive armies, and the Great Lakes will see naval battles between monstrous powers homegrown. For generations, people have asked, What will become of America? Now we know. America was a great idea, but all great ideas commit suicide by their own excesses."

"Dad, do you hate America?"

Morgan hesitated. "For what we once strived to be, no. For what we are, yes. My disdain is for our abandonment of reason the Founders employed to overcome our base nature."

John whistled. "Geeze, Dad, you're sure a cheery person."

Morgan withdrew a copper disk from his pocket and spun it in the air. He grabbed it and squinted at the disk slapped on the back of his hand. "Heads," Morgan said. "I'm right. It's always heads.

"Every cause, every person, every civilization dances with oblivion, John—daring it. In every case, the music stops. When America dissolves, it will seem another mystery of history. Such a penalty handed down to my offspring does not absolve me of responsibility. You're here because of me, to suffer. And suffer you will. But you'll suffer a lot less if you purge these idealistic notions of saving the world. You're *thirteen years old*."

Morgan flipped the flattened penny at John's face. The boy snatched it in midair. He covered it on the back of his hand.

"Well? What is it, John?"

John looked closely at a smeared image impressed on the copper. "Tails."

Morgan bent over John's hand, pointing at it. "See? I'm right. I'm always right!"

John chuckled. He put the penny in his pocket. "Laws and constitutions must go hand in hand with the process of the human mind, Dad. As that becomes more developed, as new discoveries are made, institutions have to keep up."

Morgan stared at him. "Catchy. Who told you that?"

"The nature of life is realized in the acts of living, Dad. We should take charge when he can, but don't give up just because we're not sure of the future."

"And who told you that?"

"I read it in a book you gave me that your father gave you."

"Gimme that book back."

"I guess the fall of Rome was followed by Dark Ages, Dad, but your last reading assignment said the Renaissance came next, then Enlightenment, then the Founders. Could they see what they saw, think what they thought, or do what they did without those others before them?"

Morgan looked baffled. "You may be thirteen, but damn it, you sound like a man."

"Every civilization can go only so far, Dad. Success or failure is not measured by individual civilizations, but by the sweep of *humanity* and *life* on this planet."

Dazzled, Morgan walked about John. He examined him like an alien visitor. "Say that again."

John laughed. "See, Dad, there's hope for you. Pretty soon, you'll believe in God too."

Morgan cringed. "*What?* Good grief, don't run off on some spiritual mission too."

Morgan looked for Ne Shoul. She leaned against the door frame. He shook his finger at her. "Ah-ha…Ne Shoul, do not confuse the boy." He focused back on John. "Your mother gave you potent phrases to irritate me. Fine. I get it."

Ne Shoul shrugged. "I didn't tell him anything."

"There's a lot of truth in the scriptures, Dad. Maybe it's all true."

"Scriptures cannot be read like a newspaper, John. It's not news, it's myth— Now, your mother claims myth is a kind of truth all the same." Morgan winked at her. "So I have another reading assignment for you, John, just after you finish Richard Gregg's *Voluntary Simplicity* and the usual quiz: Franz Rosenzweig, a Jewish scholar who said Bible stories are not facts but expressions of spiritual reality of our inners lives. *Metaphor*, kiddo. Metaphors are symbolic, pretend, figures of speech."

"I see the same message in the Bible, over and over. Doesn't look pretend to me."

"Really? Then why the famous variation that Saint Augustine battled for years to reconcile when he found Genesis chapters one and two report creation in a different order? It's not that each chapter elaborates different things—though they do—it's man created last in one, man created first in the other. Birds then man, or man then birds? Did Noah collect two animals of every sort, or— just four verses later—was it seven of the clean and two of the unclean? While six verses after that, two of every kind, clean and unclean march on the boat, 'as God commanded.' Huh? And what about Enosh? Was he the first to receive the sacred name of God, or was it Moses? Remember, this is a book in which Herod's murder of innocent two-year-olds is a crime, but God's killing of innocent children in Egypt is justice. This is the invariable word of God? Sure it is. God changes his mind within verses on a whim. There are thousands of such contradictions in Old and New, John." Morgan held his hand before John's face. "And don't tell me there were witnesses, because anybody who thinks eyewitness accounts constitute evidence is a lawyer, on a hunt for the next UFO, or a believer. An eyewitness counts for nothing in science."

"To trust one's faith can be hard, Dad."

"On the contrary, that's easy. I'll tell you what's hard: to accept that my father, mother, and brothers *do not* continue elsewhere; that I am refused atonement for how I treated them; that I too am fated for termination. That's hard."

John leaned back against the table. He crossed his arms. He glanced at his mother. "My beliefs are not a matter of choice," he said. "My faith is a matter of conviction to a set of beliefs I didn't choose. But I'm bound to them anyway."

Morgan glared at Ne Shoul. She shrugged. "Don't blame me," she said.

Morgan leaned in. "So, John, you were spontaneously born with these beliefs? Choice, conviction—what's the difference? If all I need do is accept the canon, to join a support group of over two billion believers with the comfort and certainty that affiliation brings—that's easy."

"How do you explain so much evil in the world, Dad, if there's no fight between good and bad as the Bible says?"

"Because there are eight and one-half billion humans on this planet, John. If one in a thousand does something foolish today, that's eight and a half million foolish things today alone. Some of those foolish things will be wicked. *Think* when you read this stuff. *Probe for unstated assumptions.* If God created humans, God gave humans the power of reason, presumably with the expectation we'd apply it.

"So here's some reason for you, John. To quote Exodus, 'At

midnight God struck down all the firstborn of Egypt, from the firstborn of Pharaoh to the firstborn of prisoners in the dungeon to the firstborn of livestock.' Firstborn of Pharaoh's *prisoners? Livestock?* Do you believe God had a *reason* to murder innocent children? Infants, toddlers, *livestock?* By what logic? Livestock flunked the nine-plagues warning test and failed to choose God?"

"Because Pharaoh wouldn't free his people, Dad."

"Pharaoh had no choice, John! Exodus 4:21, God tells Moses: 'I myself shall make Pharaoh obstinate, and he will not let my people go.' Then he commits to kill the firstborn because Pharaoh won't let his people go." Morgan laughed. "Psycho God Almighty of the universe can't devise another means? Even meager mortals will try persuasion, negotiation, sanctions, bribery. And from a God who commands thou shalt not kill? Ridiculous."

"God didn't send those kids to a painful hell because there is no hell like that in the Bible, Dad. It's not cruel. God put those kids to sleep, that's what it says. They'll wake up on earth when everything's fixed, saved from the bad world they lived in."

"An abortionist serves the same purpose, John. Why not line up all pregnant mothers, so their unborn babies get an early meeting with God's grace?"

"Because an abortion doctor would not be saving the people that led to Jesus, Dad."

"So the abortion doctor would be committing an immoral act?"

"Of course."

"With further study of the Founders, John, you'll find they revealed something vital—process matters more than their ends. If moral ends are reached by immoral means, those ends lose legitimacy, poisoned with immorality. That's why they gave us a messy democracy instead of no-nonsense tyranny.

"Consider this analogy, John. If you ran a long-distance race to win a fortune for your *church*, would you cheat to win? Would the moral end of feeding the poor, or aiding the sick still be moral? No. To do that, you cheated. Paul says to do evil so good may come is immoral. Ditto God's immoral process, John. The murder of innocent children to free others who lead then to Jesus is immoral."

John hesitated. "But God is infinite, Dad. Humans are not. Would you expect a chimpanzee to understand physics the way you do?"

"Ah, but it's not that complicated, John. Cold-blooded murder is just plain cold-blooded murder. You're mental acrobatics forces moral logic to conform to your book in order to save it. Your God is loving and jealous. He's wrathful, plays favorites, demands obedience like a human king, and throws tantrums. Does that sound like an infinite, all-powerful God, or a person? And why would that be? Because people made God in *our* image, not the other way around. Who needs to invent a devil, you've already got one and prayed to to boot. What Thomas Paine called that atheistic blasphemy, the ultimate idolatry. Who's the sinner now?"

"Sounds like you think you can judge God, Dad."

"No, John. Judge what *man* attributes *to* God, called scriptures. For me, ghosts, goblins, and witches are a short distance from belief in dead people that rise from the coffin. Whether that resurrected savior is Osiris, twenty-five hundred years before Jesus, or dozens of others in that same role before him, all virgin-born—so they claimed."

John looked away. "Jeepers...You don't believe in Jesus either?"

"Jesus as God, as most Christians believe, or Jesus as the *son* of God, as the Bible says? What I believe, John is that there can be no greater hero than a man who would live by the truth all the way to his doom."

"But that's what Jesus did."

"Oh no, if Jesus was God or a god, where's the risk in death on the cross? There's no loss. No permanent consequence to his suffering. But for the man who does this, who knows his life will end if he stands for justice, *that* is greatness worthy of worship."

John shook his head. "I guess there's more to it than that, but I don't think I can explain it."

"Excellent! You were beginning to frighten me. Tell me when you're able."

"When you are able, Dad."

"Me? Oh!" Morgan looked to Ne Shoul, hands on his hips. "You are your father's son. I'm afraid of no challenge from your Bible, or your God. Whatever it is you have to say, I'd like to hear it." John was silent. "Fine. Then I submit whatever it is you feel as a manifestation of God is not God, John, but a manifestation of *you*. The astonishing result of being alive and knowing it. Don't externalize it like these Levantine religions do."

"I don't know as much as you, Dad, but I know I need Grace to live a proper life."

"You're thirteen, how do you know?"

"You say we invented religion, Dad. Are the inventions around us not real? Planes, trains, automobiles? Maybe we are religiously eager, or whatever you said. Maybe that's the good news, not the bad."

Morgan scowled from under gray eyebrows at his son. He peered at Ne Shoul. He tapped the broom handle once on the stone wall and looked at the bay.

"Look, Dad." John motioned above haze on the horizon.

"Full moon, John."

"Think there's people up there, like you and me, only looking back our way?"

"Of course. They're Chinese."

***

Morgan and Ne Shoul sat on a couch by the fireplace, their reflection in sliding glass doors to the patio. Ne Shoul scratched the back of his neck. "I recognize that look. What's the matter?"

"It's September second, 2026," Morgan said. "It's ten twenty-five p.m. in Iowa."

Ne Shoul shrugged. "And eleven twenty-five in New York. So?"

Perspiration formed on Morgan's temple. He stood to look over shelves crammed with hundreds of books. He pulled free a volume by William Clark, *Sex and the Origins of Death*. You introduced me to this, remember? Clark taught how in old age our bodies strive for failure through programmed cell death, PCD, evidenced by wrinkles and forgetfulness." Morgan pulled the skin tight on his face with one hand, his eyelids stretched downward. "See how I used to look?"

"You look like you had a facelift. You never looked like that."

"I want a facelift. I want a body lift. I want an age…reduction."

He returned the book. Next to another about ancient Egypt, he grabbed one titled, *Fundamentals of Electromagnetic Theory*. He shook the book in his grip. "I remember," he said, "when I was proud to understand mysteries of nature few could grasp. The older I get, the better I was."

He opened the text. He slid his thumb over marginalia. "Look." He angled pages toward Ne Shoul. "Right there. See how I smudged it? Those molecules of graphite were placed there by me when I was twenty-something. They've been right there, closed in darkness, undisturbed for over forty years. From a closet in Iowa to California. Friends I didn't know I had. Do you find that odd?"

"Which part? That it happened or that you thought of it?"

"Neither. That something I did long ago remains suspended in time, like an archeological find."

He turned a page and another. "There's more." He fanned sheets of paper. Pencil calculations, question marks, and exclamations stuttered before his eyes like a paper kinetoscope. "Ooo...Look at them." Pages provoked hair on his forehead to waltz in a breeze of secrets no longer known. He whispered, "I could have been something...Something to myself."

He snapped shut the book and carried it to the couch. He sat. "Better review this. It's about time to study for *the final*, don't you think?"

Fog snaked through open patio doors, consumed by heat from the fire. Ne Shoul waited.

Morgan looked at his wristwatch. He lifted his index finger. "On this very day, thirty-three years ago, my father took his last breath...Now." He snapped his fingers. "It's ten-thirty p.m. in Iowa. I'm sixty-seven years old."

"I get it," Ne Should said. "Sorry, old man, you'll have to put up with me a little longer."

"Maybe I have to wait for ten-thirty California time," he said. "Maybe I messed up the future when I changed time zones."

Ne Shoul slapped his shoulder, smiling. "You're afraid."

"Damn right, I'm afraid."

"Oh, Morgan, of dying?"

"Not of dying. Of being dead. I'm as old as he was, and there's so much left to do, to figure out. Time to be with you—" Morgan shrugged. "Naturally, I had to say that."

"What would you say to him if you had the opportunity,

Morgan?"

"Don't know. Guys need something to do in order to have serious conversations. That way, we can talk and not have to look at each other. Maybe we'd fish. On the Wapsi—watchful of bunnies this time. It would be something simple, to the point, not fluffy. Wish I'd done that when I had the chance. Instead, I punched the man. After he just slapped the conceit out of me. Whatever caused it, I don't know—Vietnam, hippies, Nixon, aftereffects of the sixties when individualism became pathogenic."

"You were a kid like every kid, Morgan."

"Did you ever see the movie, *A River Runs through It*?" Ne Should shook her head. "Right—you weren't conceived yet. In that movie, there's a small boy told to eat his porridge. He refuses. His father, a minister, tells the boy to remain at the table until it's eaten and leaves. Waste not want not. Boy stares at bowl. Father checks progress. Hours pass. The day passes. Finally, father and family return, pray, and let the boy leave. He'll never eat his porridge. You don't defeat people like that, Ne Shoul. They defeat themselves."

"And you were like that boy in the movie."

"And that's the way I left it. That fight in the yard dominated our lives until his was over. Competing till the end."

"For what, Morgan?"

"Independence. Maybe. I dunno. It was also the era when vilifying your father was in fashion. I bought into that crap like everybody else. Plus, I was insecure. Some counselor stamped me with a learning disability. Other kids got wind of it, called me a retard. A day couldn't pass without a fistfight." He shook his head. "In the principal's office—my second home—Opal, the secretary, would cluck her tongue and say, 'You'll be nothing but a ditch digger.' I didn't know what it meant, but it was the way she said it. I couldn't fight her, but at home my father was available. People think born fighters are strong. They're not.

"I remember how surprised I was to see my brother Junior take advice from my dad, and smile about it. Like it was a gift from the wise man. To me, advice equaled insult. You thought I didn't know something? That was like calling me stupid. Time for a fight. Instead of independence, I got isolation. When I got up from that table, I did so on my own. There was no prayer. Nobody there to say, 'OK, you win.' I stood aloof with my *individual rights*, the *real me*, and lost the peace. Peace that comes to sons and fathers who become friends. That battle should have ended when I graduated from the U with my physics degree. At graduation, my dad was so full of pride. He'd just seen a show called *Cosmos* by an astronomer named Carl Sagan. And then he said something I'll never forget: 'I want to ask you about something remarkable.' But I didn't let him. I turned to someone else or changed the subject, I don't remember. That's all he said. Like some kind of truce or role reversal, as though I could tell him something he didn't know. But I didn't know another way. I stuck to the old plan, and in the end, my will prevailed. At his casket, I realized that ancient Greek caution: which is more tragic, to fail at one's great ambition, or to succeed?"

"You and John are friends, Morgan."

"But John's fuse is not perpetually lit like mine. Even when he tries to irritate me, he doesn't irritate me. Everything he does is measured, mild, pleasant. He has insight I could never imagine at his age. He's more insightful than I am now, and he's a kid. Conversely, I was an expert in irritation when I was a teen. My skills were peerless. I was rather proud of it actually."

"OK, you were a brat."

"I was a terrorist. That time my father and I fought in the yard, I never told you the whole story, because it was too awful to tell. So before it's too late for confession...An investigative journalist set out to probe accusations of American atrocities in Vietnam. He tracked down a particular platoon of marines and didn't get the story he planned for. He found them after they'd been outnumbered in a firefight. No airstrikes, they ran out of ammo, fought hand to hand until captured. One of them was Junior. So defiant, they made him watch his buddies get their throats slit one after another. When they got to Junior—" Morgan paused. He considered books on the shelf. "Arms tied to a branch, legs staked to the ground, they skinned him alive." Morgan adjusted in his seat. He straightened his pant leg. He flicked a speck of lint off the couch. "Papers published a picture from a distance. My brother dangling from a tree. Sheets of skin draped from his ankles. To the Viet Cong, that was an advertisement: this is what we do to Americans." Morgan wiped sweat from his brow. He looked at the moisture on his fingers as though to wonder where it came from. "No one spoke for a week in our house after that. My parents did not mention Junior again. Not even memories of him. I blamed my father, as though the worst insult was to erase Junior's life to ease his pain.

"With our bout in the yard, I told my father that hunting deer—what to him was harvest, learning from the Depression, using every part of that animal, like our ancestors did, including the skin for clothing—I told him it was equivalent to what the VC did to Junior. My father never hunted again after that. My accusation stuck, just the way I wanted. I trashed a way of life that was both sustenance and, for people like him, respectful. I tried to apologize, but when I did, it was in a letter he never saw." Morgan watched the fire. "Years later, I sacrificed to make those films to pay for my sins. But they didn't save the world. Or me. So does the sacrifice still count? Apparently not."

Ne Shoul rubbed his forearm. "What would you say to him?"

"Maybe how impressed I am that he was able to be who he was. After all he saw—The Depression, World War Two, 1968—all the realizations of what humans are made of, and still so respectful. He truly liked people. Among this species that's quite an accomplishment. Just look at me; except for you and John, I can barely stomach an encounter with my own race."

"You talk so tough, you one hundred percent softy. What else would you say, Morgan?"

"I'd tell him something no one today would understand; that he was a superior citizen."

"Would you want him to say he was proud of you? That of all you put yourself through, you were able to be who you are, like him?"

Morgan shook his head. "Sins never perish, Ne Shoul, and they shouldn't. We should pay for what we've done, and pay some more. Only the craven excuse themselves by sacrificing someone else to pay for their crimes."

Ne Shoul sighed. "How I wish I could convert you. So you'd understand what you can't or won't allow—forgiveness. Of *yourself*."

He waved her away with a flip of his wrist. "Forgiveness is for the perfect and cowards. I'm neither."

229

Ne Shoul rapped him on the knee. "I know what he'd say to you. It would be simple, to the point, not fluffy. He'd say, 'Even when you tried to irritate me, you didn't irritate me.' Fathers see themselves in their sons, as you see yourself in John. He knew how much you cared for him, Morgan."

"How do you know?"

"Female insight."

"You never met him."

"I've seen his picture."

"Ah, then you know all about him."

"I know him through you, Morgan."

"You know only what I told you. He was dead before you were out of diapers."

"It's not simply what you've said, Morgan. The best things can't be spoken, remember."

"I didn't say that. Joseph Campbell said it, and someone else said it to him."

"You so frustrate me!"

"But you love it."

Ne Shoul covered her face, growling.

Morgan looked at his hands. "Perhaps this PCD is a form of kindness—to finish the guilt. To pave a way for all these blameless carbon atoms in and out of living beings so many times before me. From the soil grows green life eaten by an insect, eaten by a bird, the bird eaten by a man. The man dies, and off go those carbon atoms on their merry way. Makes me wonder how many atoms in me were part of T-Rex or brontosaurus...I used to have a *How and Why* book about dinosaurs." He looked toward shelves. "I just don't want to be extinct like dinosaurs...But ants survived their times. And my grandparents on both sides lived near or past one hundred— sharp as a tack at that age. Maybe I've got their genes." Morgan's eyes narrowed.

"OK," Ne Shoul said. "That's the 'I have an idea' look."

"Is there an equivalence, dear wife, between cells of our body and individuals in civilization? Do civilizations fail, not by chance or circumstance, but because decline is *intended*, without knowing it? Like William Clark said of our aging bodies, death is worked toward, without wanting to. Is this the cause of America's deterioration, and every civilization before us? Some kind of self-destruct gene, sparked when humans live in large groups for extended periods? A way to force us into smaller groups, maybe—

"I just had an original thought. I need a pen." He stepped to the desk. He scribbled on a sheet of paper. "I'm gonna write a book. Better hustle. Clock's ticking."

Ne Shoul laughed. "I love you in new ways almost every day, you crazy old man."

Morgan wrote, nose to paper. "Almost? I can't hear you. Could you repeat that?"

She followed him to the desk. She leaned on his shoulders and read what he wrote. "I said you're crazy."

"No, the part before that."

She hugged him. "Don't you dare ever leave me."

"How could I leave a girl half my age with the best legs in California?"

"And don't you forget it," she said.

"Plus, I'm a nutty old man. Who would have me?"

"Yes," Ne Shoul said. "You're right about that."

Writing, Morgan paused to check the time. It'll be 10:30 p.m. soon—in California, he thought.

# 26. Elephant Dreams

John and Morgan raked grass in their backyard above San Francisco Bay. "No Spring Break for you, college kid. Just because you survived a freshman semester doesn't mean your visit is labor free." He pointed at John and a bag on the table. "Boy. Bag. Work."

John smiled and turned for the bag. He wore a t-shit reading, "The University of Iowa, Idaho City, Ohio."

"Tell me again, John, why you picked my alma mater? Can't be what I told you, because I didn't tell you much."

"I read this amazing story once, Dad. It was about fishing on a stream in a remarkable place, and somehow—I don't know how—I knew I'd find it in Iowa."

"You chose the U of I to *fish?*"

John shrugged. "When I got to the U, I unpacked that old rod and reel you gave me, that split-willow basket creel I found in the attic, and I got in the car with—"

"That was my dad's reel," Morgan said. "I never knew about a split basket...What'd you call it?"

"Dad, I got in the car without the slightest idea of where to go and ended up on the Wapsipinicon River. You told me about it when I was a kid. Soon as I saw that sign, I remembered. Not a name you come across often. I don't know how, but that river occupies a place rich with art and love—two things you told me don't require an education to figure out. That place I read about. Where nature is still allowed to be natural, to be wild."

"What'd you discover there, John, the Iowa Memorial Tree? Iowa's last wild place to survive the corn ethanol scam? John, that state's ninety-eight percent plowed, two percent city, can't be too wild. Most modified state in the Americas. No wonder its young people leave."

John chuckled. "Dad…It's true, there's not a lot of nature left. But what's there invites you to see more, hear more."

"More what? Herbicide? The last cougar was terminated in 1867. Elk and bison by eighteen seventy-something. Black bears and wolves were liquidated before the last Indian was shot. And with top predators exterminated, they wondered why their deer populations were uncontrollable. Until the corn ethanol scam savaged their last square meter of habitat."

John paused, almost apologetic. "Limited as it is, there's a boundless sense about it. Every weekend I fish in that first place I found. Take my books, watch the bobber on a worm line, and fly cast when I break between chapters."

"So, you're a fly fisherman." Morgan sat on the shallow stone wall, rake in hand.

John laughed. "I am now." He placed one foot atop the wall. He leaned against his knee. "You oughta see it, Dad. I walk that fly across the water like it was holy."

"My dad used to cast a fly like that. It was quite a sight."

"I cast while birds keep me company, water bugs scurry about eddies, and squirrels watch me from afar. There's conversations going on out there, Dad, lots of 'em. Conversations I can't decipher, but I don't need to because all of us mean the same thing."

Morgan smiled. "You sound like your grandfather."

"Out there all the world has the same sense, Dad. The same inclination toward this mystery of being alive. No matter how they clothe it—Christian, Hindu, Shinto, muskrat, fish, or owl—they all say the same thing, in different ways. Even the plants, the trees, those waving filaments of moss underwater, day and night. The whole world is a part of something grand. Something unseen."

"If you can't understand them, how do you know, John?"

"I didn't say I can't understand them. I said I can't decipher what they say."

Morgan held up his hand. "Explain."

"Dad, when the cat jumps on your lap, does she need to ask to be loved? I suppose it's like that. But only in the most introductory way, because what they say out there is some kind of translation

233

of…of fondness and sorrow.

"Taking the opportunity to be with nature—and, Dad, I take all I can—one becomes in tune with it again. I say 'again' because nature is the *natural* state for humans. We only think it's alien because we've kept ourselves apart from it for so long. Sequestered in our cities, we see nature as different, but it's the deepest part of us, the real part, the first part. And I don't mean to simply personify my experience. There is something real. A unity, a purpose, a meaning in concert with and supported by…No, a consequence of whatever it is."

Morgan nodded. "Some kind of unity. I saw it in physics."

"Dad, I've been there all night with a campfire on the riverbank. Then one night, I stayed without a flame. I laid on that sandbar and watched the daily reminder, the cycle, the rise and fall. The birth of light from night, and night from light, and the message just keeps repeating, but nobody hears it." John leaned in. "*The scriptures aren't only in books, Dad.*" John motioned toward the city. "In our buildings, planes, trains, and automobiles, we can't hear it, though it remains. On the Wapsi, the high Sierras, desert wilderness, or silence of an ocean deep, there's a message *clear*. It never ceased to transmit, it just can't be heard over the makings of man. All we need is a chance to listen and listen, and listen some more.

"Dad, I know now why Jesus went to the desert and Buddha to the forest. *So they could hear.*"

But for thumb and finger working his chin, Morgan was still. He scrutinized John's voice.

"I wish you could see those trees, Dad. Shoulders spread so wide on those giants they poke holes in the sky. And those stars you love so much, why, they're so thick you have to brush them away from your face.

"And do you know what else, Dad?" John pointed above, then tapped himself on the chest. "*They* are a part of *this* mystery too." John pulled one hand close to his face. He stabbed one hand with the other. "Right there. In me. In you. You warned me not to externalize it, remember? Well, the stars are as close as this. I knew it before. I feel it now. You were right all those years ago at Lassen Peak. It's the first nativity and womb of the world. The sacred mountain and a boneyard. But the good news is, *the bones have voices.*

234

"It's a sight, Dad. It's a heck of a sight."

Morgan nodded. "I'll bet it is," he whispered. "I'll just bet it is."

The lighthouse on Alcatraz winked white in daylight. Heads could be seen to peek out of Coit Tower as the slender, white Louyang Pyramid signaled a periodic red light to the sky.

John reached into his bookbag. He withdrew a roll of paper, handing it to Morgan. "I drew this one night by the campfire."

Like a tavern piano player witness to the notes of Mozart, Morgan nearly dropped the page. "How did...You drew this?" He hovered over it. "I've done my share of drawing, but never...I know what you mean. No...I feel what you mean like you said."

John smiled and leaned down to pick up a leaf. "So, Dad, I moved to Iowa, and look what I found. What made you move to California? Was it Hollywood?"

Morgan laid John's drawing on the table. He kept watching it. "It's clear Hollywood can't compare to the Wapsi," he said. "But at the time, it seemed the thing to do. My forefathers moved from England and Germany to America westward. Murdered or married natives along the way—maybe the best part of us. Maybe the reason you understand nature so well. Just kept that westward spirit alive, I guess. There were times when I thought about going home."

"Isn't this home to you?"

"Oh, I love California, but my dad used to say home is where you're raised. And I used to say, The one thing I always have to look forward to is leaving wherever I am. Maybe a home is better than a road. For years, little voices told me to return. Yet look at this vista. Who could leave it and this house your grandparents gave us? But you did, John."

"Why didn't you just answer those little voices and go, Dad?"

"Wanted to return a hero. Lot of assholes back there told me what I couldn't do. I wanted to kick dirt in their face. Instead, they'd kick it in mine for the movies I made. Least that's what I used to think. Hell, they're probably most of 'em dead by now." Morgan snickered. "Maybe I should visit you there, John." Morgan scratched his chin. "But what if I don't make it back? I am seventy-two after all. My dad died when he was five years younger."

\*\*\*

235

Marion Christian Church in Iowa was vacant and dilapidated. As with all forgotten temples, parts of this one found their way to new shrines or living quarters. The rest, useless, remained. From the anteroom, Morgan faced the chapel. A length of the nave away, a large cross hung, broken and canted from a wire, a smashed podium below it. Morgan shook his head. Even I think that's sacrilege, he thought.

Scattered pews lingered about the place, their boards separated and warped. But for water damage, massive beams arced overhead as he remembered. Heed the church bell, he thought.

He dusted a sloping pew near where he once seated himself as a boy. He sat. Wood popped. In his mind, he heard music Ne Shoul had played, the dirge of Medwyn Goodall's "Behold the Darkness."

He whispered, "The Promised Land is in Marion. That's what we believe...But just look at this place. We turned to other gods, or once again revised the old one to be something else."

He looked for donation cards and hymn books. I remember seventy years ago better than yesterday, he thought.

He bowed his head toward a pile of leaves.

"Hello!" he shouted.

"Hello!" echoed the church.

"Am I talking to you, or are you talking to me?"

With so little to absorb sound, Morgan's voice repeated.

"I suppose I'm talking to myself," he said.

He brushed dust from wood beside him. "Hmm. Didn't hear an echo," he said.

Wood walls answered, "Hmm. Didn't hear an echo."

Morgan stood and walked the length of his pew. He tried to recall what the minister had said and what he looked like. Breeze murmured past empty panes, singing notes to the church as the church once sang to the wind. Trash clustered in a corner, rustled by invisible cyclones.

"The problem to solve is the passage," he whispered. "It's the hero journey everybody takes. But the hero has to believe to succeed in the adventure. You can't pretend to be in love to feel love. You can't pretend God is real and be saved by the idea."

He looked at the inclined cross and decapitated podium. The

corroded metal of a single organ pipe endured.

The miracle is not that people found it was real, he thought. The miracle is that it saved them from the pain of knowing our story has an end. An illogical match for that seemingly illogical termination of ourselves.

Faces of long-gone parishioners drifted through his mind. He stared up at lumber layered end to end and side by side like ribs inside a whale.

"It all seems like yesterday and forever ago," he murmured. "Yes, The Promised Land is in Marion, and The Promised Land is everywhere. But that doesn't make it any easier to reach."

He assessed boney fingers, deserving hymns of praise for their function and utility, and rewarded them a valediction instead. "The church and the man," he said. "In the same condition—discarded.

"Were I a believer, this result would not seem so wrong.

"But believe what? A heavenly paradise for our family and ourselves, or God that slays his children?"

All this, he decided, from the scriptures to the hymn books, from baptism to burial, this temple itself, it's an enormous time machine. A machine to pass us through that wall of the dead. To find resurrection and live forever among our loved ones and the God of our selective imagination. Even if there is no such God or place, it doesn't matter. It's not God that gets us there, it's us—the people, the congregation, the family who direct this transit.

He turned toward the cross. "But look at you," he said. "Does it work anymore?"

He studied one arch and the next. "On that, you are silent."

In through a window frame flew a robin, its home between wall and organ pipe. Chicks stretched, anxious for food.

"So there's life in the dead church," he said.

"Is that a spark, or an ember?"

***

Accented by incandescent canisters and with a constant buzz in the air, John and Morgan walked over an iron footbridge that traversed the Iowa River. A band of oaks led toward a meander of the river's ambit to Music Hall, capping a structural cavalcade of visual, sculpture, and theater arts.

"John, I still remember the intramurals and tug-o-wars; Roscoe the religious agitator; lazy all-day rides down that river still passing by, completely ignorant of my love for it. Still flush with pesticides, fertilizer, and pig shit, I'm sure."

A hen mallard led ducklings upstream by the dozen. One turned to peck a nagging itch, floated downstream, and scampered across water for siblings.

Morgan motioned uphill. "Old Capitol steps, kiddo. West side. My dad said a sunset is the most beautiful of things, and it's free."

"Dad, you're seventy-five years old, slow down."

At the base of Old Capitol, Morgan leaned back, panting, face to the sky. He spied the Capitol dome. "Surprised the state hasn't stolen that gold to pay pension debts," he said.

"Gold leaf, Dad. Not enough of it."

Professors marched with signs before dilapidated university facilities. Staff protested cutbacks. Students changed class by the thousands.

Morgan examined names carved in stone banners about buildings: Drude, Hertz, Becquerel; window frames of wood when wood was plentiful; stacks of books through those same windows from an age when people read them.

"Despite repeated social whiplash and my dead ideals," Morgan said, "there is something beautiful about how much tradition there is just in the place. And from this very place are components billions of miles distant, still on their way to forever. Pioneer and both Voyagers, racing away at 35,000 miles per hour. This university introduced NASA to the Space Age. What a time! Those disciplines which actually had to work—engineering, science, medicine—they were still strong when I was here."

Morgan watched advertisements driven about campus on trucks, bouncing over potted roads. One urged shoppers to prepare for deep discounts and certain safety as the local mall had expanded security to ensure a murder-free Thanksgiving.

Morgan looked up and down the campus. "John," he said. "I have a question. When I was here, humans came in pairs. Don't humans come in pairs anymore? Where...are...the boys? Are you the token male at a girl's school?"

"They say girls are superior to boys in everything, Dad, including Higher Ed. Just look how girls dominate campus."

"That's like saying whites were superior to their black slaves simply because whites outnumbered blacks."

"Then why would females surpass males in school, the workplace, or as single mothers with no fathers at home if it weren't true, Dad?"

Morgan sneered. "I know how you feel, John. I was born male too. I've always felt I should apologize for that in this country, but I just couldn't find a way to raise the issue in public."

"It's what they say, Dad."

"The omniscient *they*…Don't list symptoms like some legal analyst who then writes a book to reinforce fashionable bigotry with anecdotal baloney. Find the cause—like a scientist—and you'll be famous. I've got a hunch a few reading assignments will help. Books that played a major role in our New Order. Books that made villains of boys, to weed them from education and pave the way for silencing half the population. American history witnessed the cost to human potential when women were muzzled. What will happen when the *last man* meets the same fate?"

Morgan swiveled. He inspected the students. "Thanks to our right-to-carry-in-class law, I see about one in ten of these girls are armed. Don't threaten their self-esteem by refusing a date, John."

John rolled his eyes.

Morgan scaled the Capitol's pillar-framed stairway. He sat on steps of 370 million-year-old Devonian limestone, half a century older than the last time he was here. John followed.

"This place gave me my first great gift," Morgan said. "The realization of how powerful an average human brain can be." He pointed toward the river below. "And the second gift was love. Right there, by that bridge, I found it for the first time. And the last, for three decades."

"What was her name, Dad?"

"Melody Wilson. Every day we'd meet at the same bench by the river, where I saw her that first time. And on each occasion, I was relieved to find some disaster had not taken her away. When we were apart, a part of me was missing. It was part of that whole university experience, a dream come true, and I knew it. That's rare, to be aware of the adventure when it happens." Morgan hesitated, remembering the past. "Then a few years after I left, I was absorbed by the machine, converted to alloy. And it showed. I remember when I got this wrinkle, right here. This one." Morgan turned his head to drag his index finger over a long ditch on his face.

John chuckled. "Dad, I can't make it out from all the others."

"Right there. Look." Morgan tapped his cheek. "Not this, that's an imprint of the San Andreas Fault. Anyway, I kept wondering if I could escape that machine of the workplace and go back to the U, but I felt too old. I had to get on with it. I had a late start. I dropped out, you know."

"*Dad*, I thought you were all-knowing."

"I am all-knowing, but I wasn't always this way. Early on, I let other people define me. Lot of people out there with advice for you, John. Their advice will be to live your life the way they lived theirs. Maybe you'll find another way.

"After graduation, I did what everybody did, John. I entered that world of material possessions. This is a civilization that strives to gorge every primal urge, not discipline them. So when you move to the big city where image is everything, and you're as impressionable as I was, you see pretty clearly, manhood can be purchased. So I bought it. Compared to physics, I found display very easy. I got the credit card, the debt, the car, and voilà, I was a man. Before I figured out what I'd done, I was in the strangle grip of gluttony. I was what the system wanted me to be: a consumer. When true community is lost, John, and thus there is no definition of the good, there are no virtues. All we have left is competition in that primate hierarchy.

"People told me losing that idealism would show I'd grown up. But what I found was a reversal of that, a return to childhood called *office politics*. Ass kissing, manipulation, duplicity, these are things anybody can do, but some do better. And we 'value' such people for their expertise.

"John, I tell you, life turned from exhilaration to despair in almost invisible increments. Then a funny thing happened on my way home with all that materialism. I had to pay for it. Not so much with money, but with life. And I was one of the lucky ones with interesting work. Yet still, I had to be a success defined by the usual measure: more stuff, more command over others, more status for having both. And how would I attract the opposite sex without those lures? So down the road I went. Until I was so miserable with my empty life full of things, isolated by engineers with as much social acumen as a stone, even the rule of a tyrant was preferable to my bleak existence. So I married a tyrant."

John puzzled. "Mom?"

"No."

"Dad…I'm thunderstruck. You were married before Mom?"

"Perhaps some things are best left untold, but it's true. I was married alive." Morgan restrained laughter. "Get it? Like buried alive? I dug my way out to find being happily unmarried was the only kind of marriage that could last in a place where divorce was over sixty percent. Higher now, for those few who even bother."

"Wait a minute. What about this woman? How did you fall in love? What did you have in common?"

"We weren't in love, neither of us."

"Sex?"

"No, no. She was rigorously abstinent."

"*What?*"

"John, I had just left the most magnificent experience at the U. I belonged, I had purpose, youth, meaning, true love, friends everywhere. The whole world opened before me with a sense I could command it all, know it all, have it all. Only to graduate surrounded by people eaten by the apparatus, and I was next. I assumed adult life would begin with trumpets until I found it was 'Taps' they were tooting. For the longest time, I thought I might cry like an American on TV. My confidence crashed. I couldn't buy a date. I determined it was better to be with someone, even if I were miserable than to be alone."

"But, Dad, why pick someone you didn't care for? You could of had any woman you wanted."

Morgan patted John on the back, nodding, thumbs up. "Good job…But not in that condition. Women can smell confidence. And two dysfunctional individuals can find each other in a crowd of a thousand normal people, which is what we did. She was screwed up too, worse than I was, and in ways that can't be fixed. I thought I could repair all that—never marry a project, John.

"Anyway, I got to have somebody around, she got her bills paid.

We both got what we wanted. But after all my money was lost there was a happy ending. She was that kick in the seat to find what I stood for. And I learned *The Great Secret*: it's better to be alone than wish you were."

Morgan waved one hand to push away the past. "My second birth commenced with a study of the high minds society forgot, to build my philosophical foundation through the Great Books. A small matter this civilization ignores—beyond how to be employable, I mean. Little did I realize, I was on a search for that university experience.

"Then, John, I got help from an enormous magician made of stone on the Ruta Maya. It created an impossible miracle that could not exist in my world or our times. Your mother is that miracle. Until that moment in the jungle, I'd come to believe there could be no such woman. And even if there was, I was clean, I'd beaten that molecule."

"What molecule?"

"The one that makes men do asinine things they swear never to do again, only to find themselves doing the same asinine thing."

John smiled, nodding.

"John, have you heard that ancient Greek tale about the man who's asked what it's like to be old? 'When I was a young man,' he says, 'I was driven by an irresistible force to pursue the more lovely gender. Now that I'm an old man, I feel like a madman has left my body.' Once my blood was pure, that's how I felt. Until I saw your mother. She was my template. Every man has one, even if they don't know it, and they'll destroy themselves to win her. But I got lucky. Ne Shoul wasn't interested in social rank or exhibition. She had depth and substance like no one else I'd even read about. She was born the day I met her, that very instant from a sacred center of rich earth in the jungle." Morgan shook his head. "There I was, surrounded by dead civilizations, all by myself with no way forward apparent to me. I pinched earth between my fingers and smelled it. That's when it happened. I felt…high, for an instant. There wasn't a sound. The leaves, the twigs, I could have heard a mouse at a hundred meters. Not one indication anybody was around, and poof, there she was. And then she spoke, and I was saved. I knew she was sent to rescue me the moment I heard her voice."

"Sent by who, Dad?"

"God. The real god. The god of nature."

Morgan scanned the river valley, remembering. John waited. Morgan nodded once and slapped John on the back. "That's my story. So what are your dreams? I'm not asking what you want to be when you grow up. I'm asking what you want to be *about*."

John paused. "I suppose I'll look for work in biological research after grad school, assuming I get in. But I confess an interest in larger social questions." John whispered, "I've done some extracurricular study on our nation of laws, Dad, and I've learned a lot. I've been reading Jefferson, Lincoln, the Federalist Papers, with a whole new perspective. And I've read scriptures in a way I never did before."

"Where did you find Jefferson? And you do know Jefferson and scriptures aren't exactly best friends."

"I have lots to compare now, Dad, and I'm afraid of what America's become. As though out of all possible times, I just happened to arrive on Earth to witness an unforgivable event. It feels like a tsunami's approach. It grows taller as it nears. You know you can't outrun it, so you face it. You watch in terror with a kind of curious amazement."

Morgan leaned back. "OK…And?"

"I have to do…something. I don't know what."

"I thought you were going to save the world from all these famines: Brazil, Sahel, the Mid-East."

"I know, but all the world's arable land has been farmed, and genetic technology can't keep up with so many humans. I no longer believe that can be fixed. Not with more food. Only fewer people. And food's only part of the equation. We now need two planets, just like whoever you said said that before I was born."

"World Wildlife Fund," Morgan said. "So instead, you've got some spiritual mission to chase. Remember, John, you need this degree lest you land in one of those sweatshops popping up all over this country. Or history rebuffs your options altogether when this nation implodes. You don't want to be here when that happens. I've told you before, forget this place, it can't be saved."

"With respect, Father, I've never believed it."

Morgan stuck an accusing finger into his son. "Don't make a

movie, don't write a book, don't infuriate people like I did."

"Dad, I feel I'm on the cusp of some serious understanding. All I need is just a few years, and a few insights."

"Keep your insights to yourself, John."

"But I've seen the enthusiasm firsthand, Dad. Despite thought police and campus speech codes and squelching the Constitution, people still hope in secret. Give them a reasoned argument, they still get it. Christians in Rome, Jews in Europe, intellectuals in the USSR, people only pretend to follow the rules. You told me science is about truth because nature is what it is. I want to convey that same kind of truth about society, about us."

"And nature is the judge of scientific truth, John. What's your authority in the human realm? Truth and society are never friendly."

"Well, here's a scientist who pursued truth in society." John withdrew a copy of Jefferson's letters.

"Put that away!" Morgan grabbed the book. He scanned the space around them and shoved it back in the bag. "And who's giving the reasoned argument? You'll find yourself lost in some American jail. Your name banished from the database with no amount of bribery able to find you. Oh, but you'll appeal to our nation of laws...Ha! America is a nation of liars, John. We lie about the large things, we lie about the small, we lie about it all because it's patriotic, elevates our self-esteem, keep politicians elected, and is worth a lot of money."

"It's not enough to simply witness, Father. I will stand for what is right."

"*Right?* Right by who?" Morgan checked for listeners. "Right by offspring of the sixties who embraced free speech and the rest, only to shit-can all of it once they'd crushed their opposition? Right by those missionaries of the sword who'd just as soon run you through as pray for you because you're insolent enough to ask questions? Those with power are the ones who define what right means. And make no mistake, *they* will use it on *you*.

"You will stop talking, John. That is not a request. *You...will...stop...talking*."

"Dad, you're certainly willing to violate political correctness."

"I'm old! They're not likely to hang me. Not yet anyway.

"Listen to me, John. Look at me...What are your unstated

assumptions? That these people are like you; that they really do care. You are nothing like these people. And they don't give a shit about truth or justice or any other high-minded notion you've projected on them. Challenge the intolerance of liberal tolerance, reject the Bible in science class, or question the corporate ownership of government and you'll trigger a response from believers so horrified, you risk violence. They know if the social mallet is not lifted to smite iconoclasts like you, doubt will set in. Because deep down, we realize we are an ignorant people, John, and we'll do anything to avoid hauling that to the surface. From ostracizing to character assassination to murder if that's what it takes. We *must* protect our ignorance, for if we give voice to doubt, we lose everything. Despite our ignorance, that much we know."

Morgan clutched John's arm. He leaned in to look up into his son's face. "Don't you dare tell these people the truth. The only reason you're here is to get that paper pass for graduate school in another country. This is an American university, John—liars central. March in lockstep. Keep your head down. Do not draw attention to your gender, your sexuality, your convictions. Do not stand straight, or near people shorter or fatter than you, and *never* smile like you're happy or know something you shouldn't. They'll wipe that smile off you as an offense against someone not smiling."

Morgan pointed skyward toward a constant buzz in the air. "Those bully drones need a reason to cost so much money, John. Express confidence, arrogance, or masculinity just once on camera, the Nanny State will label you a bully and make you wish you'd not forgotten suffering victims."

Morgan grabbed John's book bag. He shook it. "Never, *never* let people know you read Jefferson. And don't you disagree with popular opinion in public. Do you understand me?"

John arched his back. He looked west. "Your father said the sunset is free."

"You're not listening, John. Your tsunami's on the horizon. You'll meet it early if you don't keep your ideas to yourself."

"Perhaps mine is another way, Father. See? I'm listening."

## 27. Hell on Earth

John's plane landed at Beijing Capital International Airport. He woke with a jolt when tires squawked on the runway. He could see air turbulence whiff past wings outside, traced by poisonous fumes Beijing choked on. An even carpet of black-haired people as tall as John's chest pressed against one another, awaiting departure from the jumbo jet.

John entered a crush of humanity in the busiest airport on Earth. Almost four hundred thousand passengers per day exchanged on eight runways run round the clock. In Terminal Three, John entered 240 enclosed acres of economic statement, the world's largest building. Reflected by polished marble floors, arched metal girders above made John feel he was beneath the sky of another planet.

Bused from one near-gridlock to the next, he watched Beijing creep by. People on foot, bicycles, mopeds, autos appeared in a near stationary state of vibration. Signs painted on buildings advertised wild lion bones, said in Chinese and English to solve every problem from arthritis to sexual potency; live monkey brains to eat and tables to chain their flailing bodies; the last gorilla-hand ashtrays; the last shark fins. Anything alive or extinct could be found to devour, drink, or wear to signify The Risen Dynasty.

Three miles from Tsinghua University, John reached his apartment—a white box-like structure stacked atop two others, like every apartment within kilometers of the place. He climbed a ladder to reach its grate-metal landing, protruding like the bottom lip from a person's mouth. He ducked beneath its entry into a room five inches shorter than he was. I'll kneel when I'm here, he thought. Gives a sacred feel to my studies.

He inspected the room, as there was only one. He swept a pile of dead insects out of his sink. He turned on the tap. Good—running water, he thought. Sort of brown, odorous running water…A little PCB and methanol never killed anybody after one sip…Probably.

\*\*\*

John's first day in graduate school commenced with cell biology. All Chinese students were seated at attention. John copied their behavior. While graduate-level courses were taught in English to students from around the world, most questions were asked in Chinese, which John learned fragmentarily.

A young man next to him dropped his pen as the professor spoke. No one, including its owner, reached for it. John picked it up, handed to its owner. The young man nodded abruptly, with no expression or eye contact.

At the close of class, all stood at attention. They gave a quick nod in unison and made a sound John didn't recognize. He did the same, later than the rest, drawing attention and ire of his professor. Students giggled.

Outside class, the pen's owner approached John.

John smiled. "Hi. You're in my cell biology class."

"It my class. You visitor."

John shrugged and started to walk away.

"Don't pick up pen. Professor think insult."

John stopped.

The young man nodded once, a kind of shallow bow. "My name Lu." He extended his hand, held in space like a robot mime. "Your name."

John shook his hand. "John," he said.

"John. I want speak English. Make better."

"What do you want to talk about, Lu?"

"Ask question. I answer."

"OK…Where are you from?"

"Gansu Province. High plateau. Silk road. North Himalaya. Thousand kilometer."

"Wow. You're a long ways from—"

"Wow?"

247

"Wow, Lu. It means neat, cool, amazing—"

"Cold?"

"Cool. American slang for—"

"Slang?"

"Oh, boy…Lu, American English is full of shortcuts to express emotion or opinion without actually having to express it. Sorrier still, so much is carried in the sound of a word, or where in that word we place emphasis, it's hard to decipher. Like the word hello. *Hell*-ooo means 'I didn't know that.' Hell-*looo* means 'you didn't know that?' And hello means hello."

Lu shook his head.

"Sorry, Lu. Lost my head. That's an advanced course."

Lu checked the ground. "Head lost?"

"Here's a question, Lu. Why do I see so many Anglo-looking males here? Young men in sweatshops that look like me. As Chinese as you. Same behaviors, expressions, no foreign accent. They're treated worse in the labor caste and better when members of the educated elite, what few there are in that category."

Lu nodded once. "China sell girl for honor of a son. America sell boy for slave trade."

"Oh, I don't think so, Lu. Maybe they're European."

"No Europe. America. Labor man don't like cheap labor America boy. Compete for work and woman. Already no woman for low-wage Chinese. But university like America boy. China think Western man better man in modern world, science, business."

"But that perception is decades behind the times, Lu. Despite your real-estate bust, you people are the technological and economic light of the world now, and it's pretty clear you people know it."

"Chinese not change fast. Centuries, not seasons."

John shook his head. "I wonder where they come from?"

"America boy."

"I don't think—"

An explosion off-campus rattled buildings. John ducked. He looked for the source. A smoke cloud rose from the city. Men emerged from dorms on campus. They blew whistles and ran toward the blast. Lu walked away.

"Lu!" John called. "What was that?"

\*\*\*

An early morning wind from the city carried sounds John could not ignore. He descended his ladder in search of the screams. As he passed, several people flinched at the sight of a giant in their midst. No one but John seemed to notice the cries.

Blocks from his apartment, John crouched behind wooden crates, watching. Metal cages extended for nearly one hundred meters, stacked four high. Their bottom layers piled with years of filth and today's feces from above.

Prisoners were matted and bruised from beatings of capture and transport, half of them dead. Row after row of wire confinement bound a mud avenue. Graded with a gentle pitch toward its center, a steady trickle of urine drained into a ditch.

Some captives spun in circles about their small pens. Others packed so tightly with companions they were unable to move, dog, cat, fox, raccoon too frightened of man to regard differences.

Trucks arrived in an unremitting procession. They feed raw materials to rows of men at work, their process separated into divisions of labor with quotas. The initial group meant to kill the living—to make it easier for skinners—frequently failed their task, improving their own count.

Cargos delivered dogs crammed into a space so small their limbs stuck out from between chain-link enclosures. Men climbed over stacks to kick cages and their inhabitants to the ground. When they met pavement, legs snapped with such authority; only their shriek could be heard over the sound of cracked bones. Men laughed, poked prisoners, and probed fractures to hear the variety of pleas they could make. Eyes wide, other hostages waited their turn and scanned the scene in a twitching, sideward motion.

John's hands trembled so violently he could not stop one with the other. He turned away. He pressed his back against a crate and slid down its surface. Hell on Earth, he thought.

Flakes of dust collected on his arm. He looked up to see smoke stacks billow overhead. Their nomadic ash of once-living animals on a migration over the city; anonymous immigrants in Beijing's atmosphere.

Water seeped into John's pants. He looked down to see blood

dribble into a pool he sat in from the crate he leaned against.

Footsteps passed behind him. Indifferent conversations, the smell of tobacco, and drying muscle penetrated John's brain. A repeated squeal pierced his blindness.

John peeked over the crate to see a puppy grab the cage it was dragged from, more fearful of leaving than to remain imprisoned. The man held the dog's tail and one leg as he wrenched the animal free. He slammed the dog's head on pavement to kill it as metal tags on its collar rang like a broken bell. He tossed it to skinners.

Another man removed its collar and clipped its tail and hind legs to a thick metal hanger. Graceful motions between the tail and hind paws flayed opened enough skin to grasp with both fists. The man yanked skin down, as the creature writhed for the man's fingers to bite thick leather gloves.

The man pitched up his knife, caught by the blade, and slapped its handle across the puppy's face to crack an eye-socket. Front paws covered the animal's snout as saliva drooled between them.

Skin over the animal's body stripped away in repeated jerks, to sound like rind off a grapefruit. The creature arched, retching with a sound John had never heard and couldn't imagine. A high-frequency scream immersed him with such intensity his ears clipped the signal in saturation from sonic power humans weren't built to absorb.

The man snipped a quick circle about the dog's quivering nose and mouth. Off from its shivering body came a continuous stretch of fur ready for market. Gloves, boots, coats, collars, apparel accurately marked "Leather Free," and not accurately marked "No Animal Skins."

The man held his pelt to the sun and looked for holes. He grabbed the animal's bony legs and sailed it like a Frisbee. John's eyes followed the creature's path to where it landed on its back on a pile with hundreds of others. Regions of the stack moved like worms suffocating under water of a summer storm. The puppy's eyes blinked patiently on its quaking face, its heart pumping to organs of no use to the skin trade.

The dog's legs pawed air. In twists and shimmies, it righted itself on its belly. Threads of mucus paste connected it to neighbors. Its head wobbled to lift its barely bleeding nose and eyelids. It looked back at the men. They lit one another's smokes. They stepped over cages of other anxious victims of efficient market forces.

A backhoe scooped bodies from multiple piles into a furnace fed by the dead and dying. Voices escaped the ovens of those still alive like a low frequency, single tone song. Their chorus terminated with a hiss and crack from air in their lungs, followed by another chorus from the next bucket.

As if it suffered from Parkinson's, the skinless puppy drew its head in palsied hesitations up to nothing but the vacuum of sky. In a battle to hold its head steady, it found John.

He gasped. "It wasn't me," he whispered. "I'm not one of them." The faint image of someone's dying pet skipped through John's brain.

The rap of another skull broke John from his location. Frozen, men watched him as he fell on one of them so quickly they barely realized he spoke another language. "Stop! Stop! Stop!" John's fist hammered the man's face.

The man's knife spiraled. He hit John across the face with a dead cat, its orange tabby fur caught in his teeth. Other men jumped John in an eruption of Chinese shouts. One slashed John's arm. Another clubbed him while the man John hit escaped for his knife.

Others recoiled when Lu reached the weapon first. He swiped at them, shouted something in Chinese, and threatened enough to cause indecision. Lu yanked John back. "Go, Round Eye!"

Men appeared from a long line of cages. Men ran from their trucks toward the scene. Lu felt the crack of a stick break over his neck.

John opened one cage after another to pull animals free. "Run!"

Men chased unshackled cash. One man held John and scored hunks from his body with wire cutters. John screamed and fought free.

John hauled a collie from its cage as a man jumped on it, cracking its ribs. John locked the man's head in his arms as he beat the man's face, breaking his nose and front teeth.

Lu seized a fistful of John's shirt and wrestled him away.

John looked back at the skinned puppy, still alive. Its eyes moved back and forth as though reading words in the air, as its head sank in increments.

251

Bikes, cars, trucks skimmed by within inches of the two. Panicked, Lu jerked John through gaps in traffic and ducked items thrown by the men.

Blood pumped from John's hand as he staggered and gasped for air. "They're brutalizing animals, Lu! We've got to tell somebody!"

Lu towed John down the street. "You think nobody know? You think government save animal?"

"Yes!"

"No!" Lu pulled John close. "They kill you! Stuff hairy barbarian in barrel, no different! Embarrass Chinese with public plea or video? Skinners in new place by night, government say fixed. Like America, business and government, one and same." Lu shoved John forward. "People die here, John, on street, in dump, shanties, all day. One less rival. Think dog matter? America, Europe, Russia pay lot for skin. Export kill to China."

John pinched a blood gushing wound on his hand and ran for his apartment.

"No, John! This way!"

Lu jumped John as an explosion blew out government office windows, both of them knocked to the ground. John tried to run, but the world spun around him. Lu lifted him. "Hurry, John!"

***

Lu stuck his head in John's apartment. "Round Eye? Up yet?"

John's head was propped up with a folded towel, a wet cloth on his cheek, his hand wrapped in bandages. He was swathed in sweat. "They got me," he said.

Lu sprang in the room. "They find you!"

"No, no, Lu…What they did to me yesterday really, really hurts today." He spoke in forced fragments, punctuated with moans and grimaces. "Adrenalin wore off. Come in…Pull up a chair." John motioned toward a spot on the floor.

Lu sat. "At least you feel today, Round Eye. Could be worse."

"It is worse, Lu. They cut off my finger." John's head fell back. "Ooo…God. My hand is killing me, throbbing all the way to my toes. And to make matters worse, those men do today what they did yesterday and will do for years to come. One among thousands of

252

such places here, and around the world, I'm sure." He closed his eyes and bit his lip. "But you're right, Lu, if people don't buy, people don't produce. All that agony for displays of what people call *sophistication*. This has to change."

"Why Americans want change, John?"

"I've been around your country, Lu, and all I see is change. We call it obliteration."

"We change land, not people. China people here five thousand year, no change."

"Tell me Mao didn't change people, Lu. 'Political power grows out of the barrel of a gun,' right?"

"Change government, not people, John."

"Why were you seven kilometers from campus yesterday, Lu?" Lu looked away. "You just happened to be where pets are slaughtered, Lu. Just across the street from where a bomb went off. What a coincidence."

Lu stared at a wall.

John nodded. "I see." He examined blood on his cloth and groaned. "There are times when change must take place, Lu. Change for what is right. I'm guessing you agree."

"What right? Right to West, right to Chinese?"

"Universally right, Lu. Morally right."

"No man can say, John."

"Here's an ethics test for you, Lu. Say I came to know a heroic man with a message of how humanity should live a just and righteous life. So compelling, people know in their heart of hearts they cannot resist the truth he speaks. Someone like Jesus."

"Who Jesus?"

"Jesus. Jesus Christ, Lu."

Lu shrugged. "I from inland. We know Western imperialism, what you do with Chinese gunpowder. Don't know American celebrities."

"OK, let's say Lao-tsu. One day he is seized by police, brutalized, and executed for what he says. How could I not spread that hero's lesson, even if it means harm to me?" John squeezed shut his eyes in pain.

"Stay home, John. Test answered. What do with dog?"

"Because if I don't fight that cruelty, I am party to that

injustice."

"Those men feed child, Round Eye. Hard find cheap labor in China. All high tech now. Not all people high-tech mind. Need job."

"So do other people, Lu, but they don't torture animals."

"Not direct. Do so kinder way. Plow land, strip mines, buy furniture rainforest wood. What worse, starvation from loss habitat or what you see? Dogs not go extinct, Round Eye."

"Where I come from, we would never treat animals with such malice."

"Not true. America kill million cat dog every year. Call animal shelter. Good shelter. Shoot puma in Florida. Shoot wolf in Wyoming, Idaho, Alaska. Because wolf kill elk to eat before American man kill elk for head. Like Mongols, put head on stick."

"Well...on a wall actually."

"Kill pig, OK, John? Cow OK? Seventy-million cow per year. Nice America."

"So you know more about us than what we do with gunpowder. My father used to tell me about our reckless expansion of rights, just as Hamilton warned against. But if not animal rights, then what? What did those animals do to deserve such monstrosity? Industrial-scale, assembly line carnage, detailed right down to the chimneys belching once living souls."

"In America, dog have rights, John?"

"Over a century ago in my country, women acquired a right to vote. A decades-long thrashing to free them from dictates of men alone. But why did women deserve a right to vote, Lu? Because they are every bit as competent as any man. Gender can be acknowledged for fundamental differences, but not inequality. For all species—certainly for all mammal species—there should be equal consideration for the miracle of God's Creation. *His* Creation of life, Lu."

Lu puzzled. "So in West, animals vote, John?"

"No, Lu. But since animals have no ability to vote, it's absurd to argue they should. As it would be absurd to argue that because men can't give birth, they can't vote."

"Animals not human, John."

John lifted his hand above head-level and leaned forward. Internal blood and pressure fell to his elbow. "But are humans animals, Lu? This very university teaches that complex human brain structure responsible for mathematics and abstract thinking overlays what? The mammal brain. And where do human emotions reside? In our mammal brain and limbic system, shared with all mammals. The same emotions felt in *us* are felt in *them*, Lu. Fur seal mothers cry over remains of snow-white infants ripped free of their skin for the vanity trade. A bloody carcass she labors for three days to feed. Dolphins, with a larger brain-to-body mass ratio than humans, call for their children as men sever their spines. Infant rhinos bleat for their mothers. Shot for nothing more than her horn, pulverized and added to beer for better sex or miraculous cures—despite the fact these are myths. Animals grieve, Lu. They hurt, like us. The recognition of any wrong leads to moral logic that forbids us from treating that wrong as a convenience, a matter of taste, an economic efficiency. As with any moral impasse, we have *a duty, not a choice*." Slowly John leaned back, his hand fixed in space.

"What you feel not rule economics, John."

"I've provided a *reason* superior to my feelings."

"Can animals reason, John?"

"Because Sir Isaac Newton was superior to you and me in his grasp of calculus, would he then be lord over us, Lu? Jeremy Bentham said the question is not whether animals can reason, not can they talk, but can they suffer? Never have I seen such suffering. Humans made the problem, Lu. Humans can fix it. I will stand for what's right. Made right by God himself, ignored by man for a dollar. The Chinese are good, wise, and resourceful people. They will do what's right. Won't they, Lu."

John waited.

"You know what's right, Lu, I know you do. And maybe you know something about these persistent insurgencies upsetting the *national harmony*. Worldwide dominance everywhere but home. Injustice is injustice, Lu, no matter who or what endures it."

Lu watched the floor, silent.

255

## 28. Peri Ton Hepta Theamaton

Morgan answered the phone in San Francisco, Ne Shoul on a shared line.

"Mom, Dad, I did it. Masters with emphasis in cellular respiration. And just in time. China's about to deny entry to all foreign students."

"Quite an accomplishment," Morgan said. "With such demand, the burning question now is, Which offer will you take?"

"Like you said, Dad, deprivation reveals what is otherwise hidden. You taught me there are answers. I taught myself they don't reside in a bank account."

"Bank accounts come in handy, John. Which offer?"

"I want to hear, Dad."

"Me too. Which offer?"

"The one with promise, Dad. My offer."

"Your offer."

"My offer to know why we are the way we are and where we're going."

"You just did that, John, you finished the masters. So you're off to get a doctorate?"

"I've got all the books I need, Dad. The Bible, Constitutional studies, the founding, economic theories, census data, histories of every thoughtful man and woman to ever live. I have surveys and studies on everything from the food we eat to global warming. Even the opinions of Americans over time and why civilizations fail or flourish."

A long pause occupied their connection.

"John, you're not doing it right."

"Right for me, Dad."

"So after all the science, you'll be a philosopher. You'll end up like Socrates—old, ugly, and poisoned by your peers."

Ne Shoul cleared her throat. "Now, Morgan, I seem to recall you retreated from the standard path a time or two. Go figure out the world, John."

"Do *not* figure out the world, John. The world is not worth figuring."

"What do I want to be about, right, Dad? This is my answer."

"Until you jump in, John, you can't know any more about reality than those ivory tower dingbats who've filled your brain with mishmash these last umpteen years."

"I've decided, Dad."

"Where will you go, John?" Only low-level noise could be heard. "Hello?"

"Dad, I found a pond with a shack forty paces from the water. Granted permissions for as long as I want. Supplies are waiting to be flown in. Scheduled twice a year."

"In China?"

"Alaska. I've named it Walden Pond."

"Oh, for *God's* sake, John. Do you know how many boys have run this fantasy into the dirt already?"

"Not me, Dad."

"It's cold in Alaska, Mister Thoreau, you'll freeze to death."

"It's not cold up here anymore, and I have—"

"*Here?*"

"I have plenty of mosquito repellant, Dad. Plus, forests have fallen after the permafrost turned out not to be permanent—those drunken forests you taught me about. Plenty of lumber."

"What does a biologist know about wilderness survival?"

"Dad, did you ever see a show called *Alone in the Wilderness*?"

"A show. You saw a show...I saw a show when I was a kid, called *Jeremiah Johnson*. It was about the wilderness and some guy living in it, but I didn't run off to the woods or have the faintest notion I knew how to live there. Remember the book, *Into the Wild*? It was a show too, John. You should see it. What happened to Christopher McCandless?"

"He made a mistake, Dad. I won't make a mistake."

"How do you know? That's what mistakes are. You don't plan them!"

"OK, so there's some risk."

"Some? It's a certainty. This is foolhardy!"

Ne Shoul interrupted. "Morgan, honey bunny, sweet pea, didn't we have this conversation about risk on a sandy beach once?"

"No, Ne Shoul, we didn't. You encourage a part of your very creation to become food for polar bears."

"Dad, they're extinct."

"I'm talking to your mother."

"Morgan, he's been out of the nest for seven years now."

"How will you carry all those books to your *pond*, John?" Morgan asked.

"It's the twenty-first century, Dad. They're on my tablet, thousands of them, including your cherished titles. I even have your films on here."

Morgan nearly dropped the phone. "Oh, pulllease…"

"Scripts too, Dad. AFI has a download site. Yours were free."

"The American Film Institute has as much sense as you, John."

"I've got it all planned. Down to medical emergencies and repairs."

"You've got no electricity, John."

"Solar card."

"No freshwater, John."

"Portable filter, Dad."

"No communications."

"Dad…handheld tablet. We can talk all day via satellite. I'll hang the cam on my belt so you can see what I see."

"Nice. So I can witness the seat of your pants where your very expensive brains are just before they become rump roast for some predator."

"You can watch that and more, Dad. If you pay the bill. Pricey Chinese satellite network, but none better."

"This is crazy. You're crazy! And what do you mean, flown in? Where is this place, how far from civilization?"

"Northwest of Fairbanks by about the distance from Los Angeles to Fresno."

"About two hundred miles, John. Long walk when things go

wrong. Your tablet can't fix that."

"Just south of Gates of the Arctic National Park, Dad. Not far from Noatak Wilderness Area. Fly from here in Anchorage to Bettles Field in Evanston. Puddle jumper drops me twenty miles north at the cottage."

"The *cottage*...Ne Shoul, you better talk sense to your son, the polar bear entree."

"Dad, there are no—"

Morgan snapped, "This is not normal, John! At your age, you should be completely dominated by sexual urge. Dangerous as it is, I suggest you yield to it. It's nothing compared to a polar bear's diet."

"Dad, when you were my age, would you pass up this opportunity?"

Morgan hesitated. Ne Shoul laughed. "*So good*, John, you got him! Well done. What your father wants to say is that he is so very proud of you, and he wishes he could be there too. By tonight he'll have a command center set up in your bedroom—maps, websites, weather reports. We'll watch for your campsite online. How exciting, John. Isn't this exciting, Morgan?"

"You know, Ne Shoul, I was born at night, but I wasn't born last night. What I want to know is who paid for all this so far?"

"Don't forget to keep a journal, John. Daddy and I love you, honey."

\*\*\*

John stood high on eastern ridges of the Brooks Range above the ironically named John River. He sat on his pack. Tundra crackled beneath it. Riding an ocean of stone, mountains appeared defiant victors over Earth. Snaps of ice could be heard from receding glaciers upstream. Mountainsides echoed their sound until it bounced out of the valley.

Two gray wolves darted over gullies and scree. They disappeared and reappeared. Sprung from a hiding place, two snow-white Dall sheep, mother and kid, hopped over rocks to a vertical façade of granite. Wolves watched them leave. Observing the scene, a bald eagle shifted airflow over wingtips in a cobalt blue sky.

"God is good," John said. "Creation. Day One." He nodded and spoke to the mountains. "The John Valley. Land of lords and titans. Center of the world."

He pulled a pad and pencil set from his backpack. "Don't move."

Majesty of Earth's assembly clashed with images of man as John saw in his mind a defenseless puppy torn from its cage. John closed his eyes. Still, they plead for mercy, he thought. As I sit in the midst of holiness, man's heinous acts persist.

He opened his eyes. He felt scars on his arms. He massaged a stump where his pinky finger once was.

He spoke to the sky. "Dear God almighty above, teach me to teach men what we're truly made of."

Jupiter grazed peaks as celestial objects confined to the horizon appeared to roll about Earth's surface. Mountain shadows marched across ideas in John's mind. He whispered, "Yes...An old way. A return. Augustine looked inward then up to God to find serenity. All I need do is look around. But we see the same thing, he and I.

"The Promised Land can still be saved."

***

Thunder shook the cottage. Inside, a space between ceiling, satchels, and boxes provided a place for John to sleep. Its smallness made heating, even by body alone, quick and less taxing on fuel stores. Its height dropped with use of supplies.

On his sleeping bag, John read by candlelight to preserve his solar-powered tablet in a region slim on sunlight, allowing the electrical expense of music. Provided by his mother, Bliss played "A Hundred Thousand Angels" as John took notes, read more, and slipped into dreams of conversations between the mountains and his books. Conversations he troubled to decipher as mountains spoke from the perspective of eternity, while all of his books, including the Bible, were by comparison only just conceived.

His candle extinguished, he awoke by light of his library screen, activated by the touch of his turning. Barefoot, he stepped outside into darkness that would last for months. Fanned out from his feet were shadows shed by Jupiter, Sirius, and Venus nearly as bright as a full moon.

He went in the cottage to start a fire inside and came out with his ax. In open space sat a wolf, another partially concealed by a boulder. "Well, hello again. The Two Sisters." He bowed toward one wolf. "Lassie, how are you?"

Motionless, they studied him. He studied them. One with a full, azure mane, one without.

"Maybe you're not sisters. But Lassie, I need a name for your friend."

The second wolf barked.

"Oh, so you're rather sassy," he said.

John bent down to set upright a log and stood to address them. "Sassy and Las—" They were gone. No sound, no movement.

He struck firewood. "I know you can hear me," he said. "As you may know, there are many problems in my world. But the good news is that *every* one has an answer. Right and wrong, good and evil—these are the terrain of my home. I realize your world is beyond that. But my species left your land long ago and in so doing lost our deepest connection to God. Our biggest problem now is to rediscover what we once knew. You never left, so you know all this."

Three strikes split firewood. He carried it inside and sat with his electronic library. He called "Lassie! Sassy!"

With his flashlight, he checked scattered stands of wood through his open door. Four eyes reflected back at him from the distance.

John selected words from Chief Seattle on his tablet. He shined his flashlight on its solar cells. He played these words to the wolves: "Your dead cease to love you and the homes of their nativity as soon as they pass portals of the tomb. Our dead never forget the beautiful world that gave them being. But when the last red man shall have perished from this earth, and his memory among white men shall have become forgotten, these shores shall swarm with the invisible dead of my tribe. When your children's children think themselves alone in the field or in silence of the wood, they will not be—"

John paused the device. He watched agitated planets bound by his doorframe. "How to square our Founders' insights of a modern world with Chief Seattle?" he whispered. "Who most flourishes by their perception? The primitive, or the modern?

"No…Not the primitive…The hallowed. Moderns advance by

their achievements. The hallowed were elevated by their connectedness.

"Can these survive together?

"It's taken five thousand years since the invention of writing to sublimate the world of God by the word of man." He rotated the device in his grip that lit his face. "We've traded one for the other. The life of triumph chugs along without assistance. The hallowed, it needed help. But we are made of both worlds. Until we strike a balance, what we do to ourselves in one way, we diminish what we are in another. All we need now is a push.

"My father was right. Something's going to happen. Something bad."

# 29. Hume's Error

John sat on a train departing New York City. Images of six years in Alaska flashed through his mind. The train rocked on uneven rails as buildings passed. He reflected on his visit to Grand Central Terminal in Manhattan. Wrong crowd, wrong venue, he thought. As though anything said by mortals could make those people late for work. At least for those who still have a job.

Remembering Times Square, beneath advertisements one atop another three hundred feet high, he could neither be heard over noise nor allowed to make people late for remaining shows on Broadway.

John crossed the continent, a foreign visitor in his own country. He listened more than he talked. He worked at farms high along the northern border, shoveling manure, bailing hay. He angled south for three consecutive all-night visits to sandbanks of the Wapsipinicon River and made pencil drawings of the place. He slept under bridges or on sidewalk heat vents in cities in the cold. Economic instabilities and increased pressure from expanded populations meant finding warmth on the street was not assured, but well-protected hiking gear allowed him to bivouac anywhere. From people in these places, John learned what he would never find on his handheld library.

He met others like himself in search of a purpose, trying to find where they belonged in such a rapid changing world. They traveled together, split up, and rejoined throughout the seasons. Two in particular, Vivekananda and Callimachus, debated through the night with John on every occasion they met.

Intense Midwestern floods forced them west to the colorful desolation of the Saline Valley, a five-hour molar-cracking four-wheel ride over abandoned roads northeast of Death Valley,

California. There, John and his friends spoke to fragmented groups—unemployed engineers; the once wealthy, now homeless; survivalists; nudists; religious extremists who claimed every line of the Bible was false.

At dusk, giant fire pits shimmered off faces surrounding them. Antiquated F-16 jets from Edwards Air Base coasted up from the valley, rattling as they flew. Low to the deck, wings nearly vertical, they were so close, pilot visors could be seen to reflect firelight.

Scattered about a central flame, a dozen geothermal springs fed mortar and stone hot-tubs full of people, half of them shrouded in marijuana smoke. Repeatedly, John's friends asked that he speak to them all. Walking about the primary fire's perimeter, John asked for questions throughout his talks, yielding to Vivekananda and Callimachus as he listened.

\*\*\*

Summertime. John sat on a crowded flatbed railcar, rolling through Nevada BLM land in the night. He tried to estimate the number of white grave markers that seemed to never end; Quake victims from one horizon to the other. Next day he hopped off the train at Picabo, Idaho. A ghost town of twenty homes, Picabo had become a way station for homeless and hobos.

Walking along highway 20, he saw basalt tubes, the last signature of ancient trees surviving two thousand degree lava long enough to form a hollow shell 15,000 years ago. Just meters from his path, the world's deepest volcanic rift appeared about to swallow him and any remnant of life into an eight hundred foot abyss. The scenery of nature and that of man became more ominous as John circled the continent.

South of Pioneer Mountains, John approached Craters of the Moon National Monument. The image of two hundred humans gathered about lava cinder cones seven hundred feet high appeared like a pointillist painting of colored dots on a black canvas. They all turned to look at John as he neared. Casually he adjusted his pack and glanced behind to see what they saw.

\*\*\*

It was autumn when John advanced on Colorado's Red Rock Amphitheater and its butter-yellow aspens. He could hear low-frequency rumbles from a crowd. He pushed sunglasses upon his forehead and reread a handwritten letter from Callimachus, a product of shuttered wireless networks across the country. No mention of a large rally.

Proximity to the theater was measured by a growth in vehicle density—bicycles, pack mules, horses tied to trees or car-door handles. John stopped with no one in sight. Modulated chirps peppered with machine-gun pops from a lark bunting above warned him to go back.

I'm an hour early to whatever this is, he thought. But looks like I'm late. He shielded his eyes with sunglasses, drew a baseball cap from his backpack, and fit it tight to his head.

From above the amphitheater, John peeked around its entrance to see it crowded with people. Paths downstairs remained narrowly open between ends of seated rows. John released gear from his shoulders, held to his chest so he could sit to watch the event.

He descended steps until he spotted Vivekananda and Callimachus. Among a group of people on stage, they were arguing with each other. John turned to walk upstairs.

Callimachus pointed. "Whitaker!"

John hesitated. He kept walking.

"John Abraham Whitaker!"

Immediately surrounded by silence, John could hear the rotation of a thousand seats turn toward him.

***

Morgan sat outside, hunched under a blanket, his kitten Cooty on his shoulder. He rotated a hunk of marble and chisel in his hand. The round head of an ant took shape in stone.

Ne Shoul opened sliding glass doors to call out, "Morgan, your son has returned!"

Morgan paused. He hoisted his center of gravity over a cane.

Ne Shoul approached to hold Morgan's arm and help him inside. "*Get*," he said. "Don't baby me."

His hunched body shuffled toward the house as he watched his

265

feet, avoiding ants. Cooty rode the blanket on his back. Morgan bumped the door with his head. Ne Shoul chuckled and shrugged. He looked into glass to brush hair on his head. "I'm a prune," he said.

Inside, Morgan looked over the living area. "Where is he?"

Ne Shoul motioned toward the television.

Morgan's turtle neck stretched from his blanket shell. He squinted at the image. "Great zot, look at all the bipeds."

She giggled. "He's at the Lincoln Monument. The National Mall is full of people."

Rain moistened the Parthenon-like building mottled by sunlight, steaming with heat and humidity. John's face dominated the screen. Lincoln sat behind, his chair between columns framing John's face.

John's voice filled the room. "Morally, spiritually, intellectually, politically, we are a paper-thin people," he said. "Our families dissolved, our educational system putrefied, our government rife with sleaze, corruption, and subversion of the Constitution.

"We demand an ever-greater congestion of rights," John said, "with no moral guide for their practice. Our political order is undermined by a people with no higher interest than self-gratification. Our founding is seen as one of sand, not a rock of stability from which to brace ourselves against storms of modernity. The dark nature of power defies our grasp. We are bewildered. Fear is in the saddle now, and it yanks the bit in man's mouth."

Boos mixed with applause. Sectors of the crowd seethed. Horseback police could be seen to pull reins, their animals sensing tension in the air.

People shouted, "Noose the liberals!"

"Divisive hate speech! He's a Republican!"

Fruit hit John's entourage in a circle about him.

Television cameras observed from scattered locations. One focused on John's mouth so tightly, individual teeth could be counted. John's followers latched arm in arm about his perimeter as pressure grew.

"We now know that free society cannot survive without restraints of virtue," John said. "Without it, we suffer the post-communal era of American history. But the problems of mankind have been solved. A Renaissance is near."

Arrested by John's supporters, a man's voice reached microphones. "Revolution!" The crowd wailed in response.

John held hands high, his voice still calm. "Not a revolution. A reformation."

Roars of retribution mixed with calls for redemption from groups in circles of prayer. Factions crystallized among people as though elevated temperatures sorted common atoms into amalgams of grievance. Chants unified over the expanse. "War! War! War!"

Voices from the multitudes nearly pounded John from his podium. "Reformation of the mind, of the spirit," he said. "Will yours be reborn? Will those classic ideas of possibility spring forth *in you?* Of promise, of hope?"

Crowds fell forward like dominoes up Memorial steps. Callimachus was knocked to the ground. Vivekananda and allies closed gaps, scarcely able to stand.

Hostiles stretched for John. The microphone hit his teeth to crackle loudspeakers. "We must find again that elusive capacity to consider, struggle for, and find agreement on first principles," John said. "Reason bequeathed to man by almighty God."

People howled. "He said God is a man! Kill him!"

"He said *compromise!* Traitor!"

"He said the M word! Macaca!"

The space about John collapsed. Segments of the crowd heaved with violence. Knuckles flew in every direction.

Morgan rapped his cane. "I told him this would happen!"

Police on horseback spun, to knock down three and four people at a time. A palisade of foot soldiers stormed in. Stun guns snapped. Clouds of pepper spray filled the air. Helicopters bounced at the bottom of their descent as if tied to a string, their loudspeakers booming commands of dispersal. Higher above, blimps radioed images to bookies and gamblers in Las Vegas and Shanghai.

Speechless, Ne Shoul and Morgan watched reporters repeat in a dozen ways what they saw. "Shocking images from our nation's capital…Tonight at eleven: So you're a hundred fifty pounds overweight? How to look hot anyway—*naked.* And don't miss the mother of another murdered child cry on camera. Today's gun massacre comes from Louisiana. See it all at eleven on *You're There News*!"

# 30. The Gospel of John

Television networks assembled in Washington DC, where John was released from federal custody. Media representatives coordinated with government officials for John to answer questions before a panel of experts in the Library of Congress reading room.

Outside the library, everything from beer and homeopathic river water touched by the accused, to dolls of John hung on a noose sold from the same kiosks. Onlookers climbed every high place. From one light post, a torn banner draped over bushes below. Its wrinkled message advertised America's upcoming presidential-candidate mud-wrestling contest. The next election was only 46 months away.

National Guardsmen from three states affirmed their presence. Police confiscated small arms and assault rifles, disregarding stand-your-ground laws. Now, 124 years after students burned books said to contradict The Führer in 1933 Germany, hundreds of undergraduates burned hills of books said to challenge The Doctrine. Two blocks away free Bibles were offered at the perimeter of a smoke column churned skyward on the printed equations of science and the Koran. From Georgetown to Anacostia and Arlington to Trinidad, pacifists, anarchists, and factions of pure-race peoples—which had not existed for over twenty thousand years—marched on every street over thirteen square miles, all concentrated at the Library of Congress.

John stood beneath the library's dome, modeled on Rome's Pantheon. He looked for names of great Europeans inscribed in the ceiling, farther down for names of eminent Americans, and about his periphery for quotes from noble authors—all hidden by sweeps of discolored plaster to protect public self-esteem.

He squinted at massive windows blued by atmospheric aerosols as portals knocked through walls for the sole purpose of viewing The Four Great Truths engraved in The Ministry of Fact and Justice: Discrimination Is Equality, Freedom Is Slavery, Ignorance Is Bliss, War Makes Peace.

Rows of the wise stretched about John like fans at a concert. A public audience surrounded experts behind a waist-high wooden divider and two mezzanines above. Excluding John's platform, American flags hung from every location. A complete circuit of stars and stripes encircled the dome's base. Three fanned out before each speaker. Hundreds sequenced along table perimeters, and the moderator's plinth.

To observe it all, crowds of Chinese reporters streamed video to their Party Truth Center back home. Their pervasiveness was ignored, as to notice was defined offensive through an extension of privacy rights and the much-litigated "noticing opinion" of Supreme Court judgment. Security infiltrated the audience, from armed guards to sensors sensitive to sublimating explosives.

The moderator sat elevated behind John. The man worked gum in his mouth. Layers of the man hung over his chair. Lassoed by tie and collar, his head appeared about to pop. He tapped his microphone with a gavel and addressed the audience. "For reasons unbeknownst to me, the man before you has unsettled our national family of brotherly devotion," he said and smirked. "With too much attention to simply dispose of him, our noble and righteous leaders have allowed this little quiz. So…Mister Whitaker, how are you, sir? Now that you're out of jail."

John nodded. "Fine, thank you."

A rotund woman on the panel of experts shouted, "Such *audacity* to say you are *fine* when across this land so many are not fine!"

Audience members agreed they were not fine. They barked for contrition.

The moderator frowned. "To say you are fine is not a crime against those not fine," he said.

The woman lifted her handheld device. "Volume three, page seventeen thousand one hundred twenty-one of the Greater Victim Recompense Act states, 'One may not use the descriptive term *fine* when speaking in public where others *not fine* may intercept this message or think, imagine, dream, or wonder if they have.'" She wagged her handheld at the moderator. "*Fine* ranks as highly on The Doctrine Indignation Meter as to wish someone Merry Christmas or to offer candy canes in school."

The moderator looked over bifocals at the woman. He drummed knuckles on his podium. He motioned a team of eleven lawyers behind him. They flipped through paper stacks and storage media of the GVRA. They debated the definition of *public, speaking, message, think, imagine, dream, wonder,* and *fine.*

John checked his wristwatch. A Party Truth cameraman's head bobbed as he awoke.

The moderator reappeared from his assemblage of flesh and mind. "Mister Whitaker," he pronounced, "please cease such emotive eruptions, as others may find it offensive."

"Does the GVRA deny victims from use of the word *fine?*" John asked.

Lawyers huddled. A man in the mezzanine gave another a haircut, others in line for the same service. Chuckles, coos, and phone calls could be heard about the library as though in the privacy of their own home.

The moderator responded, "Do you have victims in your bloodline, Mister Whitaker?"

"Doesn't everyone?"

"Settled! Mister Whitaker is a victim." The moderator slammed shut a law book. Lawyers sat.

John waved at the moderator over noise in the library. "But I do not claim special rights and victim privileges."

The audience gasped.

Lawyers stood.

The panel woman shouted, "He does not embrace victim identity!"

The moderator hissed, "Mister Whitaker, do you have something of vital importance to say or not?"

The panel woman searched her GVRA. "Mister Whitaker does not embrace the preeminence of victimhood!" she said. "He cannot say *fine.* He must repent five times in public and shed three tears."

The moderator closed his eyes. "Mister Whitaker? Get after it."

"What's to become of America?" John said. "And if reason cannot be revived to save us, is there salvation?"

The moderator considered a corner of the ceiling. "That's it?" he asked. "Should be an exciting afternoon."

The panel woman screeched, "Five repents!"

The moderator pointed his gavel at a man on the panel. "You, from Kansas, stand if you can, but state your question."

The panel woman yelled, "Three tears!"

A man from Kansas blossomed from his chair built for positive-sized people. "Mister Whitaker, as a biologist—and a *liberal*—with your 'beliefs' in science, won't you be fair and balanced by accepting Intelligent Design as superior to your...evil-ution?" The man patted his belly with both hands. He smiled.

"So you believe God created the universe," John said.

"I didn't say, Mister Whitaker."

"Well, I don't believe it," John said. "I *know* it. Perhaps you also believe political muscle should be flexed to force religion into science classrooms—a blend of fact and allegory suited to the comfort of property-tax-paying parents. Or that science education should be dismantled so we can lie to our children about the facts of nature rather than, as Jesus implored you, *to seek the truth.*"

"Mister Whitaker, Intelligent Design is good science."

"Intelligent Design, Critical Analysis, Intentioned Mutation, or whatever you're calling it now, serves one purpose: to create doubt about specialties among non-specialists. But if Intelligent Design really is science, then it's quite simple to prove. Test it." John watched him. "Indeed," he said. "You contend that God created the universe and man, which is true, but you won't be able to test that, will you."

"Intelligent Design won't be proven by experiment, Mister Whitaker."

"Then why teach it as though it were a scientific hypothesis? We used to teach science in science class with an objective—to teach science. We don't teach painting in math class. Should we? They both offer ways of seeing the world."

"And the transformation of some long-extinct cow into a whale can be tested, Mister Whitaker? How long will this test take?"

"We can't repeat that specific transformation any more than we

271

can replay a specific car accident. That doesn't bar us from knowing what happened."

"One metric of science is repeatability, Mister Whitaker. Evolution cannot be repeated."

"Nor can the Big Bang, layers of sedimentary deposits responsible for iron, oil, and limestone, yet we understand them quite well. Hence, we're forced to measure what can be. Your definition is so narrow as to cast out all that cannot adhere to the most stringent of disciplines. It's *your* definition of scientific knowledge, not that of science."

"What about all those disagreements among you biologists about evil-ution, Mister Whitaker? You can't even agree among yourselves."

"And what of disagreements about the Bible or life of Christ among almost a thousand Christian denominations?" John asked. "Would you then claim that, because of these arguments, Jesus never lived?"

"Even your theories evolve, Mister Whitaker. What makes you so certain they are finally correct?"

"Science does not claim to be final," John said. "But by perspectives of science by Creationist like you, there could be no accumulation of knowledge built on past information, because everything would have to fit the old view. Which you require to be in full and finished form from the day it was born."

Beads of perspiration started down sides of the man's face. "Intelligent Design proves that creatures in nature are so complex they must have been intentionally designed to even exist, Mister Whitaker. Their parts could not have been selected for by nature one piece after another over eons, because these creatures require all their parts to work at the same time." John began to answer but was stopped. "No, no, Mister Whitaker. Consider the bacterial flagellum—the whip-like tail of a bacteria, made from no less than *forty* different proteins. Without every one of those proteins, that biological machine cannot operate. It could not wait for the fortieth protein to fall into place, because its tail won't work at all without it."

"Actually, like evolutionary stages of the eye, it did work," John said. "But not as well."

"It had to have been *intentionally* designed, Mister Whitaker."

"So test it," John said. "Devise an experiment that will verify or refute your hypothesis. Execute it. Take observations. Record data. Check results. Repeat your experiment for validity. Discuss potential problems with colleagues. If no errors appear, submit your findings to peer-reviewed journals, reviewed anonymously by scientists you'll never know and never meet. Challenge is an every day, adversarial affair in science, not some cozy consensus. If reviewers discover no faults, your work will be published. Once exposed, your experiment will be validated by others and repeated thousands of times by scientists around the world. If no mistakes are found over years, perhaps decades, then you've got something called a scientific theory, not a guess or a hunch."

"We publish on our institute's website for all the world to see, Mister Whitaker."

"What about the bacterium helicobacter pylori?" John asked.

"The what, Mister Whitaker?"

"The bacteria responsible for stomach ulcers. With a tail that performs the same function as your forty-protein whiptail, but with just thirty proteins. Voilà: irreducible complexity, reduced. And when a species is found with twenty proteins to do the job? Ten?"

"That bacteria's tail is statistically impossible to make without a designer, Mister Whitaker."

"Creationist statistics," John said. "Like the possibility of human evolution as equal to the odds of a band of monkeys typing Shakespeare's sonnets by chance. Or the probability that a jumbo jet can be reassembled from its junkyard parts by a passing tornado. Easily ingested. As much to do with reality as witchcraft." John looked to the audience. "That there remain systems in nature too complex for us to yet fully understand proves one thing: that our knowledge remains incomplete. Hardly does it prove an intelligent force behind biology. And if these designs were intelligent, why would we suffer all the medical problems we face from bodies an engineer could plan better? Because God employs *natural selection* for that." John looked back at the man. "What you've done is restored the sixteenth-century God-of-the-gaps, when God was assigned all phenomena not yet understood. Problem being that God—by man's will—was forced to retreat from each knowledge

273

gap filled by science."

The man smiled. "Life cannot come about by chance, Mister—"

"Exactly. It's called natural selection. It has no plan, though we perceive one. Genes fittest for the environment survive to reproduce, others don't. It's that simple."

"Sounds like chance to me, Whitaker."

"Consider a forest of pine trees," John said. "In heavy snow environments, trees that lean by any amount accumulate more snow than those that grow vertically. Snow has weight. Trees can carry only so much load. Trees with genes that make them grow at an angle do not stand to reproduce when heavy snows arrive—they fall. Those with genes that direct only vertical growth shed excess weight and survive. Survivor seeds populate the landscape.

"Now enter a forest where each and every tree is straight as an arrow," John said. "It *appears* intentional. Like it was designed. Natural selection *is the designer*. No intention, no plan, but not random either. Natural selection: the same blind, purposeless, deterministic selection of pine trees, humans, and every life form to ever exist. Just ask the dinosaurs."

"But they're gone, Mister Whitaker."

"*Yes*. Selected *against*, as the leaning trees. It works both ways."

"Americans aren't gullible enough to believe that they came from a fish, Mister Whitaker."

"And yet the Bible states we came from dust."

"And when scientists say we are no more than worms, how do you think this affects our youth, Mister Whitaker?"

"I suppose in a way similar to Psalm 22:6, which claims a man is a worm. Does the Bible literally mean a man is a worm? Do you think scientists would claim humans and worms are equivalent in their manner of filmmaking? In the way they solve linear ordinary differential equations?"

The man vibrated. "If humans came from apes, we are nothing but animals and thus have no need of morality! *This*, Mister Whitaker, is why our society is on the brink of ruin!"

John shook his head. "Your unstated assumption is that if apes were our distant ancestors—which they were not—then we are no different from them, with equal need of morality. But while humans and the great apes share strong similarities, we are quite different.

Do we look the same to you? Having evolved from different animals, we're no less human, as wine is no less wine when transformed from water by Christ."

The man turned toward the audience. "Reject this heretic!"

John spoke evenly. "This nation was derived from reason. Our Founders were men of science. They risked all to vanquish tyrannies of irrationalism. They would be ashamed of what zealots like you have done. Your agenda is a disgrace to their memory and a menace to their brilliance."

"Intelligent Design and Critical Analysis shall be kept by laws of The Doctrine, Mister Whitaker!"

"And Scientologists wanted their religion in science class too," John said. "Now they have it. Whose religion did you expect to keep out once yours was in? While China teaches its students science, leaving us in a Medieval-dust as we teach 'the controversy,' to let *children* decide."

John held up his finger and poked it at the ceiling. "Let me offer this barometer for Creationist consideration. Not scientists, but corporations to test evolution's validity in nature. They employ scientific theories to locate aluminum, engineer genes, unearth oil from organics buried for millions of years. Instead, why not teach Intelligent Design to ExxonMobile, Alcoa, and Cargill, so they can use your models to find oil, metals, and the next drought-resistant wheat gene. Intelligent Design will be authenticated, and they'll be happy to expand their empires." John leaned toward the man. "The science that created your smartphone is the same science that finds evolution a fact of nature—physics and chemistry—no difference."

The man paused. He wiped sweat from his face. "Mister Whitaker," he said. "My son has autism. He reveres science and can name every star in the night sky. He knows he is different from other boys, but I tell him God loves him as God loves us all. Each night my son thanks God for making him the way he is. What will I tell him when he learns science and the Bible disagree? That we evolved from something else? That he is not God's Creation?"

John considered the man. "Your son is correct in his thanks to God," John said. "Science and the Bible agree, but your reading of that library won't allow it. To deny the sphere of validated science is to deny the reason science is built on. To deny God-given reason is to deny God."

The moderator motioned to an ample woman. She trembled against gravity to stand. "Mister Whitaker, to a gender expert like me, it's quite apparent you perceive yourself as threatening, masculine. My male side knows this. Shouldn't you—"

"Your male side?" John asked.

"*Choice*, Mister Whitaker. On one day, I am lion—I am woman; hear me roar!" She growled. "On another day, I am cunning—I am man." She grabbed her crotch like squeezing juice from an orange.

"Isn't gender biologically determined?" John asked.

"Biology? Imperial, colonizing, Western bias! Society determines gender, Mister Whitaker, as *preference*. I have freed myself from such oppression."

"Are we also oppressed by gravity?"

"Your macho right-wing *conservative* aggression plays right into my hands, sir. As you probably don't know, boys are at this moment in gender equity programs. Campouts, where boys may be properly medicated, made sensitive to The Doctrine. Shouldn't you offer yourself to similar sensitivity training, as all right-thinking males do, as a matter of mental hygiene?"

"I know about the camps, professor, where nat—"

"He said the P-word! That's racist!"

The audience withered.

"Where natural male behavior is pathologized," John said.

Arms skyward, the woman spun toward the audience. "He rejects masculinity amelioration train—" Her face tangled in flags hung from a wire. Spun in circles, she fought the Stars and Stripes, finally to emerge. She unraveled a flag from her wrist and fixed the slanted wig on her skull. "And you, Mister Whitaker, think it's wrong to educate boys in equality?"

"What education? While our sons believe adults are here to protect them, our camps molest boys by age four, sanctioned by government largesse."

"*Molest, Mister* Whitaker, really." She adjusted a pair of bifocals. She lifted a notepad in front of her face. "Doctor Skipper of our most prestigious university revealed The Girl's Great Sorrow all the way back in the last century. She proved boys to be responsible for that sorrow." The pad hung limply as she looked at John over the tops of her glasses. "Mister Whitaker, it's well known how rare it is for boys to graduate high school, how so few can hold a job, how so many commit suicide. If it not for the camps, there'd be no busboys, soldiers, grave diggers to demonstrate commitments to diversity."

"Funny, you didn't mention a need for fathers," John said.

"And for those who assume that role, studies have found such men are best suited to stay at home, to keep a clean house."

"Did you ever consider the possibility our boys are failures *because* of your camps, and this society's semi-silent hatred of males? That the root problem is boys are trying *not* to be men? And why would they? Popular culture represents men as universal idiots. Every TV commercial and sitcom is composed of males made to be vulgar fools with women in the wings to study their monstrous nature or beat them in scenes with canned laughter." John looked above at the mezzanine. "Fat men clothed only in panties, bras and high heels stumble to gas up a women's Formula One race car; men pour beer and chips over their faces behind their SUV's open hatchback as a woman records their primate behavior from a forest blind; a fat man clad only in underwear does *The Twist* before a beer bottle because the cap says 'twist off;' a man on a bus struggles to make breakfast on a hot plate as women deride his stupidity, enjoying their breakfast bar. One male 'expert' on PBS declared the trouble with men is that they're not women. Televised debates prove that *men are finished.* Authors claim to have proof that even God prefers women because eighty-two percent of all fatal lightning strikes kill men."

"Oh, Mister Whitaker, please—"

"Our only other male template comes from the old Freddy Kruger films, *Texas Chainsaw Massacre*s, or any endless number of slashing males portrayed by Hollywood."

"Mister Whitaker, those commercials are funny. You could use a sense of humor."

"Yes," John agreed, "humans can be mocked without a lawsuit. But picture those gender roles reversed. Would it be comical if girls fed on a steady diet of degradation? Hasn't that already been done, long before Skipper's fertile imaginings? Boys have grown up with this media blitz for four generations. Their self-image mimics what they're told by elites who then struggle to understand the obvious.

While the concept and designation of gentleman and citizen; the notion we should educate our boys to be worthy of these honors— these ideas are foreign to us. These would impinge on self-expression, and require an agreed-upon moral standard. Imagine that."

The woman approached her seat. "You truly are the fount of almost all wisdom. You can corner the rest of it by reporting to re-education immediately. Reap the benefits of modern scholarship."

"*Scholarship*...Such as the preposterous *finding* that boys are sexual proto-predators. Like California's infamous Joseph Newton, who kissed a female classmate, punished for sexual harassment at age five. Or New York's Kurt Schumer, who hugged a girl at age six, charged as a *grabber*. All benefits of Doctor Skipper's scholarship."

"And you mean to tell us with a straight face, boys are not sexual proto-predators, Mister Whitaker? When four in five of all women in America are sexually assaulted?"

"By what definition? Desires for public outrage are satisfied because no one will ask this question. It's a long-standing campaign. In 1985, Ms. Magazine released Mary Koss's shocking news that one in four college coeds were raped, even though three-quarters of them didn't know it. While Linda Ledray's *Recovering From Rape* defined *looks* and compliments that make women uncomfortable as forms of rape. How much wider can we expand the chasm between the sexes when a compliment might be rape if someone happens to decide it is?

"I suggest some numerical analysis answers that question," John said. "Consider Katherine Hanson—director of the Women's Education Equity Act Publishing Center—who famously claimed that four million women were beaten to death every year in the US, most by men at home. Four million per year is eleven thousand women murdered per day, every day, all year long, in just one country. Wouldn't somebody notice? In thirty years, there'd be no women. While the FBI reported 4000 women per year died from violence at that time. Heinous, but short of four million by a factor of a thousand.

"Add to this," John said, "that in 2014, a CDC report found one in five women sexually assaulted. Where 'sexual assault' included 'non-contact,' 'non-verbal,' and 'sexual violence type unspecified.' A catch-all capable of the wildest interpretations. While not to deny real crimes by men against women, do these spacious definitions service genuine victims in need of justice, or trivialize them? All the while vilifying males, which is, of course, the point. The image of Emmett Till comes to mind, brutalized and murdered for smiling at a white woman in 1950s Mississippi."

"Excuse me, Mister Whitaker."

"Emmett's act would be categorized as a gender crime at any playground in America. He'd be no safer today than he was a century ago."

"Mister Whit—"

"In both cases, punishment is delivered for what? Not for our sins, not our crimes, nothing other than what we are least responsible for—our DNA. Educating young men to be useful is a basic requirement of any society. But radically reengineer their psyches in the camps, and you get what we've got: gangs that nurture a hatred so powerful that young men control inner cities even the marines fear to enter. Where the only—"

"Wholly the responsibility of those who reject The Doctrine!" she said.

"Where the only number larger than gang membership is their suicide rate. So widespread Congress quietly passed a law making it a federal violation for states to quantify it."

"Precisely why we need the camps, Mister Whitaker."

"Precisely a measure of their failure. Perhaps this nation has always required a villain—top predator species, natives, blacks, women, now men. You should be proud. You've created a whole new class of victims. Real ones."

A heavy man cleared his throat. Acknowledged, he crossed John's line of sight. He raised and lowered his chins as he nodded and tugged on his mustache. "Mister Whitaker, I want to pick your brain about this notion that humans have any large-scale effect on the planet. Are we not gnats on an elephant?"

"No."

"You assert, Mister Whitaker, that there are too many humans on Earth, but shouldn't we have more children to pay for healthcare? We saw the cost of boomers on society when there weren't enough young to support the old."

"And when those young become old and retire?" John asked.

"Then still more babies."

"And when that generation retires?"

"Keep those babies comin'! Great for the economy."

"What economy? Subsequent resource wars won't allow one. The more humans there are, the more problems we have."

The man expanded. "Whitaker's war on women!" he shouted. "He wants to sterilize women!"

John held up one hand. "Voluntary and ethical reductions in our population by having few or no children. The choice is yours. But when the time comes, it won't be me or somebody else advocating a decline in our numbers, they'll collapse all on their own. You make an economic argument for what is a moral matter."

The man chuckled. "What would you *liberals* know about morality?" He held up a calculator. "Give each person alive today a two-thousand-square-foot space to live, and what would you find?"

"Something irrelevant," John said.

"Oh, contraire. Give ten billion humans a two-thousand-square-foot residence, and you'll need only twice the size of Texas to house them all. Compared to *two hundred million* square miles on Earth, a measly two-tenths of one small percent. Are you not stunned into embarrassment to find our world is not so crowded after all? That we have no real impact on this planet, *Mister* Whitaker?"

"And as America moved west, buffalo herds were said to be so vast they would always be a hazard to railroads; forests so extensive there'd never be enough labor to cut them down for practical use; the Great Plains so wide every man could have all he wanted for free. But buffalo were decimated from sixty million to one thousand individuals; forests scalped to pay leveraged debts; only a few thousand acres remain of seemingly endless Great Plains. The more there are of us, the less there is of everything else."

The man thrust his calculator forward as though John could read its digits from his distance. "Twice the size of Texas, Mister Whitaker. That's all. Mathematical *fact*. Like those other facts you deny. Like there's a lot more river and ocean than coal ash and oil every time we spill a little." The man laughed, cellulite sealing his eyes shut.

"And among a million molecules of clean air, a few hundred of carbon monoxide will kill you," John said. "Such is the nature of a toxin."

"We pay for that pollution, Mister Whitaker. It's a matter of liberty and the American way of life." He turned to the audience. "Liberty!"

"Liberty is not an absence of moral restraints," John said. "Be those restraints applied to the environment or pornography. And people have paid to have others murdered. Paying for it doesn't make it moral."

"You liberals, always trying to scare us, so you can control us."

"What I'm trying to do is emulate my Savior. He did not force people to see the light, he persuaded them."

"Whitaker is Big Brother!"

"The requirement for doctors to wash their hands before surgery—did that rob anyone of liberty?" John asked. "Removal of lead from paint and gasoline—hamper your freedom? Though I agree, rules, regulations, and laws have swelled dramatically. Why? Because this planet is limited, while human population so far is not. Institutions struggle to maintain order and stability with a multiplication of rules. That won't change until there are fewer people."

The man waved his arms. "I've mathematically proven we have not overpopulated planet Earth. Argument settled! I win!" He dropped the calculator in his shirt pocket.

"You've ignored the fact that seven-tenths of this planet is salt water," John said. "Another ten percent is mountain, desert, or still-uninhabitable Antarctic terrain. Your available landscape is suddenly eighty percent smaller. Now, what fraction of remaining land does your calculator show allocated to each of us for the grains we consume, the animals we eat, the land those animals graze? What fraction is dedicated to each person for farms, roads, shopping malls, suburbs, megacities? I assume you have that per-person, per-year acreage for me. By comparison, the space our homes occupy is immaterial. By your assessment, we needn't even have yards."

"There's no less planet than there ever was, Whitaker. Just like there's no less water today than there was a million years ago. So, water's not rare either, as you scare-mongering libs contend."

John shook his head. "Of all this planet's water, *three* percent is fresh," he said. "Yes, that value remains constant. But there's no limit on people. The more people there are, the less water there is per person. And what do humans do when there's not enough water per person? They butcher each other to slake that thirst."

The man looked over audience faces. "How can all these people be so obese if resources are so scarce, Mister Whitaker?"

"Inactive lifestyles on corn syrup diets ensured by government subsidies."

"Whitaker hates farmers!"

"You just told me, all we require is our living space. What need have we of farms?"

"*Everybody knows* you environmentalist wackos want to destroy capitalism, Whitaker. After a hundred years of debate about overpopulation; mass extinctions; global warming; wilderness habitat lost to humans, we still don't know all there is to know. You act like it's all perfect science."

"And as imperfect as it is, science created every technology around you. Who needs perfect? We don't know everything about the flu. That doesn't stop us from creating successful vaccines."

"Another boat just got stuck in Antarctic ice, Whitaker. The Northeast froze their tails off last winter. So much for the *science* of global warming."

"Including Alaska," John said, "The United States makes up just two percent of Earth's surface. Note the word *global*. It's not 'Northeast US warming,' not 'a boat got stuck in the ice warming.'"

"*Everybody knows* we'd go broke if we fixed the world's environment. We're already broke. We can't afford to fix it."

"How much would it cost?" John asked. The man froze like a column of salt. John nodded. "You don't know...Could it be as expensive as the abandonment of New York, Miami, New Orleans? More costly than farmland turned to desert or flooded by our hyper-storms?"

The man bellowed, "The only ones to get rich will be those liberal professors with their government grants!"

A woman on the panel shouted, "He said the P-word!"

"Yes, science costs money," John said. "Are scientific findings on any topic you can name to be rejected because they cost money?

282

I'll gamble you could locate scientists who did what they did for a dollar or find one among thousands that falsified data. Does that mean after all those millions spent on smallpox, it wasn't eradicated in 1979? Was penicillin a fake? Billions spent to map the human genome didn't really map the human genome?"

The man scratched the top of his bald scalp and ordered lonely strands of hair over wide-open space. "*Everybody knows* humans have no noteworthy effect on the planet."

"And how do you know this?"

"I know it, Whitaker."

"Have you measured your own dataset to contradict two centuries of research and common sense observation? Have you surveyed measurements to find them wrong? No, you haven't. How you came to know what you know is simple: employing the Creationist playbook, you foster doubt about specialties among non-specialists, you cuddle half-truths that make you comfortable. You've decided nature is a liberal, and you refuse to take liberals seriously. You dismiss scientific evidence as nonexistent. But when quizzed on support for your position, we find you don't have any. And as we previously witnessed, you do not *seek the truth to set you free*. The science that created your calculator is the same science that proves manmade global warming a fact—physicist and chemistry—no difference.

"Now," John said, "having corrected your value of available land, how many acres are required per person, per year?" John waited. Silence and audience eyeballs pressured the man to respond.

"Given that most of this world's people live in a hut, two thousand square feet is pretty generous, Mister Whitaker."

John nodded. "You don't know. It's two acres per person per year and rising. That's thirty million square miles for all of us combined. Almost three times the size of Africa, and eighty percent of this planet's usable landmass. What's left is fractured into parcels too small for the remainders of wide-ranging or migrating animals, birds, insects, and their delicate interactions, so we've modified all of it. In these last hunnert years of the Anthropocene, extinction has claimed sixty percent of birds, in no small measure from loss of estuaries around the world, *reclaimed*—so it's called—for farms and cities. Fifty percent of mammals. Ninety percent of fishes—our oceans virtually lifeless from overfishing. And as we debate here now, in the basement of a small laboratory in China, Earth's last frog patiently awaits a female to prolong his species, while video recorders observe the death of his aspirations. Who could have imagined such an outcome? Not the wildest liberal, not the most radical environmentalist. I'll gamble not even your calculator could foretell such risk."

John turned to the audience. "There have been and will be those who use environmental decline as an argument against capitalism, achievers, and property rights. But nature has no political party, nor does it recognize borders. I do not condemn our past for invention of the internal combustion engine nor for the harvest of trees. But human numbers and our voracity, even with advanced technology, have outpaced nature's capacity. Will solutions be easy? No. But they are available."

The man thumped a tabletop. He pointed at John. "True conservatives know science and scientists are one of the four corners of evil and deceit!"

"And what do you think of those scientists who created our Constitution and Declaration of Independence, centered on the rights of man?" John asked. "Ideas from a chemist named John Locke."

The moderator looked at his list and motioned to a woman on the panel. "You're up. Our university expert on..." He looked back at his list. "Victorian rationality in the Founders' bedroom?"

An enormous woman rose. She fanned her face with a copy of *The Derrida Compendium.* "Yes...The Founders and their Declaration...Nice segue," she said. "Mister Whitaker, my expertise is in our peculiar American definition of rational thought and the Founders who initiated it to coddle the wealthy. As well as male objects who've shaped rational discourse dictated by their sexuality. Such as Lincoln's homosexual habits of sleeping with other men; the effects of diaper changing on masturbation among signers of the Constitution; Washington's—"

John cringed. "Ma'am, I'm afraid to ask, but what possible sources can you cite?"

"The Doctrine defines *ma'am* as a *courtesy*, Mister Whitaker. A courtesy is an expression of your belief in my *inferiority*."

John stared at her, momentarily speechless.

The woman appealed to the moderator. "Did you see that? How he looked at me? He touched me with his eyes. That's inappropriate touching!"

John looked down. He rubbed his forehead, whispering something. He hesitated. "Person?" he said.

She grimaced. "Excuse me?"

He looked at the space around her. "Instead of ma'am, may I call you *person?*"

"Only because I grasp the deficiencies of conservatives like you. But you should realize the Board of Fairness and Diversity, the BFD, has stated that terms such as *person* carry an esteem risk for those offended by being *persons*. While, concurrently, the Wise Talk Facility is assisting—"

"The WTF?"

"The WTF is assisting the BFD, sir, in acceptable uses for the term *person*. We await their insight. But back to my question…Given my familiarity with our Founders' sexual habits, I must ask if you practice in private or in public—"

John blushed. "Please, no, don't ask if I—" He covered his face.

"Do you practice, Mister Whitaker, inductive reasoning, and empirical research as a basis for *knowledge?*"

John peered between fingers. "Are you a Creationist?" he said.

"*Heavens,* no!"

He put his hands down. "If scientific theories based on inductive reasoning and empirical research weren't in the neighborhood of reality," John said, "they wouldn't work, would they?"

"So, Mister Whitaker, you deny the so-called rational sciences are culture-bound delusions and, therefore, subjective."

"Of course, I deny it because it's not true. Science is science no matter where you go because nature is nature no matter where you go. Science describes nature. Though I do agree, our views are influenced by our culture."

"Thank you, Mister Whitaker."

"But because culture has a strong impact on our perspectives," John said, "is not to say there exists no one able to see past it. Was Socrates culture-bound? Jesus Christ? The inventor of the wheel?"

"Perhaps the genealogy of this narrative, with its modalities, problematics, and schematisms of discourse, will help, Mist—"

John turned to the audience. "She just said she's going to give me a history lesson."

"Mister Whitaker, four hundred years ago, Francis Bacon believed the experience of our senses in the form of experiment was the superior route to truth. Then René Descartes reversed this. He believed the mind was superior through mathematical descriptions of nature because our senses could not be trusted."

John hesitated. "So nature afforded the senses its creatures possess for the purpose of deceiving them? Apparently, there's a link between our senses and reality, as our senses work rather well. Yes, we can be fooled. This doesn't mean we are in every case. Science applies a balance of both experiment and mathematics. Bacon and Descartes each saw half the whole."

"Do you cuddle *half-truths* that make you comfortable, sir?"

John smiled. "In 1948, the favored *mathematical* approach of Descartes hinted at an afterglow from some kind of explosion in the universe. No one imagined the Big Bang until a deeper investigation of equations revealed it. But that mathematical model wasn't proven correct until *experimentation* favored by Bacon was technologically feasible sixteen years later, in 1964. How could this be if science were a delusion unattached to reality?"

She shook her finger at John. "As though there were some standard external to experience. Remember, everyone has a different experience, different perspectives, values, preferences. What standard, Mister Whitaker?"

"Person, doesn't mathematics offer a universal standard external to experience? How much experience do we have with black holes? They were revealed mathematically long before they were discovered in nature."

"But, Mister Whitaker, these belief systems, which you agree exist antecedent to science, they might be anything culture to culture. How can science lay claim to truth when cultures are so different?"

"Are people in India subject to human metabolism just as you are right here and now? Any subjective character of personal experience with nature is made objective because our conclusions have something to do with nature as it is. Yes, humans are subjective, and nature is what it is, regardless of our beliefs.

Scientific models bridge that separation."

"Which models, Mister Whitaker? Dalton's, Thompson's or Rutherford's? Dalton was certain the atom was an indivisible ball. But Thomson's experiments found atoms to be like a plum pudding of protons and electrons. Then Rutherford discovered helium ions bounce off atoms, and the plum pudding model was replaced by the idea of a concentrated nucleus. They were all wrong. Do you presume science to be in a different state today?"

"I do because they were all partly right. Each was able to show what their particular experiment was able to reveal. Like the blind men and the elephant, all feel different portions of the animal. The elephant is a flexible hose—its trunk; the elephant is a sturdy tree—its leg. Are they wrong, or right? Are they incorrect, or incomplete? You view evolving theories in a state of replacement rather than refinement. For you—as for Creationists—to expand the initial idea is indictment, not affirmation."

"That's your culture-bound *preference*, Mister Whitaker."

"You don't send men to the moon and bring them back alive on preference. You don't defeat polio on preference. Either we're impossibly lucky to find all elements of a spacecraft—cars, computers, submarines—with thousands of parts that obey everything from the 'theory' of gravity to electrical circuit 'theory,' working just as we expect them to, or our grasp of nature, derived from science is close to spot on."

John looked to mezzanines overhead. A small girl held tight the railing, watching John from above. He leaned close to microphones. "I won't be able to say this enough: Do you see the similarity? Here, the liberal university postmodernist who aims to dismantle science as she impersonates scientific arguments? The conservative Creationist who hopes to demolish science as he imitates the scientific method? Are you starting to sense the costs for our abandonment of reason? Can you see how training in science and the reason it hones would resolve this?"

The woman fumed. "Science cannot lay claim to reality *as it is*. Science is not truth with a capital T. *There is none*."

"Then, how does an artist do what they do?" John said.

"*What?*"

"How does the oil painter create his image of Venice?" John

287

asked. "His painting is a *model* of reality. Initiated by reality's impact on the artist, processed in his mind in ways even he does not grasp. This model of Venice is created in a transfer of reality in his brain, filtered through emotions and sensations. He constructs his model of reality through physical interactions with the world around him—his paint, his canvas. Now, a painting of Venice is not Venice. But the painting—*if* it works—communicates something beyond a direct observation of Venice. How can this be? How can art communicate truth at such a deep level, and do so universally? Because humans too are part of that reality. *We are made of it*, of nature as it is, composed of truth with a capital T. It is *in* us.

"Likewise," John said, "scientific theories are a model of reality. Initiated by reality's impact on the scientist, processed in her mind in ways even she does not grasp. This model of nature is created in a transfer of reality in her brain, filtered through memories of experience and intuitions. She constructs her model of reality through physical interactions with the world around her—equations on a page, experiments in the lab. But this perception of nature, this theory of nature, is not nature. Do you see? The scientific theory—*if* it works—communicates something beyond a direct observation of nature. Able to reveal things we didn't know, like leftover heat from the Big Bang, hidden in Einstein's equations.

"As Picasso said, person, 'Art is the lie that tells the truth.' Art and science tell the truth without themselves being the truth. Like art, science is *transcendent*. And transcendent of what? Of final *definition*. As with any glimmer of Grace—art, science, compassion, morality—the deepest root of what makes these true with a capital T cannot be defined. The painting looks in a way that Venice does not look. Light cannot be both particle and wave, yet science shows us this unbearable duality is real. Each presents a world we know cannot be so, yet these pictures they paint communicate that which is as it is.

"These things must, in the end, be transcendent," John said, "if they are to be true with a capital T, if they are to reach that realm of nature and humanity as they are. True and real as the impossible strangeness of quantum mechanics."

She watched him. She whistled. "Wow...Whatever you just said...In your more lucid moments—'if it works,' you say—you emphasize what we progressives refer to as the *functional argument*. That is, you claim because we understand the *function* of things; we therefore also know the *meaning* of things. But consider a hammer, Mister Whitaker—a dense thing that when swung with momentum can do work. That is the *function* of the hammer. But to a carpenter, the hammer *means* something quite different than what it *means* to a murderer."

John squinted into empty space. Spellbound audience members contemplated infinitudes of their ignorance, astonished by such intellectual luster from American academia. John appeared baffled.

"*Look*...Mister Whitaker, there are many ways to define objects. Functionally, as you and other old-fashioned rationalists do, or through meaning, as the rest of us do."

"But why focus on objects?" John said.

"*Look*...It's clear, Mister Whitaker, since meaning is different for everyone, there is no true knowledge, even for something as simple as a hammer. Imagine the confusion between cultures, times, and places about *everything*. We really can't *know* anything, especially anything outside our own culture."

John nodded. "I get it. But first, if we can't know anything," he said, "how can you know we can't know anything?"

John glanced out a window at the Four Great Truths. The woman began to speak. He stopped her. "Person, you just defined the meaning of an object in terms of its use. Says who? You conflate meaning, or use, with knowledge. And since the meaning or use of a hammer is not fixed, then neither is knowledge about the hammer. It's absurd. You set the table to satisfy your argument, the way Creationists set up their statistical ruse. And your game deals with more than scientific knowledge alone; as you said, it's about knowledge of any kind."

John spoke to the audience, pointing back at the professor. "This is postmodernism at its finest. Its core project: to convince you that everything—science, law, mortality—all are part of a grand *Relativity*. Anything goes. There is no solid ground about anything. Except for the conviction that there is no solid ground about anything. While a handy convenience for postmodernist professors evading rational criticism and moral judgment, hardly a recipe for sustainable civilization. Such philosophical movements are not simply another intellectual fad for which academics give themselves awards. Philosophy can build nations. It built this one. It can also tear them down. Don't presume these ideas are inconsequential simply because they're ridiculous. These are tips of much larger hazards at the heart of our decline. It was not always this way in the humanities. They once tried to tell the truth."

John returned to the professor. "Today the public confers validity on you simply for your campus proximity to the science department. Your bewildering language is intended to inoculate you from challenge. But you've painted yourselves into a corner, engaged in a contradictory struggle to find coherence as you strive to remain incoherent. Which is evidence for a universal truth about how the human mind operates—to make sense of things."

The woman sat. Table lamps rattled. "*Look...*There are no such things as universals, Mister Whitaker. Another discredited conservative fancy."

Arms cast out in resignation, John turned to people above. "Universal, timeless human truths are why we understand Chief Seattle's lament, Shakespeare's plays, Biblical cautions, Greek tragedy, and the sad facts of life expressed by Sumer's Gilgamesh. Such examples span five thousand years of different cultures, languages, perspectives, and their own shades of human meaning. We are not alien to their experience even though we don't speak their language or live in their forever-gone cultures. We understand them still. Evidence that morality, suffering, compassion are more than mere 'social preferences' particular to each society.

"Why," John asked, "would thousands perish in attempts to free themselves from tyranny in Babylon, the Roman Empire, America's slave trade were it not for universal desires for freedom? That 1989 image of a solitary man facing down the barrel of a tank in Tiananmen Square, or Mohamed Bouazizi setting himself ablaze in 2010 Tunisia make it clear enough that concepts of universal human rights are not a secret kept only by the West.

"But what if the professor is right? Then, except for postmodernists, we could not commit to be right about anything. We could not make judgments, not only about the oppressed but about the oppressor. In that circumstance, what actions shall we take when the next Holocaust occurs? So the Nazi SS murdered twelve million

Jews, Russians, Slavs, Czechs, Poles, resistant Germans. Those people had no universal human rights because there weren't any? Ludicrous!

"Now, I admit that extermination of Jews by Nazis held different meanings for both," John said. "But does this change the reality of murder? Any more than different utilities for a hammer confounds what a hammer is? Are those meanings then simply *preferences*, neither right nor wrong, only different?"

John focused on the scholar. "With utmost clarity, this philosophical movement—born in the 1950s, strong since the 1980s—is logically and morally *wrong*. For you to settle a score with the West over its faults, professor, you have the potential, like your former Marxist allies, to open vistas of brutality you never anticipated."

Panelists whispered to others. One old man at the back of the panel hunched over his notepad. He scribbled with rapid motion.

A woman on the panel raised her hand. She seemed out of place as her body occupied only one-third of a seat for positive sized people. Acknowledged, she rose without hesitation. Panel members murmured at her sudden movements.

"John, you've written that economics must remain a free venture because its complexity denies centralized planning. You say such planning would destroy what planners set out to harness. Isn't a truly free-market economy dangerous?"

"It's also never been done, nor should it be," he said. "As the economist Frederick Hayek showed in his capitalist manifesto, rational regulation of commerce is as justified as limits on government because humans are humans wherever you go."

"But, John, while Congress makes very public announcements about regulation, that regulation is quietly massaged to allow risk-free corruption, because business interests are too big to fail. Congress—our preschool for lobbyists—represent those who bought them, do they not?" She watched his expression. "John, since we lost the 1933 Glass-Steagall Act in 1999 with its separation of investment gamblers from private accounts, we've endured economic upheavals every twenty years. Because those with the money make the laws, which ensures they make more money, which buys more laws. What regulation?"

John's eyes appeared to read pages in his memory.

"John, in 1976, the top one percent of American earners held 9% of total national income. In 2006 our top one percent took home 25% of national income, while average hourly wages dropped. Can you tell me how those numbers stack up today?" He shook his head. "Today, John, half a century later, that top one percent makes 60% of national income, and the average hourly—"

"Due to China's rise to affluence, coupled with America's current condition," John said. "We've become a cheap labor market after The Quake and subsequent crash, from which we did not recover."

"Indeed," she said. "That cheap labor hourly wage dropped to one-twelfth its 1976 value. Have we built a system that reduces income inequality, or assured it and the armed revolution it invites? And isn't this the destiny of free-market capitalism, annihilating the humane substance of society and nature with it? Aren't democratic ideals, so closely knitted with capitalism, now doomed by greed?

"The communities you seek to recover, John, were terminated by economic forces. Lost long before the Supreme Court's reproduction of individual rights pushed communal responsibilities aside. Long before centralized government replaced community organizations with welfare."

"Systems of old had their problems too," John said. "Like abject poverty. A competition ruthless for resources out of excess scarcity, not excess excess. What I urge is balance. Evils of the market won't be allayed by its elimination."

"What about moderation? With more equal—not uniform, but more equal—distributions of wealth, we avoid revolution, allowing opportunities for each to realize that indispensable value you claim we all possess."

"By what means?" John asked. "Give animals of the forest their forest, they won't become indolent. Give humans their daily bread without need to earn it, you've robbed them of purpose."

"I'm not advocating state-sponsored handouts, John, but a return to humane society. Consider what life was and what life has become. In the distant past, neighbors mobilized to rebuild the home destroyed by fire. We relied on one another. Today if I pay my premiums to strangers, an insurance company pays strangers to rebuild my house. Only when we elevate the alleged moral neutrality of *market efficiency* over *communal interactions* will insurance appear the correct manner of enduring misfortune.

"Likewise," she said, "in the farmer's home of yesteryear, connections to labor, life, and family were clear. But once work moved to factories in cities, mechanizing our roles, dissociation from self and community commenced. The Industrial Revolution, coupled with the notion of economic growth as a surrogate for social justice, made people believe all human needs could be satisfied with material commodities. Thereafter, social relations bent to that promise. What followed was homogenized training that allowed people to understand instructions of other trades, establishing a bureaucratized society of substitutable people. Communal attachments became a hindrance.

"But as Aristotle taught, John, communities are not simply associations that inhabit a common site for the sake of exchange. Communities form out of need, not for the hell of it. *Social society*, which thrived on our sensitivities of *connectedness*, was inverted into *economic society*, thriving on our *disconnectedness*. That Americans would pay less for foreign-made goods rather than more for the same product made by their neighbors is a testament to this detachment.

"Eventually," she said, "we accepted that faraway corporations would acquire local businesses because local owners ranked wealth above employees they once knew. But is the corporation morally bound to the community like the local merchant who once joined us for the Sunday sermon? What community?

"As you know, John, economists believe the best markets are those that efficiently maximize utility of calculating, self-interested *individuals* focused on their *individual* choices. Notice no mention of the communities you cherish. Even the binding agent of religion was debased. When economic machinery disbands community, it confines religious ethics to the church. Hence, these spasms of pious recovery, as attempts to press morality beyond church walls. A response to our economic system that represents the very character of modernity. Where religious teachings of modesty are obstacles to consumer spending, and ethics impose production costs, hampering economic growth.

"And isn't it ironic, John, that our retreat from ethics now folds back on corporations seeking that growth, struggling to teach their employees ethics, while corporate board members amass billions in windfalls. Because we can no longer expect talented executives to be incentivized by a mere 7 million dollars per year, not 70 million, but for the first time, a record 707 million did the trick in 2008. One man's salary, bonus, and company stock awarded by the board with commencement of the Great Recession. Is that incentive or exploitation?

"Of course, we're told such sums are attached to performance. But performance graded by the individual board member who profits from it, or from the board with whom they dine and golf. How surprising they would grant themselves perfection in every measure. And remember, these aren't inventors reaping due rewards from ingenuity and hard work, John, but helmsman of publicly traded companies. Rewards not set by shareholders—paid whether they're fired, with their golden parachutes, or tumble the world economy—hardly market-driven. Is this capitalism, or cronyism? It remains easier to pass a camel through the eye of a needle than to abate greed. Because there are no virtues, John, only laws, serving those who bought them.

"As you've said, John, there is no longer a common good. Because—but for the Amish, Mennonites, and orthodox Jews—there are no true communities from which the good is defined. With no common good, there can be no common ethic. And with this retreat from ethics, animals can be abused in the most cost-effective manner of slaughter, protected by ag-gag laws; landscapes can be eradicated on schedule, in conformance with property laws; corporations are free to ship manufacturing somewhere else, in accordance with international laws. Thus exporting tactile interaction with real things, further disconnecting ourselves, even from our own creations. These became the responsible things to do once society was inverted, once social relations became subservient to market forces.

"These examples demonstrate the swing in perspective that made us the way we are, John. From humility to display; self-sacrifice to self-indulgence; belonging to autonomy. From virtues for the common good to free choice of the me-me-me-generation.

Liberated and alone.

"This swing in outlook resulted from economic perspectives, John. Because economics is not only explanatory or predictive; it builds the world we live in when policymakers conform us and our world to economic policy. These policies change our interactions. Free-market individualism leads to life lived in a perpetual present, a series of immediate experiences. Of course, entertainment, materialism, and pointlessness dominate us with no overarching unity.

"With our societies now obedient to markets," she said, "we are alone again, greedy for our possessions, fearful of our neighbors. There are five hundred million people in this country, and we are the loneliest people on Earth. The Economy created man in its image.

"But that image took some kind of psychological turn," she said, "when in 2003 an arbitrary war in Iraq maneuvered by a handful of men at the top cost 5000 America lives, 150,000 Iraqi's and two trillion dollars only to be lost years later when we tired of managing the Middle East, that graveyard of empires. As World War One turned us against the idea that science would engineer better societies, so too, our failure in Iraq reversed American's belief in promoting democracy. Then Wall Street's Great Recession of 2008 cast the deepest doubts in the economic promise of the Market when certain individuals raked in bonuses from taxpayers they'd bankrupted. With these events, democracy itself began to look a lot like any ordinary tyranny.

"Do you understand, John, how economic efficiency is a moral matter played out in its own arena, said to be morally neutral? That how the pie is distributed is as important as the size of the pie? That excesses of the economic model will kill what gave it birth? That both democracy's individualism and its teammate, capitalist economics, will kill each other? Do you see how similar our views are, yours and mine?"

John hesitated. He processed what he heard. "And I see differences," he said. "Somehow, someway, control must be imposed. Innovation directed, change limited."

"By rate of change, John. Cohesion prioritized over modernization."

"A prescription for invasion from another country," John said.

"Change wrought by innovation is so sudden that harm is inevitable, John. It's not the innovation so much as the rate of change it promotes."

"And how will social powers determine who may buy refrigerators, while others must receive horse-and-cart delivery of ice, allowing our iceman time to find sustainable means? Doesn't a capitalistic price and wage system address all this?"

"Decided locally, John, by workers, merchants, ministers, families—not imposed by global markets. Nor levied by a faraway federal authority as though there existed some inscrutable national kinship. Rather in a manner that respects local social forces, while accepting the abstract state. Like the idea of a graduated local tax, simultaneous with a flat national tax. One influenced by human attachments, the other accepting anonymity of national disconnectedness."

John watched his podium. Air leaked from his lungs. "I need time to think about this."

"All this economizing of morality, human linkage, nature, and the animal world is a retreat of what, John?"

He squinted. "I don't know."

"Trust. Of country, of others, of ourselves. As though trust could be—"

He bowed his head. "Stop."

"As though trust could be made efficient."

"I need—"

"Trust as a commodity," she said. "Right-sized, economized—"

"Stop!" Hands up, he surrendered. "I just…need time to think."

The woman watched him. She waited.

John evaluated nearby space. "Interesting," he said, "that you and Karl Polanyi find extremes of Enlightenment's capitalistic machinery as the fault to blame for our woes. While I and Karl's brother Michael accuse Enlightenment's overextended rationalism and our reaction to it. When postmodernism on the Left makes reason the enemy of truth with a capital T, and when tribal truth on the Right becomes the enemy of reason among the common man.

"I sympathize with your perspective, really I do," he said. "We agree on the callusing of humanity, but not necessarily its cause, nor its remedy. It seems to me the exchange of capitalism for socialism—or whatever you've proposed—is a swap of one set of problems for another no less harmful to humanity and nature.

"Or perhaps I'm wrong. Somewhere out there in the cosmic void of societal evolution, there must be an answer. Or are we condemned as a species because condemnation is also part of what we're made of?"

John and the woman watched one another. She sat.

An expansive man was recognized. "Mister Whitaker, I read you're for some form of animal rights, at least for mammals—liberal. You appear to think capitalism is a match for human nature—conservative. Just what is your politics? I thought we were here to get some sense of your philosophy, which you seem to think counts for something, though who can tell for what? You're in blatant dissonance with The Doctrine. It is, after all, the definition of pluralistic society. America is tolerant of all views—both of them."

John began to speak.

"Wait," the man said. "Let's give this philosophy of yours a name, shall we? Why not...The Gospel of John?"

People laughed, teetered on their seats, snarled, or asked, "John who?" An old man at the back of the panel wrote with such force he broke the pencil he wrote with.

"Ladies and males," the man said, "*the good news* from John!" The man giggled and fell in his chair, jarring the building.

John's eyes searched his podium. He looked over those on the panel. "I promote not a physical revolution but a psychological one," he said. "A voluntary withdrawal. Not coerced, not fashionable, not from others, but from what we made. I propose an old way."

John raised his gaze to those above. "Do not disembark in a fit of fervor because John Whitaker said you should. Test my claims."

He tapped one finger on the podium and addressed them all. "*Foundation*," he said. "Begin with that. I won't be the first to suggest a sound mind in a sound body. But you won't free your mind until you abandon The Doctrine. You won't free your body until you use it like you have one. Free yourself from possessions that possess you. Be wary of what you buy, for it may own you. Purify you first."

He tapped a second finger. "*Balance*. Revive the world in a balance of humanity and nature. Keep nature in your thoughts with every decision you make, every action you take. Man is greedy for all of Creation. Instead, return to God half of what we dominate, untouched by man. Tithe a portion of profits and savings to Earth. Reduce human numbers in a voluntary, ethical manner. There are so many of us now, we want to be left alone to sense some measure of personal space as we turn privacy into seclusion. Every planetary problem, from global warming and resource shortage to mass extinctions and pandemics—all traced to human overpopulation. It's not that there are too few jobs, insufficient land, too little food, an energy shortage. There are too many people."

He pressed three fingers against his podium. *"Remember.* Morality can no longer be derived from bedrock precepts of the good for man because the authority of tradition has been abandoned. Revival is available through a patient practice of appraisal. Recover lessons of the past through the Great Books. Realize these philosophers will disagree on the most significant matters, and through that struggle for Truth, Right and Good, find your reward— the realization that you deserve to be here, part of a tradition, participant in history.

*"Recognition.* Recognize community prerogatives on individual roles and responsibilities. By *community,* I do not mean the Internet community, the NASCAR community, or some abstract national community. I do mean people and land. A person's role and satisfaction derived from it is measured by people we know, not by a vacuous national abstraction with no connotation to anybody. This is a factor in our plague of rudeness, ridiculous behaviors, public displays of immodesty as though modesty were a form of oppression—*because there is no reference.* Recognize that the system we made then remakes us. Recognize what a vital life means, what it needs, what are the costs if we lose it—that is the antidote to the system we made."

He splayed open five fingers on his podium. *"Awareness.* The peak experience of existence is reached by the richest level of awareness. Expand it with an admiration for imagination. Resurrect that artist in you. The delicate beauty of cave paintings disappeared with the advent of agriculture; the finery of Sumerian pottery vanished with their invention of the city; marvels of Renaissance expression retreated with Enlightenment analysis. Today, it's the technological saturation of the Information Age. Each stage was of benefit to humankind. Each presented novel complexities that came to dominate us. Tap into what was never dead, only buried.

"*Promise*. We must marry for life. Which is—" The audience erupted in laughter. "Which is more meaningful," John said, "sovereignty or belonging? Things or love? Choose carefully. With enduring marriage, the opportunity for trust arises, and not within the family alone. The ancients showed family is supreme, the building block of civilization. Enlightenment philosophers made individuals ascendant, assuming the family would retain its place. They did not expect individualism would undermine the home. They left requirements of moral instruction to the family, transmittable only when trust from permanent bonds allow it. That means the family is superior to individuals in it, prior to those created from it. We must educate our young in moral matters, to be wise, not merely raise them. *Quality time* during holiday visits will not replace quantity time. These are the soft parts of civilization, the small parts, the parts you can't see, like imperceptible atoms that hold up the sun."

John formed the number seven with his fingers. "Allow God's *return*. It will not be easy. We made it that way when dwelling in that new invention called the city made it easier to remove God from nature and nature from ourselves. We came no longer to see God and nature as one and the same, but nature as God's design left behind—from the sacred to the profane. *We* made God distant. And like our loss of community orientation, with no frame of natural reference, we accept ruin as normal. Like states and their ambitions, we have become our own centrifugal force. We hurl ourselves apart as we grapple to hold ourselves together. Ignorant of this miracle of existence, we stand on the Central Mountain's summit, still in quest of a high place."

John turned about a point, scanning faces. "Molecules you're made of are a sacred configuration formed but briefly in the lifetime of this universe. While we are all central to the one cosmic soul, we are also of this Earth. Made of both worlds, we must learn to live in both. Our spiritual dilemma will be saved by re-mythologizing our world through the magic of reason and faith to flower in friendship and love. And a love not only of our own but a love for *the living*, no matter how different they look or sound or behave."

The expansive man on the panel grimaced. "Even monkeys, Mister Whitaker? Llamas, lions, and lambs?"

"What we feel is what they feel," John said.

"So can we kill animals to eat? Wouldn't a world of vegetarians destroy the planet with all that extra farmland?"

"Did God not create the ideal human pair as vegetarians?" John said.

"But what about we non-ideal humans, in the real world, Mister Whitaker?"

"Six percent of soy protein goes to human consumption. The rest, animal feed, with the usual inefficiencies converting one food to another. If humans ate soy directly, we'd need much less farmland, alleviating floods that farming exacerbates as a bonus."

"What about a lethal virus, or a charging bear, Mister Whitaker? Are we permitted to save ourselves?"

"Of course. Nor do I ignore that life lives on life. But will we swallow once-breathing souls when we realize they are a *thou*, not an *it?* From all the great prophets, the message is repeated—we have an obligation to the weakest among us, the most innocent. Did Jesus not free animals from their cages when he tipped tables of the moneychangers?"

The man puzzled. "How can we embrace all life when there is so much of it? Isn't that a violation of your 'human-sized' community we're capable of seizing?"

"By embracing the sanctity of *life*—the living state, *singular*. As with the exchange of many gods for one, the idea becomes conceptually within our reach and closer to truth, personalized by each individual possessing that miracle of life."

John turned to the audience. "How will *you* respond? The Kingdom of the Father is upon the land, but you do not feel it. It lingers in spaces between us. It hints to us in dreams we forget. We can still save The Promised Land. *That* is the good news."

A panel member heaved herself from her seat. She nodded toward the moderator. She approached the audience. "Mister Whitaker, what you said, I recognize it." She tapped her chin with index finger. Her back faced John. "Where did those words come from, sir?"

"I've said a great deal. I've exhausted even myself."

"The Kingdom of the Father is upon the land, but we do not *feel* it, is what you said. Who is the source for that?"

She ducked beneath a flag and confronted John. "Do you intend to correct wrongs of the present? Or wrongs of the past?" John's face relaxed. "I saw that, Mister Whitaker. You've quoted—or nearly so—Jesus Christ according to the Gospel of Thomas. That rival to the true Gospel of John. While the disciple John claimed the Kingdom to come in heaven, Thomas claimed the Kingdom was already here, a matter of viewpoint. But the Thomas gospel was one of many texts expelled as heresy by the bishops when they voted on what books the New Testament would be composed of. And Thomas did not write that gospel, sir."

"And you know the same is true of all the gospels. No one knows who wrote them. Their names are a matter of traditional assignment. So what? Does that falsify their message? I think not."

The woman grimaced. "Do you mean to rewrite Thomas, or through a twist on him, finally, after all these centuries, correct John the disciple, Mister Whitaker?"

John returned to the audience. "I mean to bring The Word to the people, to let them hear it for themselves. What is to become of America is what we make it. Salvation is through a reformation of us, a resurrection of reason, true community, saving nature and God, one and the same."

"Do you mean to correct John the disciple, sir?"

He looked to the people above. "In this second Axial Age, the time is upon us once again to answer the soul."

"Mister Whitaker, do you mean to correct John, the disciple of Jesus Christ?"

"The news I have is the news of our deliverance at this moment," he said. "You need wait for no one. You don't need me to reach it."

"The question, Mister Whitaker!"

John hit the podium. "Did not Matthew correct Mark?"

Some people screamed. Others looked about for Matthew and Mark. The moderator bellowed for silence.

Among rumbles in the library, an old man dropped his pencil on the table. He rose from the back of the panel, his body in a battle with his cane. Hunched over his support, he signaled for silence. He spoke to the floor. "How many times have we heard this tale told?" he said. "What a joke. It is by another's influence this man has strayed against the state. Aping his mentor, he asks questions offensive to the collective." The old man exhaled, seeming about to expire. "Did you know Mister Whitaker once had *talent?*"

The audience groaned.

"And not only a talent for insult," the old man said.

The audience nodded almost in unison.

"Greedily, like the capitalists he defends, he has not offered his advantages to those more needy, more deserving of the general kindness. He has done for himself, he has seen for himself, he has thought *for himself.*"

The audience sighed and shook their heads.

The old man pointed sideward toward John. His head still bowed, part of his face appeared as though burned in a fire. "We now know that *knowledge* leads to *conviction,*" he said. "And conviction leads to anarchy. But Mister Whitaker was denied these truths because he was polluted, by me! I am to blame for his acts!"

The crowd released a unified "Ooo…"

"He is a pawn of mine because I am too old to make these attacks myself, and he seeks my acceptance."

Eyes in the audience widened. "Ahhh…"

"Truly! I watered embryonic curiosity with poisonous discovery. I assaulted him with thoughts from dead authors. I tormented him by demanding he give *correct, testable* answers, as though we could know anything beyond what we set out to find to begin with, or that I, a man, could know right from wrong. I violated his peace in weakness. I caused him to wonder. I even subjected him to that archaic bondage—to *respect thy father.*"

People howled. Some nearly fell from their seats or began to weep at the thought of such coercion.

Morgan pounded his own chest. "I am the example. Fathers are fools, beasts, born that way, just as The Doctrine teaches. Of course, we need the boy's camps to expunge maleness. Had he such guidance, he too would be safe, docile, compliant."

Applause peppered the library. People stood to cheer.

Morgan lifted his eyes, fierce on John, and spoke to the people. "No matter what he pretends, he is not the sixth prophet. He will not save you. You don't need saving!"

Ovations thundered throughout the library.

Morgan waved one hand. "Please! He is a casualty of my loathing, needful of sensitivity training. He *is* a victim." Morgan swiveled toward the bench. "Call off this stunt, Mister Moderator. Haven't we endured enough? In twenty-four hours, we'll return to the central issues of our time—the cost of gasoline, our next election, Santa's skin color."

John smiled. "How interesting this irascible fellow would become so concerned for other people's sensibilities," he said.

Morgan hoisted himself straight to face John. "Irascible, am I?"

"Though your acting could use a little polish, Father."

Morgan ignited. "I know what you're up to! If only you can keep a lid on this brewing eruption a little longer. Starting with an attempt to unfasten combustible religious views for the safer vagueness of faith. You want—respectfully—to solve our eternal problem of Athens and Jerusalem, to make reason and religion safe for one another. All the while, as you maintain this or that Biblical linkage so as not to stray too far afield from what these people can hazily recall somebody maybe might have said once about scripture. And you'll tie it all together with *transcendence*. Ha! You've muzzled opposition through another word for God.

"Remember, John, belief in ghosts and goblins are a short distance from belief in God. And you're a champion of *reason?*"

"What's your unstated assumption, Father? That the category of God and the category of ghosts and goblins are, in fact, the same category. What if they're not?"

Morgan dismissed John with a flick of his cane. "Don't forget your reading assignments, John. It was Leo Strauss who showed that in every attempt to make reason and religion safe from each other, one of them must lose."

Morgan turned toward the audience. "Reason and religion on the same team will save you? Not a chance. All civilizations fail in their own way. Ours is to be *massified*—by mass media, mass marketing, mass consumption, mass traffic, mass waistlines, mass murder, mass drug abuse to escape this disaster, if only in our minds. But we can't be rescued any more than the Maya or Rome, so go home!"

"What of Susan B. Anthony, Father? Frederick Douglas? George Washington? Every era had its redeemer."

"And today that's who, John? You? Sumer had Gilgamesh. Rome had Marcus Aurelius. And what happened to Sumer and Rome? Americans don't even know Washington is a state or named after someone of merit. Perhaps Washington is a machine that washes heavy things. These people now fail every test but survival."

"And how would you plan our exit, Father?"

"Who needs a plan? We're doing quite well without one."

John pulled a copper disk from his pocket and tapped it on the podium. He pointed at the windows. "July 1969, Father. That moon reflected off your face from the porch of an old home in Iowa. With the world in unified awe, men walked two hunnert twenty thousand miles away, side by side with the stars. You knew that if a nation could rally its resources to take such leaps, then without doubt what inspired you had foundation. Everyone felt as you did. Do you really believe that in just one long lifetime all that has been lost?"

Morgan spied the crescent moon outside. "In the length of my life, John, the distance between now and that far-off year of 1969 is as great as the distance between that moon and the stars. That was also the era of Vietnam and the sixties. When Right and Left established hypocrisy as the norm we now answer for. *Of course,* that nation has been lost. And it took only a few years, not the lion's share of a century. The public was bored with *Apollo Eleven* by *Apollo Twelve.* Do you really intend to inspire these people by reminding them of what they were? You mean to replace their loss with hope, but through the means I employed. That's what I don't understand."

"Because that's not what I'm doing, Father."

"Oh, but you are. Your active mind alone has shown them what they gave up. But that won't give them hope any more than my films. Like me, you'll only have them yawning or pissed off."

"The difference, Father, is that you stopped at criticism, with no solutions, because you saw man as irredeemable. You wanted to punish humankind for failing—not God, but you, and any hope of redeeming yourself."

Morgan's eyes could be seen to repeat John's words in his mind.

"Criticism is the beginning, Father, not the end. We're not bad because we want to be. We're bad because we don't realize how much we matter."

"Is that what you think, John? You threaten political power, owned by a commercial arrangement Americans worship as sacrosanct. And you're going to show us that we or the animals or nature or God matter for more than a dollar? You think you'll get away with that? You'll be lucky to get out of this library."

"How often have you preached the universality of desires, Father? Do you really think there's no desire to revive this nation and ourselves in it?"

"Universals, yes. Desires, yes, John. These are eternal, but their mix ebbs and flows. Why do humans keep making wars if everybody wants peace? Because resources, power, and arrogance matter. Until we've exhausted our thirst for battle. Then we're absolutely convinced humans have always most wanted harmony."

"And so the expected outcome of war is not more war, Father. Even that humans possess this contradiction is universal. Humans have a common biology. From that comes a common set of desires, which coalesce in a common set of universals. While you insist that people cannot sacrifice passions for a universal good."

"Good for what, John? The good now is what's good for each alone. This social norm is what made these people the way they are. That was the goal. Mere interests to keep us tame." Morgan challenged the audience. "Our most universal longings serviced—hoarding and fucking! We know them well! Do we not?" John bowed his head, eyes closed. "But you, John, spent half the day in one form or another bitching about Enlightenment's failure to justify morality, thus our inability to define a greater good. You already know this! The Anti-Federalists lost, and hence this nation is one large commercial republic where people are—as even Federalists feared—related by legal contracts alone."

Morgan turned to the expert on colonial diaper changing. "Do you see how the Founders tied philosophy to economics and how that set the stage for our demise?" he asked. "Our rights depend on national defense and domestic peacekeepers, but peace costs money. Money from what? Taxes. Taxes from what? Prosperity. So, prosperity pays to preserve individual rights. *That* is why our

Founders placed such emphasis on protection of economic interests. As an offset to despotism, not to coddle the rich, as you assert." Morgan scanned the panel. "And what, one layer down, is essential to that arrangement?" he said. "The natural environment. Peace comes at the cost of ripping up the natural world. But that's now the problem, isn't it? Our utility instinct never let us see that nature is a treasure of greater worth than money. Underlying the Founders' method is an unstated assumption—limitless resources."

Morgan pointed outside. "From a continent of forest and prairie to one of farms and cities. From temperance to sexual revolution. From the pony express to email. Each generation accepts what they inherit as normal. They make changes, expand the human footprint, and the process repeats. So long as there's sufficient environment to feed us and pay for peace, it's a wonderful world. But the earth's bio-capital is spent, and it just so happens civilization cannot survive on ruin. The science of shitting in our own nest just wasn't definitive enough. If we'd only known sooner."

Morgan clucked his tongue, shook his head, and sneered. "While The Great and Powerful John rewrites your religion to include nature in your prayers. To restrain your primal urge. To provide another Band-Aid. Do you sense the infeasibility of escape?"

Morgan stabbed his arthritic fist of knotted fingers at John. "And do you have any idea what you're formulating? Comforts of the body will vanish for seizures of the soul once you let these people see they have one. And when they come back to Earth, just as they were aroused by every liberator, from Alexander to Lenin, nothing will change but for those lost to slaughter.

"Don't revive their passions already broiling, John. We've got a ship of state without a rudder, which is safe. You've built a rudder to give them direction and do so directly without the shelter of a portless life. You point these people to shore after being at sea for so long; they'll annihilate it all. You think the natural world is in shreds now, just you wait until they devour each other."

"The remedy is to educate, Father."

"By who? High schools fear science because Creationists bomb those not teaching scriptures in biology class, as their brethren detonated abortion clinics. All on your own, you'll fix political subterfuge rampant in our universities—bigoted professors who stomp on the written name of Jesus but erupt in outrage over disrespect for Mohammad. They'll refer to academic freedom and diversity rules. It's all in The Doctrine, that last vomit of Satan!"

"God-given reason and faith, Father."

"Poppycock. Make the grand promise, John. Attach some quaint myth to it. They'll eat out of your hand until the next commercial break. But you'll have to decide: will you promise them universal human rights *based on the individual*, or bind them to a community where individuals are surrendered?" Morgan looked to the mezzanine. "Oh, and lest we forget," he said, "you're to shun your taste for flesh and blood, exchanged for nuts and berries…Except we've killed all the pollinators, so there are no nuts and berries."

"You're wrong, Father. Like so many of our arguments over time, dramatic and entertaining, but wrong."

Morgan's eyes razored through his son. "You would see things differently had you not shut out your father for *eleven* years after Alaska!"

"You rendered the world you railed against, Father. It wasn't mine."

"You turned your back on the only people who cared for you!"

"I made a discovery, Father. I couldn't tell you."

"Because you knew I would change your mind!"

"Because you held too much power over me! I needed to find my way, and I found it."

Morgan paused. He studied John. "But, John, if you felt—"

"Your ideas were fully developed, Father, and they were immobile. Mine may have been wrong, but I could not learn that if I let you pronounce them as false, buttressed by experience I could not match. Now I know more, and I have the confidence to face you. I admire you, Father, but I don't envy you. I respect you, but I don't want to be you. Nor follow your cold, proud practice of animus for humankind. These people, they want redemption. They merit the sound that lets them find it. I heard it; so can they."

Morgan looked out a window for a vanished moon. He lifted his notepad from the table. He nodded to some thought in his mind. He said, "They want you to promise a way out, John. To tell them you're the savior here to save them now, not that they have homework.

307

"Be the sacrifice, John. Sacrifice in their place so they can be left alone to worship your greatness without the trouble of finding it in themselves. Tell them more than books they were called to read will spontaneously jump from shelves, open to the very page that changes their life. Tell them more than they can know God if only they purchase admission to your lecture. Tell them more than this, because they've heard it all before. These schemes only separated them from their money, while deep inside remains a barely controlled sense of terror. Which is what this misdirection is intended for, isn't it? To provide a spasm of calm among the immensity of their fears."

"They will find what they need to proceed on their own, Father."

"I didn't say give them a twelve-step program. That will be like another one of their diets. I said tell them what they want—that *you* are here to save them, *now*."

"Father, if you so loved the world about to face its doom, would you send your only son to help, even if you knew he would be surrendered in the process?"

Morgan assessed John, squinting. "So you do intend to be the sacrifice...*Sacrifice*, a myth borrowed from hunter cultures, as burial and resurrection are mythic motifs borrowed from seed-planting cultures. Never mind those puerile self-contradictions, that if I commit a crime that warrants capital punishment, moral justice cannot take an innocent life—yours—for the guilty—mine—even if you offer it on a cross. So much for sacrifice. Wouldn't select that option if I were you, John."

"It's not the sacrifice, Father, but the delivery of aid. Acts of both the father and the son. Not the metaphor, the message."

"It's a puzzle, John, and a problem. Now it's your problem. You wait for light but behold the night. And it's about to get a lot darker."

"Better to light one candle than curse the darkness, Father."

"And you're it. One candle, all alone."

"All we need is a spark."

"John, you'll burn us to the ground."

"To cleanse the soul."

"Your remedy will kill the patient."

"Fire of the mind, not of buildings, Father."

"You know what, John? I wish you were the Messiah because that would mean there is a God. You're gonna need him. But demand a personal appearance by the adult this time, because no baby savior can stand up to the wrath about to obliterate us all."

John looked down, rubbing his forehead. "Goodness…There's a cheerful presence about you I'll gamble most people overlook."

Morgan froze. He bent over and sounded as if he were sobbing. "Ha! One of my many endearing qualities!"

"All can pursue truth through peaceful means, Fath—"

"My…that was pleasant," Morgan said. He wiped tears from his eyes. "Of course, John, they can. Theoretically. The Chinese preach harmony with man and nature. Is that why they drove elephants into extinction for ivory? While Christians revere Jesus for his commitment to truth. They do? They're all liars for their political party superior to Christ." Morgan held up one hand. "But fear not! John will unify us." Morgan hugged himself. He grinned at the audience. "Don't you feel a glow inside? Like this religious crank on the panel. Or you religious freaks cowering in the crowd until you find another glitch like yourself to promise your fairy tales are true and real and imminent, desperate to cover for that nagging sense *that they are not*. Or you misfits cloaked by unmemorable masses, if only the masses can be made as insignificant as you.

"Where do we go from here?" Morgan asked. "Will adherence to the holy notion that a moral vacuum will keep us free from disagreement, also keep us safe? See how this story's about to end? Think he can fix that?"

Morgan scooted sideward. "Do you find it odd," he asked, "that this *great* civilization debates whether German shepherds are racist or not? Do you muse over visions seen by this administration—a thirty-story-tall Jesus beside the White House. True, yes?"

Heads bobbed about the library, people crossed themselves, some raised a middle finger. Outside, crowds fell silent, listened to speakers, and watched Jumbotrons as sirens cried in the distance.

Exhausted merely from standing, tremors ended at Morgan's hand, directed toward the Capitol next door. "What that extension of corporate power wants is for you to shut up and buy products. Consume and dispose. *That* is your purpose. Methane burns from your tap water? PCB? BPA? You'll be fine. The CEO's multi-million-dollar gratuity is due, his senator has a campaign to run. After all, you're stockholders, aren't you? What's matters more, your child's asthma, or the velocity of cash? Common sense regulations? There's product to move. If to keep you servile requires God's approval, then, by all means, God approves!"

Morgan hobbled toward the audience. "Did you people ever stop to wonder if these things are related?" He wagged his notepad at Chinese camera crews above. "They now know we've completed that transit worn by civilizations before us. From confidence to panic. What little can it take to suffocate us? We've done the hard work for them. *The American mind is closed.* The American heart no longer beats. As China prepares to roll twenty million foot soldiers and forty million robots over this continent!"

Cameras came off tripods in a cascade. People lifted from their seats to notice, despite violations of The Doctrine. China's Party Truth reporters and their equipment punched their way through exits. Crowds surged in. People stood on seats in search of a way out. The moderator hammered and snapped his gavel in a spiral over his head. He shouted to guards, "Lock those doors!"

Morgan bellowed over noise, "Look at yourselves! Look at your neighbors! What you see is what all once-dominant civilizations saw. What you feel is what they felt. What you sense but won't admit is what they sensed and denied, for to admit it would only hasten what they already knew was drained. The system has failed because *you* have failed."

Still roiling, sectors of the audience roared approval, others shouted insults. Scuffles erupted throughout the library.

Morgan lunged his cane at a large man on the panel. He poked the calculator in his pocket. "Do you trust your neighbor not to steal your property when your alarms fail? Or not to report you in violation of The Doctrine, upon which you vanish?" He stuck the man's shoulder. "Your wife? Is she baking cookies, or fucking the neighbor? And if she is, *what*ever."

The man trembled in his seat. Morgan squinted at faces in mezzanines above, one small girl still gripping tight the rail. Visually he touched each on the head with the tip of his cane as though it were a magic wand. "You and you and you are horrified," he said. "You know the tipping point has arrived. Hear the absurdities offered from political manipulators; scientific illiterates; the cream of our university crop muttering their obsessive prattle. We can't separate a reasoned argument from a kumquat. No wonder we're bewildered. A threshold has been crossed, and you know it. Our collective immune system can no longer sustain the body of society. Fall, we will until our last dictator is strangled with the entrails of our last astrologer. Buried under bodies piled so high by war, this nation won't be rediscovered for a thousand years."

Morgan's lips flashed fangs at the large man on the panel. "When you look at your country, when you look at yourself, when you look at children who sail other children from tenth-story windows because they wondered what it feels like to do that, and these children become adults in positions of leadership throughout this society, there's not much farther to go. When we reach it, you'll understand. Like God's butchery of the innocent, no one will be spared!" He threw his notepad, turning the man's face. "Nor should you be spared. Hell's at hand, sown for a hundred years!" His cane lifted in crescendo and ticked the man's ear. *"Reap it!"*

The man crashed through chairs to maul Morgan with the lust of a carnivore who devastates the helpless. He broke Morgan's cane, now a dagger, and sliced Morgan to pieces with it.

Mental turbulence ruptured like an infection, the crowd almost airborne from their seats. Siphoned like a liquid, people corkscrewed downstairs with a deafening roar, horrified by the utmost of fears.

As guards hammered the attacker's skull with rifle butts, John broke for the scene. His copper disk skipped across tiles under a thousand scuttling feet. He tried to free his father. "You wanted this!" John shouted. "To show others the way! To set the blaze!"

Violence discharged through library doors as though they were paper. Windows exploded onto Independence Avenue by force of human bodies. Marches sprang into sprints of utter madness as cyclones of humanity touched down to ravage the city, and soldiers with their tanks spilled from invisible chambers to reinforce monuments, the Capitol, and White House

After all the hypocrisy and corruption, all the concern as a veil for loathing, at long last, from sea to shining sea, reluctance to act on their bottomless contempt gave way to satisfaction.

# 31. The Trinity in 2057

John whispered to his mother, Ne Shoul, "We're lucky he made it this far. It's what he wanted."

Ne Shoul turned to Morgan on a bed in a room he once lived in as a boy. Morgan's body was stitched, wrapped, swollen, bruised, and filled with pain medications. "You're back at your old home, old man," she said. "Swathmore Street in Marion…Can you hear me, Morgan?"

His voice raspy, "Of course I can hear you. I'm not dead yet."

"And cranky as ever," she said.

"Crankier. Thanks to that fat bastard at the library. I should have beat the crap out of him." Morgan chuckled and winced.

"The railroad bought this house as another connection to the line," John said. "A line that gets me back to the cottage. My understanding is incomplete, my approach flawed. I've got to make adjustments."

"Your father is right, John. Leave America behind."

"I confess a fear for the worst of things, Mother, but I can't stay away. I didn't choose this life; it chose me."

Ne Shoul dabbed a cloth on Morgan's cheek. Morgan cringed. "Honey, I've eroded," he said.

"This life is the anvil against which we are hammered to death, Father. Against which we are molded to our final shape, fit for passage. Fit for The Promised Land."

Morgan labored to breathe. "My anvil was a stack of books. Books saved my mind from the times I lived in with its paucity of living examples—save one, my father. And those books prepared me for love. When I met that miracle, I was ready. Then it was my *life* that was saved." Morgan looked John up and down. "Without *The Word* and a *Goddess*, you would not exist."

A low-frequency rumble shook the house. Silence preceded sirens falling in pitch. The thump-thump of blades from Peace and Apple Pie gunships could be heard overhead, soon to unload their Victim's Therapy and Self-Esteem-Support ordnance.

"Father, do you remember when you tried to teach me basic physics of the atomic world? How what seemed impossible in an unseen realm was true?"

Morgan stared at John, then turned away. "God, I hurt." He tried to massage his temple but couldn't reach it. "I've read about this condition," he said. "Near the end, we see things that aren't real."

Outside the house, Happiness-Quota-Enhancement Audio systems blared warnings of noise pollution on the north side of town. People were advised to remain indoors until clean-air standards recovered from falling debris and the smell of epidermal combustion.

John leaned over to intercept his father's eyes. "I too wanted the life we never had," he said. "To stare at a starry night sky and tell stories for no other reason than to spend time together."

Morgan looked away to study the wall beyond John's face. Maybe I'm already dead, he thought. Even his voice sounds different.

"At least a hunnert times you denied a relationship with me after I was gone," John said. "All to satisfy your over-extension of reason. And what did it leave you? No opportunity to share your life as though I were still here. Not even to ask, 'Would you be proud of me now?' And yet you wrestled with questions that you knew reason could not answer, like God's existence. Well, God doesn't care for your devotion, Morgan, your obedience, your fear. God reveres your *honesty*, your *struggle for truth and understanding*. Whether you are for or against God is irrelevant to God. Only through honesty can the truth be reached, to set you free—from you.

"Do you see, Morgan? Do you see *me?* I'm not only evidence of God's Grace, I'm proof."

John pulled an antique letter from his pocket, "Dad" printed on its envelope. "You wondered whether I got your letter, Morgan. Well, I did. I came back to live the life we never had."

Wrinkles about Morgan's eyes eased. He stared at the envelope.

"We both wanted it so much it came true," John said. "Besides, I always knew I'd make it back here, even if it took a miracle. Miracles happen, Morgan. We're confirmation of that."

Morgan's voice quivered. "Confirmation of what?"

"Years ago, Morgan, I told you about a place where all of nature speaks a different language, yet each understands the other. I tried to explain what I could barely sense myself. What surrounds us is a vast body in which each life is poured like a cup of water into the sea. What happens to that cup of water, to that life? Has it gone? No, but neither is it what it was. Together the two become as one, without oneness, a Union, dispersed through all that was and remains to be."

"What are you talking about, John?"

"I discovered the same unity you found in waves, light, and atoms. That same unity governs the rose, whales, wolves, and people. And when stars and atoms they're made from then form humans, why should we not expect this underlying unity to persist? Because emergent properties make it hard to see their source. The *soul of things*."

Morgan shook his head.

"Emergent properties, Morgan. Characteristics of a thing that come about only after there is enough of it or the right combination of things fall into place. Wetness is an emergent property of water. Less than a million molecules of water between your fingers feels dry, dusty." John rubbed fingers with thumb. "Exceed a million molecules of water between your fingers, and it feels wet." He wiped hands on his shirt. "Life is an emergent property of molecular structure. Consciousness, morality, compassion: emergent properties, all quite real. Their source is everywhere around us, Morgan. Separated by the thinnest of membranes, this unity reaches beyond the physical world. Loved by the very space and time you pass through without notice from day to day and place to place as though only a breeze.

"As I told your mother before she died, through marv—"

"My mother died long before you were born, John."

"Through marvelous cosmic generosity, Morgan, I didn't leave just because I was dead. I am a part of that truth you can finally grasp. You had a chance. It's been given again."

John stared into eyes of confusion. "Are we an inflection of the Trinity, Morgan? Now the father and the son are one—me. His son and father are another—you. And what you feel, what binds us all, could it be the Holy Spirit?"

Morgan touched John's face. "You look so like—" He turned to Ne Shoul, his voice filled with accusation. "Like Eve seeing a snake talk, you don't seem the least surprised to see your son looks like my father."

She stroked Morgan's forehead.

He growled, "Say something!"

Morgan's head fell back. So, in the end, nature is not cruel, he thought. But like the church, only if I accept it. I don't have another fight left in me. He stammered, "Give me my billfold." His hands fumbled through the pouch. He dropped the parcel.

John picked it up. He reached inside to withdraw a tattered photograph and handed it to Morgan.

Morgan pulled John's shirt. "Is it true? Was that you by the south rim? Is that you in the picture? I *know* it's not as it appears. I *know* it was a camera malfunction. I always *knew* it was, but I wanted it to be otherwise."

"You understand."

"No!"

John paused and shook his head. "I can tell you now with certainty what I told you in that far-off year in which you as a boy sent a bunny to his grave. There is salvation, Morgan, not in this world *or* another, but in this world *and* another. It is true what they say; they have been freed. You will be freed. Sacrifice the man that clothes you."

Morgan held the photograph. He felt its surface. There at the Grand Canyon was Morgan as a younger man, his father by his side, two years after his father was dead. "I thought it was a double exposure," he whispered. "One taken when my father was alive, the other, me alone at the canyon."

"All these years you wanted to believe, Morgan, but you saw belief as ignorance. *Believe*, not because it is true in our modern sense, but true in another. Believe because it makes you *complete*."

Morgan closed his eyes. He heard a boy sing "Sittin' on the

Dock of the Bay." Air pounded open windows of a Pontiac Catalina on Route 66. The scene around him looked like an Albert Bierstadt painting. Tons of rock lunged skyward, falling back in slow motion called erosion. Morgan looked at his hands, those of a child. For the first time since he was a boy, Morgan whispered, "Amen."

"Is that our traditional affirmation," Ne Shoul asked, "or a salute to one of your ancient favorites—Amen, the Egyptian god of breath?"

Morgan squeezed her hand. "Do I feel cold? The fever called living is about to break."

She stroked his head. "Oh...A quote from Poe. I introduced you to him in the Yucatan.

"John, the first time I saw your father was at Chichén Itzá. I followed him for a day and a half all the way to Uxmal."

Morgan raised his head. "You did?"

She fixed his hair. "My friend, what can I do for you?"

"Remember, fetal position, facing east and the rising sun. Flowers in my grave with plenty of pollen for the archeologists. And don't let those morticians pickle me for a dollar. Natural burial...And one pristine hunk of marble. I'll need something to do."

John gawked. "Amazing..."

"Anything else?" Ne Shoul asked.

"The urns. Sammy and Hawkeye. Even though hers is empty."

"I didn't forget. Relax, sweetie, please."

"I'm about to.

"Now, there's an apology I owe an innocent rabbit." He glanced at John. "The innocent man got his apology in a letter."

Morgan looked at Ne Shoul to memorize her face. His eyes drifted to the window. In the distance, a two thousand mile diameter stone in the sky reflected sun and earthlight.

Ne Shoul turned to see what he saw. "Man in the moon, Morgan. Big earthshine face with a grin made by our local star."

Across the street, a girl could be seen inside her house, reading a book. She read about lions and how the last one was found as roadkill along the Serengeti Highway, finally complete, improving transport efficiency. She learned how coordinated efforts between Mexico, the US, and Canada terminated one of the world's great spectacles when the monarch migration finally ended, but crops and lumber were produced. She learned about how an underground sea called the Ogallala Aquifer became an underground desert as the eight states above it approached the same fate, proud of their financial contributions to history. A woman could be seen to snatch the girl into their basement when more rumbles rattled the house.

Ne Shoul played, "Letter from Home" by the Pat Metheny Group on her music player. She sat by her husband. She held his lifeless hand. "Do you remember when..." she said.

John smiled. He looked skyward through a window. "When you graduated from university, I said, 'I want to ask you about something remarkable.' I've waited so long."

Sporadic small-arms and black-market smart-weapons fire could be heard about Marion. People were shocked at what they had done. They hoped life would soon return to its normal distortion. Homeowners who could afford it switched on their latest in Chinese high-tech security and took cover from sounds outside as darkness fell.

Diffuse hemispheres of light rose and sank on one corner of the horizon in rapid succession. Subsonic booms shook doors. Ne Shoul's music now played Alan Parsons', "The Very Last Time."

Lyrics bled through windows and receded with range from the old house. It was a beautiful night in Iowa.

Photo credit: Lesley Bohm

# ABOUT THE AUTHOR

Brett Williams spent his career as a physicist in electrical engineering and applied research in Dallas, Houston, and Southern California. He is a landscape and wildlife oil painter, and frequent backcountry hiker. He left physics to focus on writing, painting, and travel. *The Father* is his debut novel. More about Williams, his books, and blog concerning political philosophy, science, religion, and current events can be found at TheFatherTrilogy.com or Goodreads.com.

Made in the USA
Columbia, SC
19 January 2020